Manifesting the Monkey:
A spell of Transformation

Dennis Lee Dziedzic

© Magical Monkey Press

First edition, June 2011

Copyright © by Magical Monkey Press

Cover design by Timothy Daniel Dziedzic

Edited by Michael Saxe

Manifesting the Monkey, by Dennis Dziedzic. First edition. Magical-realism. ISBN: 9780615503127

To Hélène - for your support, your compassion, and your belief

I shall be telling this with a sigh
Somewhere ages and ages hence:
Two roads diverged in a wood, and I—
I took the one less traveled by,
And that has made all the difference.
-Robert Frost

0

The power of imagination makes us infinite.
-John Muir

It took almost a decade, but I made it back from my voyage into the unknown. We used to know each other. Remember? We lived in the same neighborhood, or we went to the same school, or the same church? And then my family moved...or your family moved. I'm not sure which, but somehow we got separated. That's what I remember—that we lost each other, and forgot we are the same, that despite all our apparent differences, we're all the same: people seeking to sustain happiness in our lives.

Isn't that what everyone wants?

I have returned to reunite with you from the fringes of possibility and the violence of life to be here. These words comprise my thesis, the culmination of an initiation that began with the first flush so many years ago.

The last waves of redemption are retreating now. The disease is gone, and it's gone because it was never there...but I get ahead of myself. The important thing to remember is that it's already done. The doors open tomorrow, and we all walk out into the sunshine together. The former guards released us from our cells a week ago, leaving us to heal unsupervised as the world outside restructures itself. I am excited, we are excited. Our family and friends, everyone is waiting for us. The spring is coming, and there are seeds to plant. It's our first season, and she's expecting me. She's sent a message, and everything is like we dared to dream. It's all been wiped clean. It happened...but it was close.

The ugly climax of human civilization was a long, dark night, the kind that got me pondering dawn's arrival, and I almost lost faith because I could not escape humanity's disease as it made the last surge towards our heart— driving to work, riding my bike, having sex with my girlfriend, watching movies, going to restaurants. It was everywhere, all the time, speaking to my inherited lack, and I froze, like a rabbit cornered in a cage. This malady was in the cement that held our societies together, the redundant questions we asked our spouses, the fibers with which we tied family members to our ideas about them. It spurred outrageous success in the fashion industry. It motivated foreign policies and created invisible lines that split us from them, you from me. The end was so dark, I wasn't certain we'd make it out alive, but our timing was impeccable. We were dying from this ravishing parasite, and nobody even knew it. It seemed as if we'd go on mistaking the affliction for ourselves, and blowing each other up trying to destroy it. We all pretended it was normal, but inside, if pushed came to shove, we all knew it.

Something stinks.

I didn't know what, only that something was wrong. The dis-ease was far more pandemic than any in history, and a viable vaccine had yet to be developed, though top experts toiled hours in labs around the world, searching. One way or another, most human effort sought its eradication, but then we tucked it in with our children every night when we assured them there were no monsters under the bed or boogeymen in the closet (even though we knew there were). It was subtle and objectively powerless, but it was the only thing capable of perverting the beautiful human opus. We were under attack.

Sometimes I wish I never saw it. It would have been easier to fall back into that blissful bubble and watch television. But I couldn't. I unplugged, and everywhere I looked, I saw people hurting themselves or someone else. I had no power to do anything about it, and any help I offered was met with the further entrenchment of their abuse. Then, imagine my shock when I realized I was doing the same thing, that I was just as much a masochist as anyone else. People are free, and if some choose to hurt themselves, that's their birthright and to be respected. It took me a long time to accept that, but our capacity to choose is what makes us divine.

When I left, I had no idea what I was getting into. I just bought a ticket and got on the ride, looking for a better view, some high ground to see what was really going on. And now, after surveying the terrain and making a map, I'm back. Please consider this my homecoming, my half-time of fame. My name is Ten, and I return to you with exciting stories of exotic places, impossible feats, but, most importantly, I return to you with a gift.

1

The true price for anything
is the amount of life you'll exchange for it
-Henry David Thoreau

I was always looking for what I didn't want. I saw things that irritated me, that scared me, that made me angry or sad. I stared at the things that bothered me, and I could just barely hold it together and keep the monster out of sight. In moments of love, it retreated into the shadows, a vampire avoiding the sun, but I always went searching for it, dragged it out of the basement and looked at it. I was addicted, vigilant in my search for a 23 car pile-up, intellectual failure, yellow teeth, disease, financial ruin, killer bees, thugs lurking in the dark, terrorists hurting my family, or my family hurting itself. I was a very good juggler, careful to give each of my worst-case scenarios their fair share of attention as they whizzed around my head.

Now, I live everyday thankful for my escape from that circus. I look back at the rubble of my life and wonder just how the hell I managed to survive. It was nothing short of divine intervention. What else would keep a Texas constable from asking me if I had been drinking when he pulled me over at two in the morning for an expired inspection sticker on Mardis Gras weekend? He soon discovered my lack of insurance, registration, and me, reeking of booze.

They have finally caught me.

I didn't even have my driver's license, but he never asked me the one question that would have landed me in jail and ruined it all. He accepted my passport as proof of identity, wrote the tickets and let me go. I don't know if you've ever been to the Lone Star State, but *that* is a miracle. That's God, hooking me up. When I got to my friend's after-party, I drank a beer in thanks and burned the citations.

My plane left five hours later. That was the first flush, the big one.

I grew up in one of those sprawling southern cities, poorly designed for public transport or pedestrian access. Meadows of concrete and steel, the suffocating press of the status quo molding us all into agreeable shapes. The continuous effort to keep it all from falling apart, and the inevitable scramble to patch it back together when it did. My companion goaded me into behaving, consistently unsatisfied.

Get good grades or fail entrance exams. Go to college or spend the rest of your life flipping burgers. Conform or face the contempt of society. Find a good job or sacrifice security and comfort. Get a girlfriend or spend long hours alone. Get a pretty *girlfriend or risk the ridicule of your friends, but not* too *pretty or risk someone better stealing her. Have kids or die alone.*

I was a good cog, until I realized it was poisoning my soul. Then, I learned to do it different. It wasn't easy, but I made it. I'm older now, and the world still improves every day. Just when you think it couldn't get any better, it does.

I was popular and charming, an American Golden Boy except I was more bronze than gold. I was raised in one of those upper-middle class Mexican families, a long way from the ghetto though I had aunts and uncles, nieces and nephews, cousins who lived there. They survived as best they could given their circumstances, tried to be happy, like everyone, like you. But my cousin got killed, one of those cases of wrong place, wrong time—a convenience store robbery ending the way they often do in our age of inbred violence. Carlos kept his head down, just waited for it to be over, but they shot him anyway. They shot everyone. It was normal.

In the safety of the suburbs, everything was perfect, but something wasn't quite right. No matter how good I was, it wasn't enough to silence the voice inside me, always chattering, pushing me towards conformity or away from perceived threats. I was being suffocated by a pillow stuffed with other people's ideas.

Fascinated by the digital world, I moved to Austin, and majored in Computer Science at the University of Texas, home of the fighting Longhorns. I learned to program and found translating concepts into a language the computer understood fascinating. It was manifesting, bringing ideas to life, and I was very good at it. I found a job with a respectable company and lived life like I was programmed to. I made lots of money. I worked out. I consumed. I watched my weight. I recycled and agreed with the robots on the news, reciting their lines.

I did everything according to the rules, but I still wasn't happy. By the time I admitted something was wrong, that the erosion of my soul would never stop, I was stuck. Contrary to what I had been promised, there was no 'first aid for that deep-down body thirst'. But according to all standards, I had a great life. A good job, a pretty girlfriend, friends who liked me, a 401k. I paid my taxes, my student loans, and more than the minimum on my credit cards. April was an alright fit—not too big, not too small (as my insurance against theft, I selected a girlfriend with a particularly fat bum). It could work. She was blond and blue-eyed, and that would make my dad happy because it was evidence of dissolving boundaries, the further acceptance of his culture into mainstream. It would make my mom sad because April would never be a good Mexican girl, but it made sense. She was twenty-six, I was twenty-five. Why not get married?

Someone told me once that change happens quickly. It's the preparation for change that makes it seem like your flight has been delayed forever. And for me, the motivation for departure started when I woke up sweating one moonless night. I climbed over April and sealed myself in the bathroom. I didn't dare turn on the light for fear of seeing my reflection—I couldn't bear to look at it. The dream was too strong, too true.

The suit jacket and tie. That's what triggered the revelation.

You're dreaming.

I looked down, and I was in a suit jacket and tie, cleanly pressed shirt and spotless pants, something I'd never wear to work, something I'd never wear. I sat at my desk only it wasn't my desk or my office, it was a dark cave, a cavern really, filled with a thousand whispered shouts and the occasional wail of a wandering soul. Further down in the cave, a flickering fire beckoned me. As I stumbled closer, it became more difficult to walk. I looked down and my feet were being swallowed. The solid ground had softened into a viscous slime, now alive and reaching for me. Horrified, I pulled free and set to wiping my shoes clean, but I only succeeded in spreading the organism further over my body. I continued towards the light, hopeful to improve my situation there. I was relieved to see a figure on the other side, a shadowy man despite the fire. The only detail I could make out were his bright, red eyes. I called out, but he ignored my cries for help. I continued trying to tidy myself, but the more I tried the filthier I became.

Trying implies failure.

That familiar panic of sabotage washed over me, and I freaked, swiping furiously at the ooze that was now moving all over my body. I thrashed and slowly stuck myself together. I fell and my squirming was the finishing flourishes of a very thorough trap. I came to a forced stillness, only my eyes visible and an occasional jerk to show for all the resisting. The man laughed and grew bigger, into a giant squid of terrific power. He grabbed me with a thousand devious tentacles, and I woke just as they dropped me into his gaping mouth.

Blip...

I came online, suddenly aware of what was happening to my culture, my country, and my self. The ship was going down. The plane was crashing.

Every man for himself!

So I did what anyone faced with certain existential annihilation would do: I grabbed a backpack and flushed out.

2

*All concerns of men go wrong
when they wish to cure evil with evil.
-Sophocles*

I have to kill him.

He told me his name was Jason Muscoph, but I knew he was lying. People all over the world knew him by different names—the Malayu Headhunter, Old Red Eyes, Baboulous, Dokebi, Jin Baba. He altered perception, twisted words and meaning until what I said, what we said, was nothing more than...roadkill, and disregarded as such. People never took me seriously, either because I was a clown, a felon, certifiably insane, or Catholic. There was always an excuse to ignore the obvious truth.

I never chose to save the world. I only wanted to save myself and ended up right in the middle of this universal drama. Remember? I flushed out. I bought one-way passage to Europe. When I landed in Germany, I flailed around in the river of life, fighting to keep my head above water as the unknown inundated me—wiener schnitzel, Frauleins, Bauhaus, and steins. I was disoriented for days, lingering into weeks, but gradually I made sense of the new world around me.

The slow swirl of the flush began that night when I woke from my dream just as the giant-squid-monster dropped me into his mouth, but I didn't start the descent into the vortex until I bought my plane ticket. Imperceptibly at first, time accelerated as I approached the event horizon and I would land in an unknown country without friends, family, employment, or educational structures to support me. The first swirls in the whirlpool of change were exciting, like clicking to the top of a roller coaster you've never been on—odds are you'll be fine, but there's still that curious dread.

Maybe this is the one time it all goes horribly wrong.

As I picked up speed and zoomed towards my flight, I noticed the subtle blur in my vision as moments bottle-necked on top of each other. They piled up, and I had to choose which to empower with my attention because I couldn't experience them all. Everything was amazing, novel again—colors brightened, music resonated, love-making regained its delicious peach flavor, food tasted better, and shit smelled worse. With each day, time moved a little faster, the vortex pulled me closer, and the first layers of my personality peeled away. I had four going away parties with different circles, and though nobody acknowledged my reasons for leaving (we had all been trained to ignore the evidence), a part of each of my friends wanted to come with me—the rising intonation of their voices gave it away.

Everyone tried to talk me out of my decision to go. My mom cried, my dad shook his head. My brothers made fun of me, my sister stopped talking to me, and April nagged, then tempted me. They didn't understand. Nobody understood. The last few days were a whirlwind. I packed and re-packed my bag a thousand times, putting everything into its perfect place so that I'd be ready for anything, at any time.

What was that?

I looked, but, like always, there was nothing to justify the hair standing up on the back of my neck.

Overcoming my sedentary inertia was the most difficult thing I have ever done in my life, and it took an enormous effort to animate my body into performing the necessary tasks to actually *do* what I said I was going to do. I was cutting my umbilical cord, running away from Mother Culture—the sentience born from a society's collected beliefs, values, media, and institutions. When she realized that I was set in my decision to leave her, Mother Culture presented me with all manner of pleasures to soothe me back to sleep. I was offered a promotion three weeks before I left. April invited another woman into our bed, hoping the classic fantasy would seduce me into staying. I received an unexpected check *from* the IRS. Gas prices dropped to their lowest in years. But when nice couldn't sway me, Mother Culture turned mean—a drunk driver nearly ran me over as I crossed the street late one night, my car caught fire and exploded, April had a long pregnancy scare. The constable at two in the morning was Mother Culture's last strike, but when that failed, it was over, and I was free.

I lounged in the scripted behavior of the airport and plane, like laying in a hammock, rocking in the wind with nothing to do but relax. Eleven hours later, the plane landed, and I arrived on the other side of the flush. The effects were the mirror image of the departure—maximum sensory intensity upon my landing, dwindling to the mundane. The world overtook my senses, and there was no time to think, only to react, but with each day more of the amazing dropped into the background, and the de-conditioning process continued unraveling the person I mistook for me.

That was how I ended up with this absurd mission to save the world. As I untangled myself, I learned more about my relationship to everything else and realized there's little difference between the two.

Turned out it wasn't really that big of a deal. I know, it seemed like saving the world must be some earth-shaking task, some miracle, some world-crashing truth, and it was, just not like we'd seen in the movies. There was a lag between an intention and its manifestation. It's like we were always looking into the past, into a society we had created with yesterday's beliefs. But salvation was easy (and there weren't any explosions), just a simple shift founded on two principles that both science and spirit agreed were fundamental to existence—everything changes, and observation affects change. That was it. But all over the world the weather was so ominous, it seemed silly to suggest everything would shift radically with a couple of New Age concepts.

My objective was simple in theory: I had to find the 100th monkey. I was not alone in my mission. There were others throughout the world, searching, committed to the same freedom from our invisible tyrant and the rebirth of self. The 100th monkey was the key, the tipping point.

My compatriots came in all shapes and sizes, though most found it difficult to know exactly what made us different and even more difficult to know what that difference made us.

We are mirrors, organically grown to reflect the world's beauty and grandeur.

The job came with certain challenges that convoluted the execution of our function, and the work was more difficult than simple reflection—there was much grime to polish before images were seen clearly, so much inside every mind that would smear our surface. People usually shied away from opportunities to look at themselves, afraid that what they did or didn't see might conflict with their self-image. I know I was. The necessary recalculating of identity that must follow from such insights required a tremendous amount of will power, and it was much easier to ignore anything inconsistent with our beliefs.

As the shapes in the mirror changed, people sometimes became confused. It wasn't whom they expected to see. I reassured them, said it was okay not to understand with the conscious mind, that sometimes it was actually better that way. It would all make sense in the end. This, like consciousness, was real, but difficult to express in terms that would satisfy our left brain—there was no formula, no way to touch it. As my own image transformed on the mirror of life, I learned how tricky real communication was. In our over-crowded linguistically-jumbled society, words had been inflated with meaning, diluted of any real substance.

The nature of my mission was subversive, and many gave their lives to prevent my success. It may seem harmless to reflect, but clarity meant certain deletion for many entrenched institutions, both in the micro and macro cosmos. The entire world was constructed on a fallacy most took as gospel. Setting the world free would cost nothing less than everything. And it did, but by giving it all up, we opened ourselves to receive everything back again, this time leveled on a solid foundation of authentic humanity. All it would take was a simple announcement, a declaration, a question planted in a fertile mind.

Just a seed.

Once we were enough, when we found the monkey, a wave would wash over the earth, and everything would be re-calibrated. In the blink of an eye, the world would be saved, and mankind could finally overcome its habitual self-loathing. But Jason Muscoph was working against us. He lurked around every dark corner, a dangerous ninja waiting to sabotage, and he had to be dealt with. There was no other choice. I had to kill him, and when I had taken him out, humanity would finally heal. One bad deed for a tsunami of good.

That sounds acceptable, doesn't it?

It was this root of disorder I saw everywhere. The underlying flaw that was placed next to us in our cradles, that most of us protected at all costs, hiding it safely behind security and comfort. Powering those sweeping generalizations with human emotion, this idea virus, this *meme*, turned our societies into consuming machines—to take, to grow well beyond the natural equilibrium. Eat or die. In this ravaged rush, everyone was looking out for their own, terrified a thief would snatch some valuable away in the dark. We were being manipulated. The human pack herded to its doom.

Like most others in this line of work, I began the fight when I diagnosed my infection. I was compromised, and I fought back against that foreign invader, pushed him out. It was the first battle, and I mistakenly took that long night in the jungle for the whole campaign instead of what it really was—the formal acknowledgment of one's opponent. The coin toss.

Before I saw it, the sick was nestled safely in my head, warm and comfortable. When I realized it was there, that I was possessed, I shocked. I zapped. I seized. My whole body convulsed. For a moment, I considered shattering myself into nonsense on the shards of insanity. Anything would be safer than the horror I had seen. I teetered on the brink, ready to fragment my self forever, but a song floated by on the wind, and I leaned on it as I regained my footing, recovered my balance. Then I stood up, a newborn colt on shaky legs. The disease rustled out of its comfortable slumber in the depths of my mind, and yawned in my direction, confident it would soon convince me back to bed. To it, I was just another sleepwalker. An advertising jingle, a disapproving 'tsk-tsk' would put me in my place, and if that didn't work, the Goliath would crush me into compliance.

That's how the war began, and, like all good wars, it was a necessary one. A just war.

My plan was simple—save myself. To save myself, I had to save the world. To save the world, I had to find the 100th monkey. To find the 100th monkey, I had to stop Jason Muscoph.

And I'd have to kill him to do that.

<u>3</u>

*for it flashed across her mind that she had never before seen
either a rabbit with a waistcoat-pocket,
or a watch to take out of it, and burning with curiosity,
she ran across the field after it,
and was just in time to see it pop down
a large rabbit-hole under the hedge.*
-Lewis Carroll

The flush, the actual disconnection, was simple. The preparation and motivation to make it to the plane was the hard part. After that it was pretty easy and usually fun. For sure, there were times when I wanted to click my ruby flip-flops together three times and materialize on my mother's couch, safe and comfortable, but these were the rare moments. Most times, international travel lent an exciting air of espionage to ordinary life. Buying a baguette and cheese was a deep cover mission in maintaining composure, the casual meeting with the Swedish woman at the *boulangerie* became another romantic conquest with a foreign operative, going to the ATM to continue the affair demanded finesse and alacrity. There were thieves behind every corner, ninjas in the trees, bankers in the trash cans. And they were all coming to get me.

For eighteen months, every time I got comfortable, I flushed. I'd buy a ticket—plane, train, or bus—and when I arrived on the other side of the vortex, I was in a new world. The money, the food, the language, the customs —they all changed, and I learned how to deal with my incomprehension of nearly everything. Life simplified into two fundamental questions, which after satisfying I could do whatever the hell I wanted: where was I going to sleep, and what was I going to eat? Anything else was a bonus. Nobody knew me so I could wear any mask I dared. I was a teacher, a hippie, a hipster, a bum, an intellectual, a non-smoker, an alcoholic, a patriot, a volunteer, a musician, a health nut, a computer nerd, a smoker, homeless, hungry, a chauvinist, a feminist, a bigot. They were all possibilities, and I tried on most of them at least once. Some manifested on their own in flashes of anger or bouts of depression, and others I evoked from inside, but they all shared one characteristic—none of them were me. They were only habits or roles I adopted because they were useful at some point in my life.

In less than two years, I knew I was capable of being anybody I chose. Managing those choices proved to be the longer lesson because so much of my behavior depended on the unconscious scripts with which Mother Culture had implanted me. I was getting better—I could look at myself in the mirror, I had a knack for foreign tongues, I took long deep breaths, and I loved myself. Regardless, the paradigm of doubt always crept back into my life, like a stray cat you made the mistake of feeding once. The nagging teamed up with comfort so I knew he couldn't be trusted, either, and I flushed out more often, hopping around the world like a madman, running away from anything comfortable and those goddamn ninjas! But no matter how hard I tried, I couldn't stop learning. After a year and a half of travel, my feet were firmly rooted in the ground, any ground. I was comfortable anywhere. Ironically, my dubious nature regained its stronghold, and the imp of uncertainty set to picking my scabs, hidden behind the curtains, back in the clutter of my mind.

I revealed my condition to another traveler only once. His name was Atticus, and I met him at Semuc Champey, a beautiful series of stepped limestone pools in Guatemala. After spending hours lounging in crystal-blue water, flirting with a pair of Japanese women, I hiked up a steep jungle trail, past lines of marching leaf-cutter ants and thick elephant-ear leaves to the lookout point—a small wooden deck perched on the mountain side with a spectacular view of the dramatic landscape. A dark man with long hair and thick muscles was already there, sitting on the bench and looking out over the forest of mountains.

"Here, have a seat." He scooted to the edge of the bench to make room for me.

"Thanks." I took off my day pack and sat down, winded from the exertion.

"Steep hike, eh?"

"Yeah...where you from?"

"Montreal, you?"

"Texas. How long you been out?"

"Six months, six more to go. You?"

"Seventeen months." He whistled. My clout in the traveling world gained weight with each month I stayed away. If I kept it up, I'd make varsity captain. "How's the trip?"

"Pretty good, I guess. I think I'm just starting to get the hang of it." He sounded happy, and I'm sure he was, but underneath that I could hear a deepening exhaustion.

"Yeah, it takes a while...why'd you leave?"

"You know, I just graduated, and I wanted some time to myself before I jumped into a career and then woke up married with children...I got scared my life was being decided by other people and I didn't know what else to do about it. So I left."

"I hear ya."

"What about you?"

"Oh, you know, kinda similar. I forgot what was important and figured leaving everything behind was a good way to remember."

"How's that going?"

"I'll let you know when I decide." We both laughed. "It's going, but too soon to tell, I guess." I wanted to say more, to tell him of my recurring raincloud, and the constant feeling of pursuit by some terrible menace, but he stood up before I could muster up the nerve.

"Cool...I'm gonna go down, leave you alone with this view for a while."

Atticus slung his bag over his shoulder, took one last look, then began the descent.

I stayed for another twenty minutes, mostly because I didn't want it to seem like I was following him, then returned to find Atticus.

He was at the end of the last pool, looking over the edge of the waterfall that crashed into the raging river forty feet below. He goaded me forward until I stood beside him on the ledge. "Do like I do, or you're fucked, eh?" He pointed downriver to the frothing white-water as it raged passed a cluster of massive black boulders.

"I don't know, man," was all I could get out before he jumped.

As soon as he hit the water, he swam hard towards the shore, and pulled himself out of the current to safety. The rules of pack behavior demanded I follow his example or risk the torture of being less a man than he. I had seen him do it. It should be okay, right?

But maybe this is the time it all goes horribly wrong.

It took considerable effort to move against my fear of death, but I jumped.

We got drunk on *quetzalteca*, a local liquor, that night at a bar. Honest from the alcohol, I told Atticus the dark-side of my departure, how something in my mind was eating me alive, and the same symptoms were recurring after all this time on the road, that it still had not gone away. He shrugged, waved my concerns away with his hand, and poured us another shot. "I think you think too much," he said as he clinked his glass against mine, and drank, mustering his courage to approach the small gaggle of prostitutes waiting for us just outside.

"Yeah, maybe, but does that mean I'm wrong?"

Even though I was infected, I could do anything. I had been in a Bollywood movie in India, taught English in Japan, volunteered in Nepal, took part in an orgy in Thailand, ate mushroom pizza in Laos, climbed a volcano in Guatemala, lost a week's money at a cockfight in the Philippines, ate bugs in China, swam with sharks in Honduras, and smoked the finest in Amsterdam. Now, I was in Spain, trying to fill my coffers for the next flush, a young stallion trotting through the streets of Barcelona, looking for a mare.

The first time I saw her, it was in the bathroom. It was late. I was drunk, and I walked into the women's room. The yellow and gray tile was my first clue that something was off.

It's blue and gray in the men's room.

The absence of urinals was my second piece of evidence, and the clincher was the gorgeous woman leaning over the sink, looking into the mirror and plucking her eyebrows. Her wet hair suggested she had just gotten out of the shower and the towel wrapped around her from breasts to thighs confirmed it. Her body was lean and tanned—the slender, ripe form of a young woman in her mid-twenties. Upon realizing my error, my immediate reaction was to shout an apology on my way out the door and berate myself for days at the blunderous breach of privacy, but my body would not allow me to move. It refused. I was mesmerized by this spontaneous glimpse of vulnerable beauty though it was more than her physical allure that hypnotized me. Something deep inside of me recognized something equally profound in her.

Her long brown hair fell across her shoulders as she looked at me.

"I think you made a mistake." My bemused brain couldn't pinpoint the origin of her accent. I was staying at a hostel, and everyone was foreign. I was usually quite good at the accent guessing game, and I took it as good feedback that my expatriation from Mother Culture was paying off. I could even differentiate between an Australian and a New Zealand accent.

I tried to reply, but my lips still wouldn't move. I was captivated by a cloud of freckles that began on the lobe of her left ear, breezed down her neck, then spilled onto her back and chest, stopping somewhere under her towel.

"Ah-em," she cleared her throat and tiny lines of discomfort or anger deepened on her forehead.

I snapped out of my revelry. "Uhh...yeah...I must have made a mistake."

"Yes, you did." She laughed and I heard the faint clanging of wedding bells in the distance, but they were soon drowned out by the glorious sounds of an etheric choir. My heart pounded towards her, and I thought it would rip from my chest. The singing angels raised their voices and their heavenly notes washed out my anxiety. I clutched my chest. She laughed again, and I nearly collapsed. Then she leaned back over the mirror and continued plucking.

"Well...uh, you have a good night...I'll see you around," I managed to sputter.

"Uh-huh," she said in the disinterested voice of a beautiful woman, familiar with her effect on men.

I stumbled out of the bathroom and spent the rest of the evening trying to sleep, but I was possessed by her image. I tossed and turned, worried my silly mistake cost me any real hope with her.

In the morning, I slid out of my dorm bed for work, conscious of how much noise I made. Maintaining peaceful relations with twenty-two roommates demands a diplomacy (which was often neglected by the drunkest of us), and stealth. The only person awake at 7:00 was Anna, the German woman who cleaned the hostel four days a week to pay her rent. I never understood how she managed to be so upbeat so early when she drank all night with us (amphetamines, maybe), but every morning when I entered the kitchen for my breakfast, she greeted me with a warm smile and an enthusiastic hello.

"Hey, Anna," she stopped emptying overflowing ashtrays and turned to look at me, "I met...maybe that's not the best word," I mumbled to myself, "but...I saw this woman yesterday in the bathroom. I don't know her name or anything. She's got long brown hair, green eyes, just a bit shorter than me. You know who she is?"

She shrugged. "I don't know. There's much people that come and go from here." She smiled wider, her crooked teeth shading the caricature her imperfect English had drawn in my imagination. Big-headed Anna with that silly smile, holding a tiny broom and an enormous ashtray. "Why do you want to know? And was she in your bathroom or you in hers?"

I laughed. "Thanks, Anna. I'll take it from here."

The workday was long, but I was grateful for something to do. Being an American tourist in Spain granted me no official work rights, but employment was the only reason I went there. Throughout my adventures, I had met plenty of travelers who assured me that I could find under-the-table work and earn the Euro. It took me a week and only a small breakdown before I landed my first job as a painter.

I spent that afternoon trying to concentrate on the task at hand, but mostly thinking about that woman. My boss and I had been working on a house all week, and that day I was at the top of the three-storied luxury home. Standing on the scaffolding, I saw out past the buildings and into the glittering blue of the Mediterranean. There was something hazy in the distance and I pretended that it wasn't a mirage of the smog, but Majorca or Ibiza—I'd never know the difference.

It can be whatever I want it to be, que no?

After work, I rushed home to the hostel. I cleaned up quickly and waited at the table downstairs, rehearsing my re-introduction to that mysterious beauty, the things I'd say, the jokes I'd make. I would turn on the southern charm. The lounge filled with people returning from work and others just waking from their inebriated hibernation. They cracked open beers and continued the journey into drunkenness. Normally, I would have joined them, always happy to celebrate life by numbing myself to it, but I wanted to be sober for my future wife. Somewhere in the night, I had decided that she would be the one I would marry. I had fallen in love plenty of times before, sometimes for months or years, and other times only for a night, but never had

Manifesting the Monkey   21

I encountered such a feeling as the toweled woman inspired inside of me. Since I had seen her, the daily onslaught of doubt I inflicted upon myself subsided, and a feeling of peace spread throughout my body. I was free of the something I forgot was there.

This is better than beer!

So I sat at the table and waited for three long hours, then I gave up and went to bed early that night. My liver high-fived me on the way up to the dorm.

The next day was the same. Work and then waiting. And the next day, and the next. She never came back. After four days of this torture, the sobriety was too much, and the impression she had on me faded. I had overreacted, exaggerated the whole thing. Me...married? Life returned to normal and I reclaimed my role as doubt-collector.

I wonder how long this job will last. I don't think women find me attractive. Are my teeth white enough? Does my breath stink?

Normal life to me was working and drinking. I still couldn't face the world without the buffer of alcohol. As I had planned, I earned the Euro, and then spent it as quickly, which I hadn't foreseen. After so long on the road, I didn't care much about anything except for now. I didn't have the discipline nor the motivation to save so I consumed everything I earned, usually in the form of kebabs, beer, and cigarettes.

It was a very fun summer.

As Hollywood would direct, by the time I forgot about the woman in the towel, she reappeared.

I walked downstairs to the lounge. There was loud music playing, the new rock group everyone at the hostel listened to. Klaus, the young Austrian who loved to get stoned and repeat the album until someone forced him away from the sound system, was there again, next to the stereo with glazed eyes and a foolish smile on his face, guarding the music against the mob preparing for change. I said hello to everyone, scanned the room, and my heart jumped into my throat when I saw her there. Beams of hope broke through the clouds of doubt.

She was sitting in a chair, her hands folded neatly in her lap, palms up. Upon seeing her smile, I felt my face stretch into a spontaneous grin. Her light was contagious. I watched her, saw the gentle way she moved, her eagerness to laugh, and the calm certainty with which she carried herself. She was speaking with the group of French people who stayed at the hostel.

She's French.

My heart thumping in my chest, my hands warming up, I didn't know what to do. I vacillated between spying on her from the safety of the adjoining kitchen or sitting down in the empty seat next to her. It was something that happened everyday at the hostel. Someone walks in and sits down in a chair next to someone else. It didn't matter if it was a clumsy Polish man or a beautiful French woman.

It doesn't have to mean anything, does it? It's not going to reveal how I feel, is it?

Against my better judgment and to my surprise, I stepped forward, my arms and legs moving in chaotic jerks as I tried to force my body into some false notion of normal. I sat down and said hello. Her green eyes were more beautiful than I remembered, and I had to look away and break the spell lest I be lost forever. "What's your name?"

"Aurore, and you?"

"My name is Ten." Greetings in Spain were usually awkward for me, but even more so this time because it forced me close to the object of my affection, and that made me nervous. I moved in for the customary cheek kissing, still not realizing that the tradition wasn't an actual kiss, but a touching of cheeks accompanied only by kissing sound effects. I spent many months in Europe delighting all those sophisticated cultures with my suburban naiveté and sloppy smooches.

"Ten? That's a strange name."

I smiled. "Yeah, I guess it is. Believe it or not, my parents made a mistake, and I'm actually the eleventh child." She laughed, and I was rewarded with another dose of heart-wrenching harmonics. I had to be careful —a few more giggles from her, and I'd be on the verge of a religious experience, but I had just given up Catholicism (which I still felt guilty about).

We chatted for the next half hour, and I skirted the edge of faith, ready to fall on my knees and do anything for the Divine if only I could stay by her side another hour. I had claimed love before, but it was different with Aurore —it was simple and easy. I had never felt so alive, never felt the eternal bliss of my heart and after that short conversation, I was left...whole. It wasn't like she

Manifesting the Monkey   23

fixed me because I had already learned that romance didn't repair anything for very long. At best it would only cover up whatever I lacked until the come down. Aurore was a lighthouse, shining through the fog, guiding me towards the shore of some unexplored possibility. I would do whatever it took to be with her. The doubts were gone again.

She will be my wife.

A few minutes later, our group migrated to the beach to join some friends who were watching the sunset and celebrating the summer solstice. Normally, in pursuit of a female, I would dally until my current prey settled, then weasel in next to her, but this time I was determined to let nature take its course. I plopped down without thinking where Aurore was or would be. To my amazement and the growing trust in something higher than myself, she sat down next to me. She looked over and smiled, and I knew then that she had heard the angels as well. We had seen each other. Ever so slightly, a fragile strand stretched from my heart to hers.

Our conversation continued, and I again fell into a soft lullaby. I knew a patience and a detachment that were foreign to me. Usually, I was after something, ready to steal every base I could to reach the final triumph of sleeping with my object of conquest. After that, I'd slowly (or quickly) lose interest and return to hunting. With Aurore, it was different. I didn't care about the next step. If that 10:23 pm sunset could last forever and I'd never get to see her naked breasts, I would've been a happy man, and it would've saved me so much heartache, so much loss. But the illusion of time marched forth with Aurore and I on its shoulders, carrying us into a tangled web of reflection and meaning.

When it was time for her to go, I stood up, gave her the customary peck good-bye, and lingered in her faint coconut smell and silky cheeks. She pushed her bike to the sidewalk and pedaled off. I walked along the water's edge, then ran with the intense energy that poured out of my heart.

I'm in love!

In French, Aurore means 'dawn'. True to her namesake, she was a reliable source of light in my life. I continued the chase for the next few weeks, always edging closer, the way a tide inches up the beach, powered by some far away influence. That strand connecting us thickened into a string, then a cord, and soon into a healthy rope with an immense test weight. When our hearts decided, there was nothing we could do to stop it—I didn't even have to get her drunk. After we slept together, I only became more interested.

If that isn't love, what is?

I had no maps for such a relationship—it scared the crap out of me. I was an American expatriate illegally employed, and she was a French woman on working holiday, but I had seen all the movies and was certain that there would be no stopping us from reaching our own happily ever after, that no matter how dark and twisted the story became, it would all work out in the end.

Through many countries and many adventures, we loved each other. We took an unconventional path that created great moments of stress and powerful moments of bliss. These were the good times, this was the blessed life, but like in all things, happiness sets the stage for sadness. The doubts adapted to the Aurore Effect and crept back in.

How can we hold our couple together? How can we maintain the fragile love that has supported us through so much? How can we hold that together forever?

Aurore was from southern France, a small village called *Villefrance le Rouge*. We went there together so I could meet her family—parents, sister, brother, grandparents, aunts, uncles, cousins. They were cordial, but we all knew that I was out of place, the five-hundred pound fluorescent-green polka-dotted gorilla playing the banjo in the room. But that didn't matter, anyone with eyes to see knew that Aurore and I were good for each other. We had the key ingredient to a successful long-term relationship: compassionate adaptability. We got married the next time we were in France, a year later, and although their culture prevented them from showing it in any way I'd comprehend, they accepted me. They didn't understand why my parents or siblings, or anybody hadn't attended the wedding. I tried to explain it, but they shook their heads, and their eyes went wide imagining a life without their family.

"You're my treasure," she said during our honeymoon on the French Riviera, just after we had a series of blue waves tattooed on our left ring fingers. She spoke in her slow soft voice, choosing her words wisely. "And I love you," her smile couldn't hide the tears. "But I know that one day I will lose you. Now that I have found you, now that I have my treasure, one day it will fall away from me."

I held her as she cried, reassured her with my embrace that I would never let anything interfere with our destiny. I was smart, I was strong, and I was talented. I was a man of infinite potential, in process of realizing himself. There wasn't anything that I wouldn't do to keep us together. But somewhere inside, I knew that she was right. Even if it was death that parted us, all things that exist must one day cease to exist.

4

Be gracious to all men,
but choose the best to be your friends.
-Isocrates

Although I never told anyone, the jungles of Peru and the small huts of indigenous healers was always my intention for South America. I was in search for a final conclusion to the insatiable gnawing that had driven me out of my comfortable life, from the despair that had lived in my stomach since I could remember and into the unknown. I was sick of teetering eternally on the brink of crisis. As Aurore and I continued traveling from one life to another, flushing ourselves from country to country, rumors drifted by of a special brew in the Amazon, a drink that cured a vast array of ailments and even granted esoteric knowledge to the lucky. Since I had first heard of this magic potion, I was pulled into the Amazon hopeful to finally be free of my programmed inadequacies.

We began our South American adventure with a Vipassana meditation course, hidden away in the Andes. For ten days we took a vow of silence and meditated for eight hours a day. When we were finished and words seemed more hindering than useful, Aurore and I spent a month in Cuzco, idly passing the days in long conversations with strangers. The park benches and plazas were a great place to meet people, but they were either short-term tourists or persistent touts, neither of whom had anything lasting to offer us. We wanted to know the real Peru outside the rabid influence of consumerism. When it was time for Aurore and I to leave Cuzco, we stopped by the *Oficina del Tourismo*, sure they could help us get off the beaten track and away from all the khaki shorts and homesick westerners. We chose Pucallpa as our destination, but only because it was in the jungle and a medium-sized dot on the map. Its only importance to us was that it was a crossroads. We'd head there, get our bearings, then readjust our course as we saw fit. We didn't know what to expect because Aurore and I never used guidebooks.

"Oh Pucallpa is very nice," the woman said behind her thick mask of make-up. "It is very hot, but the jungle is most...breathtaking. So to get to Pucallpa is very simple. You go back to Lima, and then you take a bus or a plane from there."

"Back to Lima," Aurore said, and her face wrinkled into an expression of baffled disbelief whose meaning to me was morphing from cute to annoying. It was her surprise that got under my skin, her naiveté. It wasn't *cool*. "We don't need to go back south towards Lima. We're going north."

"Oh...I'm so sorry, but that is the only bus route. Back to Lima. All roads lead to Lima, you see?" She laughed at her joke. Aurore and I stared at her. When the silence was awkward enough, I looked down at the map. There were towns all across the Andes towards Pucallpa. Sure, Lima may be quicker, but we weren't looking for quicker. We were looking for genuine. It wasn't that the woman was lying to us, she just couldn't see past her own programming.

I pointed at the map, to Andayhualas, the next dot the same size as Cuzco towards Pucallpa. "Is there a road from here to there?" I asked, tracing the red line, waiting for her to follow my gaze.

"No..." Her eyes glazed over for a moment, and then she looked at the map again. "Yes...yes, there is." She was dazed, lost inside talking to herself. It was the first time she had ever seen *that* road on *that* map.

I smiled at her. "Where do locals catch the bus to Andayhualas?"

So began our journey north into the jungle, one black dot to the next, on rough unpaved serpentine roads, shaking for eight or ten hours at a time in double-decker buses. We were nauseous for most of the trip, but for us, the discomfort made it real. One day we were delayed six hours because a truck had slipped off the side of the road, and there wasn't enough room for us to pass. The passengers of our bus grouped together to help the driver, brainstorming solutions with a peaceful laughter and resilient patience. Another time, a bridge was out to vehicular traffic. We crossed on foot through the mess of construction equipment and waited as our bus drove onto a free-floating dock hitched to three small boats. When the bus was evenly-positioned, the boats tugged it across the swift river, their engines screaming as they pushed against the current.

We had eleven months of money in our accounts, and no particular place to go, but I was always headed for the medicine.

If you've ever traveled with anyone, you know something about what Aurore and I were doing—chasing the exhilaration of an open road, of an unknown future and the possibility that we could be anyone we wished. We were determined to find paradise along the way, get lost and live the rest of our lives outside all this, to find that happily ever after I had been sold. Although we found paradise more than once, we never stayed. After a few days or a week, that unsettled feeling called out from the darkness below, and we were soon off into the next tomorrow. We became experts at packing our bags.

Reduction is a major characteristic of travel. The longer I had to carry something—a shoe, a psychic scar—the more likely I was to examine its usefulness. One thing about packing to go anywhere is that you can't take everything. So before you go, you're forced into a process of reducing yourself, and it continues after that, when you find out you took way too much useless stuff—three pairs of shoes, an extra belt, more than one book—but not enough socks and underwear. After a few months, your backpack is balanced, but now it's time to balance the brain. Out goes preconceptions as you realize you brought too many false stereotypes about everything—people, food, life, love —but not enough curiosity and flexibility.

Aurore and I were prepared to go the distance, to live one day in absolute freedom, and we were determined to do it together. But it happened so fast...we never saw it coming. We were pushed along, hurled into increasing novelty, and there was never enough time to assimilate what we had just been through before we were at the front door of something new.

That's how life is. Something else is always coming along. The waves never cease. Sometimes they are pounding the earth, and sometimes they are lapping up gently against her, but they are always moving, and they will always move. Change is always happening, everywhere, but it's people that adapt to the rhythm so it all seems still. Every person is born with an infinite capacity to connect to this life and turn it into a beauty for everyone, but we hadn't yet chosen that.

Always low prices!

It wasn't that the world was bad because it wasn't. It had the potential to be a wonderland, but that parasite had convinced us the party-line, while not ideal, was the best we were capable of.

5

*If you are going through hell,
keep going.*
-Winston Churchill

New Chicago wasn't our first stop in the Amazon, nor the first drink of the medicine, but it was where I finally started making sense of the images in the mirror. Our previous encounters with the medicine had been heavily tainted by the dementia of the *curandero* (healer) who had administered it. Under the proper guidance, the potion can unlock the secrets of the Garden of Good and Evil, and the patient returns to a state of glowing purity. But not all *curanderos* are created equal, and there are those who have been perverted by power. It's very much like the epic war between the Jedi and the Sith, good versus evil. Ceremonies with *brujos* (Sith) could be harmful or even fatal, and they are sly and cunning, difficult to recognize, a snake in the grass. More than one eager *gringo* goes missing in the heart of darkness every year.

A high A-frame bamboo open-aired building. A woven-palm roof, and dirt floors. That's a typical hut in the jungle. It's night and it's usually quiet, that is, people don't speak much. They're waiting for the medicine to take effect, for the *curación* (healing) to begin. It's quiet, but there are lots of sounds. The jungle bugs buzz in overtones that unfold and envelop themselves, a perfect resonance created from millions of individual melodies—the rhythm of life.

The colors behind the eyes begin to swirl and thoughts, usually dark and ugly in the first drinks, float to the surface. The patient relives the traumas of the past, the hurts glossed over by terrified youth, moments of abandonment and inflicted cruelty. Every skeleton in the closet is thoroughly examined, personal history scraped off the mirror, and as the muck we often mistake for ourselves is cleaned, the reflection becomes unrecognizable. The suffering is intense and a fever may take the body. Symptoms of sickness manifest because the mind is ill.

The *curandera*, also with the medicine but trained in its power, streamlined by its purge, begins to hum. A map of the world, of life, in minuscule colored lines, knits together as she sings, forming loops that rebound onto one another, gracious curves that are both the song itself and its seed. The *curandera* sings to the medicine, now bubbling in the gut, pulling the physical impurities out along with their invisible counterparts. All maladies have non-physical roots. Sooner or later, the sick begins to pour from the mouth or the rectum in sporadic spurts. The medicine does all the work. The patient's sole responsibility is to watch the scars surface from the psyche, back to their creation. That's all.

Just observe.

Aurore and I traveled upriver from Pucallpa to New Chicago in a long, thin boat powered by a single Kawasaki engine. There were a few other passengers aboard, smiling big, carrying their purchases—bread, sugar, flour, chickens—back to the villages in colorful mesh bags. I had to step over both people and products to claim my seat in the middle. Our trip started and the possibility of any meaningful conversation was drowned out by the whine of the engine, but I was happy with the excuse to dwell on the desperation in my heart. My light was fading, my soul dying, the once-mighty flame flickering out. It wouldn't be long before that whatever eating me from the inside finished me off. I was running out of options.

We bounced around the boat, forcing laughs to dispel our discomfort. Our new *curandero,* a middle-aged man named Lucio Vasquez, slept on the bench next us, snoring as the boat pummeled him on the rough Ucayali river.

Humans can adapt to any situation.

Lucio was bright, vibrant, and a card-carrying member of *la Asosiacion de Curanderos Tradicionales.* It seemed odd—a governmental organization that not only recognizes capable practitioners of psychedelic medicine, but also provides them with an ID to affirm their status—but the rules of reality were different in the jungle. Aurore and I had met Lucio in Yarinacocha, just outside of Pucallpa, when he came to check up on his former patients, a French couple who stayed in the room next to us at our guest-house, *Los Porcupinos.* Our first impression of Lucio was positive, but I didn't much trust into that. I didn't put much trust into anything, except that something was bound to go wrong, and for some reason, I was surprised when it often did. People who worked in the Otherworld had a powerful charisma and could easily provoke any human emotion. They had the capability to be master manipulators. My experience taught me not to trust my senses. So I didn't.

Lucio's offer for his *curaciónes* was the best deal in town—we could pay whatever we wanted. But before he left *Los Porcupinos*, he asked for twenty bucks as a deposit for his services, and, he said, we could meet the next morning to accompany him to New Chicago. I was immediately uncomfortable. Money consistently got in the way between those who had it and those who didn't. The rich were economic tyrants, and the poor were lazy mooches.

"It depends on you," the words coming from behind his gappy smile. "For the passage and to eat." I thought about denying his request, spouting reasons why such a deposit didn't make very good business sense, a very reasonable one being that we hadn't yet fully committed to the ceremony, but I refrained. Speaking my mind had gotten me into plenty of painful situations, and I was scared to pollute this new opportunity with my linguistic hunt for the truth. I swallowed and gave him the money.

Not surprisingly, Aurore and I decided to go to New Chicago and proceed with Lucio's *curación*. My previous six drinks of the medicine had further polished the mirror, allowing me to see deeper into my reflection, revealing dark, amorphous shapes beneath the surface. I knew was at the mercy of an internal saboteur who kindled a subtle, but overpowering urge to cause my downfall at the very moment of triumph. I had been compromised. This spy's exposure and expulsion would revolutionize my life. If only one thing, I wanted to leave the world of the medicine with a secure mind. If I couldn't trust myself, I couldn't trust anyone. I needed to be cured, to be cleaned of the darkness that was inside of me. If I couldn't, if I wouldn't, I'd have to kill myself because I couldn't bear another day of sleepwalking through a world out to harm me.

I put on the hopeful mask, but inside I was disenchanted with the medicine. Three weeks in San Rafael with a mediocre healer—ironically named don Juan, who fell somewhere between Obi-won and Vader on the Jedi spectrum—had scrambled my brain and disillusioned me about the potion and medicine men in general. Don Juan's lust for oblivion had suffocated whatever power he once claimed. He was a kindly old man, bent from so many years in the world, speaking only fragmented bits of Spanish that he pieced together into a motley-colored mosaic. He told marvelous stories of magic and intrigue, of astral darts and armies of anacondas. He told us of a tree in the jungle, that once brewed properly, gave command over all venomous snakes...*brujo* magic. Like I said, deep in the jungle, the reality game was played by different rules. It took us three weeks to discover don Juan was a drunk, and while his stories of the Otherworld may have been true, he had given his power to the bottle.

Though he was a drunkard, under don Juan's tutelage, I had observed a certain something growing inside my head. It started with a wavering in the black behind my eyes, a common first introduction to the Otherworld, that transformed into a mass of long thin shapes, like a mess of writhing ropes. Don Juan introduced this entity as the *soga*, a primordial form, the fertile ground of the Otherworld where the seeds of the physical world are sown. The *soga* became small dots that whizzed by, and when I concentrated on them they became flies. Next, I noticed ants marching through my head. A few sessions of observation later, and the ants traveled through a world filled with plants and then trees. By the time I left San Rafael, I perceived eyes peering out at me from the wall of vegetation. There was a jungle growing in my mind.

As we zoomed past pristine Amazonian rain forest towards Lucio's place, the shores littered with a thousand plastic shopping bags, the naive part of me still hoped I would find my cure.

The boat stopped a few times on our journey to New Chicago, and once we tied up to a busy pier for lunch. Everyone disembarked, clambering to the front of the boat, then across a wobbly plank and up two flights of near vertical steps to the top of the river bank. A couple of wooden booths sold packaged snacks and sodas (peanuts, chips, cookies, Inca cola, and Coke). We walked by the long table where five women cooked different varieties of the same things—rice, beans, chicken, pork, or fish, and always a soup. We bought rice and beans and found a spot to sit in the grass with a great view of the wide river and dense vegetation. Never before had I seen so many shades of green and so much life, growing up and out of itself, like societies building their cities atop the ruins of civilizations they had just conquered. It didn't take long for our private picnic to become public as men and boys sat next to us while the women stayed towards the edges, listening, but not participating. All the men asked the same questions at different times. Origin, age, occupation, religion, and children? I smiled, slid my Humble Tourist mask +over my face, and satisfied their curiosity. I saw it please them, and the conversation soon turned from us to them.

"You are very lucky to live in such abundance," Aurore said. Unlike myself, she was loving and sympathetic. My wife genuinely cared about the world. She felt its injustices and its ecstasies in her heart and expressed them accordingly, which was sometimes violent and loud.

"Yes, yes we are. The jungle is our mother. She gives us everything we need."

Then why do you go into town to buy your plastic junk?

The man looked at me, and my mask smiled bigger. He continued. "There is so much life here, so much beauty. So many amazing things. We live a simple life, we are a simple people.

You got that right.

He stopped again. "You do not think we have amazing things?"

I hurried to put my slipping facade back in place. "Oh, I know you do. I have been blessed to see only a few of them."

"We have a simple life, but it is a good life. We are surrounded everywhere by miracles. Here, I will show you."

He put his plate on the ground, stood up, and walked behind the counter of a booth, as if he owned it. He reached up onto a shelf, took something down, and came back, proudly holding an armadillo shell the size of a serving dish. "Look at this, my friend. Can you imagine such a creature as this, one that makes his own armor so Jaguar cannot harm him? Surely, this is amazing."

Aurore had never seen an armadillo before and she 'oohed' and 'aahed' in honest astonishment. The *señor* was content with her reaction. He moved closer so I could see better, and I examined it briefly.

"Oh yeah...that's an armadillo, alright. We got those back home...only we call them Texas speed bumps."

Manifesting the Monkey   35

His face slackened, and the man pulled the shell to his chest, as if to protect himself from my venom. He shook his head slowly and returned the treasure to its place.

In the middle of the boat three people could sit abreast, but rarely comfortably. The hard wooden benches spanking us as we bounced along the river was our first trial in New Chicago. We were only going for four days, but if the paddling we were already receiving was any indication, it would be intense. Four nights, four ceremonies. I pretended not to feel my disease as it dripped from my tongue when I filled the silence with automatic dribble, pretended not to hear it when it whispered to me, convinced me of my right to judge. Drinking the medicine was always an occasion of intense upheaval, of reality rearrangement. It would be a difficult trial, and I wanted to abort, to pull out of the vortex, but I was at the bottom of the flush, and there was nothing I could do. I was going under, kicking and screaming.

I looked at the wall of green that rushed past, sometimes singling out a tree or bush and watching it in sharp focus for the three seconds I could see it before we zoomed past. I kept my awareness away from the part of me that still believed I had a shot at salvation, afraid that my attention would only draw it out and then whatever was eating me alive would consume it as well. I came to the medicine hopeful to change a fundamental program that prevented me from obtaining lasting happiness. Since I could remember, I was pushing against a shadowy resistance, some insidious virus that silently poisoned every part of my mind. I knew that if I could just get to it, just change that crucial line of code, I would see reality different. I would *be* different. Since I first left home, I had chipped away at my programming, gathering techniques and practices that enabled a new flexibility of mind. I changed. I was evolving. I had made progress, but it was never enough. There was still something there, beneath all of me. My study afforded me with tools —meditation, visualization, dance, drums—to alter myself and reality, but they weren't powerful enough to make the change I desired. I couldn't reach it. It was too deep. Whatever it was that I was banging my head against was hard-wired into me, or even worse, it was genetic and unalterable. I either had a really long-shot at redemption, or I was screwed. Despite my better judgment, I chose to believe I was standing at a threshold, and with a small step, everything would align. I could be the man I wanted to be—strong and calm, prepared and relaxed, no longer plagued by the doubts and the worries that chased me through the playgrounds of my life.

The boat dropped us on the muddy shore of the Ucayali, and we walked twenty minutes through the jungle, past formidable papayas and banana trees, their fruits wrapped in blue plastic to protect them from flies, past fallen trees and clouds of swarming bugs, small thatched buildings and corn fields. When we arrived at his home—a grouping of jungle huts in a dusty clearing—Lucio showed us to the small raised room with bunk beds and a torn *mosquitero* (mosquito net) that served as the guest house. The beds were covered in rat shit, and the whole thing smelled as if it would fall apart at any moment. The other homes were in much better condition, but still rustic and savage by modern standards. A well was the village's only source of water, and it was light brown in color, nauseatingly reminiscent of the medicine. The H_2O + grit was normally flavored with coffee, making hydration an even bigger challenge. The jungle in New Chicago was thick, and the buzz of life was just beyond our reach, but it snuggled up and supported us.

We had only traveled for a few hours by boat, but we were centuries behind the city we had left.

6

Courage is resistance to fear,
mastery of fear,
but not absence of fear.
-Mark Twain

The guest house was falling apart, unsuitable even to our modest standards. We left our bags on rotting mattresses and walked across the courtyard to the large fire where Freddy, a tall native man and Lucio's eldest son, was cooking the medicine over a trench filled with glowing red coals that slowly consumed a massive tree trunk. Metal poles straddled the pit and two huge cauldrons sat on them, full of the boiling brew. Berto, a long-haired Peruvian vagabond, was next to him. He smiled and shook our hands, happy that he was no longer the sole patient at the clinic.

"You are here to have a *curación*," Freddy told us. His gentle words contrasted his thick frame, and I liked him immediately.

"Yes, sir," I responded behind my Eddie Haskell mask. "We've heard great things about the work being done here, and we definitely have some healing to do." Inside, I was only half-honest in my humility. Part of me was sure that I had figured out the secrets of the entire universe, that I had no need for these savages and their horrible tasting drink. Indeed, I had learned some things about life, but I refused to admit there could be more. I preferred to continue thinking I was a finished product.

Doesn't everybody?

"We all have a lot to learn." Freddy answered. A comfortable silence fell among us, a common trait in indigenous cultures world-wide. It was only in the sick places where silence was hunted and hounded by meaningless assertions and observations.

It was Berto who broke the calm. "Where do you come from?"

"I'm from France, and my husband is from Texas," Aurore answered. Freddy smiled, and I saw her effect on him. People who are open to miracles and the beauty of life are often affected by Aurore when she smiles, when she

38   Manifesting the Monkey

speaks, when she passes by in a room, or when she does anything with her natural grace.

"Texas?" Berto's accusative tone was one I had grown accustomed to with George W. Bush in the White House. Travelers abroad had to learn to suffer the reputations of their Mother Cultures. I waited for the attack. Berto poked the fire with a stick, sending a stream of tiny sparks up into the air. "They kill lots of people every year, don't they?"

"Yeah...yeah, they do." I was tempted to nibble at the obvious bait he dangled in front of me, to explain that in the context of a disturbed society, the death penalty made perfect sense. I loved to argue, but I resisted my programming.

"That's where Bush is from, isn't he, from Texas?"

"Uh...yes and no. He was governor, he's got a ranch there, but he's not originally from Texas."

"And now, Bush is killing lots of people in Iraq."

I shrugged. "Yeah, I guess you could say that."

"I don't understand why Americans have to be the policemen of the world, why they have to pretend to protect people when all they want to do is extort them out of their natural resources. America is destroying the world."

My anger flared, and this time I dove headfirst into my scripted behavior. He was right—the war in Iraq was a farce, but it wasn't as simple as he made it out either. World dynamics was a hefty onion. "Well, that's a pretty simple way of putting it. Yeah, you can say that America is destroying the world, but we do a lot to maintain order in the midst of chaos. I mean, you think it's bad now? Wait till the Chinese take over." The ember of controversy ignited the anger I kept bottled up and out of sight, like a good boy.

Berto looked at me, eyes wide. His bait had caught a shark. He stopped his mindless tapping in the fire.

I continued, the argument rose up to my heart and heated my words. "But you know what I think?" He looked at me, and I saw his fear. It made me want to laugh. "I think that lots of people like to look out and see all the crappy things the United States does so they can focus on something other than their own problems. Yeah, some of the stuff America does is really shitty, I'm usually the first to admit, but focusing on it is just a way to complain about something that we have no control over, isn't it? It's a way to avoid actually doing something about the problems that are right in front of us. Basically, it's just another of the many ways to be full of shit."

Freddy laughed and nodded in agreement. "Sure, every country has done terrible things. Peru is no exception, but concentrating on a foreign enemy is pointless unless you're staring him in the eyes." Freddy looked at me. "And I'm guessing that you're not here to spread American dogma, are you?"

"Not at all, my friend. No dogma here!"

Berto pretended to laugh with us, and I reveled in his embarrassment.

"How do you like your accommodations?" Freddy asked Aurore.

She looked into the fire and blushed. "Well...it's pretty...rough."

Freddy laughed again. "It is rough. We have not had the money to spend on maintaining the building. You can sleep in the ceremony room," he nodded towards the building next to the guest-house. "That's where Berto sleeps."

The sun set and the moon rose, nearly full. It was a few days before the summer solstice, but near the equator the solstice meant nothing. In the jungle, a fluctuating balance of day and night was as foreign as Marmite.

The ceremonies were held in a big jungle hut. Inside, a *mosquitero* encompassed the entire ritual space. The floor was lined with mattresses and blankets. An ankle-high table with a three-liter bottle of the medicine crowned the room. The red in the Pepsi logo had faded years ago. My stomach turned at the sight of it. Staring at the bottle, I saw redemption and grace. The possibility of forgiveness waved at me, invited me in with open arms. Just let go, it whispered, let go, which only terrified me, and from inside, my demons slung curses and condemnations, their eyes burning more holes into my tattered confidence. The ceremony began early, just after dark and started strong with two cups. The taste was so horrible, I barely held the second one down. After everyone drank, we laid down along the perimeter of the *mosquitero*. Lucio sat at the front, next to the bottle. Freddy, two other men, and a woman who I did not know were at the back. The only patients were Aurore, myself, and Berto. I couldn't see much, just dark shapes expanding and contracting with their breath or the momentary red beacon as someone puffed a cigarette.

We're surrounded!

To distract myself, I tried to converse with the ones I didn't know, but they spoke very little Spanish, and the only thing I knew how to say in their native tongue was the most useful phrase in any language: thank you. As the medicine washed over me, I became more and more uncomfortable, and my fiddling increased. I sat up, I laid back down. I sat up again, trying to avoid the monumental suffering that built in my gut. As the effects intensified, I broke into a fever, and my squirming increased, totally uncomfortable in my body. My panic gained momentum and left me in a state of useless terror. There was no telling what I'd see, what I'd feel, and I wanted nothing more than to run away to the warmth and safety of my mother's couch. I cursed myself for the idealogical conclusions and the naiveté to act on them that got me in my current predicament.

You're such a dumbass.

Lucio and the others began to sing their different songs. Something inside of me wiggled away from that magic brew. I didn't know what it was, and I didn't care. I wanted it out. I spent the evening over a bucket, spitting and hacking, trying desperately to get that black thing out of my body. Vomiting was a particularly satisfying part of the experience, a gratifying release of emotional knots, but the purge would not come. The medicine was working its way through my system, flowing through every part of my body, a spiritual anaconda, gobbling up negative energies in its path. Lucio and the other astral physicians swayed near us, splitting the power of their songs between Aurore, myself, and Berto. I had no strong visions, but this was normal for me, part of the disappointment I found in San Rafael with don Juan. Something covered my eyes. A black hole, slowly spreading through my energetic body, ready to use my life for its food. This was my sickness, and this was what kept me from seeing the world of light that exists all the time.

My disease manifested in many ways, all of them harmful. I was short-tempered, judgmental, angry, cynical, but I was also very intelligent and could pick apart anything anybody said and leave them feeling stupid and worthless. Blindly, I traced these behaviors back to the inner critic. I thought that was the source. He had gotten out of control and found fault with everything. I was always chiding myself, always pushing to be better instead of just accepting everything, myself included, as it was. I was a perfectionist, and my external behavior towards others reflected this internal relationship with myself.

As the doctors sang their nonsense songs to me, I got to work—I observed. During the session, three images blinked before my eyes, and I knew immediately that they were the tools of the inner critic, his weapons of choice. A golden drop dripped from the stinger of a scorpion's tail. It flashed across the psychedelic darkness that surrounded me. My mouth watered— this was the pernicious poison whose taste I had forgotten. It was the foundation of the critic's power, the weakening of my system by self-doubt. I focused on the tail, pulled it out, and stored it safely for removal. I didn't know if I would vomit, and I wanted those weapons out of my body so the only logical place to put them was in my bowels, where they would leave with the medicine in the morning. The next weapon came nearly a painful hour later, and it was a praying mantis. Segmented and alien, this was the inner critic's will to survive, strong enough to devour me, his mate. It was the cold, calculated righteousness with which the critic justified his existence and often expressed itself in my smug demeanor. I marked and stored it for disposal. The last one came just before the magic of the medicine faded into the spreading light of day—a spear. This was the inner critic's weapon of oppression with which he poked and prodded me relentlessly, the tyranny of perfection, and as soon as I intended to release this symbol, a feeling pushed down out of me.

"It took you long enough," Lucio called as I ran to the outhouse with the elegance of urgency.

7

There is more wisdom in your body
than in your deepest philosophies
-Friedrich Nietzsche

The next day, I wanted to leave New Chicago and the world of the medicine forever. It wasn't because the previous ceremony was so intense, but because I knew it was only the beginning, and whatever I found along the way to my *curación* would be no less than abhorrent, and I'd have to redefine myself to survive. As I looked deeper into the mirror, I was even more disgusted by my reflection. A thousand more doubts sprouted and flourished.

Maybe I'm not sick, maybe I don't need a curación. *Perhaps my expectations make it impossible to have a genuine experience, perhaps I'm not ready, perhaps the gentle female voice of God I heard on my very first drink, comforting me, was a hallucination and not contact.*

From all sides, the doubts plagued me, springing up from the dark *soga* twisting through my body. Every thought that went through my head had to be screened by my conscious mind, lest I be overwhelmed by my own negativity and fall further into the pit from which I was so tenaciously trying to climb

Later, I found a playing card in the dirt outside the toilet. The seven of spades. I translated that into the tarot—the seven of Swords, representing uncertainty, failure due to lack of effort. If you continue, you will succeed. I remembered the voice of Goenke from the Vipassana course, croaking the same advice to me. I took a deep breath and recommitted.

The day passed in a blur of half-reality, and before I knew it the sun set and the moon rose again, and we returned to the ceremonial hut. As we passed the wooden cup around, Freddy walked the perimeter of the *mosquitero*, singing softly and blowing tobacco smoke. I felt safe. Scared, but safe.

The medicine came on quickly, and I experienced the same feelings of dread and discomfort as the previous night. When they peaked, I convinced myself to relax and observe them. I accepted the unpleasant sensations in my body, and they immediately became less intense. I sat upright and began the work for the evening.

I had created the critic. A long time ago he had helped me survive. I acknowledged his usefulness but recognized that his purpose had mutated into a jail of limitations and impossible standards, of constant second-guessing. He was never satisfied with anything. Ever. Not once. The critic had created his home in a high stone tower where he looked down on the proceedings of my mind, judging everything. In glimpses, I saw him—short, bald, and capable. Down below, my jungle was thriving, growing thick all around his safe-house, trapping the critic. The rest of us had finally turned on him. I had revolted.

The previous night, I had successfully disarmed the critic. Now, the medicine's song slowly spread throughout my being, rocking the foundation of that unwanted guest we had all forgotten we invited. In the physical, I sat up taller. It was all easy, and I understood the power of intention. I got it. The critic was scared and digging in. The doctors knew it and crowded around me, assaulting the enemy from all sides with their melodies. From every direction came a different song, each beautiful on their own, but all mixed up they created a resonant noise that scrambled my brain. I did what I could to help my benefactors. I made myself smaller, so tiny that I could fit into a thimble, and the healers could better see the critic. After some time with that, I made myself enormous, filling the entire *mosquitero* and mashing up against the energy of the others. I flushed, drank another cup of medicine and continued the onslaught, turned up the heat. I'd burn him out. After setting the blaze and feeling the sweat pour down my face, I adjusted the thermostat until I saw my breath in the humid jungle night and felt the tremors from the critic's shivering. When all was perfect, the songs hit a crescendo, focused, and a bolt of lightening crashed into me. With a snap of the fingers, the critic was gone, and his tower was in rubble. A weight crumbled off of me, and I grew brighter. A moment later, Team Ten yanked some slimy rot out of my guts, and I vomited it into the bucket. Lucio and his assistants immediately concentrated their power on Berto. They knew that I had gotten a good grip and pulled myself up to safety. The first inhabitants of the jungle in my head, the ants, quickly took the bricks from the former tower and set about making a network of roads. I glimpsed little paradises and doors into the Otherworlds.

The critic had mutated into an intolerant tyrant, but he had served a purpose, and I felt a gap inside of me. Like it or not, I created his voice as a survival mechanism—it saved me embarrassment. His original purpose was to coach me toward more socially accepted behaviors and more intelligent ways to do things, which was a valuable asset at times. That was still something I needed so in his stead, I projected the third eye, the invisible organ of vision—dark blue and shining—down into my mind. Clear sight might meet the same needs that constant poking fulfilled. If I could see clearly, I could think clearly, and if I could think clearly, I could make good decisions, which was basically why I created the bastard, wasn't it?

When I recovered from the siege against the critic, and had installed a new force in his place, I was still with the medicine, and a violent seizure overtook me. I shook like a wet dog, surprised when wings popped out of my back. The air around me moved as these new appendages flapped slowly, uncertain but quickly learning their function. My excitement overwhelmed me, and I wasn't able to maintain the transformation. I returned to my human shape.

In the dark hut, I could just see the glint of Lucio's smiling teeth in the moonlight.

<u>8</u>

*Ask questions from your heart,
and you will be answered from the heart.
-Native American proverb*

Just after sunrise, I undressed behind a three-sided, chest-high bamboo wall and began the day with an Amazonian shower. Next to me was a large plastic basin of cold water and three empty buckets. I grabbed the largest, scooped it full from the reservoir, and dumped it over my head. I gasped at the shock of the cold water and was immediately grounded and back in collective reality.

Wake up.

I spent most of that day outside my head interacting with the community. Lucio's family was big, and their innocent curiosity drew them close to me as I lounged in my hammock. Some kids were younger than two and some as old as fourteen, but they all smiled with a purity that, in Texas, was reserved only for the youngest—by the age of six, it usually faded into the background of the personality, hidden by the nervous habit of worry, a constant stream of words, or an obsession with beauty. The children of New Chicago giggled at silly things, always looking for a reason to smile. If one did not present itself soon enough, they laughed at nothing. I enjoyed their company, but was somewhat envious of their simple, peaceful life. These poor uncivilized people had no modern conveniences, but they had something I had given away, though I couldn't remember what it was. It was the only place I had ever been where babies didn't cry. And it wasn't as if they were chided or otherwise reproached if they did. It was much deeper than that. These tiny human beings were born into a world where they fit perfectly. Barring crisis, they had no reason to cry.

I was brighter, but by the end of the day, when the sun set, the full moon rose, and the mosquitoes patrolled by in platoons, dark thoughts returned to me, doubts that I was sure should have left with the critic.

I should be done.

But it was still there. The critic was not the source of my disease.

I stumbled over this conclusion and fell further into my hole of apprehension, questioning everything. The doubts thundered in, each wave stronger, threatening to drown me. I flailed to stay afloat. First I didn't know how to trust myself.

What made you think it was the critic in the first place? You had no real evidence. You're a dumbass!

Next it was the people around me.

Who are these people in their stupid little lives with nothing? They've got nothing, but they prance around like they are privilege to the secrets of the universe. Schmucks!

Then the doubts targeted my wife and the legitimacy of our marriage.

God, I've made a huge mistake. What were we thinking? Getting married! Me, married? That was the biggest mistake in my life, and it's gonna ruin me.

Since before I could remember, some invisible mouth fed on all the things that made me happy. It leeched onto the bright times of my life and slowly sucked the light out of them, until they were dim and gray. My relationship was the latest victim of that unseen assailant. Like always, I watched in powerless horror as it oozed up to my intentions, implanted its foul heads, and began to siphon the faith from them. There was nothing I could do, and I was soon wandering aimlessly down an infinite hall of mirrors. When I entered the hut for our third ceremony, my head was in a marvelous mess.

It was the twenty-first of June, the summer solstice, three years since that fire on the beach with Aurore. The solstice is the longest day of the year, the one with the most light. It is the brightest day, but also the moment of death, when the light begins the slow fade into darkness. I was happy and sure on the surface, ready to wear that familiar mask of tranquility for the world around me, to pretend to myself and everyone else that things were just dandy, that my *curación* was finished. I lacked the courage to be vulnerable and reveal what was really happening inside, where deep down the doubts gnawed on me, and I had no idea what to do.

This was exactly the problem I had come here to solve. I lay down, disheartened, on the mats under the *mosquitero* and prepared myself for the next session.

Is this normal? Did the change I experienced last night really happen? I'm ready to be a different person, but somehow it all feels the same in my head. Maybe the change needs time to take effect, maybe I need time to perceive the effects?

The critic was gone, but I was still oppressed, weighed down by some invisible force right in front of my eyes. A fundamental switch that controlled my beliefs about the world was still closed. I nosedived towards a major freak out.

Just before Lucio arrived in his place at the head of the room, I decided to drink three cups of the medicine straight away and re-dose often. Intentions are always important with any medicine and a sincere request receives an honest answer. I asked the medicine to show me that which I could not see, hoping I could get my bearings. The effects came quickly, and they were powerful. That thing I could not see pushed me down onto the mat. I lay under the weight of that invisible force I had lived with for so long. The sledgehammer of doubt pounded me relentlessly over the head. In the background, a doleful violin wailed.

Within a matter of moments, the doubts re-targeted my relationship, the most cherished process outside myself, the thing I wanted most to keep. I watched as the troubles of our relationship—the demands, the lies, the shouts, the insults—paraded by in some painful fashion show. Then, instant comparisons were made to Hollywood fairy tales and how far we were from those happily-ever-afters. The math was done, and a briefcase materialized next to me. An accountant unfolded himself from it and handed me a curly paper from his adding machine.

Projections are not good.

He patted me on the back, leaving me the paper, then packed himself back into his briefcase, and I was alone again.

It began—a voice, subtle and clear, comforting where the critic had been disheartening.

It spoke in candy-drop words, soothing coos of security and pacifying comfort. The voice reassured me that separation was necessary, that true growth could only be achieved alone. Was it Reason looking out for my highest good? It made sense—its logic was sound, and its proof was unshakable, conditioned by so many hours of television. I teetered on the edge, ready to topple, ready to give in to the doubt. The medicine was only

48   Manifesting the Monkey

giving me what I had asked for, and answers were dangerous. I was happier not knowing. My eyes squeezed shut, and silent tears slid down my face. When I couldn't take it anymore, when the voice had convinced me it was right, that this was for the best, I sat up, intent to let the words of separation slip from my mouth and shatter what Aurore and I had worked so long to build, to destroy what we had chosen to believe in.

She was smiling and bright, having looked deep into the mirror with her first cup of the medicine in San Rafael when the demons inside of her came out shaking and screaming, then left forever. I summoned the courage needed to say good-bye. How do you let go of someone you love?

Listening to that reassuring voice, I pushed through the defenses, the barricades. I disarmed the booby traps that protected me from giving up the one thing that mattered to me. I opened my mouth, prepared to let the words flow out of me, to tell my wife that we had fooled ourselves, that our marriage, our love was a farce. But just as I called out to her in the dark, a wordless realization bubbled up out of my deeper mind, and I saw.

The lights clicked on, and my third eye opened. Finally, the shadowy glimpses parted, and I saw the majesty of the Otherworld glowing in front of me. And finally, I could see my oppressor, my infection, that disease I had lived with for so long. Its mycellium weaseled through existence, a putrid head sucking madly at my pain. I looked down at my body, now glowing white with the power of the medicine. There was something woven into me, something blacker than black had invaded me. The dark creature slithered and jerked in surprise as it realized I was aware of it. It was conscious, and this tipped me over the edge. A strong revulsion overtook me, and I vomited into the bucket. Without a word or a sound, I knew who this was. It had been with me for so long that I had forgotten I had invited it in, forgotten it was here. As I grew up, it became stronger, taking more and more control until I was the puppet, and it was the master. This dark invader had manipulated every moment of my life, and as I gazed into eternity, the medicine showed me that every human, save a few, was also infected. The boogeyman lived inside of everyone—financial loss, spousal betrayal, social denouncement, spiders, terrorists, cockroaches. We had surrendered the right to decide for ourselves, and given it to the boogeyman.

For millennium, fear had enslaved humanity, and it was such a cunning tyrant that most denied its control.

The shock thundered across me, and I vomited again, but not the kind that gets the bad out. This was a heave of disillusionment, the sheer terror of having lived a lie for so long. Photos of my life flipped in front of my ethereal vision, and in each one, I noticed the boogeyman whispering his wishes into my ear. Every decision in my life, save a few, had been made by fear, and I had masked its role in my life as common sense or comfort or safety. Facing it was too terrible to consider. What could I have done about it? But that night in the hut, it was a simple choice—life or death. Fight the boogeyman, or let fear stay inside of me and pass the rest of my days as a zombie, too scared to really live. My body would continue, but my light would be snuffed out.

This was the beginning of my war.

The Wise Old Man, a part of me I hadn't known existed, stepped out of the depths of my mind and took the reins. The innate wisdom of the human soul guided me. I hosted a parasite, and the only way to get rid of the stowaway was to cleanse myself. I asked to see the Inner Child and immediately my six-year-old self materialized in front of me, still free from the disease. He was running, his spontaneous joy perfuming the backyard.

I called, and he came to me, wearing an authentic smile, one I used to know. I introduced myself and shook his hand. The light in my head shone brighter. The strategies, techniques, methods that I had acquired over the past years in my search for a cure fit together into a complex remedy for my possession. I explained to the Child what was about to pass in his life, that he was upon a moment that would alter him forever. I cried when I told him how things would soon change, and it would be so deep that he would not recover until he was twenty-eight, not until now. I was that help. I had come to save him, to save me.

We were in my mind, and something urged me to move. I collected the child, and we opened the hatch at the bottom of my brain, climbed down through my mouth, throat, and voice box, into my heart. Here would be our sanctuary for the upcoming battle.

More than anything people want to love and be loved, and all the problems of the self and the world are cases of love gone awry—withheld, repressed, miscommunicated, misunderstood, or otherwise perverted.

From the east, a warm fire shone its light on our circle. From the opposite direction, the river of life flowed by and offered her power. Behind us, to the south, the mountains stood, supporting us, and a warm wind blew from the north and carried away the last traces of grime from the mirror. Everything was clear. It was now or never, live or die.

The black thing shape-shifted into a dragon. It circled above us, assessing the situation, preferring to fight from the safety of cover. He was not used to the exposure. I laughed as I understood my spontaneous transformation the previous night—I was to battle my enemy. I shivered and shook. The wings returned, and the rest of me transformed into a dragon, multi-colored and pissed off. My full realization was enough to untangle the fear from myself. Now, it was only a matter of evicting him from my body. The thing was black, absorbing all light, shining a vacuous nothing. The beast kept to the shadows, darting from place to place in the blink of an eye, and he was easy to lose. My power was strong, and the boogeyman knew it. A circle of hand-holding hearts appeared and lined up around the perimeter of my center, surrounding us, glistening candy-apple red, straight from some Saturday morning cartoon. The hearts danced and sang the simple words, the secret of life. John Lennon's voice boomed through my soul, *All you need is love!* The hearts encompassed everything. There was no place they weren't, and as the pursuit continued, their circle shrank, slowly pulling me and my enemy towards each other as I chased him through the infinite space of my core. I gained on him, and snapped at him with massive jaws and rows upon rows of dangerous teeth, but every time I thought I had him, he slipped away, and the chase renewed. The circle continued to shrink, until there was no place to go, and we both returned to our humanoid shapes.

I couldn't see his face. It was always shifting. Standing so close to that death, his stink overwhelmed me, and I vomited. The fear lashed out at me, wrapped his thousand devious tentacles around me and whispered into my ear, trying to comfort me back to sleep, but I pushed him away. He attacked again, used my brain against me, showed me images of my supposed worthlessness, of complete failure, and utter damnation. He intended to destroy my will, but I shook them away and smiled. He alternated his attacks —seductive words and false promises of complacency, then images that shocked—trying to force me back on my decision, to retreat back to sleep, and re-accept him as myself. In the physical, I shivered, snot ran down my nose into that bucket of filth, and I saw the beginning, the root, where it all started. The memory welled up and washed over us all, and I traveled back in time to the moment when I was infected.

I was excited, already an addict of novelty, happy to be the center of attention. It was my seventh birthday. My friends Matt and Thomas were over. We ran around the house, playing G.I. Joe and Transformers and He-Man, always on the look out for some secret spot or lost treasure or pirate's map, but found none. A snake skin and an elaborate spider web intrigued us for a few moments but lacked the excitement to hold our attention for long. Mom ordered pizza for everyone to celebrate my successful trip around the sun. We were all happy to not eat tacos again. Ordering out made us feel normal, like real Americans. It came twenty-nine minutes later, two short of being free, and Mom paid for it with a check. The smell of pepperoni filled the house, and we all shared the pizza, laughing and enjoying ourselves. I, too excited to eat much, waited patiently for my brother to finish. Of my six brothers and one sister, Diego was the most fun, probably because he was the oldest, at the moment of life when he would step into the world of adults. He was at the threshold, but held persistently to that spark of childhood spontaneity that was constantly threatened by the winds of modernization, classification, and responsibility. Diego was sixteen.

He knew I was waiting. After he finished, Diego went into the cluttered living room and grabbed my small frame, tackling me to the floor. He was only my half-brother from Mom's first marriage to a man that had disappeared, who she only spoke of in whispers when she thought all the kids were asleep. At the time I didn't know what deportation meant. We wrestled for a few minutes, me wiggling out of Diego's grasp. There was something between the two of us, some kindred spirit. When Diego looked at me, he saw himself. I climbed up him, like some great oak, and when I got to his shoulders, I enjoyed the view from a height I would never reach. We stood there together for a moment, some new creature and looked at the world around us. Outside the window, dark clouds were gathering, and the distant sound of thunder boomed into the room. This only made me even more excited. I loved the power of a thunderstorm. "Let's play helicopter, Diego."

Before Diego could answer, I climbed down the human tree and jumped frantically in front of him, holding my arms out for take-off. He debated, looked around the room and judged the situation for safety. Although cluttered, Diego determined it safe for lift off as long as we stayed away from the brick fireplace. He moved a few boxes and the ottoman from one side of the room to block the only danger he saw.

"Ready?" I nodded, looking up at my brother with total trust and love. Diego picked me up by the wrists, gripped them firmly, and began to turn, slowly at first, then faster and faster, until my feet came off the ground, and I squealed with the delight of innocence, aware only of the wonder in the world. I was still too young to see the storm coming. After a minute, Diego slowed, and I returned safely to Earth. Immediately, I jumped up and down. "Again! Again!" Seduced by my joy, Diego grabbed my wrists and began turning. Again, I defied gravity and enjoyed the wonder of flight. When I reached the highest point, a sudden clap of thunder blasted above the house, shaking the windows with the voice of God. It startled Diego, and his grip slipped. I hung in the air for a moment, then gravity reclaimed me. I hit the ground, head first.

Mom heard the fall and knew immediately that it was bad because there was no sound from me. Parents around the world knew that a scream, any scream was a better diagnosis than silence from a hurt child. She rushed into the room, already stinking of Diego's fear. He stared and slowly backed away from my still body. Mom picked up her limp child, and her fear mixed with that of Diego's, filling the room. I wasn't breathing. My heart wasn't beating. My aunts and uncles ran into the room, and their fear possessed them until they were perfuming the air with morbid thoughts of death. My soul rose up out of its body and hovered near the ceiling, watching the scene unfold below.

It was very calm.

I saw Mom sitting over me, shaking me, frantic and scared. She screamed at me to wake up, using that tone of voice, the one that would stop me and my brothers cold in our tracks. Everyone else in the room contributed their healthy dose of panic and instability, but I still didn't understand how the fear got from outside the room into my body. I saw an obscure figure, someone I never noticed before, with a shifty cloud about him, standing close to each of the adults, whispering in their ears.

Mom used the tone again, commanded me to wake up. I obeyed and re-entered my body. I always was a momma's boy. Before I hit my head, I had seen the world from a filter of trust, of love, like all innocent people. I was open, safe in the world around me. When I came back into my body, into a world thick with fear, the switched flipped in my head. I was closed. I regained consciousness in the hospital, and stayed there for four days. I was scared, distrustful of my surroundings, unsure of where the next danger lay hidden, but certain it was there.

Fear of the unknown was the Grandfather of all fears and soon enough, there were plenty of his grandkids running rampant inside me. Every moment after, I saw the world through a filter of fear, and I didn't want to see it. I recoiled and soon the world blurred. I took on Mom's handicap and began wearing glasses. A few years later, scared I wasn't enough like my father, I mimicked his allergies, learned so well to sneeze and snort and spit that I forgot I had chosen to do it—it wasn't my natural condition. Later, after enough evening news, with stories of killer bees from Mexico and the black guy down the street, after enough fear from society, I developed the habit of worry. It was then I saw the darkening skies and the imminent storm for mankind. The sky was falling.

A lifetime of acceptance and enabling had breathed life into my fear. Laying there on a flea-infested mat in Peru, with a strange doctor singing over me, I saw the situation for what it was. The fear had acquired intelligence. The alien presence poisoned my thoughts and feelings. For twenty years, fear had worked its tendrils throughout my body, determined to control. It was my very own demon.

I plucked the exposed root out of the center of my being. I vomited, and my enemy disappeared altogether. I had exorcised it. I had won.

I didn't understand why, but at this point I saw an image of George W. Bush land his jet on an aircraft carrier, give the thumbs up, and declare the mission accomplished.

From somewhere in my heart appeared countless little gnomes, green people of love, some hopping about, others fastidious bees, buzzing by, pollinating my inner world with compassion. They pulled at the remaining habits of thought, speech and belief that were tied up with fear, dependent on it for their existence. These habits, if unchecked, could lead to the recreation of the demon. Every time one of these fear-based thoughts materialized in my head, the little elves pulled, and unraveled the tapestry, revealing the bright side underneath.

I have a lot of retraining to do.

The intelligence of love creates different choices, a different world than the intelligence of fear. My switch had been flipped again, and I shone bright in my renewed state of innocence. I was open.

I fell asleep just before dawn, swaying in the comfortable embrace of the jungle vibrating as one gentle hive.

9

You are welcome, most noble Sorceress,
to the land of the Munchkins.
We are so grateful to you for having killed the wicked Witch of the East,
and for setting our people free from bondage.
-L. Frank Baum

We had one more ceremony in New Chicago before Lucio left to perform more *curaciónes* in the Rio Bamba jungle of southern Peru. Humbled and wanting nothing more of such lessons, I only drank one cup that night, happy to relax in the mellow embrace of love. The songs were light and joyful. I lay on my wafer-thin mattress, dancing my feet and hands to the music, humming and singing whatever words happened to come, watching the flickering patterns of light and color on the velvet curtain behind my eyes, safe in my cradle. Listening to the doctor's music, nestled in the buzzing womb of the Amazon, I noticed a line of ants marching through the jungle in my mind. I followed them to an old dead tree, where they disappeared into a hole in the trunk. I squeezed myself through and landed in an Otherworld.

It was much like the jungle outside of my *mosquitero,* and it's even possible that I was looking at the same physical space, but a different dimension. I'd never know the difference. A rustling in the bushes caught my attention, and I was surprised to see a little creature stroll out of the undergrowth. The shock was immense, and I almost opened my eyes, but I remembered the ABC's of inter-dimensional travel.

Always Be Calm.

I took a deep breath. My roots deepened into the earth, feeding my heart that glowed a brilliant green.

It was a small man, what people in England and Ireland know as the little people, and he reminded me of the character from the cereal commercials. He was three feet tall, dressed in tidy gray pants and a white pinstripe-plaid coat. A top hat just barely tamed his fiery red hair, and he walked barefoot through the clearing. He moved to a papaya tree and put his

Manifesting the Monkey

tiny four-fingered hand on it, whispered something, and kissed it good-bye. He proceeded to a lemon-grass plant and stroked its long, thin leaves, used his palm to test the fragile points that reached out to the sun. On his way to a banana tree, he stopped, squatted on child's legs, and commenced speaking to a termite mound. The insects waved their antennae in response, still working, each individual carrying the voice of one sentience. He said good-bye and continued to his goal, where he looked up at the fruit far above his head. He petted the layered skin of the tree, then gave it the softest knock. The wind blew, and a bunch of strangely-shaped fruit slammed to the ground. It was calm for a moment, and then, the bushes erupted into a flurry of activity as individuals similar in style to this little person rushed out from the jungle to collect the giant marshmallow food, each shape—red balloons, blue moons, clovers, hearts, and stars—were different sizes, some as small as a grape, others as large as a grapefruit. They cut their bounty from the stem with small knives, and carried as many of them as they could, squeezing the soft forms to fit into their pockets and in their belts. One woman slid a yellow star snuggly between her breasts. They left as quickly as they arrived, waving to each other, chattering for a moment, then disappearing to wherever they came from.

The little man retrieved his pen knife from the inside pocket of his coat, and cut the last two marshmallows from the stem—a moon and a rainbow.

It was then that he saw me watching him. His eyes darted from side-to-side as if planning his escape. I took a deep breath and strengthened my connection to the natural. He relaxed, considered his winnings, then nodded to the rainbow laying in the grass, offering me half his treasure. I found myself sitting next to him.

Thank you.

The moon-fruit was a third of his height. He stood it on end and cut an oval from the blue peel. The leprechaun pulled the skin off, cut a grid pattern into the soft flesh of the fruit, and returned the knife to its home. When his quick hand reappeared, he plucked a marshmallow cube, threw it into his mouth, and chewed politely.

A breeze shook the tree again. He cocked his head to the sky, and froze.

When no response came, the little man put his ear to the ground.

"No, no, it's not a problem at all. I assure you...yeah, the fruit is really

Manifesting the Monkey   57

good, luv. Thanks." He said in the sing-song Irish accent I remembered from the commercials.

He listened for a moment, and sneaked another bite. "Uh-huh...I see...okay...yeah, I can do that...no, no it's not a bother at all. I'm happy to help out. It's the least I could do, isn't it?" Then he stood up, took another bite, and lay the spoon down next to his meal. He smiled at me.

"Congratulations." He said, shaking my fore and middle fingers with much more strength than I could have imagined in his tiny body. "I'm Lucky. She filled me in on your little soirée last night. You survived your infection. Nice work."

Uh...thank you, but who filled you in, exactly?

He smiled and patted the earth. "Pachu Mamma."

Pachu Mamma?

"You know...the planet...the natural world? The trees, the grass, the rocks, the animals, the bugs. Everything."

She's alive?

Lucky laughed so hard he nearly chocked on a mouthful of blue moon. "Is she alive? Of course she's alive. What do you think that is in your hand?"

I looked down at the rainbow marshmallow and wondered. I decided to give him the benefit of the doubt.

Right...right...she's alive...of course she's alive, but she's sentient?

He nodded. "She doesn't say much in words that you'd understand, not yet anyway, but once you learn how to listen, she's got plenty to say...believe me, a lot."

She does? Wow.

"Yeah, wow's right...speak of the devil. Her ears must've been itching." Lucky returned his to the ground.

Her ears?

After a moment of listening, Lucky continued his mediation. "She says that you've done well, that you've awoken to a fundamental human drama," he looked at me, "or something like that. Words don't really make too much sense sometimes. There's more 'n more of yous who's realizing what's happening every day, d'ya know what I mean? This is just the beginning."

A gust of wind swayed the tops of the trees, swishing their leaves.

Lucky cocked his head, and when the air settled, he continued speaking.

"Pachu Mamma says this is a time of great awakening for your kind. You joined the ranks of those who have seen the tragedy of the human species. You have seen a true purpose of life on Earth—to evolve. And the engagement, the relationship to fear is a linchpin in that evolution. Healthy interactions with it manifest love, abundance, and beauty. Unhealthy strategies will manifest violence, scarcity, and filth. Collective humanity is still locked in this wrestling match, and it's too murky to see which way the scale's gonna tip."

He ate a few more bites of marshmallows, nonplussed to take his time. "What was that again?" He asked to no one I could see. "I forgot the next part." The wind blew, and Lucky nodded his head. "Got it." He turned back to me. "It wasn't always like this, you know? Humans weren't always out to get each other, you weren't always scared of the dark. Yous used to be like the rest of the natural world, a creature of flowing energies and impeccable integrity. The parasite that perverts humankind today did not exist. Yous hadn't yet given birth to your own fear. Before, mankind was more animal."

Animal?

"Yeah, yeah. Man's fear is part of what makes you human. It's not the existence of fear, but its place in life that threatens you all today. Yous accept the fear as a necessary tool in a violent world instead of recognizing it as the root of that violence that you're afraid of. Left alone, bored, fear can manipulate man to do the...silliest of things."

He paused to take a few more bites.

"Course, when I say that, the fear inside immediately speaks up, says it's bollocks. Says it's irrelevant, unrealistic. A thousand justifications surface to safeguard its position as puppet master. The most common is that you need fear to exist, that it somehow protects you, but it only protects the part of you that is not real. And it's important that people listen, really listen, cause the fear will scream and kick. It will make a terrible racket, and do everything to dilute the message so that you don't hear it or that you can't remember it forever. Even I, a living veteran, have to keep a tenacious grasp on it, lest the fear slip back down inside and reinfect me."

A veteran? You had to deal with fear, too?

"I was once like you. Somewhere, a long time ago, me people lived the

Manifesting the Monkey   59

same struggle that humanity faces right now. We overcame our own troubles, and entered into a new world. I know what it's like. There's a time before the fear, and there's a time after the fear. There was a time when mankind lived in rhythm with the world around him, a time when we were held and nurtured by love, the Source of all that exists, and it's possible to evolve into an even more glorious state of existence, another beautiful manifestation because although me kind has dealt with the fear, we are not the same as you. Humans is a special breed. You's the most sophisticated incarnations of God that have ever manifested. That's why the world seems like it's going to hell—because you have the potential to be so great, you equally have the potential to be so terrible. This duality exists in the mind of every human being and how each person resolves it will determine the fate-of-the-world."

A mouse ran up his arm to his shoulder, and squeaked in his ear while he nodded. "Uh-huh...yep...I got it. Thank you." The mouse jumped the long distance between the little man's shoulder and mine. He squeaked into my ear, then scurried down my chest and disappeared into the grass.

"Pachu Mamma said that it's important to see the difference between fear 'n instinct. If a giant saber-toothed tiger came snarling out of the jungle to have you for lunch, a physical experience would happen in your body. Your pupils would dilate as the unconscious made sense of the danger long before the you that's listening to me was even aware there was danger. Hormones would be released, and an array of changes would happen to prepare the body for some action. All of the changes would be drastic and sudden, and all of them would happen without so much as a thought from the ego. Fight-or-flight. At this moment, faced with a real danger, the only possibility is geared towards a response to the system. This is different than fear. Fear is the energy we use to weave irrelevant ideas about the world simply because we don't know what's going to happen. The projections of worst-case-scenarios or hurtful judgments or the closing of the heart to new experiences. That is fear, not instinct. Instinct is the most common cloak fear uses to convince you of its necessity."

It doesn't seem right, it seems unnatural, it's so contrary to everything we've built. It's too complex!

"But it's not. It's simple, really, cuz it's all one thing. The unknown is the first fear and death his figurehead. For a small moment in the history of consciousness, people embraced that inevitably, lived within the natural order without concern for tomorrow. As technology increased—fire, farms, finance —humans mis-interpreted their power and placed themselves on the throne of the natural world. Mankind rushed to avoid death, to push it away, to increase worldly comfort and pleasure to absurd levels. If death was inevitable, then man would live as luxuriously as possible, to squeeze every drop of pleasure out of life. It became every man for himself.

"The immediate offspring of this fear of the unknown were greed and anger. The powerful developed voracious appetites and consumed without thought of the world around. They took and took and still continue to take to this day. Their greed has transformed into a monster of epic proportions, but has been normalized to such a degree that most consider this trait inherently human, though, I assure you, it is most definitely not. Anger came next. Anger at God for the inescapable end, anger at the world around for not offering enough, anger at the body for its mortality. Anger at the natural order. From these two demons spawned a race of debilitating human emotions— depression, hate, jealously, envy, lust, shame, blame. These human traits, now mistaken as instinctual, are the most obvious signs of their Grandfather, and they have the potential to destroy human civilization forever." Lucky looked around, then whispered to me. "What I'm going to say next is me own opinion, something I learned from me own experience so take it for what it's worth...there's not enough room for both love and fear. Given enough time, one will suffocate the other because everything's the same thing. It's all One. It's that simple. But the real fucker is, you can't see One with yous eyes."

It was quiet for a moment. Then Lucky stood up and threw the empty shell of the blue moon into the bushes. He patted me on the knee. "And now you know. That's the secret to life and happiness—love or fear. "He gripped my fingers and shook them again." It was a pleasure to meet you." Like she said, there's more and more of you humans who are waking up to this reality every moment. Remember that, and if it gets dark 'n' you can't see the light from anywhere else, it may just be cause you youssself is shining so bright."

Lucky winked at me, then continued on his way, touching and talking to the natural world around him, and I opened my eyes in New Chicago.

Manifesting the Monkey   61

<u>10</u>

To love oneself is the beginning
of a life-long romance.
-Oscar Wilde

Everything changes.

Over the next days and weeks, I was a newborn in the world. The unconscious patterns that I had associated as my 'self' for so long almost tripped me back into believing the world was a dangerous place, but, with the help of the little creatures rattling around my head and heart, I pulled myself out of these relapses. Most of the time, I felt good without logical reason. The sunshine, the rain, the wind every phenomenon was justification to be happy. I radiated joy, and it was infectious. I attracted people who smiled more than they frowned, who looked for the happiness in life, always seeing the silver lining. I cared for others in a selfless way, surprised by the depth of my compassion. It was impossible for me to say no to the beggars of Peru. Without fear of my own fate, how could I deny a fellow human being in need? I gave away more than $200 in one night. After that, Aurore took control of our finances.

She smiled, and I knew that she was proud of me. Before, she sometimes urged me to be more caring to the world, but I always had a good justification for denying whatever help I could give: I was just as much a victim as everyone else and in no position to help anyone. "If you keep giving away our money, we'll be as poor as they are."

Her remark sent me into a day-dream and in it, we gave away all of our money and lived in poverty. The thought exhilarated me, and I welcomed it, still oblivious to the power of intention, a foolish wish I would soon curse a thousand times. It seemed such a free life, such a good life. After all, wasn't that one of Jesus' messages? To give and give until there was nothing more to give? Not out of obligation, but out of love.

Maybe if everyone gives and gives, everybody will have more than enough?

I slipped the small box under her pillow. Whenever I gave her gifts, I always liked to hide them some place where she'd find them on her own, sort of like a treasure hunt. When Aurore came to bed, it took her a few moments to realize that her pillow wasn't as soft as usual. She flipped over on her stomach and slid her hands under it, looking at me, knowing that I was up to something. She pulled the box out and examined it, the smile on her face getting bigger.

"Happy birthday," I said.

"But Ten," her expression transformed to mock-anger, "my birthday's not until tomorrow, and I told you not to buy me anything."

"I didn't buy it. I promise. I made it."

She smiled again and gently opened the small box. Inside, laying on a piece of cotton, were a pair of blue earrings, each made from three overlapping fish scales. The scales had been dried and bleached by the sun, then the little disks were painted blue and linked together by a small metal hoop.

"Oh, Ten. They're beautiful." She put them on, leaned over and kissed me before hopping out of the bed to see what they looked like.

Aurore appreciated the change. We never spoke about it in concrete terms, just vague descriptions to communicate the essential—that I had let go. Somewhere in our relationship, we had learned not to talk much about the things we most wanted, lest we sap them of their magic. The more we talked, the less real things became, as if the words usurped the actual manifestation of what we wanted, a hollow substitute for the thing itself. Aurore was the first beneficiary of my shift. Like everything in my life, our relationship suffered from my constant anxiety. Before, the natural protective instinct I felt towards her was perverted into a state of continuous panic, and our relationship became an insipid routine devoid of the spontaneity that goes with a well-lived life. In my new world, I was able to maintain the balance between intelligent caution and flow. When it really counted, I knew the proper time to direct our course, but most of the time, I let her guide the way. I followed the feminine, and our marriage hit a new high. We blossomed in a way that was never possible before I had opted out of my old dynamic. There were always too many doubts, too many 'what ifs' for me to keep up with—the rationalist always got in the way, and I spent my life chasing my tail.

At first, it was uncomfortable to have the empty space where the doubts used to live. Overnight, I had access to a greater source of knowledge and a profound understanding of my potential. There was an urge to do something inside my head, anything to keep busy. Intuition assured me that my efforts to do something (like reserve a hotel a week in advance, or audit our budget for the trip) would soon pervert into those little imps of worry. Better if I just took deeper breaths, continued letting go, and trust that everything was going according to plan. It was really about learning to surrender, to have faith in something higher than myself. The awareness of breath was the fundamental key to being present, the starting and ending of it all. The longer I focused on my breathing, observing it entering and exiting my body, the more I balanced my re-discovered energies.

This increasing sense of the present moment gave birth to a deeper appreciation for the world around. The sun's rays were brighter as they broke through the clouds of a passing storm and turned their fluffy underbellies a seductive violet. The colors—a thousand shades of green, the reds, blues, oranges, purples, and pinks of jungle flowers—glowed, as if they too had suddenly become more aware and vibrated with more intensity. I could almost hear them, their rainbow message of diverse equality. Even the smoke and the smog of the cities we passed through offered me a fresh insight. I no longer judged them undesirable because they were mountains of concrete and steel, great junctions of pollution and filth. These judgments could still be true, and I merely accepted them before looking at the bright-side—the tenacious reliability of public transport, the indomitable smiles of the poor, the ingenuity of modern architecture. Everywhere I looked, I saw something I liked and soon loved.

To no surprise, I often looked at Aurore. I saw her in a new light. I watched her walk through the world, touching people's hearts with only a passing gaze, a kind word, or a heartfelt hug. Her softness and care, qualities that sometimes irritated me before my *curación*, regained their true meaning as honest acts of love. She was different because I saw her differently. I reclaimed that first vision I had of her, wrapped in a towel, when I knew that she was the one for me. I looked past the assumptions and prejudices that I had stacked between us and embraced her essence as an ambassador of love.

Once, when we were still living in England, earning money for our journey into South America, Aurore walked out of the bank to find a man standing in protest. It was a big bank, one of those massive institutions that hide their sociopathic obsession of the bottom line behind whitened smiles, shallow promises, and an inflated belief in a fundamentally-flawed financial system. They tricked people into believing they actually care about them as individuals when all they cared about was profit. This man that Aurore happened upon was dressed in an English flag, and wore a placard on his chest that explained his protest in terms a third grader could understand. The bank had changed the agreed-upon fixed rates on a business loan he had taken, resulting in his eventual bankruptcy and mounting debt. His only demand was to speak to someone intelligent and in charge. He had been there every day for two weeks. A trickle of minions had engaged him, but they all fell short on one or both of his criteria. The pub across the street began a betting pool, and gave 4:1 odds that law enforcement would intervene long before the bank did. Aurore watched him for a moment, then approached, and placed a gentle hand on his shoulder for support. "It's a brave thing you're doing here. It's hard to stand up. When you're done, check this out." She surreptitiously handed him a curled morsel of paper with the address to a local Vipassana meditation center on it. "It can help you to find yourself out of the knots this has tied you in." He looked at Aurore, struck much in the same way I was when I first saw her, before nodding and thanking her. After he spent a night in jail for 'disturbing the peace', he gave up his crusade and followed her advice. He fell so deeply into the peace meditation offers that he began to teach, then to tour, offering whatever help he could to the world. Somehow, we bumped into Jim in Loja, Ecuador, at a bus station. We only had an hour before he left, but Jim spoke of how that one moment of a stranger's kindness had transformed his life.

"Thank you so much," and Jim pulled Aurore into a tight hug. She blushed and claimed that offering whatever help she could was natural.

It's what anyone would do.

Before my *curación*, when she first told me she had passed meditation on to Jim, it was another rock in my shoe. I dwelled on it, examined and sliced it to bits, until it became too much, and I told her it was arrogant and high-handed. It was another of my successful ways of starting a fight simply because I couldn't stand the tranquility between us. But in Loja, I saw her actions and her intentions in their true light. Aurore loved life, and if there was anything she could do to make the world better, she was going to do it. She was already doing it.

But her initial efforts weren't so peaceful. When we first got together, Aurore was sometimes volatile, and once, she spent months on an anti-advertising campaign. She was pissed that life had come to mean what it meant, angry that the magic of humanity had been turned into selling strategies. To her, the barrage of images and words linking ideas and natural desires to stylized products promising fulfillment no *thing* ever could ever deliver an act of war. And to war she went. Aurore didn't fight fire with fire. Instead of subverting the memes transmitted by the mass-media with her own beautiful message, she tore them down, removing the offending propaganda from the public eye. She ripped ads from walls, turned them around, covered them with bright orange construction paper. She thrashed against the world and its conceptions of who she should be. Aurore understood, though she could never verbalize, that it was her divine right to decide her identity for herself, and the constant bombardment of advertising perverted that exploration. Her efforts to change the status quo was born out of her own selfishness—she wanted to save herself.

Please secure your own oxygen mask before helping others.

This went on for about six months, and then things changed. She never talked about her transformation. Neither of us did. Things were just different, and we didn't care how or why, they just were. Aurore didn't want to fight the world anymore, and, as a show of determination to her peace, she abstained from all violent media, and no longer watched Hollywood action or adventure movies. Later, when she realized how media had corrupted her sexuality, she abstained from all that meaning-laden media as well, which meant she stopped watching Hollywood movies altogether, along with TV shows and commercials. Aside form the occasional documentary, she stopped watching because she had understood a fundamental truth in the Age of Observers:

You are what you watch.

"Do you smell that?" I asked her from the slow swinging hammock. A strange odor floated by on the wind. It beckoned memories, but they teased me from the tip of my tongue. "What is that?"

"What's what?" Aurore asked. She came from the inside of the little house we had rented for a month, perched on the side of a small mountain, overlooking a picturesque valley and the distant Mandango peak that formed the profile of a man's face looking up at the sky.

"That smell." It was still there, but fading quickly. "Do you smell it?"

She walked around me, testing the air. "I don't smell anything different. Just the eucalyptus trees...and someone down below is making a fire. Is that it?"

"I don't know." I sniffed again, but it was gone. Aurore leaned on the rail of the balcony, and looked out over as the sun painted the sky in shifting electric colors. I moved behind her, put my arms around her slim waist, and kissed her on the neck, right in the midst of the cloud of freckles that had sparked my interest so long ago in that guest house bathroom far, far away.

Aurore never passed an opportunity to experience the joy of life. Unlike my laser mind that predicted outcomes, and decisions, that analyzed the content of my life with surgical precision, Aurore rested in the quiet moment of now. She was consistently surprised. In Santa Anna, the high jungle of Ecuador, she never got over how big the oranges grew. They were enormous, and felt like miniature bowling balls in the hand, an example of life's abundance. Usually, just the very top was cut off, where the fruit attached to its stem. We placed our mouths over these holes and sucked the teats dry. It would have been a great Tropicana commercial. They were delicious, but after the third one, I was used to it. I still enjoyed them. I just knew what to expect. But Aurore continued to see the joy in the little miracles life offered her. Even after her nineteenth gigantic orange, she was amazed.

11

A question that sometimes drives me hazy:
Am I or are the others crazy?
-Albert Einstein

I only caught vague whiffs. It was there, and then it wasn't. Whenever it came, all of my attention went with it. It jostled me out of whatever I was doing. I stopped speaking in the middle of a sentence. I stopped running, eating, writing, everything.

I froze.

It was such a particular smell that I was obliged to to take notice and sniff for its source. It wasn't the relaxing scent of blooming lavender or the spice of cinnamon, for I would have soon forgotten these pleasant odors. But it wasn't an overtly offensive smell, either, like cat piss or the sulfurous stink of an eggy fart. It was mildly unpleasant, but curiously so because it offered a strange feeling of comfort, familiar, though out of conscious memory. I smelled it so frequently that it transformed from a mystery into an obsession, wafting by at all times of the day and night, in all manner of situations, without rhyme or reason.

"It's simple really, the world is going to end and there isn't a goddamn thing we can do about it."

I let his statement linger in my mind. As usual, I had lots of questions to ask, but Lucas pushed his dreadlocks behind his ears and continued, happy to sound so congruent—a rarity for him. He smoked ganja all day, every day and experienced the scattered energy of such a habit. "I mean how else can we explain the Mayan calendar, Terrence McKenna's I-Ching calendar, and the Raja yoga calendar all ending within two weeks of each other? You can't, something big is going to happen, and you all know it," he said to the half-listening group.

"Uh-huh," Lucille said automatically from the open fire and her pot of burning rice. She was Lucas' partner and contractually obliged to agree, even if only to humor him. The others—Marcos, Juana, and Dario—glanced up at him and nodded their heads. Like most times when Lucas spoke, they shuffled about uncomfortably, unsure how to say 'you're full of shit' in a nice way, something most people grapple with at least once in their lives. Lucas interpreted that as a signal to continue speaking when it really meant that they were uncomfortable and didn't know how to express it.

"It's crazy, and it's going to happen very soon. The world is going to end, everything that we're doing is going to turn to shit. Even worse than it already has..."

Lucas continued croaking, but I forgot about him. A breeze rustled the tops of the bamboo trees and in the thick perfume of coffee plants, I smelled it again. It was faint, but as I focused, it filled my nose. I looked around, hoping someone else had sensed it as well. Lucas was still talking to himself. I knew he didn't smell it, but nobody else acted as if they noticed it, either. It was so strong anyone with a nose should be able to smell it, but life continued as normal, as if this curiously foul odor was something they smelled everyday and because of its mundane nature, had forgotten. When it faded, and I returned to Lucas' diatribe, he was looking at me.

"You alright, brother?" He put his hand on my shoulder, and I resisted the urge to shrug it off. I wasn't sure why he filled me with such disgust, but I took a deep breath and let the love shine. "You look lost. I know it's a heavy subject, but it's important that we all come to terms with the end." He hung his head. "We are all mortal creatures and we will all pass on at some time."

I broke his sanctimonious spell with a laugh. "Yeah, mate, I know I'm going to die. I've known that for a long time. In fact, it's the only thing in this life we have to do. Everything else is a choice." His face contorted, and he stepped back, defenses coming online. "What you've said isn't news to me. I don't think it's news to anyone here. But what I want to know is how do you know?"

He laughed, his ignorance hidden behind bravado. "What do you mean how do I know? These things about the Mayan calendar are everywhere. It's more difficult not to know." He took a step backwards, towards his woman. "You Americans are funny, asking such silly questions." Lucille laughed, as if I was only confirming her stereotype of an American.

"That's not what I mean, mate. Of course it's easy to know about the Mayan calendar. But what is it that people know?"

He turned back to me. "Brother, we know that the world is going to end on the 21st of December 2012."

"That's what I don't understand, Lucas," purposefully avoiding the empty label—in new age mumbo-jumbo everyone was siblings to everyone else. Sometimes all the posturing made me want to puke. "How do you know the world is going to end?"

"Man, do you not listen. The Mayan calendar says it's going to."

"That's not really true, Lucas."

His eyes widened. "Where have you been, brother? Everyone knows that the Mayan calendar is going to end in 2012."

"Yeah, of course." The confusion on his face was funny, and I laughed.

"But you just said you didn't know. Are you fucking crazy, brother?"

"Well, that's not what I said. I said I didn't know the world was going to end. But you still don't see." I took another deep breath and pushed the judgment out of my voice. When I spoke, it was to clear confusion, not to be right. "Yes, it's common knowledge among people like us that the Mayan calendar is going to end, but that's it. You make the leap of faith that this planet or human civilization is going to vaporize in a ball of fire or crystallize in another ice age. The Mayan calendar doesn't say what's going to happen. It's just says that the calendar is going to end."

It was quiet, I heard him thinking, heard the panic inside of him, and I knew before he spoke that he'd say anything to convince himself that he was still right.

"Look around, brother. The world is going to shit. We've fucked each other. We've fucked the environment. We've even fucked the moon." He referenced the recent UN resolution to begin hauling blocks of compressed trash and payloads of spent nuclear fuel to the dark side of the moon. "It's all just the beginning of the end." He patted me on the shoulder. "It's obvious, isn't it?"

"It might be obvious, Lucas, that human beings are, generally, mean, dirty animals, but it doesn't follow that the world is going to end because of it. Do you know what's going to happen when the Mayan calendar finishes this cycle? Your smile tells me that you do, but what I really know is that *you don't know*, that you're fooling yourself. Do you follow?"

"I know what's going to happen." Lucas collected what little energy he could muster. "It's obvious, brother. What do you know that I don't know? What is it that I have fooled myself about?" He laughed and looked to the others for support, but they all seemed interested in what I was going to say and relieved not to pretend that Lucas was making sense.

"Well, I know something that's obvious to anyone who bothers to stop and think rather than getting so damn self-important about it. When the Mayan calendar ends, it's just going to start again. The calendar measures cyclical astronomical occurrences, and they will continue long after we are both gone. It doesn't mean that the world is going to end, it means the calendar is going to end, the same way the Gregorian calendar ends each year on December 31st. What you make of it is your choice."

Lucas laughed and replied, but I never heard it. The smell interrupted me again, I followed it until it disappeared, and when I came back Lucas was laughing. "What's wrong with you, man? Where did you go?"

I looked over at Aurore. Her concern over my more frequent outbursts of phantom smells, especially when they occurred during intimate moments, grew with each occurrence. Sure, most times I was more joyful and compassionate to the world around me, but the eviction of my boogeyman meant that most boundaries had disappeared, and I did lots of strange things that sometimes triggered her own fear.

"...I thought...I smelled something?"

"What did you smell?"

"I don't know. I can't remember what it is." I shook my head and refocused my attention. This was important. "Look, Lucas...you don't know what's going to happen, nobody does. And that scares you so you conceptualize it as some imminent disaster, but by believing the world is going to end, you'll only help make it so."

He patted me on the back and laughed. "You Americans have such funny beliefs."

People like Lucas were a dime a dozen. All over the world they believed that the end of the Mayan calendar would only herald the ultimate destruction of mankind, the return of God's great flood. It was the only possibility in a fear-based world-view. Any major galactic event must herald the cataclysm, right? Like so many, Lucas had taken an inevitability—the sun rising between the Earth and the galactic plane—and transformed it into the boogeyman. Maybe it would happen, or maybe we'd ascend into a golden age,

Manifesting the Monkey   71

or maybe the sun would rise like it does everyday and life would continue as normal. It was anyone's guess. It could be major. It could be minor. It could be nothing. Destructive or creative. The truth was that nobody knew.

The smell continued to come and go like this until I became habituated to it and began to forget it. As soon as I stopped paying attention it, the smell came more often and lasted longer, as if it was coaxing me to remember its origin. Now, it stayed long enough in my nose and in my mind that I could almost orient myself to it. Instead of just stopping abruptly in the middle of a conversation and gazing into space, I would take a few steps in one direction, then the other. The people around thought me even more mad as I would suddenly began prowling around them, some bloodhound picking up a faint trail. Before I could ever locate the source, the smell was gone, and I was left with a confused thought of something and a hasty explanation. It got to the point where Aurore didn't even bother. She would wave her hand at me and sigh with unabashed exasperation.

The only choice I had was to ignore the smell. It had gone on for weeks now, and what else was I supposed to do? I was sure that I was going crazy, that I had taken one step too far over the line. This, I knew, was how the world of magic worked. All the power, all the insights were founded on the ability to walk an edge between what was considered normal and what was actually possible—that's where magic lived—and one mis-step could mean insanity. This smell was the latest challenge on my path of power. I ignored it, and the smell grew stronger, filled the air around me. The longer I ignored it the more pressure built between me and that external stimulus. The air thickened with it so much that I felt like I was walking through a cloud of gnats. And no one else noticed it.

Then something else happened. A small sound accompanied the smell. I could hear it only when I ignored the smell long enough that the odor was everywhere, all around me and insistent. At that point, I heard a voice whispering. I couldn't make out the words, just a continuous mumbling. There was more than one voice, but they all shared the same qualities—a nagging, whining tone.

Then one day, the pressure was too much. The wall broke, and my mind flooded back to the memory of that smell, to the same memory I had relived in New Chicago, back to that moment of rebirth, when my spirit moved back into my body, and I was first infected by fear.

My eyes fluttered open, but I still couldn't see anything. There was something pushing me down, keeping me from focusing on the world around. It felt like I was suffocating. I had no words, no experience for my brief journey into death, and the extreme shock left me wide open. When I noticed the smell, I still couldn't see. It was thick and pungent, like the curious odor of rotting flowers, sweet mixed in with the sour, turning my nose and enticing it at the same time. The room was flooded with it.

I pulled back when I heard my mom's voice, "Ten, Ten? Are you alright?" As she opened her mouth to comfort me, the smell splashed out over me. I choked and sputtered, tried to sit up, but she pushed me back down. "Help is on the way. Just lay there." My eyes focused, and I could see her clearly, see my aunts and uncle from the corners of my eyes, see each of their boogeymen next to them, whispering, and I seized in horror. A black cloud of swarming insects surrounded everyone in the room, visible in the spirit, but hidden to the physical. This was the source of the stench. No one cared about the bugs covering them. They didn't even know they were there. I looked up at my mom so near to me and screamed. I could only just see her eyes—bright and pleading—from behind the veil of invisible black bugs. They were feeding. I followed their trails and fainted in horror when I realized that I was covered in them as well.

The memory faded, and I returned to the present. Now that I had exorcised my demon, I was sensitive to the fear around me. I could smell it. Not all the time, not yet, though it would soon evolve to that as I accepted my role in the human drama. And now that I knew what the smell was, I saw every situation differently. If the smell was strong, I knew that people were afraid and that their actions were motivated by their fear. Suddenly, I lived in a completely different world in which I was the only inhabitant.

<u>12</u>

The past may not repeat itself,
but it sure does rhyme.
-Mark Twain

Two friends we made in Spain that summer we fell in love joined us in Popayan, Colombia. Alec and Isabelle were on a short trip from their lives in Belgium. They had come over to vacation with us, finding Mother Culture too thorough a mistress to escape for long. Their allotted window was six weeks, and it was with great joy that we found ourselves together in the mountains of Colombia.

"It'll take us a while to get there," I explained. We were in Cordoba, a brisk mountain village where the locals had bright purple costumes and friendly manners. All throughout the south of Colombia, people were welcoming and warm, a far cry from the drug dealers and prostitutes Miami Vice programmed me to believe were the main composition of the Colombian population. Of course, there were plenty of drug dealers and prostitutes, but in no greater percentages than anywhere else in the world.

"It's okay with me. I want to try it for myself," Alec said. Isabelle agreed.

If we were to drink the medicine, it would require nearly a full day of rough travel. For Aurore and myself, we were going backwards on our route. The first alarm went off in my head.

Never go back.

"I don't know." Aurore said. I saw her squirming on the inside, recoiling from her fear. I didn't know what it was, but it was strong. It was big. I wanted to warn her, but caution stayed my hand. I made a mental note to speak with her about it and tacked it to the bulletin board among all my other forgotten reminders.

"I don't know," her soft green eyes glanced at me, "I want to drink the medicine. I do. But I also want to go to the Caribbean. You know? We've been going to the beach for two months now." It was true. For the past seven weeks, we declared the coast as our destination, but had gotten side-tracked along the way by all the marvelous sights and adventures of South America. Aurore was ready for that post-card beach—white sands, palm trees, turquoise waters, and plenty of coconuts. "You know...I need a vacation from my vacation." The final admission of the inner turmoil slid off her shoulders and crashed to the ground.

That's probably what I smelled, right?

Long-term travel is a strenuous initiation into a broader perception of life and its purposes. I had already dove into that world, but this was Aurore's baptism. She had lived in other countries, but hadn't cut loose of all structures —friends, family, work, school, taxes, media—that a long journey requires. She was in transition.

Our pack prowled aimlessly, in search of direction. Alec said he wanted to go, but he really didn't care what we did. He always held a perfect poker face, and as long as there was pot and alcohol, he was happy, or so at least he pretended. We spent the next two days arranging our options on the table. Aurore was acting strange, as if only half of her attention focused on the external world, and the rest of it chased some elusive phantom in her mind. I assumed it was the stress of travel, but something kept nagging me. I was still green in the world of magic, and I didn't see its true nature until too late.

"You okay," I'd ask her in our quiet moments. She'd always nod and smile at me, but I could see that there was something else there. I assumed it was something trivial, and that all was well. It was a foolish assumption, but I was still high from my freedom.

The pack gelled, and we journeyed down into the valley of Sibundoy in search of the medicine. Two months had passed since my last drink.

As promised, the trip was long and uncomfortable, like watching hours of video shot on one of those clunky, first generation VHS recorders operated by a drunken cameraman. Our path led us to a small town called San Cristos, and the next round of alarms clanged in my head. Our black experiences with don Juan in San Rafael happened right outside of a another small village, also called San Cristos. The allure of the medicine had drawn thousands of occidental patients, would-be shamans, psychedelic travelers, and an enormous amount of money to that part of Peru. This massive influx of financial abundance gave force to the Dark Side, and many tourists fell to Sith Lords posing as compassionate Jedi. We had witnessed one soul-stealing in particular, when our lively Japanese friend came back from a ceremony devoid of his former joy and passion for life and its adventures. When he cut his trip short and returned home ten days later, he was still a zest-less shell. But I wanted nothing of such evil energies and pernicious omens. I beat fear. I was done so I plopped my head firmly into the sand.

Happily ever after.

Despite my inhibitions, the Universe beckoned us forward and offered us free lodging with a local man name Jose Vargas, twenty-four and lonely in his role as caretaker of the family home. He opened his house to us, pleased for the exotic company—not many Westerners made it to the jungles of Colombia. Jose offered us two rooms and the kitchen to use as we pleased, for as long as we needed.

When my friends were asleep, I went outside and put my nose into the wind, but there was nothing there to raise my concern. The premonition about the name of the village was a lingering cough of fear—I had cured myself, I was well, but my body was still freeing itself of phlegm. When I looked inside, I saw light and love, a marvelous jungle of positive thoughts, beautiful expectations, and an abundance of life. There was no sign of infection. Alone, I often smelled myself, like some eager teenager before a first date, but aside from the occasional body odor (I had given up deodorants with the first flush), there was never even a whiff of the rotting flowers. I never considered that my misgivings were an honest intuition. I was a newbie, and I assumed the disturbance in the Force was just the lingering effects of a lifetime of mind-fucking myself.

There were no other tourists in San Cristos so the locals received us with the good-natured interest and welcome of small-towns the world over. Our first conversations with them lasted hours, touching on one subject after another, like a long aimless walk in the woods with a good friend you haven't seen in years, and the excitement of reconnection lifts the shroud of everyday life from your eyes, revealing a world filled with common surprises. As our presence echoed to the far reaches of town, our pack faded into the background of everyday life. The days were spent gently inquiring for a *curandero*. The medicine hadn't yet attracted the money and corruption into Colombia. We asked with the respect and courtesy of intrepid explorers seeking the wisdom of God, and the community received us with a warm embrace.

In our free time, we spent a lot of time in the kitchen, and many of our strolling conversations took place there, seated on counter-tops, munching raw vegetables and the occasional bag of chips.

"Have you learned much about dreams," I asked. Isabelle studied psychology in Brussels.

"A little. Tell me."

"Tell you what?"

"Tell me your dream," she ordered.

"How do you know I've got one?"

"Nobody asks about a dream unless they've got one they want to talk about."

I laughed. "So I was dreaming that Aurore and I were in a boat, in a canoe and we were rowing it towards this group of houses floating on a platform just off the bank of a river. And there was something coming after us, something chasing us. I saw it go by in the water, and it was an enormous Anaconda," my smile widened. Myths and legends of spiritual snakes had captivated my interest since I had flushed out into the world. "As the snake attacked us, we jumped to grab onto a group of houses floating next to the shore. I made it, but the Anaconda had Aurore, and it was dragging her down."

"She died?" Isabelle whispered, anxious of what it meant for a husband to dream the death of his wife and more concerned what that would do to our tribe.

I smiled bigger. "Let me finish...I turned and looked. I saw Aurore sinking down, fading away as she went. Her face was terrified, and she reached up at me, screaming to me, screaming for help." I shuddered at the image. "But in my dream, I wasn't scared at all. I was calm, and I knew exactly what to do. I dove in, swam down, and I took Aurore back from the Anaconda. I brought her back with me...I saved her, and it was so simple."

Although the exact meaning of the dream was unclear to me, I had an overwhelming positive feeling about it. I had faced some crucial danger, and faced it confidently, calmly and successfully, exactly how I wanted to behave in

Manifesting the Monkey   77

'real' life.

"Very interesting..." Isabelle said as she chopped carrots for the soup. "What do you think about the Anaconda? Quick, quick. Say the first thing that comes."

"I think of the medicine, the *soga*. The raw power of nature."

"Okay, okay...And the lake?"

"Uhhhh...it's dark and murky. Unknown, I don't know. Seems dangerous."

"Uh, huh," she pointed the knife at me, "and Aurore?"

"She's my love...but more than that...she represents what I hold dear, what I've chosen to create and believe true in this world."

Isabelle returned to her carrots, pleased with my answers. "Very good, very good."

I waited for her reply, and when I realized that it wasn't coming, I pushed. "So...what's that mean?"

Isabelle looked up at me, and laughed. "I have no idea."

"What?"

"Only you can determine what your dreams mean. In all your broad travels across the world, surely you've learned that."

And I did know that, but sometimes I didn't remember what it was that I knew. This caused me all sorts of interesting consequences.

Finally, we met our *curandero* (*taita* in local terms) a man named Ishmael Florentino. When we found *Taita* Florentino, everyone had a confident feeling that he was a good fit for us and our intentions. Upon meeting him, I detected nothing alarming, and we arranged to see him that Friday evening, at his normal office hours where he administered the medicine to the surrounding community. His flat rate for local and gringo alike was $10, a far cry from the inflated prices of Peru. (I once knew a man who paid $1,000 for a single ceremony.) We walked the three miles back from his house excited and joyful. But something still wasn't right.

It's our fifteenth drink.

I knew it, but I ignored the significance. In the world of the Tarot, fifteen was the Devil's card, meaning the separation of conscious and unconscious, of man and woman by the illusion of the physical. What came together in six, The Lovers, was split in two by the Devil. The hair stood up on the back of my neck.

We celebrated the accomplishment with a walk up into the foothills and enjoyed the panoramic view of the gorgeous valley, next to a babbling brook that eventually joined with the Rio Putumayo, which then thundered down into the jugular artery of the rain forest. In equatorial South America, all rivers lead to the Amazon. Watching the sun set into an incredible purple, everything was beautiful and perfect, calm. My friends chatted, but something called me away. I moved a few hundred feet up the slope, and squatted on a rock next to the water. I imagined big, purple bat-ears slipping over my own, and the more I listened, the more I heard. The sound of the water, which began as a pleasant white noise, aligned into a beautiful harmony of overtones, and then transformed into a woman's voice, high and clear, singing some forgotten language. For a moment, I felt held and protected, as if I was back in the womb.

When we returned back to our new home, Jose was sitting on the couch. He was slouched like any human in their early 20s, relaxed in his space. "You'd better go," he said to us. His blunt statement slammed into our joy and trounced it to dust.

I thought we could stay as long as we pleased.

"What?"

"The FARC are coming. They've already blocked the road from Mochoa. Soon they'll block the road to Pasto, and you won't be able to leave."

"What?"

Jose repeated himself and laughed. "This happens sometimes."

"Are you scared?" Aurore asked.

"No, I'm not scared. They won't come into the town. If they block the road, and I can't leave for one or two months, what do I care? Everything I need is here in San Cristos." He shrugged his shoulders and folded his hands on top of his head. Our pack passed a few moments yelping at each other in trilingual chaos.

The initial reaction was fear, and it wafted strong through the house. I cringed, then gagged. Something was afoot.

"I'm leaving." Isabelle said. She was determined, hyped-up and aware with the sudden crisis, rank with her fear. Suddenly, life was very different, and it was all serious. It was possible for us to be stuck in San Cristos for two months, maybe even more. Jose assured us that it was safe, that our lives

Manifesting the Monkey   79

would be secure, unless we did something stupid like try to leave until the roads cleared. As a general rule, the FARC had stopped holding tourists from rich western countries hostage. It was too much trouble. They found it much better to take South American hostages.

"Yeah, that's for sure." Alec agreed immediately with Isabelle. "For sure." He nodded, gazing into the distance as if preparing to deliver some tragic Shakespearean soliloquy.

I looked at Aurore. The rush of emotion surged over her. She hadn't yet given into it, but she was dangling by a thread. Alec was consoling Isabelle, assuring her that they would do whatever she wished. He was the Protector, and he would protect. All of a sudden, everyone had an excuse to abandon our mission. The smell came stronger, and the pack tightened. The fear manipulated them. I felt the cloud of invisible insects pushing against me, looking for a way in, to move my lips, speak lies, whisper poison words of security and comfort. I swatted at at bug buzzing around my face.

I took a deep breath, my roots extended into the Earth, and it all faded. "Well, we don't even know if it's going to happen," I said. "Or when it's going to happen. Tonight is Wednesday. On Friday, we go see the *Taita*. And then we leave on Saturday morning."

It got quiet as they weighed their words. Alec was the first to speak. "C'mon, Ten. We leave tomorrow. We don't know what's going to happen."

"That's right. We don't know what's going to happen." My temper rose. Sometimes, Alec was an especially irritating mirror for me. We were too similar. When he had joined us in Popayan, he talked so much of magic and walking the path—New Age crap that made my skin crawl. He talked so much that I found him hard to take seriously. Weren't magicians dark and mysterious? If not dark at least mysterious? If not mysterious at least discrete?

"We don't know what's going to happen, you know? We *believe* something, but we don't know anything."

Maybe I can unlock them with a little guerrilla ontology.

"Okay, okay, whatever." Alec threw his hands up, unable to prove me wrong. I was always there to remind him that he didn't know, never to pester, just to show him the space of 'I don't know,' where the real magic lives. I was irritated by his constant automatic assumption that he knew something he only thought to be true. This was my biggest annoyance, and I found it prevalent in the French language. Over the years, my observations had led me to form the opinion that a small linguistic habit made a large contribution to the Arrogant-French stereotype. As a matter of routine, they labeled ideas, beliefs and opinions as hard facts. They said *'en fait'*, in fact, the way Americans said like—unconsciously and often.

In fact, this chocolate cake is delicious.

Surrounded by so many facts, righteousness wasn't far away, and the only difference between righteousness and arrogance was time. "I don't know, okay," Alec waved his hands in the air, "I don't know. I just really, really, *really*, believe that the FARC are going to close the road, and I don't want to be here when they do."

"Look," I spoke calmly, hoping that tranquility would succeed where logic failed, "we don't know what's going to happen. We do know that right now we can leave, but I think we can agree that we're not leaving right now. It's 9:30 at night." I waited for their nods. "Let's see what people have to say in the morning."

"Yeah, that's a good idea." Aurore said.

Can she smell the fear, too?

The next day things were peaceful around town. People had lots of things to say about the FARC, but the vast majority claimed that they weren't closing the road yet, and it probably wouldn't be closed that day. Nothing happens quickly in South America. Not one thing...except pick-pocketing.

Throughout the afternoon, we roasted this issue. Should we stay or should we go? I was the only person who insisted we continue as we intended, though I had my reservations. I believed that fear was sabotaging us, creating this scenario so that I would leave and miss the opportunity to further my evolution and perhaps help the others to see their own self-imposed tyrants. I would stay, even if I stayed alone. It seemed like the right thing to do, though in hindsight, it was a really dumb idea.

Although every person we spoke with assured us we were in no danger, the egos of my friends used the emotional energy of physical harm to charge the case to leave. If we drank the medicine, we would be forever changed. And we all knew that. The more fuss the others made about our departure, the more clearly I saw the situation. The fear was strong in them, and it wanted out of the ceremony. It was fighting for its life. I rested in the quiet certainty of my decision.

Friday morning, we still hadn't decided, but everyone packed their bags, myself included. Either way we were leaving Jose's house, it was only a question of where—either to the city of Pasto or to *Taita* Florentino's.

"Anyone want to look at these?" Isabelle blushed, holding a pack of tarot cards. "I got into them while we were studying Jung. You know? Archetypes and stuff." One-by-one, we all agreed.

"I'll go first." Isabelle shuffled the cards and laid them down in a diamond pattern, explaining what each position meant. The top card was the light, what could be seen. The bottom was the shadow, what could not be seen, and the one on the right, the action. On the left, what needed to be experienced. Her cards were ambivalent, indicating that life wouldn't change much if she stayed or if she went. Surely nothing suggested that a kidnapping by the FARC awaited her if she remained one more night in San Cristos. Alec was next and his cards showed the same thing. The Justice card urged him to do the right thing, to weigh the options carefully before he made a decision. Aurore's cards culminated in the seven, the Chariot—how she guided her powerful emotions would dictate the outcome, and she'd have to be strong and aware to follow her road safely. None of the readings hinted at their fears being made into realities and the subsequent incarceration by the FARC.

My reading was strong, by far the most foreboding. Six, the Lovers, lay in the shadow position, suggesting the marriage of my conscious and unconscious, my union with Aurore, had brought me to this moment. But the experience card was its opposite—the fifteen, the Devil, predicting illusion, isolation, and separation.

Oh, shit. I really don't think that's good.

The Devil was prominent in the middle of the card. On his left, a male figure—the same man from the Lovers—wore a crown, and a greedy smile as he looked at the wealth of gold coins at his feet, oblivious to anything else, even his partner. She strained towards him, but a chain held by the Devil, collared to the woman's neck, prevented her from reaching him.

The fifteenth ceremony and we pull the fifteen? I've got a bad feeling about this...

I was the only one not afraid of the drink, but the cards suggested, and my intuition confirmed, that this ceremony would bring me face-to-face with the Devil. I had no fear, but I was the only one with a good reason to be afraid.

Fucking irony.

<u>13</u>

Every man carries an enemy
in his own bosom
-Danish proverb

Half an hour after three cups of medicine, I stepped through the threshold into the Otherworld. I was in a cave. Rain splattered outside, and I shivered.

It's the same cave as before...

The light was dim, but I saw a flickering further into the tunnel. One hand pulled my tattered coat together, and with the other, I guided myself along the wall, my feet pulling hard against the muck that threatened to capture me. I soon came upon a young man in a wide-brimmed hat and a long trench coat, shivering next to a small, smoky fire.

"Who are you," he demanded. I froze and looked behind me, but there was no one else. "Yeah, I'm talking to you."

"Me, well, I'm..." Something pulled my name back into my mouth each time I tried to say it.

Does the Devil know if you're lying?

I said the first thing that came to my mind. "I'm October." Technicolored growths on the pulsing wall morphed into faces, screaming for help in silence.

"October?"

"Yeah...the October Man." I stood up straighter, realizing for the first time my identity as a superhero.

His red eyes were glassy, raging with anger. Three parallel scars ran from the hairline just above his ear to the opposite side of his chin. I sniffed and smelt only the dampness of the cave. I placed a timid foot forward.

"You came anyway." He hissed. "I'll never understand your kind. You looked in the mirror. You knew I'd be here. But you came anyway?"

"May I sit down?" was all I could think to say.

I interpreted his silence as consent and took a place across from him, with the orange glow of the fire between us. "Who are you?"

He looked up at me and smiled. "If you're the October Man," he laughed, "then you can call me...Jason...Muscoph." He laughed, and a mob of bats unhooked from their perch on the ceiling and screeched out of Jason's lair.

"What are you doing here?" I asked. My roots extended into the ground. I was safe, yet somehow out on a limb. I wasn't sure what I had gotten myself into.

The sound of the crackling fire filled the cave. The smell crept in and thickened around us. "I have come to realize your horror, October Man." He spoke the words like an artist putting the final touches on his opus. "People need fear. They cling to it. It's the one thing holding our miserable planet together. And you want to take it all away." As he spoke, the fire grew bigger. "What gives you the right? What gives you the right to strip people of the one thing they can depend on, the one thing that gives them a sense of security? The boogeyman keeps people in line, moving in the right direction. Without it, the world would be chaotic, people would do whatever it is they wanted. There would be no limits! You have disrupted the flow, the natural balance of things, and you shall now be punished."

The alarm ran up my spine and hammered inside my skull.

Jason was holding a small hatchet that glinted in the twinkle of the Otherworld.

I vomited.

This is it. There's no dodging this one. Here comes the train wreck.

I stood up, but the ground awoke, slithered up and grabbed me by the wrists and ankles, pulled me close, and held me down. Jason leaned over me, laughing.

That's not good.

I extended my roots into the cave floor, but the sentient slime holding me spit them out just as fast. I tried to shake, to transform into my dragon, but I was too tightly bound.

"Some lessons, October Man, must be learned the hard way." It was then I noticed the thick silver rope in his other hand. I looked down, and my heart was a web of these cords, all different sizes and luminosities connecting me to everyone I cared about. A switchboard. The rope he held was the biggest, and it was rooted right in my center. Jason smiled, and I followed the cord to its other terminal, to Aurore's heart. I looked her in the eye one last time before he raised the hatchet high above his head. The first blow slammed into our connection, and I screamed as my heart was gouged. Jason hacked at the rope until it finally broke, leaving me with only a few loose strands of a once great love. And in that last look, I knew that Aurore and I could do anything, everything together. A thousand paths led to beautiful, happy endings, but then the separation was finished, and those possibilities blinked out, like a strand of Christmas lights with a faulty bulb.

The Otherworld faded into collective reality. Aurore was looking at me, and she was crying. "I have to go. I don't know why, but I have to go. I don't want to, but I have to. I have to go, Ten." She looked at me, and the spark we had shared was dead. She kissed me on the forehead, squeezed me into one last hug. Then, she left the ceremony hut and retired to her sleeping quarters.

I spent the rest of the night and the early evening doing my best (which wasn't very good) to stop the bleeding from my heart. Alec tried to help, but there was nothing to do but let it clot on its own.

In the morning, the wind picked up. The cocks and the macaws announced the arrival of the light. When the sun rose, I was alone, and my eyes were red from crying, but I was happy. In spite of all the misery I had been through the night before, I was happy to have the experiences that I did, happy that Aurore and I had shared our lives together for so long. I was lucky.

Broken hearts build character.

I understood better. I cursed my naiveté to think I could defeat such a powerful force in New Chicago, that twenty years of infection could be cured overnight. My fear had stayed alive, had left my body and lived inside of Aurore, had grown and waited for the next moment to strike. After drinking the medicine, Jason Muscoph, disguised perfectly as *Taita* Florentino, started whispering to her, and towards the end of the night, she believed him. How could something that we had worked on building for years crumble from so few words?

My love for Aurore was as strong as ever, but we couldn't reach each other.

The Devil.

For now, with the sun rising and the macaws squawking, we were done. Jason Muscoph had won. But it was just beginning. I knew that now.

Aurore opened the door and stepped out into the courtyard, looking refreshed and happy. She glowed in the same way as the day I fell in love with her. For two months my fear had eaten away at her, and now that it had passed, she shone with her characteristic brightness. Once realized, there wasn't much inside of her for the fear to feed off of, and she was left with only her own silent, relatively balanced boogeyman. Aurore was and always will be a creature of light, a rare angel who travels through life loving no matter what terror the world throws at her. I smiled at her, pained that I was no longer privileged to sneak behind her, put my arms around her, and surprise her with a kiss on the nape of her neck. When she saw me, anger filled her face and plunged daggers deep into my heart. Why was she angry? What had I done that was so terrible? But anger was the support she needed to carry out her decision, and she wore the mask beautifully.

Taita Florentino came out of his home soon after, smiling as well.

"Hello, my friends. How did you sleep?"

"I didn't," I said, searching for some clue to his true nature.

Friend or foe.

"I slept great," Aurore said and another strand fell from my traumatized center.

"It was a strong ceremony." The *taita* looked at me. "But it is over now and what is done is done. We can only trust God that it was what was meant to be. How else can it be different? This is what is, this is what is meant to be. Same-Same."

A few reasons to debate him crossed my mind, to dissect the words and leave the finality of the night's decisions in tatters, but I refrained. As painful as it was, I knew that this was the way. I now walked alone. The wind picked up even more.

The *taita* continued. "We are all walking different paths, and sometimes they are close to the path of those we love, and sometimes they are very far away. In life, acceptance is the key to success, to accept what is in front of us, what is happening now because it is all that we will ever have. And only by being grateful, by really loving what we have, can we have room for more. Last night the bond that you spent years of your life growing was cut." A surge of emotion rushed up, and I stepped forward, desperate to plead my case one last time to Aurore, to unveil Florentino for the traitor that he was. But the *taita* put his hand on my chest and stopped me. "It is done, my friend. The bond has been cut, and no words will make it whole again. You are on your path, and she is on hers and last night was the fork in the road. She's just there, you can still see her, but in a moment, her road will make a sharp turn. And she will disappear around the next bend and be gone from your world." The finality of his assessment cemented the reality. For now, it was finished. My words were powerless. I had nothing left in my world, except my war.

I have to kill Jason.

His words deflated me, and my legs no longer supported my body. I sat on the small stone wall around the flower bed, and my shoulders slumped. "Remember, my friend, that this is all the work of God. I have seen in your soul that you know this to be true, and you are on a new path, with new responsibilities. You must go on alone. And besides, my friend, we never know what God will want with us tomorrow. As easily as He splits people, He may bring them back together." I looked up at the smiling *taita*.

"You think so?" I was too confused to be sure of his role in this drama. Was he an unwitting puppet or a conscious player?

"I don't know, my friend, I don't know." He laughed and for a moment, I thought I saw three faint scars running across his face.

Is he a Jedi or a Sith?

Taita Florentino continued. "The truth is that we never know. You have much work to do, much work that is bigger than yourself, and you know that. For now, you must forget her."

He left me sitting there and went inside. He returned a minute later carrying an old yellow umbrella, patterned with ducklings holding umbrellas which were decorated with more ducklings holding more umbrellas, ad infinitum. He handed it to Aurore.

"This is for you, my friend." He hugged her, then stepped back.

She looked up at the clear blue sky, surprised again. "It's not going to rain."

"Sometimes, things are not what they seem. Sometimes we mistake the flame for the entire fire." The wind was howling now and the taita whispered something into Aurore's ear. She looked at me and smiled, the sweet, soft smile both asking for and granting forgiveness. Then she opened her gift and stood there battling the wind for it. A strong gust whooshed past me and filled her umbrella. Aurore was holding it with both hands, and the next surge carried her off her feet, over the house, and out into the distance. I watched her small form, legs kicking, shrinking until she disappeared beyond the horizon.

14

You've got to learn to survive a defeat.
That's when you develop character.
-Richard Nixon

After that, I limped northward with Alec and Isabelle, berating myself for my ignorance. I had plenty of opportunities to see the imminent disaster, but I ignored them, preferring my rose-colored spectacles to objective reality. The boogeyman had taken advantage of that inexperience to strike back. In my delirium and self-pity, I headed towards the only place I had ever called home, back to Texas and the artifacts of my former life. I wasn't sure why, but something pulled me there. In those moment before sleep, I heard a soft lullaby, soothing me to sleep. Was that Mother Culture calling me back? I had almost forgotten her. Along the way, I walked a razor's edge, sometimes drowning myself in the endless loops of 'what if' and 'but how' and other times searching for that new strategy with which to face the world. I tried to ignore the smell, sick of knowing the intimate motivations of people, sick of novelty and magic, sick of the incomprehensible scope of possibilities that exist in every single moment. I only wanted my old habits and comfortable limitations. Fox News and my local bar.

Crossing the threshold from south into central America presented an interesting opportunity. Due to the undeveloped wilderness and a number of dangerous smuggling routes, there was no land connection between Colombia and Panama, leaving only two ways to cross the threshold—by sea or by air. Dazed and confused, stumbling out of the jungle, we opted for the sailboat. It was a six-day journey, four and a half of which were spent in the heavenly San Blas archipelago, aboard the Siren, captained by a man named Nigel. He spent the high-season ferrying tourists back and forth between Panama and Colombia, playing host and offering his passengers a small taste of the Jimmy Buffet lifestyle. All for the reasonable price of only $475! Nigel supplied the boat with food and plenty of rum, and by the end of the trip, Alec and I nicknamed him Captain Drunk-As-Shit. We spent the days basking in the sun, diving into crystal waters with white sand bottoms, watching red fish and blue fish swimming through their paradise. We caught barracuda, and Nigel grilled them on the barbecue. We scoured uninhabited islands for coconuts and made pina colladas. Alec and Isabelle took advantage of our remote location and spent a day alone and naked on beautiful tropical island. It hurt to see the smiles on their faces when they came back on the boat, fresh and glowing, but I kept it to myself. One day, we docked near a bigger island and went into a village. There we met the local Kuna Indians and saw a glimpse of how the recent introduction of alcohol turned fine spirited young men into powerful demons who fought and flailed at the world around them, blindly possessed by anger at their inability to save their dying culture. We were quick to re-board the boat and numb our encounter with truth by mixing strong cocktails and cranking up Bob Marley while Nigel sailed us to the next little paradise, where we could forget again.

Reluctantly, I left the warm daze of the Caribbean and entered Panama, and that's where my friends and I parted ways. That's one of the hard parts of long-term travel—you're always saying good-bye to someone you love. I hugged Isabelle, enjoying the warmth and safety of a female. Then Alec pulled me aside, "if you need anything, send a mail, alright?" He looked me in the eyes, and I remembered, although our similarity often caused me some discomfort, it was only because I loved him very much. They stayed in the city to visit the Panama Canal, and I left on the next bus. The stench of fear was now a part of my assessment of the external world, and this new map bred new behaviors. I had to change my way of doing things. It wasn't a question of if I wanted to or not, it was a question of comfort. I swatted at a fly buzzing nearby.

Who wants to live next to a dump?

So I did the obvious. I went towards places that didn't smell bad. Inevitably, those were the smaller places. Cities were choked with fear, and on some level, everybody remembered that moment when they were infected. Everyone knew why else would people douse themselves with perfume? Or hide their true form behind liposuction and Botox treatments? Why else would people spend so much money on entertainment, to distract themselves from any sort of stillness? Why else would they run away from themselves?

I bussed up through central America, learning quickly to take the little routes along the coast, to take my time, village by village, to push quickly

Manifesting the Monkey   91

through the bigger cities because Jason lurked around every corner in those putrid nests, and I wasn't ready. I wouldn't survive another fight with him, not yet. The next trial would find me dead of an apparent suicide. I still had no weapons to battle him, just an uncomfortable radar. How was I to fight an idea that only existed in people's heads, yet was powerful enough to rule the world? I caught shadowy glimpses of him, his wide-brimmed black hat, flapping trench coat, and red eyes. In the smaller rural towns, he was there, but fainter, still extending his influence, like some experienced prospector sure of the next big thing.

Swimming in the ocean everyday built my strength. I started and ended each day in the Pacific, terminating my play in the water by listening to the melody the waves sang as they tumbled over each other to connect with the shore. Every day, the ocean sang a different song. I ate well and smiled often, despite the mending hole in my heart. When I thought of Aurore, it hurt. If I stayed too long with her memory, I started bleeding again, and the center of my shirt would soon stain a bright crimson. That only invited the concern and curiosity of the people around, and the more I talked about it, the more I bled so I kept my attention on other things, like how I was going to kill Jason.

Eventually, I had to leave the beach and enter the city. Even a metropolis as lovely and peaceful as Oaxaca was practice in maintaining my boundaries in a hostile environment. This was it. In three days, I would be back in the States—a homecoming five years in the making. It was time to try and insert the round peg into the square hole. I smelled ahead and sensed a hive of programmed insecurities and intolerance—an army of boogeymen.

I was early for the Kundalini yoga class, a style practiced to strengthen the life-force through rapid breathing, so I sat down in the metal chair. There was already an older Mexican woman at the table. She flipped the pages of a brightly colored esoteric pamphlet, promising the resolution of life's fundamental tragedy through continual forgiveness. When I sat, she looked me right in the eye and smiled. I smiled back and noticed the smell of jasmine.

"Hello," she said.

"Hello, how are you?"

"I am fine. The weather is beautiful."

The passing conversation quickly turned profound. It was refreshing to talk to Christians in South America—generally, they were far less hung up on the church and much more open to God and the essential teachings of Christ. Most were happy to talk only about the beauty and love of the divine.

What more does religion need?

"I'm fine, too, *gracias a Dios*." I enjoyed letting those words of praise roll off of my tongue.

"You have faith?" She asked.

"I do." It felt good to answer truthfully to that question. Once, while I listened to the Pacific, her song explained that any action against fear was fruitless unless it was connected to a bigger source of love than the individual. Somewhere along the way, it was important for all of humanity to humble themselves before something greater, even if it was humanity itself.

"And what are you doing here? You're American, right?"

"Yeah, from Texas."

"That's great! We are neighbors!" I was surprised that she jumped right over the Bush controversy and subsequent complaining.

"Yeah, I guess we are."

"And what are you doing here?"

"I'm on my way back home."

"That's far away."

"Well, I started a lot further away so right now it feels like I'm just next door, and I'll be home for supper."

"I like that." She leaned closer to me and whispered, "so...what has your journey taught you?"

I laughed. "Well, a lot and I don't know how much time you have, but —"

"I've got about a quarter of an hour."

It was unnerving to open up in front of a stranger, but I hadn't felt safe in a long time so I did it. I didn't know when I'd get another chance. "God, I learned about God. I mean, don't get me wrong, I grew up consistently educated about God. Do this, believe this and you'll go to heaven. Do that, believe that and you'll spend the rest of eternity burning for your mistake. But that's not true at all. God is Love, and always loving, never punishing, and I learned that when I imagined God to be angry with me, I was really only angry with myself. Now I'm starting to understand what it means to have faith, and I am so thankful for that lesson." A fervor of passion overtook me, and my words came faster. "And I learned that the world is sick. I mean, I know why it's sick. It's sick because we take so much and give so little. It's sick because those that have the money, and therefore the power...not all of them, you see? There are no absolutes. Some of the wealthy do amazing, beautiful things with their money, but generally the powerful make selfish decisions that affect the entire world, and then that power is diced up into small bits and fed to us. The institutions that are created are so big, and the struggle to survive is so constant, that the Average Joe has very little opportunity to make something better for himself. In the end we all give our consent when we participate in the world as it is. We all swallow and agree to those decisions because it seems so impossible not to. What other choice do we have? Dropping out of the status quo is a serious investment."

The words rushed out, and the beliefs behind them formed into distinct shapes for the first time. I thought it might have gone over her head, but she smiled and nodded. Apparently, the tragedy of the human animal was common knowledge in that part of Mexico. "Yes, of course."

"Obvious, right? But then I saw deeper. I pushed a little further, the veil gave way, and I saw what was really going on. I saw the wizard behind that greed and anger and security. It was terrible. Our whole world is created because of a flux between love and fear. When fear was born, we were doomed to reach this point of critical mass. It has pushed us out over the edge and into the wild blue yonder, but not to soar, only to fall. And now we are at this point of ultimate crisis. We are the first species in the history of more than a billion that may force itself into extinction. The world is going to shit, and it's going to shit because we're afraid to be still and look at ourselves. We're afraid to admit we're wrong or, even more difficult, that we don't know.

"That's what I've learned. I've learned that all of this hangs in the balance, all of history is about to be blown away by our fear. What if we didn't do it like that? What if we did it in other ways? I've seen the disease and seen the answer, and it's a simple one that complicates things. The answer is, of course, to love everyone in beautiful ways, especially the ones that are so easy to hate. It's Jesus' message along with every other true spiritual leader in history. It's nothing new, just something that we're constantly forgetting, or diminishing, or rationalizing away, something we push back there, out of the way where we don't have to take it seriously."

I stopped talking, and she looked at me for a moment. "Wow...that's a big lesson."

"Yeah, a huge lesson, let me tell you. And it hurts. I'm still figuring out what to do with it."

She was quiet for a moment. "That reminds me of something. I'm going to ask you a question, and you have to answer with the first thing that comes to your mind, okay? Are you ready?"

"Yeah, I'm ready." She repeated her instructions. "The first things that comes to my mind. I got it." I took a deep breath. "Ready."

"What animal are you afraid of?"

15

The whole object of travel is not to set foot on foreign land;
it is, at last, to set foot on one's country as foreign land.
-G.K. Chesterton

What animal are you afraid of? Que raro!

I saw a little brown bunny. I laughed, but it terrified me, and not because I thought it was that horrible beast from Monty Python's Holy Grail. Most things about rabbits I enjoyed—their soft fur, cute pink noses, and outlandishly long ears. But the bunny I saw was frozen, cornered in a cage. It didn't know what to do, so it did nothing. I thought it was funny until that woman explained that her question was somewhat of a psychological evaluation. In a nutshell, I was scared of the bunny because part of me was the bunny, cornered with no way out, frozen in the face of the unknown. Powerless in the world, powerless in my war against terror.

But then the border loomed in front of me, and I forgot about the bunny and what it meant. I crossed the Rio Grande and was immediately in the throes of a bad case of reverse culture shock.

If the outbound flush is weird, the inbound back home is fucking bizarre. Leaving is intense because it's all sorts of new images—cows chewing their cud in the middle of quick traffic, a man bathing himself on the side of the street, 12-year-olds already established as businessmen (and con-men), removing your shoes any time you enter someone's home, eating on the floor, eating with your hands, wiping your ass with your hand. The outbound is weird because you never know what you're going to get. It's like grab-bag at the school carnival, surprising and, usually, at least mildly enjoyable.

Try it. Go flush yourself. Buy a plane ticket to a place where you know nobody, where you have no connections, and go there. But stay gone. Get used to where you land. When everything is normal, just when you think you got the hang of it, do it again. And again, and again. When even the most bizarre flush is a minor blip on your radar, flush yourself back home, and get a good look. No matter who your Mother Culture is, it'll be weird. But where the outbound is exciting-weird (shagging a French woman with hairy armpits) the inbound flush is creepy-weird (creating lifetime product loyalty by advertising to 6-year-olds). That's when you get your first real glimpse, your first peek behind the curtain. And if you make it to that point, if you've polished your mirror enough, wiped away the grime, then you'll see it. And once you see it, you're screwed...because you can never *un-see* it. You're obliged to carry that light. It's your responsibility to illuminate the way for others. In whatever way you can, it's your job to shine.

She knows when you come home. Mother Culture always knows. At first, she'll leave you alone. She'll even point out some of her overbearing absurdities. But she knows people. She knows how we work. Just after you think you're immune to her advances, she'll start whispering to you, and you won't even notice, not for more than a split-second, and then it's only a matter of time.

Can we stay awake long enough to get out?

When I arrived in the United States, things weren't the same, or I wasn't the same. Life went on as normal—people went to work, came home, went shopping, watched television, had 2.3 kids—but it all seemed fake to me, as if at any moment, everyone would snap out of their trance, and (after dancing in the streets) we would get to work making something more beautiful instead of chasing our tails, hording our treasures, and wasting our time pursuing happiness from outside of ourselves.

But that didn't happen. I looked around San Antonio and saw the public, saw people sleep-walking, having believed most of what they had been told. I didn't hold them accountable. It wasn't their fault. Mother Culture slammed the messages into us all the time, and there was no avoiding them because they were literally everywhere. Everyone was sleepwalking. How else could a human being agree to live in such circumstances? To work forty hours in a week making some CEO rich while struggling to keep up with the demands of their programmed consumption. I walked through the city, with wads of toilet paper shoved up my nose to lessen the stench, bewildered at how effective Mother Culture kept people from realizing how short their stick was. I compared this American lifestyle, touted as one of the best in the world, with the poor tribal cultures I had met in Zimbabwe. It was difficult to say whose was better, but I guess it depended on the standard. If happiness was the measure, then Zimbabwe won easily, if instead we used comfort, then the USA kicked ass.

I tried the computer programming thing again, but found I couldn't sit in front of a screen for more than a few minutes at a time. It only took a couple of days before I snapped and left the office, screaming about the loss of human connection in our modernized world and how it was eating our soul. But nobody really cared. I was just like the crazies they had been warned about on the news, and it was even exciting for them, to be so close to the action.

I tried to live back home, but that didn't last long, either. *Mi mama y mi papa* were always hovering near me, happy to fall back into their role as parents. They had never gotten over it, never understood that they were more than a mother and a father, that they were people, and that being alive meant finding new ways to define themselves after their children left the nest. My mom cooked a lot, and I have to admit that the smell of *carne guisada* wafting through the house filled me with a nostalgia for the days of youth, when everything took care of itself, and I was safe in my parents' house, back when the world was still a beautiful wonderland, and everything was possible. I ate a lot, enjoying the treats of homemade Mexican food—tacos, enchiladas, pico de gallo, tortas, beans, rice, and guacamole. Then one afternoon, I bolted upright on the couch after a big lunch, just before I drifted into the warm embrace of sleep. Someone was whispering to me. The persuasive comfort that tempted me to let everything go, to forget and fall into oblivion, that was Mother Culture. I left the next day, and this time my mother didn't cry. She knew that something had changed inside me, and I don't think she liked it.

Afterwards, I got a job as an electrician's apprentice. It was good, honest employment, but I knew it wouldn't last very long. I enjoyed it, but I worked with people I'd never understand. There was no common thread, no link between us. They hadn't so much as realized Mother Culture existed. I was an outsider, some alien stuffed into human form, with excess flesh pushing through the creases of my costume. Alone and confused, I didn't want to know the boogeyman was real. It wasn't hard to see that the world was superficial, that something was missing, that most of what we heard was only marginally true at best, and very often a complete misrepresentation, a one-sided story, all manipulated by Jason Muscoph. I understood his role better, now that I saw Mother Culture again. Jason was her right hand man, the tool she used to propagate her agenda.

I knew it wouldn't be long before I broke, but I had to try. I grasped at the straws of my once meaningful life. I called old friends and not so pretty girlfriends. I had a clandestine meeting with April. She was able to slip away from her husband for an hour. We hugged, and both said it was good to see each other, but we never acknowledged how strange it was to look into the eyes of someone you once loved, only to find a stranger looking back. When I asked her why she had to sneak out, she shook her head, and said, "he wouldn't understand." I didn't think it wise to explain to April that her husband wouldn't understand because the boogeyman was whispering in his ear, keeping him afraid that betrayal was on the horizon, a perpetual inevitability.

I had a foot in two worlds—one here, coping with the modern American dream and the other in some plane I couldn't see, working below the surface. In the jungles of South America, my supernatural sense of smell fell within the broader range of 'normal,' but in the States such things were impossible, and any claims to them were denounced, ridiculed, or condemned. Back home, it only brought isolation. Flight and invisibility were the superpowers I wished for, never a nose that sniffed out people's pain. I felt what they were going through, what emotional scar they had hidden first from themselves, then the world, but I could do nothing about it. Any attempt only burned bridges.

People don't like to be touched where they are wounded, even if the touch intends to heal.

The breakdown of my interpersonal relationships started with my best friend. We had just returned to his house after a long run and stood outside enjoying the transition from day to night.

"But why?"

"What do you mean why, dude? I'm just doing it. I'm doing it because I want to do it. I'm doing it because I love her. Why else does anyone get married?"

"Of course there's something else. There's always something else." But

Manifesting the Monkey 99

I knew he had never taken the space to see that. A fish never discovered water.

"Whatever, dude." Matt started to walk away. I grabbed him on the shoulder.

This is important, if he knows where it started, maybe he can heal it before he builds more of his life on this pain.

"Look, man, I'm sorry about all this. I know it hurts, but that's life, man. That's growing up. Believe me. I know that if you can see why you're doing these things, if you really saw yourself, you'd be able to make a leap forward. You'd be way ahead of the game."

What I was offering was true—looking in the mirror was a difficult thing to do, accepting and loving that reflection was incredibly hard, but it always brought healing. Shining light into the darkness is more an act of love than correction. The way of healing, health, and happiness is simple—look inside, accept, and love. After enough glimpses into the soul, this process is naturally applied to the outside world, and what happens is first a transformation of meaning, then of reality.

"If you're sorry, why do you keep coming after me? You've been gone for years. You just bailed. And what news do we have of you while you're gone? Next to nothing. A few short emails, most of the time asking for a loan that you'll never repay. You come back, and you tell everyone how to live their lives while yours is fucked up. Is that why Aurore left you, Ten? Because you kept telling her how to live her life?"

His truth slugged me in the stomach, and I slumped down onto the grass. He stood over me and smiled. I noticed too much, how his posture was only a few adjustments from a proper fighting stance, noticed the fire in his eyes that suggested he wanted me to push him so he would have an excuse to kick my ass. Matt was an amateur boxer and trained all the time in constant fear of the enemy he created. I shook my head and tried to forget the emotions racing through me, tempting me to bite him back.

"You're right, of course. Aurore left me because I was a jerk because I was never satisfied with the way things were." It wasn't the whole truth, but Matt wouldn't understand exorcised demons stowing away in my partner, waiting to strike, then severing our connection with a rusty astral hatchet. "I'm surprised you're using that as a weapon. I never thought you'd be the one to use my separation against me."

100   Manifesting the Monkey

"Well, dude. I never thought you'd be such an asshole." That broke the tension, and we laughed. We had known each other the better part of seventeen years, and it was easy to step out of our roles and return to being eleven again.

It was knowing this that convinced me to push it.

"It's your mother."

"What," his voice tensed, his defenses immediately online again.

"That's why you're doing it, that's why you're getting married after knowing Jenny only four months. When you were young, your mom left you in the car when she ran into the shop just for a minute." I shifted my position in the grass, surprised that he was allowing me to continue. "Sure, nowadays it's considered negligent or even abuse, but in 1984 humans weren't as afraid. It was okay to leave kids in cars for a few minutes. You were sleeping so quietly that she didn't want to disturb you. You were so peaceful. But you woke up when the door closed and all you knew is that you were alone. It was the longest seven minutes of your life, a deep fear that left its imprint on your soul. And since then, you've been trying to fix it, and because you don't know how to fix it, you've hidden it with hand guns, alarm systems, and pit bulls. You've been searching for someone, searching for security. And that's why you're going to marry Jenny. Because you don't want to be left alone." The odor of fear that wafted by on the breeze confirmed the accuracy of my statement.

The silence was tense, and I looked down at the ground between the paint-splattered running shoes I had bought at Goodwill. When Matt spoke, there was a deep growl beneath his voice, and I heard the cracking wood as that old bridge burned. That's when I knew I went too far and things would never be the same. "Fuck off and don't come back." He turned and walked up the steps.

I stood and followed him. "Hey..." Matt turned and punched me in the nose, but not as hard as he could because he didn't break it.

"Fuck off and don't come back." Betrayal lit his eyes, and I heard the hiss as the last planks of our friendship dropped into the oblivion below.

I walked the three miles back to my apartment, disgusted at my audacity. I didn't know what to do so I got really drunk. Part of me was happy at Matt's reaction—for the next week, my nose was congested and unable to smell anything.

According to my skepticism, I assumed that Matt's reaction was a fluke and proceeded to unveil everyone's pain to them as soon as it became known to me. I explained to my cousin, Ricardo, how the shame of his Mexican heritage began when he heard two older white guys calling his sister a 'beaner-whore' at an early age. I diligently showed my brother Augusto that his alcohol and drug problems were understandable coping mechanisms for a constant identity crisis and the feeling of incompetence generated by his ambiguous place in the world. I revealed the relentless berating of our father as the source of Martin's weight problem. I kept going and going, like some tripped-out Energizer bunny, beating my drum of righteousness. Within three months of my return to the States, only a handful of friends and family still talked to me. And I continued to dream true.

The first time it happened, I convinced myself that it was just a fluke. Because I understood that everything in my dream was a reflection of some facet of my life, I figured that it was some repressed material re-surfacing or perhaps experiences from a past life (though I didn't really believe in reincarnation), but then it happened again.

It was the ants that I noticed. They reminded me of the days in the jungle with Lucio, during my first *curación*. I saw them in a dream, marching along one of the roads they had built. I followed them to a massive tree, where they continued down into a hole in the ground. I stopped and watched them disappear into the Earth. Then I took a deep breath and jumped down.

I found myself on a tundra. The wind blew snow across the horizon, but I heard nothing. Everything was muted.

Conscious dreams are an extension of the Otherworld, and changing any aspect of the dream—surroundings, characters, tone—is only a matter of attention manipulation. For example, to turn into a giant, I'd often imagine Paul Bunyan then hold my mouth shut and blow as hard as I could. The pressure would increase my size until I was stepping gingerly over mountain passes and tiny cities.

In the silent frozen desert, I tried to fly up and get a better look, but my jump ended like any other in collective reality. I tried turning the distant mountains on their heads, but that didn't work either.

"Who are you?" The female voice was kind, but demanding—a fair caretaker who had discovered a trespasser lost on property.

Manifesting the Monkey

I turned, but there was no one. The voice repeated. It came from nowhere at once.

"My name is Ten."

"Ten? What a strange name that is. How did you get such a name?"

"It's a nickname from middle school. Some stupid joke about my last name. A double entendre. Who are you? Where are you?"

The voice laughed, the kindly cackle of an elderly woman. "I'm everywhere, *this is* me."

"What do you mean this is you? Where am I? What am I doing here?"

"I was hoping you could answer that for me. You see, this is my mind, and you are the intruder here."

"Your mind? Uh...shit, sorry...how is that even possible? I don't even know how I got here. I just went to sleep and...voilà..."

"Hmmm...that is strange." The voice was behind me now. I turned, and a wrinkled old woman dressed in furs stood smiling at me. "It looks like you've gotten yourself lost. My name is Ahnah, and I think I know why you're here."

She took me by the hand, spun me around. The scene swirled, colors blurred together.

It was dark and cold. As my eyes adjusted to the low light, I made out the shape of the room. I was in an igloo. Three people whispered to each other and another lay in bed. All of them were bundled in thick layers of fur. I looked at Ahnah and she smiled at me again, then pushed me towards the figure on the bed. "Don't worry, they don't see you. We're in there, after all," she pointed to the person lying still and giggled. I moved closer, and I leaned over one of the others, but he didn't notice me. I was invisible. On the bed, sleeping smiling, was Ahnah.

I looked back over at her, and she giggled louder. "I told you we're in there."

"But how?"

"I'm asleep."

"...why are we watching you sleep?"

"Because, Ten, this is my family, and I want very much to see them."

"Well, why don't you see them when you're not sleeping? Are you away from home? Don't you see them everyday?"

Manifesting the Monkey   103

"Yes, tonight is special because I won't ever see them again."

"You're leaving?"

"I'm dying."

She pulled me away and moved towards her family.

I listened to the soft words of care, understanding nothing of their language, but all of the compassion. The family around her was sad and happy at the same time. It was an expected death at the end of a long life of good living, but that didn't make her imminent absence easier to bear. Ahnah touched each of them on the head and whispered some words of encouragement or kindness that they would remember sometime long after she died.

Then she came back to me. "Now we must deal with you." We walked out of the igloo into a purple world of dusk. I could hear the wind this time as it whipped past me, blowing snow through my hair. "Have you ever been to the Caribbean," she asked. "It's just that I haven't got much time and I've never been. I saw a postcard once, and it seemed so...impossible."

I smiled at her. "Yeah...yeah I've been to the Caribbean." She took me by the hand and spun me around.

The same sun was still setting when we focused on the beach. The sand was white beneath our feet, the water turquoise just ahead. A light scattering of clouds intensified the dark red of sunset. Behind us palm trees, laden with coconuts, swayed in a breeze just strong enough to keep the mosquitoes from landing on our skin. I knew where we were. It was my memory of the San Blas archipelago. We were on a small island and could walk the perimeter in half an hour at a leisurely pace. The sailors who passed through that spot called it the Aquarium—a ten-foot-deep white-bottomed wonderland. A hundred meters behind us, a reef broke the force of the sea, leaving the 365 islands of the archipelago paradisal and humming with the constant singing of the sea. Out in the distance we could see islands, one so tiny there was only a small shack and two palm trees on it.

Ahnah beamed, absorbing the magnificence around her. Shining in the sun, she looked at me. "Thank you, Ten. It's perfect."

"It's amazing."

"What's that?" She pointed to the green lump in the sand.

"It's a coconut," I walked over and picked it up. It was nearly the size of a pumpkin, and Ahnah took it with both hands, her eyes and mouth wide in wonder. "Wow, and all this time I thought they were brown."

"Well," I chuckled, "they are, but this one is immature so it hasn't turned. There's less meat, but more juice. We need to open it."

"Open this?" She knocked the hard green skin and looked at me in disbelief. "How are we going to do that?"

I scratched my head. "That's a good question...we need a machete."

"What's that?"

"It's a long knife, almost a short sword."

"You've used one before?"

I nodded. "Plenty. It's really handy."

"Well go and get it," she stared at the tall thin palm tree. "Think of it and you'll find it behind that...coconut tree. What a strange place this is. It's hard to believe it's on the same planet where I've lived my life. It's so foreign." She looked down, and began wiggling her feet, quickly learning that her motion was enough to dig herself down into the sand up to her ankles.

I laughed when I returned with Nigel's machete—I had used it plenty of times when I had made the crossing from Colombia to Panama. "Let me see that," I took the coconut from her, and she continued to play in the sand with the gentle curiosity of a child.

"It feels so strange, coarse, yet soft."

I walked to where the small waves were washing up, put the strange fruit on a rock, and hacked into the green flesh. In seven slices, I had the top cut off and had poked through the soft shell of the young coconut.

"Wow," she giggled again. "That's amazing."

I handed her the the natural juice box. "There's nothing like it." I was honored to offer an old Inuit woman her first coconut on the eve of her death. Ahnah searched for the best way to drink the liquid. She tried holding it above and pouring it into her mouth, but hardly any made it to its goal. Finally, she put her lips to the hole and took a sip. "It's good!" But then she was spitting. "The sand gets everywhere, doesn't it? God, I bet that becomes such a nuisance." Her face turned into a momentary grimace of disapproval, the common expression of someone outside their comfort zone.

"Yeah, it is for a bit, but then you get used to it."

When she was finished drinking, I split the fruit in half and showed Ahnah how the shell would harden into the round, brown form she had seen in photos. I handed her a wide, flat sliver of the green skin and demonstrated how she could scoop the jellied pulp. She took a bite. "It's good,...but gooey." She held half the empty shell long after she had finished, and stared out into the horizon. "I'm going to miss this world. It's amazing, Ten. I know that you know that, somewhere inside, you know this. To have arrived in my dream as you did, you have to know. You're a monkey. Not the 100th, but you're a monkey."

"A monkey?" I asked, but she only waved my question away.

"The world is blessed, though right now it's hard to see that. The seasons are changing, the light is coming, but before it comes it's going to get darker and out of that darkness mankind will be reborn. And it's important that we remember who we are. When the darkness is greatest, then we must remember who we are so that we can be reborn in our true image. If we hold onto the terror and greed of the world, then the next era will only replicate this one. And that's why you're here." She took my hands and smiled. "You're here to embark on the next phase of the path. It's up to you to find the 100th monkey."

"What are you talking about?"

"It goes a little something like this. There's an island with ten thousand monkeys on it. One of them learns to wash his food before he eats it. The next day, another monkey sees the first washing his food, so she learns to do the same. Then two more learn, and four more, then twenty. More and more, the food-washing starts to spread through the population. And when the 100th monkey learns how to wash his food, all the rest of the monkeys instantly know it." She paused for a moment. "You see? Once enough of an idea has reached the collective unconscious through the minds of the individuals of a population, it can't help but manifest into the conscious. And that's what you're to do—find the 100th monkey, push humanity past the tipping point, and that will start a chain reaction and unfold love onto the world. We'll return to the Golden Age."

She reached into a pouch she wore on her belt, removed a small amber vial, and gave it to me.

"What's this?"

"It's whale oil."

"What shall I do with it?"

She squeezed my hands. "Find the 100th monkey."

I put the bottle into my pocket. "How do I do that?"

She laughed. "I have no idea, sweetie." She touched me on the shoulder, "But I know you can do it, and you'll have to figure how to deal with Jason, too."

"You know about him?"

"Yeah, he's a real pain in the ass, but he does serve his purpose. He won't let you succeed. It would mean the death of him so you're gonna have to find a way to...defuse him. Ten, I send you out into the world to do good, to help others, to spread the message, to help us remember who we really are, what we are really capable of. That is what you are to do." She squeezed my arm and nodded, then looked out over the water. The sun was disappearing into the sea. "I guess you'd better get going now."

An intense tangle tied up my gut—she had the answers I needed. "I don't want to go. I need to know more."

"Honey, you can't stay here with me. There's not going to be any here to stay in anyway. It's time to say good-bye." She laughed. "I'll see you on the other side, someday."

She squeezed my hands one last time, then turned and walked into the water.

She turned and called out to me. "How is your heart like a parachute?"

That was easy, but before I could shout my answer to her, she was gone and I woke up. I looked for the vial, but it had disappeared with my dream.

The journey to Ahnah drained my resources, and I didn't dream for awhile. But eventually it happened again. That was how I knew about Matt's trauma from being left alone in the car. I had seen it in his own head.

16

What you can do, or dream you can, begin it;
Boldness has genius, power, and magic in it.
-Johann Wolfgang von Goethe

My life got weirder and weirder, and I desperately wanted to turn it off. All I had wanted was to get rid of the nasty voice in my head that constantly spelled out the reasons I wasn't good enough. And I had succeeded, but that success had landed me in the middle of a human soap opera, and a dying Inuit woman had now charged me with finding the one person capable of saving humanity. I had no idea how to find the 100th monkey, but I knew it had something to do with the engagement of fear. I assumed pointing out the moments when someone had contracted the infection was enough to uproot the boogeyman and heal people. I had plans and blueprints to save the world strewn about my apartment, taped to the walls, half-finished flow charts that all culminated in this monumental microscopic shift that I knew was possible. If it happened for me, then surely it must be possible for everyone as well. But my initial trials told a different story.

My dreaming continued to reveal people's scars—molestation, negligence, embarrassment—and I kept waking up, finding these 'patients' and poking them right where they didn't want to be poked, expecting them to turn into monkeys. I picked their scabs, stubbornly continued showing them the wounds they had purposefully forgotten and wondered why my social life fell apart. But I didn't know what else to do so I kept poking. If nobody had the strength to face their demons, how could we expect humanity to survive the imminent shift? My hopes shattered, and I became despondent, drinking more and dreaming less.

Ironically, the answer came to me in a drunken epiphany, one of those fleeting moments of insight that alcohol seldom yields. For months, I had been dreaming myself into other people's minds. I saw their pain, only to wake up and show it to them, hoping that somehow they would change, that being stripped of all their armor would initiate healing. I thought exposing their vulnerability was the way to health, but it only closed them tighter around themselves. I was traveling into the soil of people's minds, where the seeds of their personalities grew. I saw the weeds that choked the very life out of them, leaving hollow shells of automatic behavior, most of it protection from one fear or another. Then I would wake up, expect to bypass the thorns of their conscious minds, and pluck the offending belief from their garden. I was blinded by my own conception about what was and was not possible.

At first, the dreaming was always with someone I knew, and the next time I followed the ants I found myself in my aunt's head.

It wasn't the kind of snow that had been around for awhile, the kind that began to gray and brown, and drive away all hopes of spring with its ubiquitous gloom. This snow was beautiful, eternally fresh, the kind of snow that makes everyone, even the old and dying, feel like they are a kid again and marvel at the miracle of nature. The kind of snow that energizes and excites. It was the kind of snow that stops traffic and motion, that halts production and erases individuality from days.

I found myself above them on a cliff-top, standing next to my aunt, but she was oblivious to my presence. Down below in a valley, five children ran through this winter wonderland, laughing and throwing snow at each other. Aunt Vicky's face was lit with joy as she watched the children playing in the snow down below, happy enough only to witness the vitality of youth. Laughter filled the valley. All was well.

"Aunt Vicky," I said, but she remained fixated on the group below. "Hey, Aunt Vicky!!" Shouting had no effect either. I waved my arms, clapped my hands, but I was invisible to her. I even jumped up and down while screaming her name, but she only leaned to the side for a better view, as if hypnotized. It was only her intense fixation on the focus of her dream that prevented her from realizing I was there. She continued smiling at the group, laughing with them, content to pass her time there.

The valley stretched out before us, lengthened and the group of children turned to tiny black specks in the distance. As they moved further away, my aunt became more and more anxious, and I knew the scarification would happen soon, that she would again decide to carry whatever trauma had occurred here. Something drew my attention to the mountain peak far away, and I saw Jason Muscoph there, in his wide hat and coat. An image from an old G.I. Joe cartoon flashed in my head. I looked behind a small mound of snow, and there was the rocket propelled grenade launcher. Looking through the cross-hairs, I saw the boogeyman give me the finger. I fired. It was a direct hit, but he disappeared before my projectile exploded.

For a breath it was calm, and then a great mass of snow grumbled loose from its perch.

Shit.

I put my hands on my aunt's arms, tried to shake her loose, interrupt the pattern, inform her of her power in this place, of her responsibility, but nothing I could do would break her from her trance. She still didn't see me, but she kept adjusting her position to keep her eyes glued to the imminent tragedy. The grumble became a roar, and my aunt stared at the scene below, her face transforming into that mask of terror I had seen on the faces of so many I loved. The snow was beautiful and slow as it began the descent, but as it picked up speed, it turned into a meaningless act of devastation. The soon gushing avalanche, dotted with the odd tree, car, or house, rushed down the valley towards the children. Giving up on my aunt, I changed tactics and bounded down the slopes to save them. I still hadn't the necessary control to fly within someone else's mind, but I was able to jump great lengths, and I reached the kids just before the flood of snow crushed us all.

I saw their bodies being tossed around in that thick, unforgiving sea of snow, but the avalanche pushed me up on top of it like a glitchy video game doing its best with some unexpected input, leaving me safe to watch the destruction. The strength of my aunt's trauma pushed me farther and farther away, and the only thing more powerful was my dismay at my incapacity to affect change. The snow settled, and an eerie calm returned, but that was soon broken by my shrieking aunt as she crumpled on the mountainside. I woke, sweating in my own bed.

This wasn't going to be easy. My former approach of illuminating scars to those I cared about was not the way forward. That only brought pain, but I was sure that it was crucial for us all to see our pain, that true healing must be done conscious of our wounds.

Could I be wrong? Can people heal without knowing what it is they're healing?

Two nights later, I followed the ants into my little sister's head. I never pretended to be a psychiatrist or to know how people were thinking. All I ever wanted was to help, and my inconsistencies and faux pas were only symptoms of the learning curve. But sometimes it didn't take years of training to see things, to know which were the points in life where people were traumatized. I think it was pretty obvious with my little sister. She had been molested by an older boy at school when she was seven. The administration didn't want to call it rape, and I guess technically it wasn't, but Cristina was never the same again. After that, her light dimmed to a flicker, and my family centered its energy in search of a way to brighten her back up, but it never worked. She was never there again, never completely present, always lost somewhere in her mind, building walls to protect against another trauma. She finished school, then got a job at a dry cleaners, but it was only half a life.

So I wasn't surprised to find myself in a red-lit elementary school bathroom that needed a thorough scrubbing and reeked of the boogeyman.

Where is he?

Thick vines grew up out of the sinks and the mirrors were cracked windows that lead to even more dismal scenes of self-abuse. The doors to the stalls were missing or soon to fall off. Inside one, my sister sat in a clean white dress, her hands gripping her rosary, mumbling her prayers. There was no one else there, no demonic boy ready to take Cristina's innocence, ready to infect her with his disease, not yet. In the stall next to Cristina, her favorite teddy bear sat perched on the toilet, swinging his legs nervously, looking at his watch, waiting for the encounter he knew must come.

Still a ghost, my sister couldn't see me as I knelt in front of her and tried to talk to her. She kept reciting her prayers hoping for the countless time to avoid her pain. I shook her, screamed at her, banged the wall, but nothing happened. Tears streamed down my face as I remembered the hurt and the horror of this trauma, and how it had been the final blow, the one that had ended our dreams of 'normal' forever. Life wasn't ever the same again. Everyone in the family woke up into a nightmare that wouldn't end. Eventually, time had dulled the sharp edges, but we were forever changed, each of us carrying this scar in our own way. Now, I had a chance to help her, but she was catatonic to my presence, a sleep-walking robot following the designs of its program. A tiny gnat buzzed around my face, and when I looked back at Cristina, a cloud of them swarmed around her head. I heard the door swing open. I didn't have to see him to know that her attacker had entered, and I smelled Jason right behind. I rushed forward to tackle the boogeyman, but I only slammed into the wall. A demonic laugh erupted from him, and I had to hold my hands over my ears. When it passed, I reached for a sliver of mirror and plunged it into his heart, but my hand only passed through him. I tried again—to cut, to stomp, to smash, but I could not touch the boogeyman. Cristina tensed and froze, some cornered rabbit too terrified to run. Helpless, I leaned back against the wall and heard the clink of glass in my pocket. I reached in and retrieved the vial of whale oil Ahnah had given me.

Jason Muscoph morphed into a nine year-old boy. The awkward expression on his face suggested he had not yet convinced himself that his course of action was a good idea, but there were internal forces pushing him forward. I pulled out the cork, sniffed it, and cringed. The smell was strong, and I recoiled, but it was so pungent I couldn't smell the fear any more. I waved the vial under Cristina's nose once, and she pulled away from it, but I followed her movements and kept the vial just beneath her nostrils. I passed it a few more times and smiled as consciousness returned to her eyes, and she blinked. She waved away the gnats and looked up at me.

"Ten? What are you doing here?" She looked around, saw the boy. Jason's stench swirled around her, and I held the vial under her nose again.

"It's not important. What's important is that you understand that this is just a dream." The boy took a step forward and offered a vulgar comment, and I could tell then by his tone of voice that he was only acting out some pain he himself had experienced. Cristina's fear surged. This time I touched the oiled bottom of the cork, then rubbed my finger on her upper lip. The fear vanished and alacrity returned. The boy and the room with him began to fade away. Cristina was waking up into collective reality. I would have to be fast.

"Hey, Cris," I said in a gentle tone. "I know you want to wake up, and you can in a minute, but I wonder if you want to stay here with me for a few moments, okay?"

She looked at the boy. "Of course I do, of course I want to see you...but not with him."

"Well, okay. I understand that. Why don't you do something about that?"

She looked at me, her eyes wide open. "Me? What am I supposed to do about him? You're my big brother. You do something."

I smiled. "Believe me, I would if I could. But this is your dream, and it's you who have to take care of him. Anything I do here won't last. It's you who have to change it."

"It's my dream? How is this a dream? It feels so real."

"It just is, you know? It's your dream, and in your dream you can do anything you want. The only limitations are those you choose. And right now, there's somebody here you need to deal with."

She fixed her eyes on mine. It was still the seven-year-old Cristina, but I could sense her grown self in there somewhere. She turned to meet her attacker with a courage most adults had long forgotten, the open-hearted love of a child, the innocence that we had all lost to one fear or another. She stood up, and as the boy grabbed her, Cristina fought back. She pushed him towards the door. In his eyes, his own fear was burning bright, and Cristina could see it too. "What is that?" She asked me.

"That, my dear sister, is the one thing that keeps men and women out of paradise."

"It's sad. It's sad to see it inside of him."

"I know. But that's okay, too. Everything happens for a reason."

As she stepped towards him, the boy flinched, and I saw that his fear had sprung from physical abuse—an alcoholic mother who only remembered to love her son in those rare moments of sobriety and spent the majority of her inebriated time beating or ridiculing the boy because she was never able to cope with the life she sacrificed to have her son. Cristina grabbed the boy and pulled him close to her, wrapped him in a big hug and whispered in his ear. "I'm sorry that this has happened to you. That you have to live with her anger. I can see it inside of you, eating you up. I know it's what made you do what you did to me. And that's okay. I forgive you. It's even okay that I held onto it for so long. But now, now you're no longer welcome."

She let go of him and took a step away from him. "You're going to go now, and you'll stay away forever." She gripped her rosary and began saying the Hail Mary louder and louder. The room brightened, filled with a warmth that centered and took shape—a massive winged man with emerald eyes. He smiled at Cristina and myself and walked toward the former attacker. The angel kindly took the boy by his hand. The light intensified, filled all of us, and then receded. When I could see again, Cristina and I were outside on the school playground. The sun was shining. She ran to me, and I picked her up,

Manifesting the Monkey   113

spun her around.

"You did it, Cris. You did it." I managed to say through my crying.

"Thank you so much, Ten. Thank you." The little girl turned into a little woman of 23 years, and then I woke up.

Although the dream had been so real, I wasn't sure if it had worked until Cristina called me a couple of hours later. "You were in my dream last night."

<u>17</u>

Everything that irritates us about others
can lead to an understanding of ourselves.
-Carl Jung

After that night with Cristina, it was obvious why my previous attempts failed—I tried to heal people instead of creating an opportunity in which they could heal themselves. Before that night, I had never done anything I could really be proud of. I was as capable as most—smart, charming, and strong—and I had experienced plenty of interesting things, but nothing I had ever done felt like it did in those dreams. I had found my calling.

Maybe to retain some balance, or perhaps as part of the Great Cosmic Joke, as my dreaming life increased coherency, my life in collective reality fell apart. Midas soon discovered the golden touch was a curse, and I soon realized the gift of knowledge was a heavy burden to carry through the world. At the job site, this manifested itself as well. I always saw a better way to do things than the others, even those who had been electricians for decades. At first, my co-workers got a kick out of it. I was a young man with wild stories of impossible feats in the jungle who learned how to wire a house in two weeks. But after a few days of my constant interruptions, I was looked upon with fear and doubt, and the boogeymen came out to play. My boss 'asked' me to stop coming to work. It wasn't that I was lazy. I worked faster and harder than just about everyone in the company, including the boss, but to say that I didn't integrate would be an understatement. I smelled Jason as soon as I walked into Mr. Switcher's office.

"But I'm the most productive employee you have, and I'm learning fast. I could be a journeyman in three months."

"Yeah, you're right. You're right, but it's not about that," he chose his words carefully, "it's just that you're really...abrasive."

"Abrasive?"

"Yeah...none of the other guys feel comfortable working with you so

Manifesting the Monkey   115

I'm either going to have to double up a team and have an employee wasting his day, or I'll have to force someone to work with you, and it won't be long before they quit. So the way I see it, if you go, then you go, and that'll be that. Everything will...harmonize. I may not have anyone that will work as fast as you, but I'll have a group of guys that get along, and that's far more effective than one man."

I walked off the job site, a new build in a luxurious suburb, a castle really. It was a house for one family, with a full-size gym, a movie theater, and a number of other obscene luxuries. I laughed when I thought of how many Mexican families could live there comfortably. It would be a village.

Outside of work, my righteousness only accelerated the disintegration of my personal life. Nobody likes people who are right all the time. It just doesn't work like that. People are happier sleeping, happy to be comfortable and ignorant rather than exposed and uncertain. It takes a strong man to admit that he's wrong, and a stronger man to admit that he doesn't know. I could reduce the problems of the world to an outbreak of fear, prescribe a simple cure, but nobody was willing to hear that. Nobody was willing to admit there was a problem.

Most people believed they knew things that they could only believe. Human beings were generalizing in dangerous ways. An arachnophobe 'knows' that she's afraid of all spiders because she had a scary experience with a daddy-long-leg when she was thirteen. She generalized that one encounter to every spider in the world. In America after the 9-11 attacks, many people 'knew' that all Muslims were terrorists. They generalized that one experience to every Muslim in the world. Sometimes it was enough to provide a counter-example, but many times it wasn't because the generalization happened at an unconscious level, and no amount of conscious discussion would change those deeper patterns. People believed their limiting concepts because it kept the world familiar and safe.

This dangerous case of mistaking a belief for knowledge was the cause of every major conflict in human history.

The Holocaust.

Jews are subhuman and not fit to live.

The Crusades.

God wants us to save the Holy Land.

The Gulf War.

Iraq poses an imminent threat to the United States.

Every act of war was powered by people believing they knew something they couldn't know.

That's how I was abrasive—because I insisted on separating knowledge and belief. That's why I lost my job and what was left of my social life. Any time I met someone, they would mis-classify a belief as knowledge, I'd point out the difference, and, soon, I'd be alone again. I knew that to save the world, I had to find the 100th monkey, but I couldn't even find a friend.

The world didn't want any help from me. I drifted out to sea and into nothing. I was living in a country that valued things I knew to be unhealthy, and I didn't know how to deal with that fundamental clash so I talked about it to anyone who would listen. And most people often replied, "well if you don't like our country, then get out."

This was a most common reaction to any 'foreign' invader—get out. Which worked until the whole world was telling me to get out.

I wanted to laugh with someone honestly and in the moment, not the mask of laughter I had begun wearing, when it seemed socially appropriate or particularly advantageous. I wanted to feel that rush of excitement as I got carried away into a moment of joy. Bars seemed like a good place to do that. Throughout my travels, I had learned that although they served different beer, had different posters on the walls (remarkably, all of them displayed a beautiful woman with large breasts), and spoke different languages, bars all over the world were the same.

"Did you see the rack on her?" The redneck next to me asked.

I put on Prowling Man and nodded while I sipped my beer. "C'mon, mate. You'd have to be blind not to see her, and even then I bet you could hear 'em bounce." I laughed and slapped him on the shoulder.

When our laugh subsided, I took a sip of my beer, and he took a sip of his.

This is rapport. He's mimicking our gestures, most likely unconsciously. People like people who are like them.

"Where you from," he asked.

"England. Brighton, actually." I had gotten into the habit of speaking with an English accent, and most people never questioned it, despite my skin tone. My plan was simple really and, so far, fairly successful. I understood that my disconnection from the values of my culture caused my current interpersonal crisis. I was a man embodying new ideas trying to live in an old paradigm. Unconsciously, being an American, I was agreeing to certain things, and when I spoke in my natural accent, people grew hot because they felt betrayed. One of their own had left the pack and was even talking shit about it. But it wasn't that I was anti-American—I was anti-last-3000-years-of-'progress'. Somewhere along the way, mankind had made a decision, had moved a belief into the realm of knowledge. It was the single greatest mis-assumption in history. Speaking in a foreign accent transformed me from a traitor to an interesting mystery.

"England, wow." He stared at the glass shelves full of colorfully tempting bottles on the wall behind the bar. His eyes dilated, and his breath deepened as he wandered into a memory of a fantasy. "I'd luv to go to England. Or France. Or Spain."

"France, what d'ya want to go to France for? It's full of frogs, mate." I laughed, and he laughed with me, but I could tell it was his Laughter Mask. Most American's didn't know much about the historical feud between *the frogs* and *les roast beefs*.

He was quick to cover his ignorance. "Well, there are lots of nice things in France."

"Yeah, mate. I'm just takin' the piss, is all. France is a beautiful place, innit? I'm English and am obliged to ridicule the French every opportunity I have."

"You've been there?"

"Oh yeah, we'd go on holiday all the time when I was a kid. It's right next door, mate. They've got cheap flights nowadays. But now, they've got the Euro, and it's not like it was before, is it? Bloody expensive. Spain's where it's at now. That's where the English spend their pounds these days. Down on the coast, putting up condominiums like you wouldn't believe. Bloody disgusting, it is."

I took a sip of beer, and he followed. "Oh yeah, yeah." A small silence fell, and in it, he gathered the courage to ask me a question. He looked at his own ignorance, accepted it, and even expressed it. He was brave. "Why is it disgusting?"

"You know, mate. The environment and all that." I waved the glass of beer in front of me. "People spreading like flies." The judgment poured out of my voice. I pumped the brakes, tried to steer myself off course, but it was already too late. I was skidding out of control, and it wouldn't be long before my ego crashed into his. "It's disgusting is all."

"Well...well, that's the way it goes. That's what we humans do."

"Yeah, and that's the problem." I took a sip, and he didn't follow.

Can you see how our movements are becoming less aligned? He's no longer following us. We're losing rapport.

"What do you mean, the problem?" He sat a little taller in his stool. His face was scrunched tight around his eyes.

"Oh, nothing, mate. It's nothing."

He wouldn't let me off so easily. I saw him put on the mask of Tolerant Listener. "C'mon, now. Let's hear it. Consider it a cultural exchange." He sipped his beer.

"Well, it's just that, you know, we've gotten things all wrong."

"Who has?"

"Everybody. The Americans, the English, the Japanese, the French. Everybody has gotten it wrong. We've all been fooled, been tricked by the devil." I laughed alone.

"But how's that? Pardon my ignorance, I've never left the country. Hell, I've never left the state. Why leave paradise?" He smiled at the bartender who had crept over to listen to our conversation. "You'll have to explain it better than that."

I looked him in the eye. He was awake and engaged. He was present, he was here, but only partially. I had provoked him, poked him in a soft spot, and he would see me torn to pieces.

"Alright then, bruv. It's obvious to anyone willing to look at it. We live in a world governed not by what's right or benevolent, not by what is humane and decent, but by profit. Everything has been monetized. Money is god these days, and people live and die for it. We have become pathologically obsessed with the bottom line. I'm not saying money's bad. I'm just saying it being the most important thing may not be the best idea for us all, as human beings, you know?"

"So now you're an expert on what it means to be human?"

"Not at all. I'm not an expert, mate, but I've done a fair bit of living."

"And I haven't? Is that what you're saying?"

"No, that's now what I'm saying. I'm just saying somewhere ...somewhere along the way, we got it all wrong."

"But how did we get it wrong? You're making some strong claims, but you're not backing them up with much."

"Alright, it's right there if you're willing to look, really look. Most people live in cities, breathe dirty air, and eat unhealthy food. They live this detrimental lifestyle either to survive or to continue on one path of addiction or another—drugs, sex, comfort, whatever. We live in capitalist societies, which means either we grow or we die. Our model of the world is based on economic growth, constantly growing, and that will just never work. Sooner or later, we're going to hit the ceiling, maybe even kill ourselves." I felt his gaze on me as I sipped my beer, but his laugh surprised me. It was cold and vicious, and although I was accustomed to hearing it from people, I wasn't used to provoking it so early in a conversation. Always an overachiever, I was getting better at being abrasive. "Is that it, then? Why didn't you just tell me you were a tree-hugging hippy faggot?" He laughed and the bartender laughed with him.

That is rapport.

I slumped in my stool, confused how things had turned out so badly so suddenly. I just wanted to laugh with someone, to connect for one moment with a real person and remember what it was like to be human. God, if only Aurore were still there. She'd understand, she always understood. I mustered what spirit I had left and responded. I knew it would be fruitless, but even confrontation was better than the cold silence creeping in my soul.

"Well, I wouldn't go that far, bruv. It's just an observation is all. You don't have to take it personally."

I was sure that his fear would drive him away. A couple of gnats buzzed near his pint of beer. The smell of his fear thickened, but he kept at it. He insisted. "That's what I don't get, is people like you. Gotta save the world, gotta get in everybody's business."

"It's not that I want to get into everyone's business. It's that everyone's up in my business. I mean, look around. Look around at the stupidity of man. We're the first species in the history of the planet who are on the brink of killing ourselves, of wiping ourselves out of existence."

"Bullshit. That's probably just something you read on the internet. Bullshit."

"It's not bullshit, anyone with an open mind can figure it out. Look at the world around us, look at it. We're surrounded by natural systems that keep themselves balanced, that are balanced by the world around them. If there are too many wolves in an area, the available food supply will dwindle until there is less food, some wolves die, and the balance is restored. It's natural."

The man laughed, reeking with fear. "Well, there's your mistake buddy. You're comparing us with fuckin' animals. We're not a pack of wolves, and we sure as hell ain't no chim-pan-zees. We're human, goddamnit."

"Okay, we're human, but that doesn't mean we don't have to abide by the natural laws of the Universe."

"Well, we don't actually. Don't you ever read the Good Book? It says very clearly there that man was made master over the animals and the plants. This is our planet to do with as we please."

I stared at him in disbelief. The logical flaw many take as gospel had passed from his lips as easily as 'hello', and he had no idea what it meant. I dropped all of my masks, including the accent and laughed. "That's what I don't understand about this country. George Bush was re-elected after a terrible first term. He fucked the economy, committed war crimes, and lied to the American people, but then he wins office again. Why? Because so many bible beaters are afraid of gay men stealing their values or socialists stealing their money. And people still believe that we have the right to rape and pillage the planet, to stuff ourselves because God granted us the right from on high. When will it stop?" I laughed again.

"Well, boy. I don't know what y'all do over there in fancy England or wherever you're from, probably fuckin' Mexico, but here, in God's country, we kick people's ass for talking shit about the Lord. You know what, if you don't fucking like it over here, why don't you get the fuck out? Take another swim across the Rio Grand-aye."

"Hey...that may not be such a bad idea..."

I had returned to Texas so that I could be close with my friends and family. I wanted to share this with them, share this special medicine that I had found, but they weren't having it. None of them were having it. At all. And now I was in a city stinking of fear, with toilet paper shoved in my nose most of the time because I was doing something I felt obligated to do. I laughed again and finished my beer.

"Well, thank you for the conversation." I nodded at him and the bartender, both of whom stared at me with malice in their eye. In today's world, speaking out against the norm was heresy and, apparently, punishable by an good ole' ass-kicking.

I left the bar and walked with my hands shoved in my pockets. He was right, though. As stupid and ignorant as he was, the redneck was also right. I had no business being someplace that made me so miserable. It was my responsibility, everyone's responsibility, to do what was necessary to be happy. There wasn't much else to it. But something in the back of my mind was bothering me. Sure, life wasn't like I wanted it to be here, but would it be right anywhere? Was there any place that was still free, still moving forwards in life? It was easy for him to tell me to fuck off if I didn't like his country, but was there even one country that I would like? And would they let me live there?

I walked back to my crumbling apartment and prepared for an imminent departure. I wasn't sure where I would go, but that was fine with me. The less I knew, the better. It would keep me on my toes, keep me moving in the right direction.

It only took me a few hours to prepare. I was unplugging again, letting go of something, taking another step into the great unknown. A few changes of clothes, a journal to write the most harrowing of dreams, eating utensils, a homemade alcohol stove.

What else do people really need?

Although I was ready for departure, for the next flush, it took me a few weeks to actually do it. The wind kept blowing against me, counseling me to stay put. Just a bit longer, it whispered.

<u>18</u>

Not all men who walk in the street naked are crazy.
-African proverb

I guess it was natural to think about Aurore all the time. Not only because she was my wife, but because she was always someone I could talk to. I guess that's a big reason I married her, and it may seem like an obvious characteristic of any relationship, but I don't think all marriages were as lucky as mine to have such healthy communication. It took a lot of effort, years of slowly chipping away at linguistic ambiguity and assumptions, but the resulting intimacy was worth it. I missed her and fell further into loneliness and isolation. I was slowly sinking into the sludge of society. A misstep would have me in a mental institution, and maybe that's what was left undone. Jason Muscoph had taken Aurore from me, and now he shattered the rest of my world.

It happened in a grocery store, in the self-checkout lane. Efficiency and profit margins were pushing out another round of workers. In the future, people wouldn't even exist—there'd be no need for them. The flies swarmed near me again, a constant nuisance. I was batting my hand at them, pushing them away, more and more nervous about the length of the line. I hated being in there, with the faint hum of the fluorescent lights subtly squirming into the cracks of my mind. The supermarket was another place we gave up consent, sacrificed our connection to the food source. That was when we agreed it was okay that we had been turned into cogs in some machine, when we bought it in the supermarkets. And I hated myself for participating.

I'd like to say that I had no choice, but there's always a choice. They're just not always easy.

I batted my hand at a fly. I figured there was a rotten bunch of bananas: the vast fruit section was only a few meters away, where the tropical treasures convened to feed our desires. The woman behind me, wide and black, looked at me from the corner of her eye. "Whachya doin'?"

Manifesting the Monkey

123

I felt it, I knew it then, but I hid from it—it couldn't be. "Something is bothering me."

"Well what, cuz you swingin' yo arms all around's startin' to botha me."

"Uh..." The four check-yoself stations were still occupied. I was next, but it wouldn't save me from the coming shock. "...the flies. Fruit flies. Yeah, they must be fruit flies. They're everywhere."

She looked at me, looked around. "You crazy? I ain't see no flies."

"You don't?"

The surprise was phenomenal, and a detached part of myself watched in curious amazement as the pressure wave passed through my psyche. I had never experienced a shock so great. I don't know why I didn't classify the smell and the faint whisperings of fear as evidence of my insanity, but there was no way to avoid the meaning of a consistent visual hallucination. That was a whole other level of dysfunction, a very precarious perspective. I had to leave, or they'd put me away. A minor slip-up, and I'd be institutionalized 'for my own good.' And there was no way I would let that happen. I would decide my fate, not the doctors and their standards of sanity, their prescriptions, and their hospitals, those structures doomed to crumble. What could I do, but run?

I left in the middle of the night. That's the best time to run away. I could have gone during the day, and nobody would've stopped me, nobody would've noticed, except her. But it's fitting to go at night, shrouded in darkness. It makes the disappearing easier. What I was doing was inconceivable to anybody around me, and they'd never understand. They said that when Columbus' first ship arrived in the new world, the natives couldn't see it. They could tell that something was different, but every time they tried to focus on it, their eyes darted away. They called the medicine man. He was experienced in the unknown, capable of seeing things previously un-seen. And as soon as he put a name on it, the ship became visible. I knew that people couldn't see what I was doing, but it wasn't them that I was running from. They were only a symptom. I had to get away from Mother Culture before she caught me. I was too dangerous to her.

There are many Mother Cultures in the world. And they all want to keep their children at home, next to them. She's the culture that we grow up in, the society that forms us, that implants her ideas into our minds in every

124   Manifesting the Monkey

waking minute. Mother Culture is all around us, so present as to be invisible. She's the school system, the tabloids at the checkout counter, the media outlets, the government officials and their speeches. She's Hollywood films, television, and radio. She's there in all the commercials convincing the masses they need another product to be happy, and even the preacher on the podium spouts her doctrine. Once we are conscious enough to decide for ourselves what's important in life, we are already loyal subjects to her imposed reality. But every so often, there are the individuals who wake up and see things as they are. They see that nationalism will only lead to suffering and death, that consumerism will only lead to exhaustion, and that righteousness will only lead to isolation. What most people assume is that Mother Culture isn't alive, but she is. She is sentient and she knows when someone is thinking outside her box. At best she will make their life difficult, and at worst she will destroy them.

That was why I had to leave in the dark—because she was watching. I pushed out, let go and sailed out once again into the unknown. I left that night, left the city, and the life I had built, the person I decided to be.

It must have been easier for Aurore. Sure, more intense in the short term, flying away like some mad Mary Poppins, but at least she didn't have to go through the painful waiting that I did, the slow build of pressure before I popped, the preparation for change. For her, it happened fast. Aurore was always like that. Most times she just did things, moved by the Holy Spirit or Shakti or Inspiration, and poof she was off somewhere else, someone else. Aurore was a shape-shifter. I knew that I'd see her again, I just didn't know if I'd recognize her or not.

I walked out of the city, headed west. When the wind blows us out of our nest, if we are to evolve, it must blow us in the right direction. For me, it blew west. I didn't see the sun break the horizon, but I felt him on my back not much longer after he made his first appearance. I put out my thumb, caught a ride a few hours later, and zoomed away out into nothing. Behind me, I could hear the grumble of Mother Culture as she realized that I had escaped again. It would be much harder for her to find me now, but she'd come after me. She'd send Jason. I was sure of it.

The first night, I got out of a pick-up just before dusk. I was on the edge of town at a crossroads so I did the sensible thing. I calmed myself down, then took a long deep breath, a big sniff. I could smell the fear a long way off, could smell it from each direction. I picked the road that smelled the least and walked down it. The farms weren't too far apart. I kept walking till I smelled one less stinky than the rest. Then I knocked on the door. An old man with his blue-plaid shirt buttoned all the way to his throat wobbled to the door with the aid of a cane.

"Can I help you, son?"

"Yes, sir. I'm headed west and, well…I ain't got no money for a hotel." I hid the Spanish touch to my accent, lengthened my vowels to make it a bit more redneck. "I was hoping that you might be so kind as to let me sleep in your barn." I heard Jason whispering to him, saw a gnat buzz over his shoulder, and I was soon headed back down the road. I tried two more farms before I gave up. The weather was nice, and as the space between farms grew, I squirmed through a barbed wire fence, picked a spot under a tree, and slept there.

I must still be too close to the city. The fear is too strong.

I had a normal dream that night and in it, I was a snake, a harmless brown snake, pushing out of the skin that had grown too restrictive, revealing a new pattern—glittering colors and a bright red snout.

<u>19</u>

And once she remembered trying to box her own ears
for having cheated herself in a game of croquet
she was playing against herself,
for this child was very fond
of pretending to be two people.
-Lewis Carroll

I went wherever people were going. In dreams, I understood how to heal people, but in the waking world, I had no idea how to maintain even a pleasant conversation so most of my rides were either silent or very short. I was alone in an unknown world. If my new programming would have allowed it, I would have been scared, but seeing as I had left all of that behind, I trudged forward into my life and convinced myself it was exciting.

There's no biological difference between excitement and fear. It's only the thought behind the experience that changes one into the other.

I used caution when it was appropriate and bravado when it helped. I was on the path to freedom, or so, at least, I hoped. It must seem so ludicrous, to leave everything behind again, this time to sleep on the streets, and it felt that way, but something quiet inside assured me that it was a step forward in finding the 100th monkey, the unexpected move that my enemy could not predict.

Human beings can adapt to anything, and life on the streets came to me easily, at first. It was like an extended camping trip, and it reminded me of that adventurous spirit I once knew as a boy when my parents would take us up into the hills on those brisk autumn weekends, after the Texas heat had snapped, and we could tolerate being outside of the A/C for more than a few minutes at a time. On the road, I always found a place to sleep just before dark, and I loved listening to the song of the Earth, as day transitioned into night. Out there on the road, Mother Culture didn't know how to find me. I was free and safe. But after three days, the bubble popped, and the waves of my reality tumbled over me.

This is the worst camping trip, ever!

Manifesting the Monkey

127

I spent a day raving mad at myself for acting on such a stupid, shortsighted impulse. I had chosen to become homeless. Ridiculous. Surely, I thought, I had made the wrong decision, but I'd never know, not even now, in retrospect. There was no real way to tell if a decision was the 'right' one. It was impossible to compare one against another because as soon as I chose one path, the other disappeared, with only 'what ifs' as evidence it ever existed. When the bubble popped and I became disillusioned with my choice, I freaked out. I cursed and screamed, I cried and shouted, but I was already out the door of the plane and crashing towards some unknown planet, looking for my parachute. In that free-fall, the only issues I could pay attention to were those of survival. In a few hours they went from minor voices in my head to screaming children, crying to be fed. I wanted to go back, to rebuild the bridges I had torched. I knew it would be a shell, a grand mask that I'd hopefully forget I was wearing, but I couldn't. So there was nothing to do now except admire the view and channel the...excitement that I felt.

Although the rational part of me was pissing his pants, my concerns of impending institutionalization faded away. I was free of Mother Culture and her intentions for me. It wouldn't last forever, but maybe long enough for me to come up with my next move. Since the first flush, I had gradually and sometimes suddenly changed the ideas and the beliefs in my head. While in the city, I was living a lie, going through the motions because I didn't know what else to do. Now that I had left behind that false stability, I clutched to a splintered plank of sanity in a turbulent sea. Adrift in an eternal swell, constantly cresting and crashing over me, a power far greater than my own, I searched, always on the lookout for land. I had left behind my old way of life, and I badly needed a healthy replacement.

I thought about Aurore a lot, tried to dream myself into her bed, but it never worked. I had no idea how to control where I went. I just followed the ants.

I fantasized and saw her smiling bright under the sunshine as she worked in her garden, or the relief that flooded out of her on the last day as a 5th grade teacher. I saw her enjoying the full silence of the great outdoors and the wild rhythms of a night on the dance floor. I did dream about her, but they were the foggy dreams, the ones I soon forgot. I didn't know where she was, but she had sent a message from somewhere in Guatemala, and she was alright. That was the last I heard from her, and maybe I should have just let her go, but I didn't want to. She was my wife, my partner, and we had what it took to go the distance. As far as I was concerned, we were only on a small hiatus. Okay, a long hiatus, but one day it would end, and we'd find a way to reconnect our hearts.

Maybe I can put it all back together?

On the road, outside the system, survival was the only priority. Of course it was a priority inside Mother Culture, but a misplaced one, lost somewhere in the junk drawer—now associated with the ideas of social status, beauty, wealth, and no longer connected to actual biological survival. I left with a handful of cash and spent the last of it on some beans and a can of SPAM a few weeks later. After I ate them, I was still hungry and didn't know what to do. I froze into that familiar cute-brown-bunny trance, helpless in a world out to harm me. If I didn't have any money, how was I going to eat? The injustice of our world was upon me. Play the game or starve. It was the money that sustained us, not food. Or better yet, we were connected to food through money, which may seem justified until you find yourself in a moment with nothing, and you don't know what to do. That's when it becomes obvious how few options we really have, and while talk of equality in America has the comfortable feeling of most illusions, it's not real. Ambition and hard-work are commonly touted as the only necessary ingredients for success, and they are, but the fact remains that not everyone has access to the same resources— namely a stable environment and a healthy education. Without knowledge of one's potential, ambition and a strong work ethic are about as valuable as a burnt-out light bulb. If you've never seen a map of the world, you can't be expected to navigate yourself to China, can you?

It only took two days of hunger to break my pride, and I started begging. Most people ignored me, some scoffed, and a few gave me their spare change. If I spent all day asking for money and I was at a good place, then I could feed myself for that day. But being in rural areas wasn't really a good place to panhandle. The most logical spot for me to be was at a gas station or a truck stop, but the owners soon told me to piss off or sometimes, they called the police straight away. I even spent one night in jail for vagrancy and understood something else about our society and money. Not only was our survival connected to money, it was a crime to be broke. If I didn't have any money, and I couldn't ask anyone for it, how could I eat? One day, I found a half-full bottle of cheap wine. I drank it, then begged for enough change to buy another, and then another, and then another. I sobered up five days later, shivering despite the warmth, with no recollection of what I had done or where I had been. I was miles away from my last memory. That was my first real dip into darkness, and as disturbing as it was to see only black when I looked for the memories of that time, I found it oddly comfortable. There was something inviting about tipping over the edge and reveling in the oblivion of alcohol. It was an escape, a cheap way to avoid the reality in which I had landed, a way to numb myself from life.

How often have I drank as a coping strategy for my life, to keep me accepting the bullshit I had been fed?

Panhandling exhausted me, leaving me disheartened and humiliated so I started browsing the trash cans of the small towns I passed through. I was a pro in few days. Most times, there were only a few things in the bins—a half eaten sandwich, a rotten apple—but once in a while, outside a grocery store, I found a buried treasure. When food reached its expiration date, and often two days before, a store-wide culling took place and all that perfectly edible food ended up in the dumpster, separated, and sealed in a trash bag. The first time I found one, I had fruit for four days, but that diet soon brought up toilet issues. If I had one bag like that a week, I ate well. Usually, I found three a week.

After food, there were other survival and hygienic matters to consider. It wasn't as bad as in the city (where there were more eyes to see my transgressions), but even in the countryside going to the bathroom *au naturel* was an event, and it had to be planned carefully lest I be caught. The small stint in jail had taught me very well that it wasn't a place I wanted to be. Absence of freedom was my personal hell, my nightmare, and maybe then, I knew I'd have to live it some day. So when nature called, I found a clandestine spot and answered. Off the side of the road, under a bridge, behind a dumpster. When you've got to go bad enough, just about any place will do. Bathing wasn't very difficult, either. It was just a matter of finding a natural water source and getting naked. But again, extreme caution was my protocol. If someone saw me squatting with my pants around my ankles or naked in a river, I was sure the sheriff would be hot on my trail at any moment, labeling me some crazy pervert, instead of a man who needed a bath. In the course of civilization, we had come very far in terms of what we could and could not do. The natural had been judged obscene, and I knew Jason would whisper to those rural judges, amplifying my discretions into depraved, outlaw behavior.

As it always does, time slipped by.

Within two months I was accustomed to living the homeless life, and I even enjoyed it. I was free. I couldn't move very quickly without the help of kind-hearted strangers, of which there was an abundance, but I was as free as anyone could be. I was living a hard life by all common standards, but an easy life compared to most of the rest of the world. There were billions of people who lived on less than $1 a day. One day, one dollar. What could you buy for $1?

In my nocturnal adventures, I learned to better disguise myself as a part of the dreamer's own unconscious instead of announcing myself as a foreign entity, which I learned could be dangerous. One evening, after alerting a man to his imminent moment of choice, he became outraged that I had dared to breach his privacy, and no amount of explaining kept him from chasing me through his dream as he tried to smash me with an enormous fly swatter. After that, I told people that I was an archetype from their own unconscious, and that I had been summoned by their own desires to heal. Most times it worked because no matter how often their egos denied it, people's unconscious' knew there was something wrong, and they genuinely wanted to fix it. It could've been true, for all I knew. The illusion of separation had thinned for me, and although I understood that each soul lived its own distinct life, that wasn't the fundamental reality.

In the same way every aspect of your nightly dreams—the characters, the setting, the wildlife—is a representation of some part of your life, in the waking world, we are all different representations of one greater self.

In this deeper reality, human beings were more connected than we were separated. From a macroscopic view, we were all one soul, one divine being, and from that logic, I *was* the part of each one of them that wanted to get better.

I had no control over whose dream I entered. I just followed the ants. I often went to bed focusing intently on Aurore, or Matt, or my parents, or the President, hoping that I could hop into their heads and affect change on a greater scale. It never worked, but sometimes I got close. One night, I fell asleep trying to enter a popular congressman's head, and I materialized somewhere very different, though it was the mind of someone with a lot of political influence.

The scene was dark—black and red the only colors in a foreboding landscape of looming structures. I took a whiff, Jason's stench filled my nose, and I gagged. Dark silhouettes, with red glaring eyes patrolled the uniform streets of a massive city, looking for the dreamer. I wandered, unsure if I had moved at all. Each time I turned a corner, the next street was the same as the one before, clean and neat, with an ominous feeling of imminent betrayal. I followed some of the shadow soldiers, hoping they would lead me to my goal, and I'd have time to help whoever created this nightmare before I got lost forever. I paused for a moment in front of the one building with color, a blue three-storied house with a picket fence and a manicured lawn, its difference so great as to hurt my eyes, like the mid-day sun on a white sand beach. A small dog yapped at me from the safety of the porch, and a woman, her plastic face frozen into a perfect expression of someone's idea of femininity, peeked out from behind the cracked door of the house, which could have fit in any American suburb. Her eyes widened in fear. I looked back, and a swarm of these homogeneous silhouettes converged on the house. She screamed. They climbed all over it and pulled the structure apart, brick by brick. When they were almost finished, the family came out of the front door and were immediately surrounded by these soldiers. The woman screamed again, but she and the rest of her family were transformed into more of those shadows in only a few seconds. The former residents turned and helped with the destruction of their home, the last unique thing I could see. When it was finished, I watched the trail of these soldiers as it went a few hundred meters off and reassembled the pieces. Just as quickly as they had leveled one house, they constructed another, this one all right-angles, washed of color and of any identity that separated it from the rest of the buildings lining the streets.

More and more of the soldiers joined the ranks.

We must be close to the dreamer.

I jumped to the head of the platoon and sure enough, in the distance, there was a rickety green shack. I phased through the wall.

Inside were six kids of various ages, filthy and doing household chores—folding clothes, sweeping the floor, taking out the trash, washing the windows. A woman stood in front of the stove, and the expression on her face displayed the permanent grimace of an uneducated life saturated with poor

132   Manifesting the Monkey

decisions. She took a drag from a cigarette, rubbed her pregnant belly, then stirred the pot of boiling corn. Based on their differences, I guessed the children shared the same mother, but there must have been at least three different fathers among them. Although the kids were hard at work, the inside of the house was a mess, trash littered the floor—overflowing ashtrays, half-empty beer cans, and long-forgotten plastic soda bottles. Piles of laundry were stacked on each of the chairs around the kitchen table, a piece of plywood balanced on wobbly legs. The woman shouted some profanity when one of the younger children wouldn't stop tugging on her dirty shirt tail.

Which one is the dreamer?

I noticed a wooden ladder leading up to the loft, and thought myself up through the rotting planks. Sulking on a foam bed was a chubby boy, with dark freckles and an aquiline nose. The cloud of gnats buzzing around him told me that he was the patient that evening.

What's he afraid of?

"Luke!" The woman called from below. A cloud of cigarette smoke wafted up through the hole, and the fat kid waved it away while he stuck his tongue out at his mother. She continued. "I told you once, boy, and I ain't gonna tell you agin. You come down here and you share that candy with your brothers and sisters...NOW!"

I saw the struggle in his eyes. He retrieved the crumpled brown paper bag from beneath his pillow, and stuffed his face with gum-drops before he slumped his shoulders and climbed down the ladder. When he got downstairs, his siblings had mutated into the dark shadow soldiers. They jumped towards him, and the chubby kid threw the bag on the floor in front of them. They devoured it.

I dabbed a drop of oil under Luke's nose, and he spluttered as he became alert in his dream. He looked at me, then the shadows devouring his property on the ground, and scrambled back up the ladder. I was sitting on the bed, waiting for him when he arrived.

"Who are you," he asked.

"I'm the October Man, and I've been sent by your unconscious mind to help you."

The soldiers outside had begun dismantling the house, taking it apart board by board. I watched as a dark hand slipped through the roof, ripped off

Manifesting the Monkey   133

a beam, and jumped down to the ground, carrying away its treasure.

"They're taking it all! They're taking my stuff!"

And they were. The shadow siblings were now upstairs with us, removing all of Luke's clothes from the cardboard box in which he stored them. The leaning bookshelf was soon empty as well. I looked down at the boy. His head was in his hands, and he was crying. I lifted his chin and dabbed more of the oil on his upper lip.

How are we supposed to help him get over his fear of people stealing from him?

"Look, Luke...that's your name?" The boy nodded. "Look, we don't have much time. Tell them to stop."

"What?" His confusion quickly turned to irritation. "Like that will ever work."

"Just do it."

"stop."

"C'mon, man, like you mean it!"

"Stop...STOP!" And everything in the dream froze.

"Wow, it *did* work." He grabbed a book from one of his former siblings and put it back on his shelf. "Ungrateful little shits," he mumbled.

"So why are you afraid of people taking your stuff?"

"I'm the oldest, and my mom lets the younger ones have anything they want. They come in, and they take everything. I've got no privacy, nothing that's really mine."

"I hear you." I looked at his portly midsection. "But, you know, it seems that you have plenty."

He looked at me with rage in his eyes. "Who are you to say when I've had enough? I earned that candy, worked hard for it."

I poked him in the fat around his waist. "You're right, you worked hard for it, and it's yours, and you shouldn't have to give anything away you don't want to."

"That's right. Tell that to my mom."

"But they are your siblings...so I guess a good question is, why don't you want to share with them?"

"Cuz I worked hard for it, and they didn't do nothin'. What does it matter if they're my brothers?"

"Well...maybe it does and maybe it doesn't. But do you love them?"

"Yeah, sure, I guess," he said reluctantly.

"You guess? C'mon, imagine if," I pointed to the still shadow who had taken his book. "What's his name?"

"*Her* name is Tanya."

"Imagine if Tanya died."

"But she's right there!"

"I know she is, but humor me and pretend. Pretend that...she got hit by a car and died."

"Okay." It only took a moment for him to construct a gruesome scene, and it flickered on the wall in front of us as if from an old movie projector. In another minute, his heart softened and the movie displayed images of Luke and Tanya laughing and playing together.

"Do you love Tanya?"

"Yeah, I do. She's a lot of fun."

"So if you love her, then why don't you share your candy with her?"

"Because it's mine. I earned it."

"Yeah, you did. But if you eat all of it, you're just going to get fatter than you already are. And that's not healthy."

"I'm not that fat. Big-boned, really."

Luke inflated and in an instant, he was his adult self, and it was then that I recognized him as the host of the wildly popular talk show, *Canon Fodder*. I wondered how I missed his whining, nasal voice. "It's my candy, and I'll do what I like with it."

"You're right, it's your candy, and nobody likes some greater authority telling them what to do with their candy, making them share when all they want to do is eat it alone, or with the people they choose."

"That's right."

"But maybe that's because you're not looking at the big picture. Maybe your mom wants you to share the candy because it will help the family to be stronger. And a stronger family will eventually make you stronger as well. It's in everyone's benefit for everyone to do well in life, to have plenty. And maybe you don't see that having candy isn't possible without your brothers and sisters. I mean, what are they doing while you're out getting some candy?"

"Mostly playing."

"Mostly?"

"Well...they've got their own stuff to do around the house."

"Alright, so you're out getting candy, and they're here taking care of your mom and the household chores. Basically, the stuff you don't want to do, even though it needs to get done, right?" I took his shrug as consent. "Have you ever offered to take some of your brothers and sisters to go with you on your candy missions?" He shook his head. "So, Luke, what I don't understand is that if you love them, if you love Tanya, why wouldn't you want to share it with her, not all of it, but enough so that she can enjoy it as well."

"Because it's mine. I earned it."

"Yeah, I hear you, I understand, you earned it, but why don't you help Tanya to get her own candy. I mean somebody taught you how to do it, right? Someone helped you along the way. And they're here doing the jobs that you don't want to be doing. I mean you don't want to take the trash out everyday, do you?" He shook his head. "But somebody's got to do it, right?" He nodded. "So is it hard to imagine that because Tanya's here helping out with this stuff, she doesn't have the opportunity to learn how to find candy? So why don't you help her? Or share the candy with her?"

"Because they don't deserve it," Luke spat the words.

"Why not?"

"Because they didn't earn it."

"But you love them."

"Love don't matter for shit."

"Isn't that more important than working for candy?" I asked

"No, you get candy because you work for it."

"But maybe your siblings have an inherent internal worth. Maybe because they are human beings, they deserve as much as anyone else. Maybe if you offer them some candy or help them learn how to get out of the house more so they can find their own, it doesn't have to be a terrible thing, maybe it can be a generous thing for you to do, one that means you love your siblings and that you understand helping your family will only make you a stronger, healthier Luke. It doesn't have to mean you're not going to have enough. Maybe the more you give the more you'll receive."

He looked at me, and I thought I got through to him, but the rage in his eyes flared, and he reached back and socked me in the jaw.

"I fucking hate communists!"

<u>20</u>

Every mind must make its choice
between truth and repose.
It cannot have both.
-Ralph Waldo Emerson

"Well...what-what-what do I do about it?" The lanky man called frantically as he ran past. Soon after, a giant three-eyed troll rushed after him. The monster's gaping mouth spilled drool from rows of monstrous teeth, but it smiled.

Some people really enjoy being trolls.

"You could turn and tell it to stop," I offered

"No!" The man shook his head and was gone again. I dematerialized and appeared ten meters in front of him.

"Give him a hug?"

"No way!" He sprinted past, and I jumped forward.

"You could fly away."

"That sounds great. How do I do that?"

"But I don't really recommend flying away. He'll come back. You see, you live this dream over and over again because you don't ever deal with the root of the problem. That's why your friend is there to chase you. You're running away from something."

"No shit! Him!" The man zoomed by me. Now, the surrealism of the dreamworld kept us next to each other, despite the fact that I was sitting cross-legged under the shade of an oak tree, mindlessly chewing on a long piece of grass, and he was running for his life.

"But what is he?"

"He's a troll!"

"Yeah, but who is he? This is your mind, and everything in it is a reflection of you and your life. So, who is the troll in your life?"

"My boss. No, my wife!"

I laughed. "If you can't tell the difference between your wife and your boss, buddy, you're going to be running for a long time."

"It's my boss." I looked back at the troll, and its appearance changed. The eyes transformed from the tall, narrow pupils of a reptile to a more human shape and color. The tough leathery skin turned into a proper business suit, complete with a flapping tie.

The costume makes the man.

"What do you want to change about your boss?"

"I'm tired of him running me ragged."

"Okay, right, but what has to change inside of you for that to happen."

The man slowed down and stopped in front of me, hands on his knees, panting. The troll was nearly upon him. "You've got to stand up to him, and I promise there's no better place to do that than here," I said.

"What do I do?"

"What's that?" I pointed, and the man was surprised when he pulled a rattle out of his back pocket.

The troll charged and roared towards the man who looked down at the small rattle, wondering how something so benign could stop a monster. "It's all dream," he muttered to himself. He widened his stance, took confidence, and just as the troll was about to bite his head off, the man shook the rattle. A sound much too large for such a small instrument echoed across the dreamscape, as if armies of long-dead warriors were beating their war-cry, coming to the dreamer's aid. The troll stopped in its tracks, and blinked, surprised that the endless routine had altered radically. Sensing danger, the troll-boss turned and tried to run, but the man was too quick. He grabbed him by the tie and held him still while he shook the rattle. The troll shrank, smaller and smaller until he was the size of a mouse.

The man raised his leg, but before he could drop it down on his helpless prey, I grabbed him by the arm. "Look man, take a deep breath. Compassion goes a long way here. Do you really want to answer his violence with more violence? It's your mind and you have the power here so if that's what you want to do, then, by all means, do it. Just think about it for a moment first."

"You don't know how long I've been dealing with this."

"You're right, but I do know that if you're not careful with how you resolve this, you'll only create another troll somewhere else. Maybe your wife next time. There are times when we must accept the presence of trolls and just let them be trolls, okay? You've done the most effective thing we can do to the monsters in our heads—you've made him ridiculous."

He put his foot down and took a deep breath. "Okay, okay. I get it. What should I do, then?"

"Take another few deep breaths, take time to get to know your troll, appreciate him. For all the trouble he's caused you, he's also helped you survive in some ways you may not have realized until now. Be thankful for that, and then I'm sure you'll think of an appropriate way to handle the situation."

He stared at me for a long moment before speaking. "And who are you? If everything is a part of my mind, then which part are you?"

I flashed him a big smile. "Well, sir, let's just say I'm the part of you that's looking out for our best interest."

"What?"

"I'm a manifestation of your unconscious, the part of you whose sole focus is to heal and to integrate the traumas of life so that you may realize your full potential. I call myself the October Man." Just before I phased out of his dream, I called to him. "Oh, and one last question...how is your heart like a parachute?"

The man shrugged. "Is this a test?"

I woke up and left him to deal with his demons as he wished. It wasn't my job to tell people what to do, only to offer them a light within which to make their own choices. They had the power and decision—both crucial to their healing.

I rustled out of my homemade bed, disappointed that collective reality had not become more comfortable while I slept. I was running out of time. In the last days, I had felt the near-misses of Mother Culture's tentacles searching for me, and it was only a matter of time before she found her lost sheep. The stench of Jason was stronger, thicker than normal, and that could mean only one thing—they were getting close. My days as a refugee were numbered if I didn't come up with something, but I had no idea where to go from there. Making myself homeless seemed like such a good idea, but what next?

I packed my things and hoisted the pack onto my back, then, I went to the road and put my thumb out. I didn't get a ride for a few hours so I started walking. I walked all day, and nobody picked me up, but I didn't mind too much. I figured the less contact I had with people, the less chances I had of getting caught. As the sun was setting, I hit the edge of a tiny town, Saint Christopher. I knew immediately that something was wrong. The wind picked up, and the stink of rotting flowers surrounded me. The people I passed all looked at me with their evil eye, and I knew that she was watching. Mother Culture had found me. As soon as I realized that, my mind started reeling, and walking became difficult. I teetered back and forth like an experienced drunk who somehow regains his balance just before he tips over. Suddenly, my mind wasn't my own. I no longer had control over my thoughts—nasty images and gruesome worst-case scenarios flipped through my head, habits I had worked so hard to release came back to haunt me.

Mother Culture crashed down around me in waves, threatened to pull me out to sea, and drown me. Everywhere I turned, everywhere I looked, Jason was there. I saw him on the evening news as I leaned on the diner window for support, watching people eat their meals. He was talking about the black boy that killed the white girl, or the mother who drowned her babies, or the Arabs and their oil, or Al-Qaeda and their bombs. I passed by the movie theater and saw lines of people waiting to get a healthy dose of the boogeyman. Was it insane that people stood in line, that they paid their hard-earned money to watch human beings hurt and kill other human beings? Or was I the crazy one for even questioning such a practice?

The line between sanity and insanity is often not about health, but about convention.

The boogeyman was twisted up in the words that spilled automatically from people's lips, silence too terrifying a prospect. On and on, the boogeyman pushed. Cultural conflict and AK-47s, hatred and greed, detachment and isolation. Every manner of depravity. The human race was beset on all fronts by crises, and Mother Culture pointed them at me right there on main street of some God-forsaken place.

Jason's stinky tendrils filled my nose, yanking me closer by all the hooks with which Mother Culture had implanted me, hooks that I could not release. They were too deep, tugging and tugging on me, but I kicked back, pulled away from the boogeyman. The barbs, in the form of memes—'raise your hand if you're sure!'—threatened to rip me apart before they would give way. They were the messages of lack or inadequacy that I had seen or heard everyday for years. And they all stunk of Jason Muscoph because they were all trying to convince me that I wasn't good enough as I was, that I needed to spend my money on something outside of my self to be happy, or adequate, or attractive. They were buried throughout my entire body, so deep as to seem fundamental.

I got to the other side of town and found a small bridge to sleep under. I lay down in my sleeping bag on a used cardboard mattress. I was feverish and delirious, but I clutched with whitened knuckles to my choice. It was the only thing I had left, and I held it close to my heart. The boogeyman had no power over me without my consent. In all of this, in all things, I had a choice, and I kept it tightly in my fist. Behind closed eyes, squirming masses of black slithered towards me. I was done for, lost, sure to remain on the streets for the rest of my life. The fear had crawled in through my nostrils and pushed towards my heart. It would be there in any moment, and with the unconsciousness of sleep, I would wake up tomorrow once again inside the collective fear-body. I would be one of them, but never allowed to walk among them and enjoy their comforts. I had misbehaved, and I would be punished, always sick, like some recovering alcoholic, doomed to the fate of his label, pushed to the extremities. My fight, my knowledge of the man-behind-the-curtain was too dangerous, and Mother Culture would keep me where I couldn't infect anyone else. I would be a bum.

With the eyes of the Otherworld, I saw a vision of my fate grow out of the blackness snapping towards me. After I succumbed, the fear would turn me on myself. My drinking would continue as a coping mechanism for the sharp points of reality around me, then it would slowly consume my mind, transforming my once great potential into nothing more than the memory of a cool breeze on a hot summer day. But the self-hate would smolder underneath it all. Through the haze of alcoholism, I'd remember how I lost, how I gave up the one chance I had, the one chance humanity had. Slowly, my soul would suffocate, manifesting as drunken mishaps. I'd wake up with a sprained ankle or a gashed knee, but no recollection of how it happened. Sensing my blindness to the cause, the resentment would motivate my mouth and limbs. Soon, I'd be nothing more than the angry homeless man, lost in a world he once claimed to conquer, shouting his vitriol on a dirty street corner, smelling of booze and looking for the next bottle. I'd become an enemy to a life I once loved, and still the self-hate would burn. My drunken mishaps would turn more dangerous. I'd wake with a bleeding skull and a broken arm, missing teeth and a growing shadow where I once had memory. There'd be no outlet for me, no rescue. I was beyond help, and in my helplessness, the fear would make its final move. I'd begin to cut myself, only a little at first, small incisions with a dirty knife, just enough to relieve the pressure when the alcohol wasn't sufficient. They'd get bigger, and bigger, leave thicker scars, until one day the boogeyman caused my hand to slip, and the knife plunged too deep into my skin. I'd know instantly that I'd never be able to stop the bleeding in time, that help was too far away, and just before death, I'd be cursed with a moment of clarity in which I could see myself, see how it all began right now in that present moment with the one choice I still clutched in my hand with all my life. I'd see it all so clearly, and I'd see my weakness for allowing Jason to replant his fear inside me, for succumbing to the torment of Mother Culture. And all because I didn't know how to choose differently. I didn't know how to save myself, or to find Ahnah's damn 100th monkey, or to stop the boogeyman. In that clarity, I would see how I'd choose to be reinfected because that was far easier than treading the road less traveled.

My vision faded into collective reality, and I looked for the choice I had clutched in my hands, but it was gone. I had forgotten the prized possession, my consent. Somewhere in my delirium, I had let go and made my choice. It was done, and I went to sleep cursing my laziness, but somehow happy that it was over. Even the life of a beggar was more comforting than the unknown. But just before I slept, sensitized to the frightening black mouths that reached towards me, I was surprised to see flecks of light. They had been there all the time, but the sirens screaming in my head had distracted me so thoroughly that I didn't notice them. And so, I fell asleep looking for the light.

I was surprised to see the ants because it must have meant that I had fought off the infection. I followed them to a clear lake and dove in. When I materialized in someone's mind, a rush of relief raced through my soul, brightening it with faith and self-worth. Somehow, in the darkness, I had chosen the light. I had pushed back the disease. For the time, I was safe, and things were back to weird. I was under a cartoon sea. I looked down at my hand, now like some character from my childhood Saturday mornings. The water was clear, and I could see quite far. Schools of motley-colored fish swam by to examine me, and I waved. A few waved back.

Walking along the bottom of the sea, I passed coral formations, eels, octopus and squid, some of whom where welcoming and chatty, others,

142   Manifesting the Monkey

standoffish and paranoid. I was again astounded by the power of the unconscious mind to generate such complete realities as to fool the dreamer into believing them. I glanced upwards, and the surface of the water was only a dozen or so meters above my head, a distant shimmering, the threshold between worlds. I felt something in the water, a slight turbulence, the distinguished thrashing of someone uncomfortable in the aquatic realm. I followed the vibrations, and as I bounded over a giant coral formation, I saw my dreamer. It was an old man wearing a red trucker's hat. His eyes were wide, and his white hair floated calmly beside him, like a grounded school mistress talking down a distressed boy from his perch on the monkey bars. The man's feet were embedded in a block of concrete.

I landed in front of him, but he was blind to me. I reached for the oil in my pocket, but realized that it wouldn't work. The man's face said it wouldn't be long before he 'drowned,' and my window for change would close.

I had an idea and immediately set to manifesting a piece of gum in my mouth. I chewed it, and when it was ready, I blew a bubble. It took all my concentration, but it worked. When it was big enough, I placed it gingerly around the man's head.

He spat and coughed the water out of his lungs, filling my rescue bubble half-way. While I held it for him, I inflated another, and when it was ready, I replaced it. He was waking now, and began to flicker out from one reality to another. If he was to overcome his fears, he would have to calm down, and stay in the dream. In front of him, I took a deep breath, illustrated the motion with my hand. After the second time, he understood and began to breathe with me. I filled another air balloon and put it around his head. Then, I concentrated and kept blowing into it, expanding the bubble. It grew larger over his head, moved down past his shoulders until his whole body was inside of it, wet and shivering, but alive. When it was a little bigger, I stepped inside with him.

"Thank you, thank you," he spluttered. "My God, what has become of me?" He trailed off into incomprehensible mutterings. Although he could see me, he was still disoriented. I dabbed a bit of the oil under his nose, and instantly, he was alert. "What's going on?"

"You're dreaming."

"Yes, yes, I've figured that out, but what are you doing here?"

"Well, I am also you, an emissary of the part of you that wants to get

Manifesting the Monkey   143

better. You've had this dream before?"

"All the time."

"What is it? What are you scared of?"

"Isn't it obvious? Drowning?"

"And the cement shoes?"

He looked down and noticed them for the first time. "I don't know about those."

"Who gave them to you?"

"I can't remember." He was silent for a moment. "I can almost see him, but as soon as I get closer to the memory, it clouds over and it's gone. All I can remember is a wide-brimmed hat."

I looked out into the sea. There were three big sharks circling our small bubble. This could get messy. "Are you afraid of sharks?"

"Who isn't?" And the bubble started to stink.

"You know that you're dreaming, right?" I reminded him

"Yeah, I told you, yeah," and the smell disappeared.

"Well in a minute, this bubble's going to go. I can't maintain it much longer. But you need to understand that as long as you remember you're dreaming nothing can hurt you. You can do anything you want. Take courage."

"Anything?"

"Yeah, anything, but it's best to learn to crawl before you walk. Start with something simple." I looked down at the block of concrete around his feet. "Do something about that."

"What?" A jet of water streamed into the bubble. I plugged it with my finger. Another formed behind him. Soon, we'd be flooded. I could feel myself flickering awake. "I don't know. Use your imagination. Turn the concrete into sand. Or just pull them out. Become a ghost. Turn into a giant...do something!" Leaks appeared all over the bubble. Just before it gave way and the ocean crashed down upon us, the man shot up out of his trap and into the free water. I watched him as I slowly faded out of the dream. The sharks, dark and menacing, raced towards that strange pink fish, and I thought he would fly past them and explode up into the beautiful blue sky beyond, that he would find the love in his heart to free himself. But instead, he froze, like some helpless bunny, motionless, waiting for something to happen.

I looked away from his gruesome end as I dissolved from one reality into another. The last thing I saw was a yawning oyster. Laying in its mouth was a blue earring. The same fish-scale earring I had given Aurore for her twenty-sixth birthday. I focused my mind, but I could not hold that reality together. The dreamer was awake, and this world would only exist for another blink of the eye. I reached and snatched the earring just before I was completely gone.

I woke up, still clutching that last precious gift.

21

The world is a dangerous place to live;
not because of the people who are evil,
but because of the people who don't do anything about it.
-Albert Einstein

I stared at the painted fish scale.

How did it get inside the dream...how did we get it out?

I had no idea, but the meaning was obvious—I had to find Aurore.

The sky was brightening and so was my mind. The ominous storms of yesterday had passed. I had dodged the latest assault by Jason and Mother Culture. I was alive and free. As usual, I took my time with breakfast. I filled the stove with denatured alcohol and put half a liter of water on to boil. In seven minutes, my tea was steeping, the rest of the water was cooking my oatmeal, and I was focusing my intent. I created a movie in my head—a joyful reunion with Aurore—and replayed it again and again. That was the core of manifestation: to be able to see and feel what I wanted as if it had already happened. I squeezed a bit of lemon into my green tea and sipped it slowly. When the oatmeal was done, I sprinkled some cinnamon and drizzled lots of honey over it, then, I said a quick word of thanks to God and to each hand that participated in making my simple meal a reality. Then I ate. I always preferred a slow start to the day. It seemed more civilized.

I reached the highway just as the sun made its first appearance, and I found a good place to hitch. It was at the bottom of a hill— there was enough space for any passing cars to see me well in advance, but not enough space for them to think too much about it. If given the time, most people could talk themselves out of doing good for another. It was best if they could see me for three or four seconds, that way their decision would be quick.

A beat-up pickup drove by an hour later, but the old man didn't stop. Now with breakfast finished, I focused my mind on the incredulous events of the dream. My analysis was mixed. I had brought something with me from that world to this, a concrete manifestation of the Otherworld.

How had it gotten in the dream?

I tried to come up with a rational explanation, but I failed. Either, I tricked myself into believing I had pulled it out of the dream (making me crazier than I thought), or my experience was accurate, and I had actually brought something back from the dream into collective reality.

Like it or not, some phenomenon do not have rational explanations.

For the thousandth time I pulled it out of my pocket and stared at it. Surely it was an omen, and its uncertain meaning hounded me like some mistress looking to upgrade her status and usurp the rightful woman of the household.

Have I really done this? Is this one of Jason's pranks? Is this real?

By far the most disturbing question was this: if it was indeed Aurore's earring, how did it get into the dream? And I wasn't concerned with astral-quantum-mechanics, either. I wanted to know how it was removed from her possession. Another car drove by, but I didn't bother putting my thumb out. I was too involved in my thoughts as I stood again on the edge of the known and peered over into the incomprehensible.

A half-hour later, an old red station wagon stopped, despite (or maybe because of) my lack of effort.

Sometimes the easiest way to get things done is to do nothing.

I put my bag in the backseat and sat down next to an attractive woman, about forty-years-old, wearing a blue floral print dress. Her salt-and-pepper hair just touched her shoulders. She looked at me with bright green eyes and winked. "Howdy!"

Well, things are looking up! Usually lone women, especially attractive ones, don't pick up hitchhikers...especially Mexican ones.

I gave her a sniff and discovered only faint traces of Jason, just that lingering odor of the smallest of compromises.

"Where you going?" she asked with a sweet southern twang.

Normally, I'd pick a place further up the road and claim that as my destination. People were more open to someone with direction. They found a footloose wanderer with nowhere to go disconcerting. I knew I had to find Aurore, I just didn't know how to do that. I was lost, and there was no more reason to pretend that I wasn't. That would be silly. "I don't know."

She laughed. "One of those days, huh?"

"Yeah, you could say that, one of those days...or one of those lives."

She laughed. "I'm sure it's not as bad as you convince yourself it is. I'm headed to Junction. I can give you a ride as far as that."

"That's a long way. That'd be great."

"What's your name, nomad?"

"The Oct...Ten. My name's Ten."

She looked at me for a moment. "You sure about that, cowboy?"

"Yes ma'am. Today, I'm sure. Tomorrow might be another story. What's your name?"

She stuck out her hand. "I'm Dawn."

I laughed. "Dawn?"

"Yeah, Dawn. What's so funny about that?"

"No ma'am, I'm not sick in the head. It's just strange is all. I used to be married to a woman named Aurore, and in French *'aurore'* means 'dawn'. And I even had a dream about her last night...well kinda about her."

She whistled. "Well I'll be...yeah, that's...that's a pretty strange coincidence alright. Don't you just love life?" She smiled big, as if such synchronicities were a daily occurrence.

She put the car in gear and drove away. The next three hours were the most enjoyable time I had experienced in almost a year. Dawn was the kind of woman who laughed easily and loudly, the kind of laugh that kept the fear at bay, the kind of laugh that Aurore had, and while it didn't evoke angelic harmonies, it helped still my soul.

Is that why she smells so good?

Dawn had an open heart and listened as much as she talked, another rare trait in a community pumped full of catch phrases, one-liners, and famous last words. Comfortable silences were an endangered species, and it was still open season. With Dawn, it was different. The coincidences stacked up—it wasn't only a name she shared with my absent mate. Dawn majored in French at university, and she studied abroad just outside of Montpelier for a year, very near where my wife was born. Dawn was passionate about the destiny of the human species. She shared that with my wife as well. They both saw a fallacy of modern civilization, knew that man had constructed a world around him with at least one really bad assumption—that human beings were masters of the natural cycle and not a part of it.

148   Manifesting the Monkey

"I don't want to be the bee in anybody's bonnet, but building up the world on such a...foolish conclusion means that everything after it is flawed as well. You can't have a stable house if it's built on a shaky foundation." And she laughed like it was no big deal.

I tried to stop it, but there was nothing I could do. Dawn, this older fractal of my wife, became dear to me in a matter of moments. She filled the cavern that had been gorged out of me when my wife had blown away on the wind. I fantasized about staying with her, about being invited into her house and reclaiming a stable, 'normal' life. To forget, then to sleep. This was my second chance to be a good cog. The street and my nomadic ways were cold, foreign, and far below my potential.

Maybe this is the moment I evolve into something better?

The ride neared its end. I saw the green sign flash by—Junction 15—and I prepared myself to say good-bye, the good-bye I never got to say to my wife.

"Where should I drop you?"

"Uh...usually near the edge of town is the best. That's the easiest place to catch a ride."

"That makes sense, I reckon. Where you gonna go?"

"I have no idea, I guess where the next ride is going. It was really nice to meet you, and it was great talking with you. I hadn't had a conversation like that in a long time. Thank you so much."

She laughed. "It was good for me, too...look, I don't normally do this, you know, pick up strays, but I've got some work around the ranch needs doin'. Lord knows there's always something to do. What do you think? Stick around for a couple of days? I can't pay you much, but I can feed you plenty."

"Wow..." I scratched my head.

Did I do that?

"Yeah...I mean, if you're serious—"

"Of course, I'm serious. You think I'd go off and tell you that, try to get your hopes all up, and then just dash them to pieces. What kinda person do you think I am?"

I laughed. "No, I don't think you'd do that."

"Well, what d'you say?"

"Yeah, absolutely. That sounds like a great idea. I haven't stayed put

Manifesting the Monkey   149

for a long time."

I had seen the set of her ranch in plenty of movies—old dead equipment rusting in the weeds, chickens out back, and a melange of junk in the yard. It offered that warm, homey feeling promised in the films, that place you could always go and be accepted for who you were (as long as who you were could work a few hours a day). I hopped out, opened the gate, and closed it after she pulled the car through. Then I followed to an old two-story house, with faded yellow paint. A coyote crouched next to a pile of metal tubes, and growled at me. I took a step back, froze. The faint ringing of an alarm bell echoed through my heart.

"Maya, knock it off. That there's Ten, and he's going to be staying here with us for awhile so you're just gonna have to get used to him, you hear?" Then she turned to me. "Don't worry too much about her. She's a man-hater, but she's harmless. She'll get over it in a couple of days, and it'll be alright. She won't leave your side." She winked. "You'll be the best of friends, won't you Maya?" I heard the alarm again in the distance. She rubbed the coyote's head vigorously. "I found her up on the ridge, cryin' when she was a pup. I raised her, and she's been family ever since. C'mon, I'll show you to your room."

The house smelled like a grandparents home—old, musty, and friendly. Magazines, newspapers, and mail cluttered the desk in the corner. Clothes were strewn on the back of the couch. The whole house felt wantonly confused, but joyful nonetheless. My nose had to reach hard for that rancid smell, but it was back there. It was always back there. Some of it lingered on an old photo of Dawn and her mom, some littered among the pile of bills, but generally, the normal fears of modern life were balanced by her laugh, no doubt.

Follow your nose, it always knows!

And I remembered the cartoon bird in those old commercials for Fruity Loopers. It seemed like good advice.

"There she is. It's not much."

I smiled in glee at the bed before me. It was narrow, just big enough for one, covered with a patched quilt. "That's great." I laughed like a kid on Christmas morning. "God, I haven't slept in a proper bed in months. That is absolutely perfect."

"Make yourself at home, just relax. I'll make lunch, and then we'll talk work." She patted me on the shoulder and went to the kitchen.

I plopped down on the bed, amazed at my turn in fortune. I took out the earring and looked at it, sure now that I better understood this sign. I had found the deeper meaning. I kissed it and put it back into my pocket. Everything was fine. I'd just pick up where I left off with Aurore.

When I walked into the kitchen, Dawn was putting a dish of lasagna on the table. She smiled at me, and for a moment, I was looking through a window into the future, at my wife twenty years older.

Is it possible that Aurore flew into the future on that umbrella?

"It's nothin' special, just some leftovers. I didn't want to take too much time fixin' up a proper meal. The day's a'wastin'.'"

"Yes, ma'am." I sat down in the wooden chair.

"And you're going to have to stop callin' me, ma'am." I smiled at her, and she held my gaze long enough to stir up a cloud of butterflies in my stomach.

A home-cooked lunch, even leftovers, filled me with an energy and a trust, and I accepted my good luck at face value. It was the second time my ignorance got me into a heap of trouble. I could remember such a feeling, but it was in a fog, somewhere in the past, creeping out.

"It's nothing fancy. Just some labor, and none of it that hard. This place misses a man's touch." Our eyes met again, lingered at the edge of comfort, and my anatomy assured me she was a suitable mate.

I spent the day digging holes for a new fence. She had the proper tools, and that made the job a lot easier, but it was still sweaty work. My mind spent its idle time thinking about her, wondering if this wasn't some alignment, some correction, returning my life to the way things had been. It was perfect. My heart hadn't felt peace in months. For a brief moment, I was happy.

Is this a reconciliation?

When the day was done, I took a shower. When I came out of the bathroom, Dawn was sitting on the couch dressed in a red satin see-through negligee, broadcasting her intentions, not only with her lingerie, but also by the way her thighs couldn't stay together. They slowly waved, swaying closer, then farther apart, as if she was in the midst of an internal struggle between desire and propriety. In a few moments the glances and subtle approaches turned into gazes and sensual touches. She was the first woman I slept with since my wife had flown away on her umbrella. And it nearly killed me.

I made love to Dawn with the energy and motivation of a fit adult who had been too long since indulging in the carnal pleasures, and she engaged me in a similar tone. In the heat of it, she scratched my chest from shoulder to opposite nipple. Her eyes were closed, lost in bliss. A feral gesture in the fire of the moment. Nothing out of the ordinary, right? That's what I thought, even though the scratch burned and tingled, but I soon forgot about it as her rhythmic rocking sped into a strong gallop.

I woke in the morning with a red gouge where she had taken the skin.

By then, it was already too late.

I walked into the kitchen. Dawn was at the stove preparing breakfast. I tiptoed behind her, and just before I slid my arms around her, she growled at me. I jerked still, shocked. I had never heard such a savage sound from a human being, let alone someone as graceful and endearing as Dawn. It was long and guttural, like the coyote outside, but marked with the cold, malicious intelligence of a person.

"There'll be none of that kissy-feely-bullshit," she said without turning, her attractive southern drawl gone, replaced by a sharp, authoritarian voice. "Sit down and eat your breakfast. You have work to do, and you'll need your energy. I bet with a bit of moderation, you'll last a few months...though I never was good with moderation." She said it like some addict who no longer fights against her disease, but instead accepts it as a fact of life and, sometimes, a source of humor.

I responded without my volition. Some invisible force animated my body and moved it for me. I sat down and ate, but it wasn't me who put hand to mouth. When she turned around, Dawn gave me the passing look one offers an unwanted, but useful dog, just before she kicks it.

When I had finished eating, I regained control of my body.

"What's going on?" She ignored me as she laced her boots. "This is fucked up," I yelled, still shocked by the strange turn of events and the momentary possession of my physical body. "Thank you for the food and the bed, but I'm outta here." I walked towards the guest room.

"Stop." She whispered, and my body stopped. I strained against it, but I was disconnected. My body was no longer my own. "Come here." And I

152   Manifesting the Monkey

lurched backwards towards her. She leaned closer to me and whispered in my ear. "You are mine." Then, she pulled away and gave me a soft slap on the cheek. "Now get to work."

I touched the burning, blistered scratch on my chest.

What has she done to me?

I spent the next weeks literally being ridden all day and all night. True to Dawn's word, Maya served as my guard and didn't leave my side, threatening me with a growl, and even a nip if I strayed too far from acceptable behavior. During the days, I worked hard—lifting, chopping, digging, cutting, moving. As my Chinese zodiac predicted, I worked like a horse. Anything manual and Dawn would send me to do it. And in the evening, she rode me. After that first night, she dropped the niceties. She spoke to me only to tell me to do something, or to warn me again against escape. She had taken a piece of my flesh, and if I did manage to get away from her and Maya, she would use that fleck of skin to torture, then kill me. Her appearance had changed. As a result of her energetic-theft, she became younger every day. The salt-and-pepper of her hair retreated, then faded all together. The skin around her eyes had tightened. Her legs were firmer and breasts perkier. With a week of feeding, she had taken five years off of her life, and I was an empty shell. My joints ached as if I had aged ten years, and I suffered a continuous exhaustion like I had never known. But I didn't know if she was telling the truth.

I don't know. Probably. I mean, take a look buddy. It's some pretty fucked up shit she's doing already, and there are countless documented incidents that claim such a thing is possible.

One night, she showed me the fetish, a small corn husk doll that looked nothing like me. Buried somewhere inside was the small scrape of flesh she had taken from me that first night. It was the bridge she needed to manipulate me. She flicked the doll in the groin, and I tumbled to the floor in agony. The blow shook loose the memory of my first encounter with the sensitivity of my testicles back in the 4th grade, when Julia had kneed me in the library for no reason other than her own understanding of how easy it was for women to control men.

Why are they so mean?

At night, Dawn would drain me of my life-force. Although it could've been a dream come true (demonized wives are hot!), in reality, it was a nightmare. The nocturnal feedings threatened to kill me. Three or four times a night, I was forced to perform. And no matter how much I resisted, she was able to trigger me. My mind was cluttered with sexual references, innuendos, memories, and taboos—a thousand products sold! She spoke to my body in a way I could not resist, and my penis was in cahoots with her. I needed to keep my strength, save my energy and figure out how to get the hell out of here, but after only a few moments of her seductions, I was ready to give her what she wanted.

Is there a better way to die than being fucked to death by a sexy she-devil?

It was the craziest sex I've ever had in my life, and I hope that I never have to live through that again. She was everything I had been programmed to want. Trust me, it was terrible. The detached observer was fascinated at how tangled up my own sexuality was, so much power and tension intertwined around itself. My body responded to her no matter how I tried to distract my mind—math problems, capital cities, the backwards alphabet, but it would not obey for long, and my dick soon followed.

Some of that was natural. I was an animal first, and my body would do whatever was necessary to see my offspring in the next generation. Shrouded among these normal biological imperatives, my mind was working against me. I did everything to avoid those sessions, but my body would betray me in two minutes or less. Guaranteed. All she needed was the right trigger—Catholic school girl (I entered puberty in Catholic school—there was no getting around that one), or the woman in the beer advertisement with a balloon bosom and a tinsel thin bikini, or the nurse who couldn't quite button her blouse all the way, or the French maid whose particularly short skirt *almost* revealed the sensual delights of the flesh. Or the cowgirl who rode bareback, nude (except for her hat and boots, of course). Or the reprimanding teacher. Or the librarian...or the astronaut.

Put tits, lipstick, and a vagina on it, and anything is sexy. Hell, I don't even need the lipstick.

Dawn saw into my mind and knew exactly which buttons to push. All it took was one moment, one reference inside my head, and I slipped. It wouldn't be long before there was a demon huffing and puffing on top of me,

154   Manifesting the Monkey

sucking me dry. I was programmed, and she was manipulating my code. For my entire life, the sexual act had been cheapened, sliced up, bought and sold.

It's so powerful.

This degradation went far beyond the conscious mind and the moment of decision. The normal American unconscious was filled with images and ideas, connections between sex and some authority—the church or the corporation—and it took much more than just wishing to realign those beliefs with something more natural. It took more than just knowing. There, at that ranch, I was at the mercy of my mind and its institutionalized perversion.

My body ached in a way that I had never felt before. Some previously untapped reservoir was being drained, and if something didn't change it would soon be empty.

Would too much sex kill me?

Of course. Too much of anything will kill you.

How?

Most likely, a heart attack. A stroke is a possibility.

A physical thing?

Yes, but there are many esoteric philosophies behind the physical demise. According to the Taoists, the body is composed of three main types of energy—chi, jing, and shen. Jing is the sexual energy, the creative force, and humans are born with a finite amount of it. Once depleted, you'll die.

Late one night, after her fifth feeding, I caught the first glimpse of myself in a mirror in more than a month (I had been quarantined outside with the animals except when it was time for her to feed), and I couldn't believe the man staring back at me. Instead of my true age of twenty-eight, a man of nearly forty stared back at me, complete with tufts of gray hair at his temples and deepening crow's feet around his eyes. My heart raced as I examined my face.

Where did my life go? What have I done to myself?

I was going to die. She was eating me alive. A panic overtook me, and my survival mode kicked in. When Dawn called me the next night, I pinned her down, my knees on her arms, and I tried to suffocate her with a pillow. It was the furthest I had gone. I didn't want to kill anything, let alone a person, but there was no other way. It was me or her. I had to get out. And it was only then that I understood how dangerous the world was, when even love and sex, two of life's gems, could be turned into weapons.

Dawn fought for a moment and then went still. I could hear her laughing so I pushed down harder. I would do anything for my freedom, but, then, she was gone. She just wasn't there anymore. She had vanished, and an instant later, she was behind me, spitting and biting, that deep growl filling my body with the certainty of its imminent death. Just before I passed out, either from the beating or the shock, I got a good look at her. She had dropped the human appearance altogether and taken on her natural form: more beast than human. The brown coyote-like fur was matted down in places by a black slime that seemed to ooze out of her skin. Her fingers terminated in thick claws. Her face, now covered in a brown fuzz, retained only a hint of its former humanity. The ears had taken an elvish point, and the mouth had lengthened, lined with rows of sharp teeth, and that same black sludge dripped from the edges of her mouth, filling the room with the stink of fear.

22

No demon deserves forgiveness.
-Irish proverb

I stayed calm and looked for the light. I had to nurse its embers, but I was able to get the flame in my heart burning again. The only thing I had was faith. The Universe would provide me with an opportunity. The only thing I had to do was be ready when it got here. For the most part, Dawn let me be. She was an unconcerned master, certain of her power and my impotency. She was right. I didn't know how to escape, but I was going to figure it out.

This is a tough one. A succubus is, supposedly, a mythological creature, and the literature that does exist is rooted in Christianity. And exorcism is pretty simple. Just repeat the name of Jesus Christ along with some key scriptures over and over until the demon flees. Could take hours, could take weeks.

What else?

Looking deeper, I see there are more options. Some suggest just asking her to leave, but I don't think that's gonna work. There are numerous pagan candle spells. Gold and salt will help to protect against an attack. There are many suggested solutions, but the one unifying factor of them all is that the user believes they will work. Modern occultists agree, for the most part, that it is <u>the belief</u> in a tool, a spell, a practice, or a god that grants the power to affect change, and not the thing itself. You can do anything, create any magic, and the engine that will determine its success is your belief in it.

Like always, she called me after the sun had gone down. That time, I did not comply. If I was lucky, she would only use me once, but that was the rare occasion. She called me again, and I resisted the urge to go to her. Something inside me was obeying, pushing me towards her, but I pulled back and sat squarely in my circle of salt. Instantly, the foreign drive to go to her was dampened.

She laughed when she saw me. "Is that what you've been up to? Salt?

Come, come, you must do better than that."

A wet popping sound accompanied her transformation. She approached my circle, then she huffed, and she puffed, and blew my little hope of safety away. I looked back at her after she had reverted to her human form. She offered me her hand. "Haven't you ever heard of the big, bad wolf?" She winked at me, and her eyes were kind, endearing, and familiar—my wife's eyes. I broke down. "Come on, lover. You have some work to do," she whispered to me in Aurore's voice. I stood up and followed her into the bedroom. That night, I was listless and uncaring. It didn't matter what happened to me, I was drained and ready to go, ready to toss in the towel. Everything was empty

When she was finished, she whispered in my ear, "don't give up hope, my dear. You taste so much better when you hope."

I woke up, alone, in her room, and that was strange. Normally, she would send me back to my sleeping quarters, now a pile of hay on the porch, with the dogs and the fleas, always under the watchful eye of my relentless warden, Maya. That morning, it felt good to be in a warm bed, normal, and for a moment, I forgot where I was. When I remembered, I tried to forget again, but that never worked.

For fuck's sake, I have the worst luck. A nose that smells the boogeyman (who no one else believes is real), a missing wife on a runaway umbrella, a homeless life, and now I'm fodder for a sex-demon.

I took a moment to snoop, searching for the fetish. If I found it, I could free myself. Under the bed, in the drawers, top shelf of the closet. Nothing. On my way out of the room, I noticed a plain envelope. Something about it attracted me, and I reached my hand inside and pulled out the object that was inside—my wife's other blue earring. It couldn't be the one I had found—I had hidden that safely away on the first day of my imprisonment. The return address was a P.O. Box in Lecoeur, California to none other than Mr. J. Muscoph. It was postmarked three days before I got a ride with Dawn.

I took the earring, put it in my pocket, and left her room.

Dawn was in the kitchen, finishing her breakfast. "Today you will finish painting the wooden fence. Then, you will chop firewood and continue digging the ditch along the south pasture. Do you understand?"

"Yes."

"I am going into town today." The announcement surprised me, but I hid my reaction. "And I will be back before nightfall. If you are to leave this property, I shall remind you of the fate waiting for you." She showed me the fetish, then with a sweet smile, she flicked her finger into its groin again. The blow knocked me to the floor and into a groaning fetal position. She stepped over me on her way out. "Have a nice day."

But I had a plan. I worked my ass off during the day, enough to make progress so that she would not be suspicious of my time spent while she was gone. It was hard to find moments to myself. Maya was never far away, but every once in a while she was distracted by a sound or a smell, and I had a few unsupervised minutes. While feigning some task, I harvested the wood from a weeping willow down by the creek. Then, during the heat of the day, I leaned up against a tree as if to nap. I felt Maya's eyes on me, but after a moment she must've bought it because I heard her walk off in search of something more interesting. I knew that she was close, but she was still far enough away for me to act. As I wrapped the flexible willow branch around itself, forming a hoop, I focused on my intent, put power into each twist, all the while aware of the wrinkles in my hands. When I began tying the knots of the string around the circle, a small song bubbled out of the jungle of my mind, and I sang softly to myself. With each knot, I felt stronger. I only had one shot at this. I made five dream catchers, all of them laced with some personal item of hers—a hair, a fingernail clipping. When I was finished, I tucked the hoops inside my shirt, and walked towards the house. Maya growled at me, but I waved my hand at her. "I'm hungry, and I've got to take a shit." I kept walking, and she continued growling, but she didn't do anything else. Inside, I placed four of my hoops in the bedroom, and kept the fifth with me to spring my trap. As promised, she arrived just before sunset, with an armload of groceries. "Unload the rest." And my body obeyed.

Two hours after dinner, she called me to her room. I stood in front of the door for a moment, letting my roots extend into the ground, connecting to Pachu Mamma, praying to God for strength and clarity. I didn't know what else to do, and somehow it seemed appropriate to call the forces of light into that dark place.

She stared at me for a moment. "C'mon, Ten. Be a good boy and give me my medicine. Her seductive smile sent a shiver down my anatomy and the sleeping serpent awoke.

Why do you betray me?!

I closed my eyes and recited the last words of the invocation I had begun while she was away. "In this circle of love, let the demon be contained." I repeated three times.

Her eyes flamed bright, and she rushed towards the door, but I had already hung the dream catcher just outside. The circle was complete. She moved towards it, but could not pass. I was careful to keep myself out of her reach, lest I be dragged in. In the blink of an eye, her human appearance dissolved and revealed her true form—fur, teeth, and claws.

"The fetish? Where is it?" I demanded.

She only growled. I tried to get her to talk, but she only paced and knocked things about. I waited all night, but she still wouldn't say a word. My circle would hold her forever, as long as it remained intact. I slept on the couch that night. In the morning, she had nothing to say so I slept the rest of the day. She didn't want to talk the next morning either, so I searched for ways to leverage her, feeling the strength return to my soul. But would my youth return to me as well?

I don't know. It's possible we will revert back to our natural age, but there's no way to tell. As for leveraging her, what if we made a fetish of our own?

I walked out of the house to assemble the necessary materials. Maya's growl betrayed her attack as she leaped towards me. I tried to dodge, but my body no longer responded with the immediacy of youth. She landed next to me, ready to attack again, but I forced myself away and to my feet. I picked up a garden hoe and used it to fend her off. The coyote was hunched, snarling, and looking for an opening. She lunged at me a few times, but they were only the intelligent feints of one looking for the weakness in their opponent. She tried it again, but this time I stepped forward and swung the hoe into her side. She yelped as the thin edge embedded itself into her flesh. The coyote looked down at her wound, then up at me. She showed me her teeth, growled, and a thin trickle of that black filth fell from her mouth. She shook the edge out of her, and bounded off into the fields. I had won, but I knew we weren't finished. I threw down my weapon and collected the materials I'd need for the fetish.

I set about making the doll. It was a simple thing, similar to Dawn's own, made of corn husk and string, with her hair entangled in it. When it was finished and charged, I walked to the door of her prison, relieved that our roles had been reversed. Already the demon showed signs of fatigue. The first bits of salt had reappeared in her hair. She had not fed for two days. She was thinner, looser. I showed her the doll and smiled, then gave it a flick on the head. She tumbled onto the bed. Despite all that she had done to me, I felt guilty about the power I held over her. It only took a few flicks of my finger for her to reveal the location of the fetish. In the cellar, behind a small wall was her altar, and on it was the doll. I wrapped a handkerchief around it and put it into my pocket. Her tools were there as well—a bowl, a knife, a candle, and a bundle of feathers. I didn't want to touch them directly, so I used my shirt tail as a barrier, and I scraped them into a sack.

How do I disarm it?

There are various methods, but they all prescribe a very gentle dismantlement of the fetish. You'll want to make a circle, then untie the fetish, spread its parts out over the water and the earth, then take a small piece and burn it. Throw in a Jesus Christ for good luck, and that should do it.

After I was confident that the fetish was safely unloaded, I packed my bag patiently, turned the stereo up, and made breakfast tacos even though it was the middle of the afternoon. Anytime was a great time for breakfast tacos.

I didn't want to do it, but I saw no other option. It wasn't only myself that I was protecting, but my wife and any of Dawn's future victims. I built a fire outside, and when it blazed, I walked around it three times, then I dropped the fetish into the middle of the burning wood. Her shrieks filled the air. I saw her burning body through the window, flailing and a few moments after she dropped dead, the house began to burn. I put my pack on my back and walked down the road.

<u>23</u>

Do not pray for an easy life.
Pray for the strength to endure a difficult one.
-Bruce Lee

I tended the fire inside my heart, blew on its coals until it burned bright and hot. The aimless wandering had come to an end, and I headed towards Lecoeur, happy to finally have a destination. With a strong gust of wind, I was gone, headed West. To me, California was valley girls (like, oh my God), and rich snobs, it was stoned surfers (whoa, dude) and far-out freaks, it was gay-pride and cloud 9. Regardless of these stereotypes, California had always been the frontier. Since the birth of the United States, we had been pulled further and further West, drawn by the allure of new beginnings and awaiting abundance. California had been the place for revolution, where ideas were born and nurtured or promptly aborted. Even though the last physical frontier was well-mapped, California was still the horizon for new ideas and lifestyles.

Back on the street, my flimsy confidence shattered. My nose, a formerly reliable signal had failed. It had been so easy for the succubus to trick me, knowing exactly which of my buttons to push. At night, I slept in barns, in ditches, on the side of the road, always invisible to the outside world, another forgotten soul pushed towards the extremities. As long as I kept my head down, bowed to the superiority of Mother Culture, and kept moving, nobody would take much notice of me. It was when I spoke, when I stayed too long in one place that people became uncomfortable and forced me out. It was then that the boogeyman could locate me. I held a radical perspective in our world, one that threatened the ruling paradigm.

I'd often meet others living the same lifestyle. They couldn't smell fear, but they moved along and lived a life of wandering and wondering, wayward ghosts in search of their tombs.

Hobos.

Sometimes, we'd journey together, but most often we said good-bye as quickly as possible. There were some that grouped together, but those were the ones who were afraid of being alone. The free ones never stayed with anyone too long, lest their paradise be corrupted by compromise. Jogo was one of these. He called me 'sir', and it took a confused moment to remember the years the succubus had stolen from me, and, immediately, I felt it again— the aches in my lower-back, the fog in my mind. It was almost as if my age was in my head, and it was only when someone reminded me of it that I felt as old as I had become. Jogo and I had met at a crossroads, and we shook hands before setting up to hitch, ready to catch the next ride. I knew he was on a similar path by the tattoo he had on the side of each of his index fingers. 'PAY ATTENTION' reminded him in elegant cursive to be in the present moment. I guess that was how he got to be where he was. Any serious commitment into being present and honest would inevitably unveil the obvious corruption and disease of the prevailing world-view, and the only real option was to opt-out.

Stop participating.

Jogo was on the opposite side of the road as me. He was going East and me, West.

"California, I'm headed to California." I shouted.

He smiled. "I just left."

"How is it?"

"Crazy, compadre, crazy." He smiled bigger. "It's like no place on Earth."

"You know a place called Lecoeur?"

"Yeah, I know Lecoeur. About three hours north of San Fran. You going for the Season?"

"What season?"

He just laughed. "It's a hefty hitch, you know, to Cali. You may get lucky with a long ride, but if you want to get there sooner rather than later, your best bet are the big rigs."

"Yeah, that's what I figured."

"There's a truck stop about 90 miles south, just off I-10. You could get a ride from there."

"Yeah, but I really haven't had much luck at the truck stops." The best

Manifesting the Monkey   163

way to get a ride was to talk to people, and I wasn't good with the small talk. After only a few minutes, it was obvious that I was from another dimension. If I pretended to be like them, they sensed that facade and wouldn't give me a ride. "I'll just take my chances on the back roads."

"Oh, you'll get there." He smiled big to the driver of a car as it zoomed by. "There's another way. It's a bit more dangerous, but it's the most reliable way to get anywhere in the country for free."

"What's that?"

"Freight trains."

"Freight trains? People still do that?"

"All the time. It's the way forward, my man."

"Then why aren't you riding them?"

"I'm trying to get somewhere the train don't go. There's a track about a mile that way," he pointed through a grassy field. "If you take that three miles east, you'll find a freight yard. Ask someone where the trains are going, be polite, and they'll probably help you. Stay discrete and you'll be alright. If it's already moving, be careful and never hop a train you can't keep up with easily. Throw your bag up first and jump on. Be smart and you'll be fine. Be stupid and you'll be a peg-leg or worse." A car approached. Jogo stuck out his thumb and smiled. It stopped a dozen meters away. He scooped up his bag and ran to the car. "Watch out for the Bull," he called over his shoulder.

Feeling the need to expand my map with a new experience, I took Jogo's advice and headed for the railroad. The sun set, and, soon after, I was walking in the dark. The moon was new and the nights were black. I always tried to find a place to sleep before the sun set. I didn't like moving around when I couldn't see. Finding a spot to call home in the dark was an exercise in courage and trust. But that night, I continued walking, hastened along by new-found purpose.

After a few minutes of relative peace and serenity, I heard a sound. It started as a soft grating of rock and the rhythmic crunch of grass—the distinct sound of a footstep. An electric chill tingled up my spine. I froze and listened, but heard nothing save the thumping of my heart. Satisfied, I walked on, but after only another minute, the sound returned. I focused on it while I walked, noticing its proximity and its near invisibility among the noise I was making. I thought it was an animal, a cougar or a wild boar, but after I listened longer, I determined that it was clearly the gait of a human being. Whenever I stopped, the sound stopped. When I began again the steps followed me, so much like the sound of my own as to think I was crazy for hearing it. The tingle in my spine became a surge threatening to throw the breakers. I turned, expecting to see an enormous man in a hockey mask, wielding a bloody machete, but there was nothing, only thick darkness and a sky full of twinkling stars.

I walked faster now, with the firm conviction to arrive at the rails and then, the yard. I relaxed when the sound faded away. Surely it was my imagination. A quick sniff told me there weren't any humans near by. Every person I had met since the beginning with this supernormal sense always had at least a whiff of fear accompanying them. I kept walking and only silence followed me. I took a deep breath and the night regained its friendly demeanor. A cool breeze wicked the hot out of me. The owl's cry took an amicable tone. The night wrapped around me, comforted me in her arms.

Faintly, far away, getting closer, the definite sound of heavy footsteps in the grass reached my ears, again, as if someone was running at me. A wave of panic crashed down, threatening to overwhelm me. There was nothing there. There was never anything there. The sound had disappeared in the night, and I was alone.

Blood pounded in my ears.

"I can hear you!" I screamed into the night. "I know you're there! C'mon, you motherfucker!" I stood there panting in the cool night, my spine electric, my mind empty except two objectives: territory and survival.

This is my space.

After several moments of alert waiting, I turned and continued walking, whistling this time to hide my vulnerability. The noise continued, the footsteps of this invisible pursuer grew louder to compensate for my whistling. My mind shed another priority, and I was left with only the most basic instinct: survival.

I ran.

With my pack slapping against my back, I ran as fast as I could for as long as I could, but the footsteps stayed with me. All I thought about was moving out of right now into a tomorrow that might never come. My life was in danger. I found the tracks and began to walk on the rail, hoping that by silencing my movement on the cold metal, I would lose my pursuer. I turned as I heard the first step onto the fist-sized rocks around the tracks, but I saw nothing, just a black velvet curtain behind another black velvet curtain. The sound had been only a few meters away, but that was infinitely further than I could see. I stood there, holding my space, waiting for him to continue, but nothing happened. My heart constricted, closed to protect itself. "What do you want?" But there came no reply. I continued on my way and accepted its inevitability when the steps followed me. When I saw the dim lights of the train yard, I walked away into the field of waist-high grass and sat down, wide-eyed and watchful, waiting for some sign of my silent enemy, happy for him to attack, if only to get it over with. I sat like that, unmoving, for half the night, then fell asleep into a foggy dream.

I was in the cave again, back with Jason Muscoph. I couldn't move, didn't have the lucidity I needed to be anything more than an observer. The man was sitting on the other side of the fire and the stench rose up from him, strong and thick. He was laughing at me, pointing and laughing at me, laughing that I was covered in his filth. The fire grew brighter and hotter, and I dissolved into the waking world just as my skin began to burn.

By the time I remembered where I was and what I was doing, the dream had faded. I closed my eyes and smiled at the warm sun on my face, somehow surprised that I had survived. I stood up and looked around, shocked at what I saw. In the night, I had created a very distinct trail in the tall grass. The path that I made was clear. It started at the tracks and ended at the small circle that I had unintentionally made with my bags and my sleeping. That was normal and fine, it was the second trail that I was having difficulty accepting. The hair on the back of my neck stood at attention. The other path started from the tracks about a meter away from mine and stopped at the circle I had made. It was identical except it did not enter the space in which I had slept. Whoever had followed me had stopped just a foot away from me, and then, sometime later, departed to the north. I shivered and now felt even more exposed because of the sunlight. I was visible. There was a train just starting its slow trudge, headed west.

Where is that train going?

To California.

Perfect. I jogged alongside of it, threw my bag up into a box car, then hoisted myself aboard.

Flush.

"Who said you could come up here?"

The voice startled me, and I almost fell off the train, but a strong hand reached out and grabbed me. "Well, I ain't sayin' you gots to go right now. Let 'er slow down a bit first."

I looked up at a grizzled middle-aged man. The paw steadying me was greasy and his beard braided and beaded. There were two other people in the box car, a young couple, both as grimy as the man in the floppy hat. Yellow armpit hair poked out from his sleeveless shirt. He smiled. The girl was wearing a brimmed hat, and a spirally tattoo accented her big smile.

My guess is that she's a glass-is-half-full kinda girl.

I had never seen anyone with a tattooed face, and I forced myself not to stare. Her boyfriend was short and plump, with a shaved head and a dirty face.

"Sorry, I didn't mean to intrude." I stood up. "It's my first time."

The middle aged man laughed. "A real virgin. Shit, I didn't think none of them existed no more. Especially one your age. You havin' one of 'em mid-life crisis? Tryin' to re-discover your youth?"

I laughed. "Yeah, something like that."

"Well, hell mister, where ya' goin'?"

"West, to California."

"That's where we're going," Ms. Optimist said. "You going for the Season?"

"Which season?" It was mid-September. "The grapes?" She giggled. "No, I'm not looking to do much work. Is that why you're going?"

Her partner spoke up quickly. "Yeah, we're going there to work."

"Sweet." I pushed my bag into a vacant corner and leaned against it. "What about you?" I asked the man.

"Me, I'm just a'goin'. I'm just ridin' to ride. I'll get off in California, find something to eat, screw around for a couple of days, then get back on and head back east. Livin' the tramp life, there ain't nothin' like it. What's your name?"

"Ten. What about you?"

"Me, sir," his chest puffed, "I am King Arthur of Albany, the last true crusader for what is right and decent in this world."

I laughed, "seriously?"

Manifesting the Monkey   167

"Whaddya mean, seriously? Think I'm a'kiddin'?" His tone sharpened.

"No, no, King Arthur it is."

"King Arthur of Albany." He corrected me.

"And what about you?" I asked the couple in the opposite corner.

"I'm Daisy, and this is Max."

"Pleased to meet you. How long until California?"

King Arthur of Albany spoke up, "Not too long...about a day and a half...you got anything to drink?"

"I've got some water." King Arthur shook his head, grunted and returned to his space.

The world clickety-clacked by us. Chugging through narrow passes and spaces of raw nature. It was good to see my country go by, to remember that it was still alive, that out there in the fringes, things were good, even great. The earth was still waiting for us. Of course we'd pass through cities as well, gray scabs swelling up on her skin. The train made a few stops, and the others risked leaving for a while, but I stayed put and pissed out the door while everyone was gone. I had food, and I enjoyed the space I was in. That was the best part of the flush, when you're on a plane or a bus or a train and you don't have to do anything but watch the world go by. Being carried. That was my favorite part of travel. In Phoenix, the train chugged away before King Arthur of Albany could get back on. I watched him running towards the train and wanted desperately to help him, but there was nothing I could do.

How do you stop a freight train?

He gave up, put his hands on his knees, breathing hard and cursing.

"Throw my pack!" He yelled. I let it go gently, but it tumbled roughly to the ground. I yelled out the riddle just in case. "How's your heart like a parachute?"

"Oh that's easy..." But his answer was lost in the wind.

The sun set and the steady rhythm rolled us ever westward. The wind blowing through my hair and my heart cleared out all those cobwebs and muck that had accumulated inside of me. I was going to California, and in California everything was possible. I woke up in the middle of the night from a foggy dream. By the time I remembered where I was, I wasn't sure if I had seen that scarred face in the dream again, or if I was only remembering it from before. Jason was everywhere. It was dark, and I crept along the edge to the door and sat down, letting my naked feet dangle out in the free air.

"It feels good to move," Daisy's voice nearly pushed me off the edge.

"Yeah, it sure does," I said, hiding the jolt she had given me. "How long have you been doing it?"

"Oh, Lord, for a long time, nearly as long as I can remember. I was riding the trains with my momma, before she got killed."

"How did that happen?"

I couldn't see Daisy's face, only the vague outline of someone sitting next to me, but I could hear the smile, and wondered if she had somehow tattooed her voice as well. "She lived her life on the trains, and that's what killed her, too. She fell when she was trying to hop a train. She was seven months pregnant with my brother. Not fit to ride. But she did anyway. She always did whatever she wanted to, and pretty much every time a friend or a family member would tell her that thing she was planning was a bad idea, she'd be sure to do it anyway. That's how she died. Someone told her hopping trains while she was pregnant was just plain dumb. She fell and got caught up underneath. Chewed her up pretty good."

I imagined the cold steel cutting quite easily through flesh and bone. "I'm sorry to hear that."

Isn't that what I'm supposed to say?

"Oh, that's long gone, now. Nothing for you to be sorry about."

And that's what she's supposed to say.

The clickety-clack came between us and filled us with a space to breath and to think. "What's taking you to Cali?"

It was my turn to laugh. Could I tell her that I'd found an earring from my wife in a dream and then another in the bedroom of a succubus? "I'm looking for someone."

She interpreted the awkward silence accurately. "I hope you find her."

"It's my wife."

"Oh." I didn't know her, but I wanted her to reach out to me, to touch me. I needed the comfort, the human connection. How long had it been since I had touched a real woman in a meaningful way?

Three-hundred and twenty-four days.

"Where is she?"

"I think she's in Lecoeur. That's why I'm going there."

Manifesting the Monkey   169

"Uh-huh. So she left you?"

"I guess you could say that." Actually, she flew away holding an umbrella, but I didn't feel comfortable saying that either. Daisy seemed like a nice woman, and it was obvious that all of her traveling had granted her some wisdom, but there was something cold about her, as if the road had taught her not to open too much to the outside world because it wouldn't be long before she had to say good-bye.

"And what have you been doing with yourself in the meantime" she asked.

"You ask a lot of questions."

"Sorry."

"It's okay...no worries, really. What have I been doing since? Well, like anyone with a decent head on their shoulders, I've been trying to save the world." I laughed.

"Good for you. We need more people like that." I caught a glimpse of her face. I wasn't sure if she was smiling or if it was just the effect of her tattoo.

"I've never seen a tattoo like that before."

"Yeah, facial tattoos aren't too popular. I understand. I saw a picture once of a guy who had a skull tattooed on his face, his whole face. Sure it makes sense when you're pissed off at eighteen or nineteen, but it's really short-sighted when you're thirty-two and looking for a job."

"Exactly. But what about you? What helped you decide to get that one."

She looked out at the night flowing by us. "Well, I guess it started with hopping trains. I was never in a system for very long, never went to school very long. I never felt too much a part of mainstream America. So getting my face tattooed wasn't that big of a leap for me. I was already an outsider. The tattoo just makes it visible to everyone else. It clarifies things for myself and the rest of the world, you know? So we're on the same page. And the design? I chose it because it's pretty, and it's simple, and it's spirally, three things I think are really important. And it's accentuating my smile because I want to remember to be happy, and I want people to think that I'm happy so that they feel good around me."

"Wow. Hands down, that's the best reason for a tattoo I've ever heard."

"Yeah, I guess." We listened to the clickety-clack for a few moments. Then she continued. "So ever since I saw you, I've had this feeling that I've seen you somewhere before. So I thought about it, but not too much cause I don't want to upset Max. He would hate it if I was thinking so much about somebody else, even if it don't mean nothing. But the more I thought about it I realized that I didn't know you, but I knew something inside of you, like I'd seen it before. Then I figured out what it was. I could see the same energy in you that I'd felt in myself."

"What's that?"

"You're lost."

"I'm lost?"

"You're lost."

No fucking shit!

But instead I said, "yeah, I guess that's a fair thing to say. It's that obvious?"

"Yeah, you stink of it. But like I said, I notice it because I've been there before, and since I've been there I can smell it on you. The big thing about being lost is knowing that you're lost. Once you can admit it to yourself, then you've got awareness, and awareness is key."

Awareness is key.

"How do I get unlost?"

She laughed. "I wish it was that easy, but I don't have a map or a compass that will work for you. Those are tools that you've got to find. There's no one who can get you out of this except yourself. And you can do it, but you've got to do it. In the past year, you've had lots of changes?"

"You have no idea."

"That's what I figured. You're up against something, yourself really, and it's up to you to find your way out. The thing about being really lost like you are is that you're not guaranteed to get out. You've got to get yourself out, and I've seen people who take a lot longer to get out than others, and some who don't get out at all. There's a lot like that on the streets and on the freights. They never figured out how to cope with their new way of seeing the world, with their new vision so instead, they stay lost because somehow it's comfortable, but they're never quite there and never quite here...just ghosts waiting to die, really."

After a few minutes of silence, Daisy stood up. "Just remember, the map is not the territory."

Manifesting the Monkey   171

"What does that mean?"

"It means what we sense and think and believe isn't the real thing. It's just the way we interpret the world, and not the world itself." She handed me a piece of paper. "When you get to Lecoeur, go here. The professor may have what you need. Now, I'm going to get some sleep."

"Sweet dreams." I put the paper in my pocket.

Stupid lessons.

She was right. She didn't tell me anything I didn't already know, but somehow I was more open to hearing it from an attractive woman than myself.

The map is not the territory.

24

All the works of man have their origin in creative fantasy.
What right have we then to depreciate imagination?
-Carl Jung

I arrived at the address Daisy had given me and rang the bell outside a wooden gate. A tall man, nearing sixty years answered. Judging by his smell, he was relatively free of fear. He wore a faded red trucker's cap, and white hair peeked out from its edges.

Where have I seen this man before?

He was clean-shaved, except for a small tuft of hair just under his lower lip, and he dressed in loose fitting clothes, as if he had just finished a yoga class or Tai Chi session. Immediately, I had a positive feeling from him, like he was a force for good. The sparkle in his eyes confirmed he had seen something of the world, that he had gone past the surface in search of a deeper meaning. I felt at once that he was an ally, although there was a quality to him that defied my attempts to classify it. I just hoped that this time, I was right, and he could be trusted.

There must have been something reassuring about me because he opened his door and let me right in. I knew that I had landed, that I had found some respite. I had grown tired of my adventure, first thinking I was the one chasing Jason, then realizing I was the prey, and fear was tracking me down, relentless in its pursuit to snuff out my influence on the world. The boogeyman was behind every corner, ready to destroy me anyway he could— death, insanity, addiction. It was with relief and a little caution that I walked through the gate, optimistic that at last, I had found sanctuary.

"Welcome, friend." He shook my hand and held it for a moment, and I had the sensation that he was reading something about me. Magic was possible, and it was at the edges of belief where you'll find it. It was there that the beauty of the world was revealed, in that space where conscious language played only a supporting role. I knew from the moment we shook hands that this man had been there, had traveled to the edge and back. There was something about him, a special way he moved his body as if the laws of physics were subtly different for him. His colors stood out, like he had been drawn that way by some divine artist.

"Hello, sir."

"Come in. We've been waiting for you."

"You have? How..."

"That doesn't matter, does it? Come in, set your sack down there. We'll get to the rest of this as soon as we can. You must be Ten."

"Yeah, I am. How did you—"

He held up his hand and smiled bigger. "I told you, it doesn't matter."

I tried to silence the barrage of questions assailing me. I appeased myself with the obvious one. "What's your name?"

"I am," he performed a traditional half-bow, "Professor Ping-Pong."

"Seriously?" His laugh was the only consolation he offered to my bewildered expression. "What is this place?" The complex was long and narrow. From the gate, I saw buildings and open spaces.

"This, my friend, is the Ping-Pong Club of Lecoeur."

"Seriously?"

"Yeah, what, man, you don't like Ping-Pong?" His voice had a particular vibration in it, as if he was on the verge of laughter.

Truth be told, I didn't really like ping-pong at all. I played it sparingly, and I usually lost. My former friends always used my clumsy efforts as ammunition to ridicule me, a traditional bonding behavior among male domesticated primates where I came from. Ping-pong seemed like a silly thing, to knock a tiny white ball around with flat pieces of wood. "I haven't really played much, and then I wasn't very good."

"Oh, I see," he led me into the first building, "you only like things you're good at."

Isn't that how things generally work?

We entered a dimly lit salon with cool concrete floors. "Have a seat," he motioned to the table cluttered with glass bottles of different shapes, sizes, and colors; condiments; and a basket of fruit. The professor entered the kitchen and put a kettle on to boil. "Black or green?" He clasped his hands together and rubbed them while his lips played with the hair below his mouth.

"Green, please."

"You got it, man."

His voice was happy and melodic. I imagined he was a living example of the 60's and the revolution that happened in the west, that he had surfed the wave Hunter S. Thompson watched crash. I wanted to know more. "So what's this place all about?"

"All about, man?" The clink of coffee mugs accompanied his laugh. "It's about ping-pong, the greatest game in the history of all games." Excitement carried through in his voice.

"Really? What about football? That's a good game."

"Yeah, if you like violence. Okay, it's a great game for the strategy involved, the necessary calculations to achieve your goal, but it's all about war, the primal, brutish side of man. It doesn't hold a candle to ping-pong when it comes to flow. And flow is what it's all about." He stood in the doorway of the kitchen, waving an invisible paddle. "There's no time to think when you're playing with someone who is your equal or better. You've got to be on it. Really on it, man. In the moment. And that's what it's all about."

I was beginning to feel the Zen aspect of ping-pong had gone over my head.

Could such a banal game really be as full-on as this...professor claims?

"It's about energy, you know? It's about using it, meeting your opponent's energy and then exchanging, seeing what works with another and what doesn't. It's about the exchange, the constant movement we're going through all the time. Even when it seems so still." The kettle whistled, and the professor turned off the gas. He filled the two mugs and set one down in front of me, a small paper tag hanging off the side, before sitting in the chair opposite me. I had the immediate impression that I was undergoing some sort of diagnosis, like he was looking at me with more than his eyes.

"So where'd you learn to play ping-pong," I asked, picking up my mug, sipping it nervously though it was scalding.

He smiled and waited before answering, still examining me. Then he shifted, re-arranged himself in his seat and began telling me his story. "When I was in my late-20's, I moved to Taiwan. I just had had enough, you know? I needed to get away from the Nixon era and all that war crap." He shook his head. "I graduated from Berkley, full of great ideas, but knowing quite clearly that I could do nothing to put those ideas into practice. The whole system was against me. Sure, things were bad, but it wasn't the obvious things that made

Manifesting the Monkey   175

me realize that. It was the subtle things, the little ways, the small ideas that are transmitted, passed around, and shared like a virus. Memes, you know? Mind viruses. I saw the love movement would never win because people were too god damned afraid, you know?"

I laughed. "Yeah, yeah, I really know."

"Afraid to let go of knowing long enough to create something new. So I said screw it. I bought a plane ticket and moved to Taiwan. I spent five years living in a monastery as a monk. Five years meditating in that special silence, that present moment that is everywhere we go. Five years of playing ping-pong. And after five years, I decided I needed to keep going. I needed to give something back to the world, so I studied Chinese medicine. I did that for three years, really learning it, and then, I came back to the States to see what I could do about helping. I had no grand hopes, you know, I didn't think anything would ever really change, not the way that it needed to change, but I figured that it was better than nothing, you know? I really had to do something. If I did nothing, then I was part of the problem. And I just couldn't believe that, couldn't live with that.

"So I set up shop here and began practicing, helping people get out of the addictive cycle of Western medicine, man, with all its drugs and all its users. Never trust a pharmaceutical company. There's no incentive for them to cure anyone. Sure, they'd gain in the short-term, but, eventually, they'd destroy their market. That's not good business sense, and that's what they are first—businesses." He sipped his tea, then continued. "No, man, I knew from a long time ago that the natural way was the way forward so that's what I did. I started planting my cannabis crop—" I choked on my tea and coughed. The professor laughed.

"Yeah, man, cannabis. So I planted my crop and I started showing people how to use it medicinally. It's a strong plant, and it has lots to teach us, you know, but that doesn't mean it's always good. You've got to be smart how you use it, and that'll show you every time. How you use it. There's lots of fakes and phonies, like everywhere. They're here, too, you know? We grow 'em on trees in California. The medicinal marijuana thing has lots of leeches attached to it, lots of addicts, but it's easy to tell who's using the plant as medicine, and who's using it as a drug. I mean, you don't take medicine everyday do you? Of course there are some exceptions, but, usually, you don't. Not if you're treating the root of the disease. That's the big difference between our system and the Chinese. Here we cut the branches and are surprised when new ones sprout up, but in Chinese medicine, we pull out the root of the illness."

"How do you tell if someone's using cannabis as medicine?"

"Well, if they take it everyday for weeks or months or years, you can be pretty sure that they're more addicted to this or to that aspect of the plant. They may say it puts them into contact with their creative side, which it can, or that it's good for pain relief, which it is, but except in extreme cases, you're not going to use it all the time for that. Or, like anything, it becomes a crutch. We need to work from the belief that the human body is capable of a great many miracles, and healing itself is the first of them. If we look at medicine through that lens, then we get a different diagnosis, a different prognosis. So with cannabis, there's two things to look out for—method of ingestion and frequency. If you're smoking it, then chances are you're not using it medicinally. How can something that really damages your lungs be considered medicine? And that's okay. I've got nothing against people using it as a drug, just call it that. If not the word medicine is going to get diluted until it means nothing."

"Yeah, yeah, I see your point. So you eat it?"

"Yeah, you eat it. You make cookies or brownies or hash oil or whatever, but you ingest it orally. Usually, smoking it will only plunge you into more self-hate."

"Pardon?"

"You know, man, people that smoke. Tobacco, cannabis, whatever, there's something about it, some self-loathing. Why else would a person willingly inflict damage upon themselves?"

He laughed, but I didn't know what was so funny. The way profit had replaced healing as the prime motive for the nation's health industry really bothered me. It was so polluted by Jason Muscoph. I smelled it on the professor as well, back there in the back, but he was managing his fear, instead of it managing him. I could tell that he acknowledged his fear, that he accepted it, and that somehow he actually used it. I didn't know how, but he did.

"And that's about it." He leaned back in his chair and folded his hands in his lap. "What about you?"

I laughed. "Me? Uhh...what about me? Well, the quick version is that ever since coming back from South America, my life has slowly fallen apart, you know, the typical country song—lost my wife, my job, my friends, and my dog died. But there have been some good things happening as well. Really beautiful things that I know are positive—"

"Like appearing in people's dreams and helping them get over their fears?"

I looked at him, speechless, as the memory washed over me. The hat, his face was the same one I had tried to help, but failed. This was the man with his feet embedded in concrete, the one who was ripped apart by the sharks. It was in his dream that I found Aurore's earring.

Professor Ping-Pong smiled at me. "Thanks for trying. It didn't work out, but you gave it a good try."

"I'm sorry I couldn't help you."

"Like I said, don't worry about it. You gave it a good try."

"How did it get in there?"

"How did what get in where?"

I pulled the earring out of my pocket and showed it to him. "It's my wife's. I saw it in your dream, just after you were eaten. I reached for it and grabbed it, and when I woke up, I still had it in my hand."

He leaned over the table and looked at it. "I've never seen it before. And you're sure you brought it back with you?" I nodded. "That is a mystery, isn't it? I have no idea how it got in my dream."

"Do you know who Jason Muscoph is? You know...the boogeyman?"

I expected him to laugh, but instead his face grew more serious. "Oh, Jason? That's what you call him? To me he will always be Old Red Eyes. Well, I know he's real if that's what you're after, but I don't know what he has to do with your earring there."

"I think he put it there."

"Why would he do that?"

I told him about Dawn, my capture, and my eventual escape.

He whistled in response. "That's pretty heavy, man. So you're not as old as you look?"

I shook my head. "I'm twenty-eight."

He whistled again. "Wow, she did a number on you. You're lucky you got out when you did."

"So that's pretty much my life right now. Looking for my wife, trying

178   Manifesting the Monkey

to kill Jason, and living on the streets. I've been there for a few months and as free as it is, it's not where I want to be anymore, you know?"

He raised his eyebrow, "free?"

"Yeah, free. I mean, if the system is corrupt. If everything is a sacrifice in liberty, a compromise I have to make to survive, then what choice do I have but to choose not to participate? That's the freedom and sure, I can't go wherever I want whenever I want, but that's not real freedom either. I've got all the time in the world to do what I want."

"And what is it that you do with all that time?"

"I've been, you know, thinking about things, figuring things out."

"And what have you figured out?"

"Well, I've figured out that I don't want anything to do with the American dream, that it's just a ploy to keep the masses content and in their places and the elite in riches."

"Yeah, of course. And you're right. What you're doing is a freedom of sorts, a freedom that limits you because you'll never be able to do certain things, and some of them could be really beneficial to you and, more importantly, the rest of the world. Right now is a time of change, and we've got to start influencing people, we've got to be in positions where people will listen to us because if not, we'll all be screwed. It's good what you're doing, what you've done. Most people never take time for themselves. In our world, we go from crib to school to college to job to marriage to house to kids without ever taking the time to unplug from our culture long enough to find out for ourselves what we want in life. It's always good to get a different perspective. It takes a lot of guts to unplug, to pick up and go somewhere else. Three months, six months, a year and everything changes, you come back with a new point-of-view and suddenly you've got a choice—to be apathetic or an activist."

He stood up, took our tea cups, and placed them in the sink. "Let me show you around."

Professor Ping-Pong gave me the grand tour of the Ping-Pong Club. In another life, the building we were in had been a creamery. There was still the walk-in cooler sealed on each side with heavy metal doors. There was also a small lounge, and a room the professor sometimes used as a study where he counseled patients. Just outside was a massive RV bus, filled with someone's junk, the professor claimed. "You can get to work tomorrow cleaning that out.

Manifesting the Monkey

179

How does eighteen dollars an hour sound?"

"That sounds great." I wasn't really looking for a job, but a little hard work would do me good.

Next in our journey down the property was the pavilion, a massive metal building. It was essentially an open room with a section netted off where the three ping-pong tables were. On one side of the 'court' was a lounge with many plush chairs, different pieces of fitness equipment, and a piano. On the other side of the net was a vast library spreading over two walls. There were books on all types of healing methodologies, Chinese language primers, and eastern philosophy.

We left the pavilion and passed his workshop, which looked in need of a good organization—tools and extra pieces of machinery were littered over every available surface. The next building on the right was the healing center where the professor gave treatments. Steam, sauna, acupuncture, and herbal counseling. "The body knows how to heal, we just need to give it the time, space, and love to do it." He introduced me to another man, Linus, who was staying at the center. He was older, but had the graying ponytail of someone trying to hang onto a past he never had, but always wanted. Linus was the center's main horticulturist and earned his way by tending the gardens.

"And now for the medicine." The professor opened a door to a greenhouse and the thick, sweet aroma of marijuana surrounded me. Inside were six tall plants. I had never seen one before, and I was amazed at their size. They were at least ten feet tall, and it would take five people hand in hand to encircle one of them. I walked through them, admiring their psychedelic flowers. There were more than fifty hefty buds on each plant. The professor smiled in pride. "What do you think?"

"Amazing. They smell so sweet. My mouth is watering, and I don't even smoke."

We continued on our tour, and the professor showed me the hoop house where most of the edibles were grown. Squash, kale, swiss chard, carrots, cabbages, onions, garlic, cucumber, zucchini, spinach, broccoli, cauliflower, eggplant, lettuce. The goal was to provide most of the food the community needed and to trade for the rest. They were after sustainability. We came to the end of the property, and the professor introduced me to an older couple, Lester and Jackie. They lived in an old, one-room shack.

"Where you from, Lester?"

He looked at me over the rim of his glasses and stopped sanding the piece of wood in his hands. "Alaska. Wild country. Big game." He said in a gruff voice. Lester stared at me a moment longer, smiled at my growing discomfort, and went back to sanding. I watched Jackie cook dinner in the 'kitchen', a gas stove next to some wooden benches posing as counter tops. "What are you making?"

I was talking to Jackie, but Lester answered.

He held up the slender piece so that I could see its shape. "A spoon. I've made thousands of 'em." He pointed to the canvas bag on the front of their tandem bicycle. It was full of spoons. He handed me another lying on the table in front of him, with a face carved into the handle. He smiled big, "they're Santa's elves, you see? Christmas is coming and they'll sell like hotcakes. A spoon like that will get fifty to a hundred bucks depending on the place. I'll write up a little story, give that face character, and there you go, a one of a kind spoon. The perfect holiday gift." He leaned over and continued sanding.

"Wow, that's so creative. How long have you been in the spoon business?"

"Years, and years really. God, longer than I can remember. I've been up and down the west coast on a bike. Man, people all over know me. Say that you know Lester the Spoon Guy and they'll know who you're talking about. I'm a fuckin' American icon, dude."

"That's amazing."

"Yeah, it sure is," Jackie agreed as she stirred something in her pot with a hand-carved spoon. "Lester has had a pretty amazing life." Jackie spoke with the reserved glee of a woman constantly living in someone else's shadow, although I learned that it hadn't been Lester's for very long. They had been together less than a year, but they both claimed to have been waiting their entire lives for each other. When they spoke, whiffs of fear spread around us, and it seemed to me that their statements, although beautiful and sentimental, were said in a desperation to give their lives meaning, rather than in truth.

The professor and I walked back through the complex without speaking, letting the soft sunlight shine down on us. Its wasn't cold yet, but sometimes the wind would blow and foretell of the imminent chill.

"You can sleep in the loft of the pavilion."

"Thanks a lot."

"And you can get started tomorrow on the bus. Eighteen bucks an hour alright with you?"

"Yeah, that'll be great."

I spent the rest of the day wandering around the small town. Locals seemed to be of two varieties—the strange and the paranoid. Throughout my little tour—there was only one stoplight in Lecoeur—the strong odor of Jason encroached on me, and even once or twice I saw his silhouette creeping in the shadows. I knew that the fear was there, that it was entrenched, and somehow I knew that I'd find Aurore right at its center. Or at least, I hoped. That's how it always happened in the movies.

<u>25</u>

Man who stands on toilet is high on pot.
-Chinese proverb

Nobody had seen her, at least nobody I talked to. I spent a few hours each day at the Ping-Pong Club cleaning out the bus, and doing other odd jobs supporting the community. During the rest of my time, I hung out at the coffee house or the pub meeting people and showing them a picture of Aurore. Nobody had seen her, and most disappeared soon after I showed them the photo, usually leaving that distinct odor behind them.

Upon my arrival in Lecoeur, I learned that I had landed in the middle of the Emerald Triangle, three adjacent counties in California—Mendocino, Humboldt, and Trinity—that produce hundreds of tons of high-quality marijuana, and what people had been referring to as "the Season" was the marijuana harvest. In late September, people from all over the world started showing up to the towns along Highway 101 looking for work, the bulk of which didn't begin until mid to late October, depending on a myriad of factors from the weather to the patience of the grower to the possibility of a police raid. The work was long and tedious, requiring hours and hours of trimming the worthless leaves from the flower, leaving only the final product—a manicured marijuana bud, ready for sale.

California was one of fifteen states that had medical marijuana on the books, and although there was much medicinal value for the plant, most people receive marijuana recommendations from doctors for reasons as vague as back pain, loss of appetite, or general discomfort. Now that it was semi-legal, people who wanted to smoke weed replaced the word 'drug' with the word 'medicine' and could carry three pounds of cured product with no legal consequences.

Lecoeur was an eclectic town full of former hippies and new age hipsters, and there were a lot of interesting projects. The New Center for Creative Spirituality taught that all spiritual experience was subjective, and the best way to contact your own divine world was to describe it in ways

Manifesting the Monkey   183

personal to you, a user-defined spirituality. The Art-Car Collective had weekly meetings to show off their outrageous cars—that El Dorado painted like the ceiling of the Sistine chapel, the maroon Chrysler van that had transformed into a permanent battle ground for platoons of little plastic army men. The Dykes on Bikes was a particularly popular group and attracted lesbians from all over the Emerald Triangle to their bi-monthly meetings, before pedaling around town shooting any on-lookers the grimace they had worn since they freed themselves of male oppression.

Marijuana funded all of these projects. In California, the industry was worth fourteen billion dollars a year, but the money came with a price. Never had I been amidst paranoia so thick. Generally, the people of Northern California were liberated, more evolved somehow, and Lecoeur was no exception. Most people had faced their fears—fear of loss, of success, of failure, of love, of rejection—and called it done, not realizing that without constant vigilance, the boogeyman would return. The marijuana itself aided Jason Muscoph's campaign. Although it was a powerful plant capable of great change and positive experiences, cannabis could be dangerous, and it was easy to become entangled in its webs. Paranoia found the perfect soil to bloom in the constant abuse and easy access to the plant. And the boogeyman just piggybacked along. If people lived in that part of the world long enough, they either had a healthy dose of paranoia simmering on the back burner or an active strategy to keep it out of their minds.

The more I asked about Aurore (locally known as snooping), the more people thought I was some undercover agent, waiting to spring his trap. And I guess that I was, except that my plan was meant to free everyone from the traps we had built around ourselves.

26

Failure is unimportant.
It takes courage to make a fool of yourself.
-Charlie Chaplin

The Ping-Pong Club of Lecoeur was sanctuary, one of those rare places of profound safety for wandering souls. In my previous life, when I was lost or otherwise in need of a break from the world, I went to the library. All those books, all those stories, comforted me until I felt better able to stand up to the world and its demands. Although I had been free on the streets, I never felt completely safe. Living out in the open and exposed to the elements was dangerous. On more than one occasion, I had woken in the middle of the night to the muffled shuffling of someone moving in the darkness around me. In these moments, I had two main strategies. Either I would take whatever I had for a weapon—stick, rock, or bottle—and play possum, or I would take whatever I had for a weapon and scream like some demented banshee on crack. Both methods were effective.

In Professor Ping-Pong's domain, I was safe, comfortable, and welcome. Everyone at the club had something to offer, and although I could smell their fear, I knew that they were good people, that they were on the same path as me. They had balanced their boogeyman. It was when fear was ignored for years that it festered into some puss-filled wound that slowly consumed the soul. Maybe the residents of the Ping-Pong Club didn't know that, maybe they couldn't put it into the same words, but I could see it in their eyes and feel it in their hearts. They wanted to be loved, they wanted to love, and they were doing what they could to spread that feeling. Everyone knew love to be the highest ideal any human could move towards. Jackie, the woman who lived in the shack at the back of the property, was a talented musician—she sang, played the piano, the Irish drum, the guitar, and the harp. She wrote music, and in the evenings she would often play for whoever listened, casting a sleep spell. When she finished, we'd all leave to our beds, happy, content and ready for the dreamworld. A peace filled my heart, and I realized the contentedness I felt was the gentle effect of a well-lived day. My light burned brighter. Feeling safe and secure, my nights were busy healing the world, and sometimes, I went into two or even three different dreams a night. I never saw another sign of Aurore in the dreams, but I saw Jason all the time. If I looked carefully enough, the boogeyman was always there.

The house was dark and creepy, the only light came from the dull glow of an aquarium on a metal stand. On the couch, a body rustled and then sat up. It was a girl with golden hair, a sweaty brow, and a feverish glaze in her eyes. She looked around, terrified of something, but I was unable to determine what. It all seemed mundane to me. Her eyes widened in panic. Then, I heard the buzz as it grew louder. It was coming from the fish tank, and it was annoying, but hardly anything to be scared of. The girl bolted off the couch and began fumbling with a knob on the back of it, trying to turn it down, but she only succeeded in making the noise louder. I approached her and waved the bottle of oil under her nose. She became alert and blinked at me.

"Who are you?"

I bowed. "I'm the October Man."

"What are you doing here?"

"I'm an emissary from your unconscious, a part of you that wants to help."

"Help me do what?"

"What is it that you were so afraid of a moment ago?"

She looked at the fish tank. "That noise. It's so loud. It's going to wake my father." She whispered and slipped back into the fear. She looked down that infinite hallway, I waved the bottle under her nose again, and corked it when she had regained consciousness.

"Your father? What has he done to you?"

"Nothing. Not really. He just gets angry, he yells, and—" She froze. A low rumble began from the depths of the hallway, and the girl stepped back. Her fear returned, and I dabbed a drop of oil under her nose. As it approached, the rumble became a booming roar as her caricatured father burst into the room, snarling and chomping, waving his hairy arms. I noticed the facial scars immediately. The father stopped and smiled at his daughter, and then looked at me with recognition in his eye. "Still at it, October?"

"Same as you, I see." I stepped between the girl and the boogeyman.

"Did you have fun with my Dawn? You're looking a bit older than I remember." He laughed.

"You know my father?" the girl asked.

"Not exactly." I turned and took her by the shoulders. "It's not exactly your father. You see, this is a memory you've had, one that is related to the birth of fear in your life. It started with your dad, but it has mutated into something else. Now, that fear lives inside of you." She drew back. "Look, I can do nothing for you here, not anymore. My only real power is to wake you up, to bring you present with your fear so that you may do what you wish. The choice is yours, and it's time to make it. Either you remain awake, strong, and full of love, love for yourself and for the whole world, or you fall back asleep and keep living in fear. I promise you that if you stay awake, if you find some healthy way to deal with this, then you'll wake up in your bed, wherever that may be, and you'll be better. You'll be a stronger, happier, lighter person. Everyday that passes your heart will bloom open with love. But if you go back to sleep, if you let the fear push you down, push you back from being who you want to be, then your life will go on pretty much as it has since."

"Well, what should I do? How do I deal with it?"

"Your dad yelled a lot, and that scared you. Is that it?" She nodded. "Well, stand up for yourself. I mean, you're worth it. Love yourself, love your dad, but tell him you don't like that, tell him he needs to find a better way to deal with his anger, okay? And if that doesn't work, try something else. But keep going until you are strong, confident and full of love. When you are like this, there is no room for fear. It has nothing to feed on. And if you do this, you win. We all win."

I turned back to the boogeyman father. His eyes were on me, and a cruel smile passed across his face. "We'll be seeing each other soon, October. Very soon." His sick laughter woke me up.

I had money in my pocket, and that was a very strange feeling. While on the streets, my day-to-day options were limited, but I had connected with something long forgotten, with a primal humanity. At first, returning to the world of the highly valued green paper made me uncomfortable, those notes that most of the world was so eager to spend their time and energy collecting. I knew why they did it, and it made perfect sense, but that didn't make it easier for me to deal with. I was sure that money as intermediary was getting in the way of something, interfering in the connection with my own being, but I also knew if I was to do what I wanted, money was a necessary evil. Since being at the Ping-Pong Club, I understood that, like it or not, I was part of a system, and my only real chance of influencing that system was to play by at least some of its rules, and money was a very useful one.

I spent most of my free time away from the club, trying to catch wind of Aurore. Though there was no sign of her, I was content to wait. I was on the right path, and I knew that she was close.

Life at the Ping-Pong Club turned into a comfortable routine. Although I wasn't going anywhere, I knew that there was something for me to learn, something for me to do before I could leave and continue my quest. I just waited until it showed up.

"You're either apathetic or an activist. So which one are you?"

It wasn't like the professor to pose such a direct question. We often spent hours discussing the world's miracles and messes, but he never put such a choice in front of me. Most of our conversations were thought games and exercises in logic, where I teased out my own conclusions. Like many, the professor was sure that we were on the brink of something, either great victory or explosive disaster, and that it was too early to tell. He didn't believe in the Mayan calendar end date, but he did believe change was coming.

"So which is it? And I'm talking about in the physical world, not what you do in your dreams."

It took a moment for me to admit the truth to myself and another to summon the courage to speak it aloud. "Apathetic. Although I care very much about the world and want to help. When I'm looking at it, at all those massive institutions that create the world, I find it impossible to do anything. I freeze. I just don't know what else to do. It's all...too big."

"Yeah, it sure is. That's part of the intimidation. Look, I'll give you another chance to answer that question in a couple of days, but first...but first, we're going to have a little fun. I've seen you, and I've heard you speak of fear this and fear that, about how fear is running the world and how we are nearly powerless to stop it. And all of this may be true...I don't really know, but I do know that you're focusing on exactly what it is you don't want, and that's only going to give you more of the same thing, right? Right. You get what you focus on. So...what is the opposite of fear?"

"Love," I said without hesitation.

"Right, love. Fear is the closing of the heart to the world, and love is its opening. So how do you love the world? How do you open your heart and let the love shine out onto the world?"

I shrugged. All my talk aside, that was the last thing I wanted to do. I wouldn't last more than an hour before I was thoroughly trampled by the cynicism of the world.

"Well, I'm going to show you. And it all starts with this." He showed me a red, rubber clown's nose, then held up his hand to stop my question. "Not now. No questions now. First we must remember how to play, then we can decide if we want to know what it is we're doing."

"When I say clowning, I'm not talking about circus clowns, or balloon animals. I'm not talking about Bozo or Goofles. There's no real way to put in words what it is I'm talking about, but I know that some of you are addicted to the intellect so I will do my best to appease that incessant voice inside of you." The professor paused and scanned his audience of eight. "Clowning is a process of being. This kind of clowning is not a gag or a set routine. It's not a pie-in-the-face or a whoopee cushion, at least not intentionally. Clowning is never planned." As he spoke, I noticed an almost imperceptible shift in him, a slow phase from one state to another, like ice melting. "It's a return to that place of being we all experienced as a child, before we conformed to the rules and norms of the society around us, before we assimilated the way things are and forgot the infinite potential of life. The journey that you are all embarking upon now is a journey to that place, to the clown inside each of you. It's a return to that state of innocent vulnerability where everything is possible." He stopped his flourishing and pacing, and looked at us all. His phase shift continued,and he became less solid and more something else. "There is no right way to be a clown. Each of you has your own unique way of clowning, the same way that each of you are unique in your personalities. It's imperative that you never try to clown like anyone else. It's imperative to the work that you do not try to be anything except what you are feeling in the moment.

"It's about letting go of what you expect to be true, letting go of your ideas of what you should or should not do. It's about returning to this place of vulnerability and being amazed at the world around you. And in the end, it all returns to love." The professor looked at me, and I felt a surge of youthful

Manifesting the Monkey

189

energy in my heart. "It's about learning to love the world again, to live in a place free from judgment of ourselves, of others, and our surroundings. It's about loving life, about being playful and free. And if we continue down this path, if we are not put off by the fears that may well up inside, if we are successful at connecting to that playful energy then we'll return to our hearts, we'll return to that trust we once had in ourselves and in the world around us when we looked upon it in awe and wonder." He paused and smiled at us. "Any questions?"

Mine was one of the four hands that shot up. The professor smiled bigger. "Good. Let's begin."

"I'm going to play some music and we're all going to move continuously towards the open spaces. Your focus is solely on the space around you and not the people. You are alone here. Any questions?" Lester began to say something, but the professor started the music. "Go for it!"

And that was how it began. We walked around the small garden, moving into the empty spaces that appeared and disappeared, a constant flux between existence and non-existence. As soon as I arrived in an empty spot, it was no longer empty, and I had to move to another. Obvious or not, it became a sort of Zen riddle. Full and empty. Sometimes, the space I was headed for would be occupied just before I arrived, and I would have to adapt and change my course. The professor stopped the music after two minutes. "Alright, very good," he said, "very good. It's very common that we go through life without thinking of where we're going, constantly worrying about what we're going to do later instead of where we are now." The professor molded his body, bent his back, hunched over and began mumbling to himself as he shuffled clumsily around the garden, supported by an imaginary cane. The phase shift I had witnessed was complete—he had transformed into a fumbling old man wearing blinders. "But if we're able to wake up and be where we are, then we can connect with the present moment." He stood up straight and returned to that potential of neither-this-nor-that. "Okay, now, we're going to play a similar game," he rubbed his hands together. He was shimmering. It was a subtle effect, as if his edges weren't solid, as if he was made up of something different than the rest.

Am I the only one seeing this?

"It's essentially the same. You're going to move around the space,

190   Manifesting the Monkey

moving towards the openings, but as you pass someone, I want you to meet them, but only with your eyes. I want you to make eye-contact. I don't want you to do anything but look each other in the eye. Got it?" Nobody bothered trying to ask any questions. The professor hit the button on the CD player and the graceful melodies of a piano moved us.

I walked to the open space and passed Lester along the way. We looked each other in the eyes, and I noticed something inside of me, a flutter insisting I look away, and so I did. When I was changing directions, I met a woman, and the fluttering became stronger. I tried smiling, but that only forced her eyes away, as if I had admitted to seeing something I wasn't supposed to. This continued for the next three minutes, silent meetings and that panic to hide from them. I wanted to put something up in front of me, I wanted to wear a mask, say something to distract them so that they wouldn't see the ugly part of me that I had spent so long hiding from the world. I wanted to explain myself.

The music stopped.

"Okay, what did you notice?" Nobody answered. We were all sure that he would ignore our questions anyway. He laughed. "No, I'm serious, what happened?"

"I was uncomfortable." Lisa, a tall Australian woman, said. "When I was looking people in the eyes, there was a feeling that I was doing something wrong."

"Yeah, me too," Jackie agreed. I looked around the group and noticed for the first time that of the eight participants, Lester and I were the only men.

"And why is that?"

"It's because we're all wearing masks," I offered.

The professor smiled. "What do you mean?"

"I mean that we spend our days pretending to be this or that person. We're always playing a role. We've forgotten that we are not the personalities that we created. They're only tools, generalizations we've created to deal with the world, and they're not really us."

"What does that mean?" Maggie, a woman with gray hair said. "I don't wear any masks."

I thought it better to remain silent than to argue with her. I had lost most of my contacts with friends and family for pursuing righteousness, and I wasn't about to set fire to any bridges-under-construction. My experience in

Manifesting the Monkey   191

the world confirmed that truth for me, and that was enough.

"But he's right," the professor answered for me. "We do go through our lives hiding something from the world and even from ourselves. We hide it with masks. We hide it behind the mask of 'good employee' or 'tolerant boss' or 'faithful wife' or 'mischievous son' or 'sexy woman' or 'real man' or whatever stereotype we have taken on for ourselves, whatever person we have chosen to be. True, these roles serve us and speak some truth about who we are, but they are not *the* truth. They are only a rough estimate. That's why we feel this discomfort when we meet a stranger's eyes. We have this immediate fear that they will see into us, that they will see whatever secret we are trying to cover up. We rush to look away, we rush to cover the moment with needless words or automatic phrases. Anything, really. But it's this discomfort that is the beginning of the road to your clown. It's this discomfort that you must follow to find out who you truly are."

He rubbed his hands together and for a moment, the professor transmogrified into a cartoon character, just like I had seen in his dream. The shimmer around his edges was more distinct and the colors of his body became more vivid and pronounced. "Next, we're going to do the same thing, but this time I'm going to stop the music, kinda like in musical chairs. And each time the music stops, you have to make eye-contact with someone and freeze. If you don't have a partner, it's important that you make yourself visible...hey, look at me, look at me!" He jumped in place like an excited child. "And the ones who already have a partner can help by staying perfectly still and becoming as invisible as possible, while always maintaining that eye-contact with your partner." The professor froze, and without moving, he made himself nearly disappear. Nothing changed, it's just that I forgot he was there, and my eyes began to wander around the garden. "Okay?"

For the rest of the day, we played. It was simple really, but very difficult. There was a force in my head, years and years of conditioning and habit, of self-conscious awareness that prevented me from letting go and being present. I wanted to look 'cool' or 'intelligent' or 'calm' or 'confident', but these games would not allow for that. I could not enter them with a pre-existing thought of what I was going to do or how I was going to do it, much less how I would look to the rest of the group. I could only be there and respond to what was happening to me, however I happened to respond. We practiced moving in these spaces, in noticing an object as if we'd seen it for the first time, as if we were amazed by some mundane rock or particular patch of grass. We practiced making random gestures sounds, then leading the group in these movements.

Although I never considered myself a clown, these games came quite easily to me, and I immediately understood the professor's teachings. The clown was that inspirational, spontaneous character, that person we were when our lust for life hadn't yet been dimmed by corporate strategies and our own eagerness to be like everyone else. That afternoon, I realized that I had sacrificed my clown for my lust to be 'normal.'

We began again the next morning. The professor stood in the middle of our circle, dangling a rubber nose by its elastic string. "What is this?"

"It's a red nose."

"Yes, of course, but more importantly this is the mask of a clown. It's the smallest mask in the world, and it is the mask that reveals everything underneath it. That is the beauty of the clown—his transparency." He paused and that shimmering returned as Professor Ping-Pong re-entered the field of possibilities. "Our lives are filled with roles, most of them unconscious. The beauty of a clown is in the revealing of his masks to the audience and showing the authentic human beneath. It is in this honest disarmament that we can connect to the person below, and then we can reconnect with our own humanity. A clown is a mirror. It's riveting to watch someone have the courage to be who they are, the courage to cry in agony in front of us, to scream in fear, to squeal with pleasure, or to laugh in selfish delight. This is what attracts people to clowns—their courage to feel and express the things that we have been taught to suppress or to dampen or to otherwise pervert because it is just not comfortable or acceptable to express them honestly. The clown feels the emotions we are afraid to feel in front of others, even afraid to feel when we are alone, terrified how that feeling might rearrange our identity. But all that will come much later. First, we must become acquainted with the clown, we must enter his world and learn to play in that space. Whether you remember it or not, you've all been there before. It is the world of childhood, the world of the imagination."

The professor divided the garden in two by laying a red rope across it. The concept was quite simple to grasp, though embodying it was much more difficult. On one side was the audience, and on the other, the world of the clown. And once there, to be successful, it was essential that we follow the clown's motivation:

Be present and genuinely express whatever emotion you're feeling.

Our goal was simple. The professor placed a blanket in the middle of the stage, and we were to enter, walk towards the blanket, and then, touch it. And once we had made contact, we were to follow whatever ideas and images came—the thread, as he called it. The really difficult part of this was that we were to throw out any ideas that came before we touched the blanket. While sitting in the audience, if I had an idea, I had to throw it out. If I had an idea on my walk over to the blanket, too bad, I couldn't use it. Anything I thought of before I actually touched the blanket had to be discarded because it violated the rules of the clown. If I thought of it before, then I wasn't present.

The professor gave a demonstration. He took a few steps towards the blanket, now glittering with some previously dormant life. "Ooooooohhhhh," he looked at us and wiggled his finger in delight, "that's a great idea, but sorry, I can't use that one." A few more steps. "Nope, not that one either." He was standing behind the blanket, with it between him and us. "I must only nurture a curiosity and allow that to pull me towards my goal. And then," he reached his hand out slowly towards the cloth, "I touch it." And as he did, his eyes went big, and that shimmering came back, his colors became more vivid, more outrageous. "It's murky at first, but I can feel it coming," his eyes squinted shut, and his face scrunched in effort, "I must stay present, must hold off the panic, that expectation to do something, anything and let the idea come, let the thread come, I've almost got it." With a gasp, his eyes opened. The professor switched his gaze back and forth from the blanket to us as he spread it flat on the floor and smoothed its surface of wrinkles until it was just right. And when it was perfect, the professor looked at it, parental pride filling his eyes, then shifted his gaze to us. In that connection, the veil between worlds parted and the garden was infused with a comforting light. Now, the blanket was no longer a blanket, but a thick, woven rug. With another glance at us, the professor seated himself gingerly in the middle with his arms and legs crossed regally. His loose-fitting clothes had been replaced by fancy silks, topped by a royal turban. Then, his magic carpet took off. The Raja looked at us and smiled with the glee of success. His trusting the unknown had opened the Otherworld. A warm glow radiated from a tiny chink in reality on the ground where the professor had first arranged the blanket. The transition knocked something heavy from my shoulders, and my lungs, released from some of my emotional baggage, opened up and filled with air. The weight tumbled down away from me, and clunked gently towards the hole in the ground, where its corner eventually lodged, sealing the crack into the Otherworld. For a moment, the light dimmed, then went out, as if a gargoyle thundercloud had sneaked out over the sun. The professor screamed as his carpet lost power and tumbled towards an Arabian market and a messy end.

But then, the embrace of the Otherworld overcame the inertia of my baggage and squeezed it through the hole, where it disappeared forever. The light flooded again through the tiny hole, recharging the professor and his steed. His carpet regained life. It bucked and shot ahead at cheek-shaking speeds. The hole in reality continued to pull bits of muck off of me and into the Otherworld, back to source. But I barely noticed it. Most of my attention was fixed on the fine-robed Raja zooming and looping through the garden on his runaway rug. The fulfillment of trust had unlocked the imagination dimension, and I suddenly remembered my own. Even then, I knew I had found the strategy to solve my problems.

The Raja looked around, down, and when he regarded us again, fear glazed the glow of his eyes. He dug his fingers into the fine Kashmiri threads until his knuckles whitened with the strain. He struggled to control the wayward rug, and when it was close enough to the ground, the Raja took a risk and jumped off. He rolled head over feet towards the rope separating us from him, to the edge of the fragile membrane his trusting had created. He finished on his bottom, looking at us, the crooked turban adding clarity to the bewilderment on his face.

Slowly the threshold dissolved, the light faded, then left with a faint pop.

The hole on the floor was gone and normal life seemed dull from the lack of spiritual light. My own understanding of imagination dissolved soon after. I reached for it, but only succeeded in knocking it faster into oblivion.

He was still for a moment, before a deep, divine laugh exploded out of him. It was contagious medicine, seeking out the seeds of our own joy somewhere in the soil of our bellies. One-by-one, our laughter fruited, shyly at first, but it only took a few seconds before we all shook loose our ideas of propriety and let the feeling overtake us. It washed over the garden intoxicating us with pleasure.

When it subsided and reality sharpened, the professor clapped his

Manifesting the Monkey   195

hands. "Who wants to go next?"

No one volunteered. Slowly the professor scanned his students, until he motioned to Jackie. "Would you do us the honor?"

She opened up her mouth, the protest loaded and ready to fire from her lips. But she stopped, and her eyes brightened. She looked around, sniffing, trying to name whatever pleasant aroma had sparked the delightful memory running through her head. She took a deep breath, walked to the rope, and put the red nose on. After another breath to steady herself, Jackie stepped through the boundary, onto our imaginary stage. She looked nervous, timid, and meek, and I could smell that she had already lost track of whatever memory had possessed her to refrain from avoiding the professor's choice. When she touched the blanket, she scooped it up immediately and draped it over her self. I had the vague impression that she was wearing a cloak, but it lacked any reality. She marched around, but there was no light, no crack in between worlds.

Trust is a skill.

When she was finished, she sat back down, and it was quiet for a moment.

"When did you think of that idea?" The professor asked.

"When I touched the blanket." Jackie replied.

"Are you sure?"

Jackie blushed. "Maybe just before."

"I know. We could see that you thought of it before you actually made contact. It happened so fast. There were moments in your walk over that were brilliant, that were really clowning because they were honest and truly present, but they were fleeting. We saw your premeditation."

The Australian woman, Lisa went next, and she was more relaxed. When she reached the blanket, she touched it, felt it for a moment before it became a cape, and she flew away. There was a flicker of light that momentarily carried Lisa through the air, but as soon as she realized what happened, she thought about it and toppled down to the ground.

When my turn came, I was amazed at how nervous I was. My task was simple, but it seemed impossible—my hands were sweaty, and my heart pounding. I put on the nose.

Flush.

196   Manifesting the Monkey

Suddenly, my senses opened up, flooding my brain with information. I staggered back from the force, resisting the temptation to reduce the experience to my description of it. It was if my senses had never really worked before, or that I had forgotten their depth, and the nose reminded me that the world was much more than I thought it was. I crossed onto the stage and took a step towards the blanket, feeling self-conscious, like some napping student forced to the blackboard. The weight of all those eyes, all those judgments peering down threatened to pop the fragile bubble that swelled out from me and nudged up against the border between me and my audience. I looked at them and swallowed. The sound was unintentional, and I was surprised by the chuckle it created. The surprise widened my eyes and the chuckle became a laugh, strengthening my crucible. I returned to my quest and kept throwing out the ideas that came to me, like some desperate sailor bailing water out of his sinking lifeboat.

How many things can you do with a blanket on the floor?

I forced myself to remain in that space of not-knowing, trusting that, somehow, something would come out, some magic would manifest. I kept looking back at the audience with my honest emotion—nervous surprise— and their authentic attention fed back and energized my imagination. I got close to the blanket and was overcome by an immense curiosity that drowned out any lingering wonderings of what to do or how I should look in front of people. I simply did not care because I was so absorbed with the non-blanket.

It could be anything!

It was the most incredible thing I had ever seen, and that feeling exponentiated the opening of the Otherworld. I was amazed by this blanket that wasn't a blanket, but there was something else, something just out of sight. I poked the blanket and a surge of critical voices argued in my head. I began to change my strategy, but the professor whispered to me, "stay with it, follow the thread." So I did. I ignored the doubts and the self-abusive remarks that echoed out of my subconscious. I kept poking the blanket, then got really involved with poking it. I sat cross-legged in front of it and kept poking, this time with both hands. I had the fuzzy feeling of something buzzing around me, but I could only focus on the blanket as my poking became fevered. The buzz climaxed into a thunderclap, and my fingers exploded into a wild frenzy of typing. The blanket had become a typewriter and with a flash of light, I was

Manifesting the Monkey   197

in a new world. I looked around. I was at a desk, in a home I would one day own. I felt good there, and the typing continued to accelerate as page after page of my stories and ideas piled up on the desk until it was covered with the products of my passion. I had finally found a compassionate way to share my truth with the world. The pleasure of such an opportunity filled me with a happiness that spread my face out into a child's bright smile. I looked at my audience. They laughed, and I pushed the tube back over and kept helping the world design a new paradigm.

<u>27</u>

Out beyond ideas of wrongdoing and rightdoing,
there is a field. I will meet you there.
-Rumi

I went to sleep and followed the ants into a turbulent world of shifting images. I watched from above as naked women of all shapes and sizes, all colors and races moaned, groaned, and screamed in ecstasy and agony. Big breasts, small breasts, no breasts. Red hair, black hair, blond hair. Dominatrix lingerie, French maids, naughty school teachers, mischievous cheerleaders. Shaved, trimmed, bushy. Blonds running on beaches, breasts bouncing in sync. Catholic school girls biting their lower lip and blushing. The girl next door in Daisy Dukes, popping her bubble gum in boredom.

Immediately, I knew it was an army of succubi sent by Jason, but I couldn't concentrate for very long. The images were too appealing. Some women were engaged in lesbian acts of the most lascivious nature: strap-ons and ferocious 69ing. Penises—connected to amorphous, faceless men— repeatedly penetrated any available orifice of the droves of eager women, who pushed and shoved to have their turn. Some screamed in painful pleasure as gangs of unidentifiable men defiled them, and some only derived pleasure from pleasing and took on the task of touching and sucking five bodiless tools at once.

I floated above, transfixed. I couldn't move, couldn't make sense of the mass of flesh below me. I was caught off-guard. All I could do was watch in shameful pleasure, and I soon forgot where I was. A familiar lust filled me, threatened to burst me apart. I was unable to think of anything but my own sexual satisfaction and the many varied ways of accomplishing that climax. I approached the dream images, moving from my disassociated perspective up high. I drifted down into that wonderland, feeling marvelously lucky to live in such a sensual world. I was powerless to the blasphemous images about women and sex I had been force-fed. Our nature, the very instinct that a man had to reproduce, had been turned into a tool to manipulate, indoctrinate, and sell.

That's not good.

I approached an unoccupied blond with tender C-cups and a pair of crotchless panties, who was fondling herself, a bored look on her face. She smiled at me and moved to her knees. When I was in front of her, she looked up at me while she slowly unbuttoned my pants. I ran my hands through her hair and tilted my head back waiting for the pleasure I knew would come. And just before she put me into her warm mouth, and I would be lost forever, I saw something moving up in the sky, a white dragon flashed across the horizon, and it was then the smell of fear wafted upon me. It took every ounce of strength I had, but I pulled away and contained myself. The women of the dream converged on me, threatened to overtake and fuck me to death. They touched me, clawed at my clothes, pulled and tore them from my body. They were drunk with lust and would have their reward.

Remember what happened last time. You know...the coyote-woman?

I made myself immaterial and became a ghost in the dream. The women looked concerned over my sudden disappearance for a moment, but they soon went back to their work of rubbing, jerking, and enveloping. I moved about the dream world, followed the scent of fear and looked for Jason. He was here somewhere, and I had to find the dreamer so that I could wake him up and get the hell out of there before I did something I'd regret. The dream was too tempting. Any slip in consciousness and I'd be fornicating forever.

The women went on and on. It was a never-ending playground of pleasure and perversion. I passed pockets of violent rapes, and then romantic teenage love-making, in soft green grass. I walked by women servicing a donkey and being showered in his gifts. It was at once stomach-turning and highly-erotic, a playground of taboo images. I wasn't sure what the dream meant, or what I could do to fix it, but I understood. Since forever, humans had been drawn to exactly what it was they were not supposed to have. The longer a taboo was ignored, pushed down, the greater its gravitational force until it surfaced and pulled us down into it, like an existential black-hole.

With each step, temptation was stronger. I stopped (just for a quick look) and watched a gorgeous lesbian couple soaping each other up in the shower. It was only when they beckoned me to join them that I realized I had become solid again. Immediately, all of the beautiful women around rushed towards me and started to pull at me again, insatiable in their hunger for my penis. It was incredibly flattering, but I summoned the strength to tear myself away again and return to my incarnation as ghost. The women blinked at each other, then rearranged themselves, and continued moaning in forbidden pleasure.

The dream was strong, and I knew it was the special work of the boogeyman, a trap for me. I smelled him close to me, but I would not fall for the same trick twice. I unhooked my emotional connection to the images in front of me and observed how much of my own sexuality lay buried, suppressed, and poisonous. Repressing any material only limited the self and could even create a ticking bomb that would one day blow up in a very unpredictable and perilous way. This was the danger of fear, and its continual integration was the only solution.

After a few more near misses, the pressure in my loins was monumental. I wanted nothing more than to split into an infinite number of selves and enter every scene at once and release my passion onto the world, but that would condemn me to damnation. It would be the end of me and perhaps the end of the world.

I'm still not sure where one stops and the other begins.

I closed my eyes, stuffed my fingers into my ears and hummed myself a song. I sniffed and followed Jason's stench. It was in this way I found the source of the fear.

When the smell was strong, I opened my eyes. I was up on a hill, outside the bordello of flesh. I turned around and looked at it below me, a massive undulating mountain of humans (and some animals), all trying to get off. Although it was still appealing, the urge to dive in was only mildly present. In front of me was a boy about ten years old. He could not see me and thankfully so. His pants were around his ankles, his shirt pulled over his head, and he was in the process of pleasing himself as he frantically flipped through an old copy of Playboy, his head jerking between the magazine and the scene below, trying to take it all in at once. I sniffed and confirmed that he was the dreamer. In the course of my work, it was usually obvious how to help someone get over a fear. Most times, it meant dealing with an outside factor. Something external coming in to scar and cripple, but with this boy, I had no idea what to do or how to do it. It was obvious his fear was related to sex and women, but more than that I could not know. I was an amateur in this arena. I imagined if I woke him up with his pants around his ankles, he'd not be the most willing to talk about it.

I looked around and saw something dart behind a tree. Jason Muscoph had come to feed. He was always there to feed. A small platoon of his gnats buzzed by.

I sat down on a rock and waited for a more appropriate time to intervene in the boy's dream. I closed my eyes, and trusted I would open them at the right time. I lowered my breathing, moved it down into my diaphragm. Slowly, my body transformed. From my root chakra, thin red roots inched out and gripped the rocks, then dug into the soil underneath until they were firmly planted in the ground and thickening. They pulled energy up from the Earth into my internal energetic system. My heart opened up as a beautiful green flower, pulsating light and love to everything. The energy continued upwards towards the branches of the tree I had become, and a small egg cracked open. A royal blue bird jumped out of my third eye, chirping and saw the world around him from its elevated perch. My heart flower opened wider and vibrated out a divine love for all things.

My eyes flicked open. The boy was buttoning his pants, and standing up. He looked at the magazine, and his fear thickened. He shut it quickly and looked to see if anyone was around. Still invisible, I stood up and walked towards him. He was looking down at the frolicking females below, staring at them. He stayed like this for a moment, and then slowly, he began to unbutton his pants again.

I pulled out the bottle of whale oil and dabbed a drop on his upper lip. His face contorted, and he shook his head trying to escape the smell. His body shivered, and, then, he was awake.

When he saw me, he recoiled and moved away. "Who are you?"

In a flourish, I removed my hat and bowed before him. "I have come from the depths of your unconscious to help you deal with your fear. You may call me the October Man." When my ears confirmed that he had arranged his pants, I stood up and smiled.

He looked behind me. "Who's that?"

I didn't need to turn around to know who he was talking about. "That, my friend, is your fear."

"My what? I'm not afraid of anything." He folded his arms across his chest, the unconscious gestures confirming his heart was closed and overgrown with fear.

"Oh, of course not. But there it is anyway." Jason moved closer. "What about this...how is your heart like a parachute?"

He looked at me. "What the fuck is this, a test?"

"Never mind."

The boy looked out over the mass of writhing flesh and shuddered. I stepped next to him.

"There are some interesting things going on down there," I said.

"It's gross. Disgusting. I mean, look, there's a donkey...and look what she's doing to it."

"Yes...it's quite disturbing. This is your dream, you know? You could make it all go away." I knew it wasn't that simple, but if we reduced the stimulus, perhaps he'd be able to wade through and find the root of his fear. I had no idea how else to help him except for a 'birds and bees' talk, but what good would that do? More than likely, he was an adult man with competent knowledge of the human reproductive system.

"It's kind of exciting, too." And there, faintly, was the fear.

"So it's the women that bother you?" He looked at couple making love very conservatively on a plush Victorian couch, and shrugged.

"Yeah, they do. I don't know what it is about them. I mean, they're gross, of course, but it's more than that. I mean, I'm attracted to them, you know...I want to do all those things with them." He laughed. "I don't even know how to do them." His voice had grown deeper, and when I looked at him again, he was older, what I presumed to be his current age of twenty-seven. "But they're beautiful, I want to go to them, I want to take them all." A fury entered his voice, the suppressed aggression of the modern male as the natural forces in his body, manipulated by years of conditioning, worked against him. "But I don't know how. I mean, I know how, it's easy to know how to do it. Insert tab A into slot B. But I get the feeling there's more to it. I don't know what to do with them. I have this very strong feeling that just fucking them isn't enough. Just making love to them isn't enough. No matter how many orgasms I give them, it's just not enough, and I don't know what else to do. I'm just not enough. And it feels so terrible. It feels like something's missing, like the more I go towards them the more incomplete I am. It scares the shit out of me. Ever since I can remember I've felt broken, incomplete and

Manifesting the Monkey

203

very, very unsure of how to proceed, but pushed forward anyway, sure that every way I do proceed will only shatter me further. It's terrible. There is something beautiful about every woman. I know this. I can see it, and it's not just physical. I mean, sometimes it is physical, but sometimes it's not. There's something else there, something I don't see with my eyes...some...mystery." He took a deep breath and looked down at the confusing scene. "And that's what scares me. Women are this enigma, this unknown energy that I have no idea how to interact with, but yet I'm supposed to interact with them. It's just plain crazy. And you know what it is? It's not that it's even unknown. I mean, I've dealt with plenty of the unknown in my life. Lots of craziness, and some really intense moments."

As he talked the writhing crowd of ecstasy began to thin. Slowly the women were disappearing.

Not the lesbians!

"The unknown I can handle. Once I get there, I'll know. It's only unknown for so long. But with women, with women. I don't know how to know them...that's it! I don't know how to know them. For me, it's not that they are the unknown. It's that they are unknowable. That's what scares the living crap out of me. I mean, I'm a married man. I go to sleep next to my wife every night. And I love her, but I don't know her. Sure, I know what she likes and what she doesn't like. I know what to do to piss her off and what to do to excite her, but there's still something in there. I can feel it. There's something inside of her that I haven't even touched, some mystery inside of her that is waiting for me to be the man who solves it, and I have no idea how to get to it. She doesn't even know it, but deep down she does, and she's waiting for me to get there. There's something I'm not doing, something I have no idea how to do, and no idea how to learn how to do it. And it's been like this since I had my first hard-on."

The man slumped to the ground, crying. Down below there were only a few conservative sexual demonstrations going on. I sat next to him and put my arm around his shoulder. I had no idea what to say. Everything he said resonated with me. Women were terrifying. They were this unknown mystery that I felt totally ill-equipped to handle.

Let me handle this:

"You're right. You're absolutely right. They are a mystery, and they are an enigma. But they are not unknowable. There is something inside of you that is profoundly masculine, and that profound masculine wants nothing more than to merge with his counterpart, the mystery that dwells inside your wife, inside every woman. You can't know how to do it because there's nothing to do. It's not about doing or knowing, it's about *being*. The key to all of this is remaining aware. That when you are with your wife, all you have to do is remain aware. Stay in the present moment, stay alert, and open. When the worries come, don't follow their trail because you'll just get lost. Sure as shit, you won't even know you're lost again until it's too late. Let them go, and stay present. And this strong consciousness will call to the mystery in your woman. The longer you stay aware, eventually, I think, the mystery will reveal itself to you. It's not about you knowing her mystery, it's about her mystery opening for you, to you. The less you do, the better." As I talked, I began to understand my own struggle with the feminine. "You don't have to *do* anything. In fact, the more you do, the further you will be from that union you so desperately desire. Just be there, and keep being there. Then one day, you'll be surprised when you draw out the mystery of your wife, when it reveals itself to you, reveals the secrets of the Universe."

He looked at me and wiped the tears from his eyes. "That's it? That's all I have to do." I nodded and he thought for a moment. "Simple, really simple...shit...I have no idea how to do that."

I laughed. "We don't know how to do that, for sure because we're doing everything. We live in a world that teaches us to do all kinds of things, but never to just *be*. Once you get started, you may find it's really, really easy. Start by just sitting, and paying attention to your senses. To the information you get from your senses, and every time your mind wanders off of that, come back to the senses. Just be aware. Then let it all fall into place."

Awareness is key.

I looked down and the clearing was empty, save a young couple engaged in a deliberate act of sacred sex. I looked behind us and saw Jason walking away.

Manifesting the Monkey   205

<u>28</u>

*I object to violence because when it appears to do good,
the good is only temporary. The evil is permanent.*
-Mahatma Gandhi

You're dreaming.

I looked down, and I was in a suit jacket and tie, cleanly pressed shirt and spotless pants, something I'd never wear. I was sitting at a desk that used to be mine, but it was twisted by the imagery of the dream into a surreal table of torture, complete with dried spots of blood that swirled into menacing faces and clawing fingers. My former coffee cup turned into a rusty shackle, its mouth gaping open and clamping shut, reaching for my arms. I was in that dark cave filled with a thousand whispered shouts and the occasional wail of a wandering soul. Further into the cave, a flickering fire beckoned me, its flames turning into hands waving me closer. I stood up and headed towards the light, but it became more difficult to walk. I looked down, and my feet were being swallowed. The solid ground had softened into a viscous slime, now alive and reaching for me. I pulled free, and set to wiping my shoes clean, but I only succeeded in spreading the organism further over my body. I continued to the light, hopeful to improve my situation there, and I was relieved to see a figure on the other side, a man enveloped in shadow despite the glow of the fire. I called out, but he ignored my cries for help. I continued trying to tidy myself, but the more I tried the filthier I became, just like the last time I was here.

Trying implies failure.

The familiar panic of sabotage—that insane feeling of unwittingly, unknowingly destroying my own opportunities—washed over me, and this time, I just observed as it inundated my soul, threatening to drown me. I didn't identify with it. An intentional breath, a deepening of my roots, and the wave retreated as quickly as it came. While living in France, I learned that if I stared at the piles of canine feces dotting the sidewalk, I saw shit everywhere.

But if I ignored those biological hazards, I would eventually step directly on one of those organic land mines and have a slippery mess. However, if I acknowledged the shit, gave it only a cursory glance, and then chose to shift my attention to the interesting architecture, beautiful women, or delicious smells, I could safely navigate the streets without worry of any unfortunate encounters. In the cave, I applied the same principle. I looked at the muck spreading up over my body, but then I noticed how much of me wasn't contaminated. The more I focused on those clean parts of me, the bigger they got. It wasn't as if I ignored the disease trying to re-infect me. Rather, I chose to give my attention to what I wanted: clean shoes.

I looked down, and they were spotless. Jason Muscoph was there on the other side of the fire, his bright red eyes and scarred face suddenly astonished that his trap had failed. Regardless, he puffed himself into that giant squid, and began lashing tentacles at me. The first few knocked me back, but I remembered my lesson, and focused on what I wanted—light. The fire grew hotter, brighter. The giant was barraging me with blows, but I felt nothing. They passed through me, and soon he stopped altogether. Jason shrunk, shivering next to the fire, and continued to get smaller. The blaze blotted out all darkness, and I admired the motley-colored fungus that grew on the wall, the pretty way it reflected the glow of the fire in purples and pinks, sometimes in quick flashes of orange. I looked back at Jason, but if I stared too long, he stopped withering and started growing.

You get what you focus on.

So I concentrated my attention on the wall and the fire, happy to inspect their natural wonder, but I looked at Jason every few minutes, just to acknowledge the reality of my environment. If I took a quick glance as a part of my normal way of observing the world around me, he was not empowered by my attention, but when I stared at him, I gave him strength. So I spent the night in the cave, enjoying the bright light, comforting warmth of the fire, and the final key to the riddle of happiness.

Just before I woke up, I found myself alone in a brightly lit cave. That was the secret. The battle against fear wasn't a battle against fear. To push against what we feared would only cause it to push back, and we'd soon be lost in that eternal dynamic. We'd forget that we could opt out at any time by simply observing what we wanted in life. Resistance to resistance is resistance.

Turn the other cheek.

Violence begets violence. Jason was still out in the world, terrorizing people from the shadows of their own minds, but I lay down my weapons and ended my war against him. And if I didn't fight him, eventually he'd disappear. I'd still see him, but less and less. It wouldn't be long now. As more monkeys awoke to that reality, he'd slowly fade into the background until he was gone forever, like a bad case of poison ivy.

As difficult as it is not to scratch, it's the fastest way to recovery.

Once I found the 100th monkey, all of humanity would understand the puzzle, and it would take only a little time as the world restructured itself. Physical reality would need a few weeks or months to catch up with the programs of the mind and heart, but soon, we'd drop all the things that no longer served us, and start building the world again, this time founded on an authentic humanity centered in compassion.

29

*Anyone not shocked by quantum mechanics
has not yet understood it.*
-Neils Bohr

Everything changes.

Somewhere along the way, my heart had healed, and I noticed a fresh silver thread that extended from its center and disappeared into the distance. It was still small, but it grew a little everyday, and on the other end, Aurore was waiting for me.

Seeing the world through the clown's eyes revolutionized my life. I saw the love that is always there, and I smelled it, too, the sweet aroma of jasmine. I heard the soft whispers of support and courage that were always there just underneath the violence of self-criticism, and the more I noticed the butterflies, the more they fluttered by. Clowning thrust me back into the space of a child, where innocence and curiosity flooded my system. As I spent more time in that space, my youth returned to me. Each day, the gray faded more from my hair, the skin grew tighter around my eyes, and I had greater access to a boundless energy. I learned to change my focus and find the love in people. I was no longer bombarded by the constant reek of fear and its effects, though they were still present in the sum total of sensory information that constituted my reality. As with all things in life, the more I noticed those instances of love, they multiplied. Teddy bears and rainbows crawled out from the cracks and smothered me with their affection.

This is a great mystery of the universe—what you focus on is what you get in your life. The world is an enigma, constantly shifting, morphing and to ride this wave successfully, it's necessary for us to look for the healthy aspects of life, lest we get caught in a tailspin of doubt. To look for problems is to invite them, and while it may seem a daunting challenge in times of great upheaval, it remains a fundamental aspect of an entangled reality.

"How do you do it?"

"Do what?"

"Turn into a cartoon."

Professor Ping Pong laughed. "Is that how you see it? A cartoon?" He carried a tea pot and two mugs from the kitchen, sat down and leaned back into his chair. "I've never heard that one before, but then again, most people don't see it."

"See what? Why do I see it? What is it?"

He held out his hands, palms facing upwards, as if he was balancing something. "Eastern or Western?"

"I beg your pardon?"

"Eastern or Western. They say the same thing in different languages so I ask if you want to hear the language of eastern mysticism or western science. We live in a world that has come full circle. Ouroborus, the snake eating its own tail. It's not reached the consciousness of the general public, but it's on the way, and when it does, it will change everything. As Terrence McKenna said, 'it will be the end of history.'"

"Eastern...no, wait, Western."

"That's a smart choice. In our culture, science is the bedrock for all thinking, and it will be much easier for you to digest, at least intellectually. Putting the belief into practice, well, that's something different."

"What belief?"

"So, quickly, we live in a materialistic world, and I'm talking about the very basis for thinking. In our current scientific model, as it's manifested in the world around us, consciousness is merely a byproduct of the molecular interaction in our brains. An accident. The world is materialistic, meaning its fundamental essence is a solid, material thing. We live in a world of machines, and science has taken the task of knowing about our world by dissecting the wholes into the parts, into looking at the little bits. We've done that with physics, geology, chemistry, biology, everything. The vast majority of modern science is built upon the notion that everything is a machine, and that we can know all about it through careful dissection. And in the support of science, we can know many, many things through this way of thinking, and human civilization has benefited greatly by the pursuit of knowledge through that particular scientific lens, but it is ultimately flawed."

"How's that?"

"Because the whole is greater than the value of its parts. An automobile engine disassembled for inspection on the ground is not the same thing as the entire unit even though they are in essence the same physical things. The assembled engine has something the pile of parts lacks."

"Yeah, that seems obvious enough."

"Just when it seemed like we were going to figure it all out through materialistic, or Newtonian science, exploration into the quantum world began. As we looked deeper and deeper into the atom, it became evident that the microscopic world didn't behave like we thought it would, or like it should according to our materialistic models of the world. The quantum world did not follow Newtonian rules. One of the most important realizations that arose was this: the observer affected what he observes. I'm not only talking about live animals or people cognizant they are being watched. I'm talking about everything. This table," he knocked on it, then poured tea from the pot into the mugs, "this tea. Everything is entangled with the consciousness that's observing it. And observing it has an effect on it. Now, how far that effect goes is uncertain, but it's agreed as true—observation affects change. Scientists saw that light could be either a wave or a particle, depending on how they constructed their experiment."

He paused, and although my left brain assured me it was impossible, my soul encouraged me to believe. Such a belief allowed a wider range of possibilities.

"You see, Ten, everything exists in a state of potential. Everything. It's all a big cloud of infinite possibilities, and it's only the observer and his expectations or beliefs that collapse the infinite into one thing. Sure, it happens at a subatomic level, and there are experiments that suggest this even happens on an atomic level, but it doesn't really matter if the effect progresses farther than the subatomic. If the building blocks of our world, the quantum, are in a state of flux, what does it mean for the reality that is constructed from them?"

He paused for a moment, then sipped his tea and place the cup into the saucer with a soft clink. "Does it make a difference in the finished product if you build a house made out of ice or straw-bales or wooden logs or bricks or cement?"

"Yeah, I mean, they're all going to result in a house, but very different houses. But what does that have to do with clowning?"

Manifesting the Monkey 211

"That's what you see as the cartoon. In clowning, we temporarily forfeit our beliefs about the world and gain access to this wave of possibilities, and it does things to us, it changes us in a way that is both terrifying and unbelievably rewarding. It grants access to that space of potential. That's what the clown reminds us of, that we are movements, that we are all processes, and that we are all blessed with infinite potential. It's only a matter of expressing that potential in useful ways."

He leaned back and played with the tuft of hair under his mouth. After he saw the lights click on in my head, he folded his hands into his lap. "Do you see now?"

"Yeah, I get it. I mean, I have no idea what it means, but I get it."

<u>30</u>

Be the change you want to see in the world.
Mahatma Gandhi

Jason's neutralization was simple. I only paid him the most cursory attention, and his effect in the world slowly diminished. I crossed that objective off my list, but I still had to find the 100th monkey before I could reconnect with Aurore. As the silver cord grew bigger, I felt tiny tugs pulling me towards my wife.

It terrified me so much I had to laugh. I hadn't allowed myself to process 'excitement' as 'fear' for so long, and now, something so benign frightened me like a little kid with just his eyes peeking out from below his blanket.

How can a flimsy piece of rubber scare us so much?

It was simple, small and round, like a red squash ball that had been cut open. An elastic string was attached to either side of the round mask, and my first clown nose fit nicely over my head. I took a deep breath, laughed, and slipped it onto my own sizable hood ornament.

Flush.

The change was instant and deep. A weight slipped off my back, and crashed onto the floor behind me with a bang. My clown jumped. He looked at the collected pounds I had carried for years, laying in disarray, as if someone had ransacked my life. Pleased, the clown smiled and dusted the grime from his hands and set about investigating the world in which he had landed, starting with himself. Adjusting the antique full-length mirror in front of him, the clown looked himself over. His ultra-cool silver hip-hop shoes clashed nicely with his orange and black striped socks that almost matched his too-short purple slacks that didn't go at all with his blue and white striped mime shirt. He let out a low whistle and smiled in admiration at the handsome fellow reflected before him. After a few poses, and flexing of muscles, the clown inspected the room. It was gloomy and dismal, with spider webs monopolizing every corner. Boxes and trash bags filled with old clothes and knick-knacks cluttered the floor around him. The clown began to feel uncomfortable in the room, and his face melted into a look of profound panic. He pulled his arms closer to his body and twiddled his thumbs, trying to distract himself. His face continued sagging into an expression of utter hopelessness. The clown wasn't sure why, but the space made him feel bad, as if he couldn't breath. He looked at the only source of light—a broad, half-circle window—and felt a glimmer of hope shine into his soul. The floor was wooden and made spooky creaking noises as he walked towards it. With the force of the sun on him, the clown relaxed and regained his confidence. His posture opened up, his grimace turned into a bright smile, and suddenly, it seemed as if everything would be fine, maybe even better than fine, quite possibly spectacular. Right now, he was okay, and right now was all that mattered. Curious, he looked out the window onto the street below.

It took a lot, but I managed to burst into the clown's mind for a moment and remind him that we were on a mission. We had things to do. He assured me that he had it all under control (God help us), and pushed me back down into the dark. He straightened himself, adjusted his clothes till they were sufficiently crooked and marched down the stairs and out into the world to spread love and light.

Clowns.

These are but one of the agents of change in the new paradigm, only one kind of mirror that reflects an authentic essence of humanity. These humble creatures of love and tranquility are beacons of light in a darkening world. They work to bring their change to the world, to add their nonsense to the chaos, always sure that everything is going according to plan, especially when all evidence points to the contrary.

As humanity hurtled to its meeting with fate, it was my duty to allow the clown out.

"It's really great what you do."

I was sitting on the sidewalk, my eyes closed, enjoying the warmth of the sun on my face. I had just finished clowning, and it was very easy to be present. I looked up. I had seen her before, but we had never spoken. She owned a window-washing business, and if the name written on the side of her

Manifesting the Monkey

van was correct, she was called Cathy.

"Thank you very much," I said, "but it's not really me who does it."

She smiled big and tossed her hair back with a quick flick of her head. Judging by the gray streaks in her mullet, Cathy was nearing fifty, but she looked at me with the eyes of a curious child, constantly darting from one spot to another, trying to put the pieces together and solve the great mysteries of life. "What do you mean it wasn't you? Do you mean it was another you, like a trans-dimensional shift or something? Like you opened a doorway and you went in and someone else came out? Or are you possessed?" She stared down at me, her mouth open in anticipation. Clowning was beginning to affect my 'normal' life. I received her questions and waited until I was ready to respond. I stood up and leaned on the wall, exhausted from the clowning. It hadn't been long, but it had taken a lot of energy. Clowning was difficult enough, but going at it alone on the street in a hostile environment was a serious drain. As open-minded as Lecoeur was, the heavy undercurrent of paranoia took its toll on me and, presumably, everyone else.

"Well, it's not exactly that, but I guess that's as good a metaphor as any."

Cathy wasn't satisfied, and she stepped closer to me, her face scrunched as she tried to get her idea out. "Well, what is it then? I mean you said it wasn't you, then who was it? What was it? It was beautiful. I mean, man, it was great! Just perfect, I hadn't felt that since I was a kid. Hell, it was like I was a kid again! And I didn't do anything. Where did you come up with this stuff?"

I held up my hand and laughed. "Whoa, whoa, one thing at a time. When I said it wasn't me, I was telling the truth, and I was lying. It's not the me that's talking to you now." I held up the red nose dangling from my neck, "I don't know...when I put this on, something happens. I go away, and the clown comes out."

Cathy's tossed her mullet again. "I don't get it. I mean, I've seen a little clowning at the professor's place, but he doesn't come out on the street like this. Nobody does, and I still don't get it."

I thought for a moment. "Okay, okay," I said, excited by this challenge, a real opportunity to communicate with someone patient enough to listen and brave enough to admit ignorance. I stood up straight and prepared to deliver what I hoped would be a great shock which would get my point across. "It's really common, nearly universal, for the ego, for the 'I' to mistake itself for the whole mind."

Her face contorted again as she processed what I said. It was true—to some degree, we were all ego maniacs, mostly oblivious to the other facets of personality dwelling inside of us. We believed the captain to be manning the entire ship all by himself.

"Okaaay, okaaay, I follow you," she laughed and hitched up her pants. "So what you're saying is the 'I' is not the whole of me, even though most times I think it is?"

"Exactly."

She put her hand to her chin. "So what you're saying is that when you put on that red nose, you're allowing other parts of yourself to come out and animate your body."

I bowed, and spoke in an elegant English accent. "You have solved the mystery, my dear. That is exactly what is happening."

She slapped me on the back, guffawing. "Wow, that's so cool. So cool. I mean, if a clown can come out of there, what else can come out? I mean, there could be so much in there, so many people, so many different ways of being."

"I know, kinda intimidating, isn't it?"

Cathy stood very still, smiling, but serious. "It sure is, my friend, but really, it sounds like a good way to go crazy."

I laughed. "Let's hope not, Cathy."

We relaxed into a comfortable silence for a moment.

"So what do you do?" I asked.

Her eyes grew wider, and she spoke in a soft, reverential tone. "I wash windows. I've got my own business, and it's doing great." Her eyes filled with gratitude for a life she perceived as blessed. Therefore, it was blessed.

"That's excellent."

"But that's not all," she shook her head as if she were saying this for the first time as well, "I also fix bikes."

"That's great." I felt the clown pushing up out of the depths, but I restrained him. The more often I let him out, the more he demanded to be let out, like some ungrateful cat who learned the freedom of the street and would never forget them.

"Yeah, that's my real passion. Saving the planet. I know it's not that big of a deal, but getting people to ride bikes is important."

"Of course it's a big deal."

"But that's not all. I've got a new idea. Let me show you." We walked around the corner and stacked neatly together was a dryer, microwave, and television.

She put one hand on the dryer and leaned into it, proud of her possessions.

"These are yours?"

"Yeah, but not for much longer. You know, the way I see things is like this. We live in this great big comfortable society, right?" Her voice filled with the emotion of a twelve-year-old girl, sure she had found some precious key that could help so many.

"Right, the most comfortable culture on the face of the planet."

"Exactly, and also the most wasteful. I mean, it's crazy how much waste America produces. And when you say that, people get all defensive and come up with reasons why it's okay that we selfishly control the majority of wealth on this planet while people die from starvation every day. People get defensive because they feel guilty, and they don't want to be blamed, and I'm not blaming them. I know that we didn't decide this life. We were just born into it. I mean, it's not okay, but it's not our fault."

She moved closer to me, and whispered, "And when I get into these debates, and I get into a lot of 'em, let me tell you." It was then that I became charmed with Cathy's authenticity, moving through her life unconcerned with other people's opinions. She continued, "After I tell this to people, they often accuse me of not doing anything about it. I tell them that I fix bicycles so that people will use their cars less. I tell them that I don't watch TV so that I can think for myself, but they always shrug that away as if it isn't important. So this is what I'm doing!"

She patted her pile of consumer appliances.

"What exactly...are you doing?"

She whispered to me. "I'm boycotting, man, I'm boycotting. I'm going to stay out here and boycott, and if I'm lucky, if God is with me, then maybe someone else will come over here and join me. And then maybe two more, then four more. I don't know. That's all I can do. The only way to really change the system, to enact the changes we need now, is to stop participating as much as we can. I don't mean that we all have to move out of our houses and go live in the trees. It doesn't have to be that drastic, but we can boycott a lot without

Manifesting the Monkey

217

sacrificing too much. We really don't need most of the shit we have. So we stop using it, we reconnect to our food source, and there you go," she snapped her fingers, "we'll live in a new world."

31

I remain just one thing, and one thing only,
and that is a clown.
It places me on a far higher plane than any politician.
-Charlie Chaplin

All absolutes are subject to exceptions.

Clowns never try to be funny. The humor of the clown emerges in the form of his honesty. Everything funny is true. If it's not true, and appears to be funny, a deeper examination will reveal that it is either true or, in fact, not funny. It's a clown's job to walk, sing, dance, grumble, or complain through the world with an open heart, shining on the world, and it is this vulnerability that attracts an audience to the clown's spectacle. It's this unconditional loving that manifests itself into laughs. The Universe is a funny place, and laughter is its best prayer.

I wasn't always alone. Other clowns came out, and we played on the street corner by the Irish pub, a block down from Cathy and her things. Having someone to reflect off of made those days easier. Our clowns found something, a facet of an authentic feeling glinting in the sunlight and went towards that, following the thread to see and to share that vision with others. Sometimes it didn't work. Sometimes the glint of light that they saw was nothing, or sometimes it was ugly and grimy, and no one wanted to look at it. But regardless of what the clown saw, his audience usually laughed because life was funny. Anytime his only intention was to 'be funny', the clown immediately lost his capacity to crack reality.

The car alarm went off again. It came from a dusty black BMW, and it had been going off all day, even before I started. I considered moving to another spot, but I refused. I was a territorial animal and had spent the better part of two weeks 'pissing' on that corner with my red nose. Unless the perpetrators were invisible, no one was trying to steal the car. The alarm went off sporadically because machines break down. Like all things, they will die one day, and this alarm system must have been on its deathbed. It usually only lasted a few seconds, but it pulled all surrounding attention to it immediately.

Isn't that the idea?

But we had reached a point of saturation where most people immediately assume that the screaming car alarm must be malfunctioning. In all my years hearing them, I had never seen anyone dash out of their home to chase off potential thieves. We had been sensitized by the constant calling 'wolf.'

How quickly I had changed.

To be fair, we didn't change very quickly. Unless you only count the moment of transition as change. Looking back, you can see that we've been preparing for this change for years, since before you left, back when you were still with April.

But it felt like it happened so suddenly, like it all fell into place overnight.

It both has and has not. It all depends on your perspective, depends on whether you consider the fire to be only the flame, or the coals and heat that make that flame possible.

"Hey Ten!" Jack jogged down the alleyway, his plump belly swaying with his strides. Jack had just celebrated his fiftieth birthday and had only recently begun his journey into clowning. After twenty-eight years of marriage, his wife kicked him out of the house and told him to find Professor Ping-Pong. He was not welcome back until he learned the ancient art of the absurd. Apparently, his wife was fed up with his extreme seriousness and would take no more of it.

"Hey Jack, how's it going?"

"Pretty good." He stared at me. "Is it just me, or are you getting younger?"

I smiled, relived that the youthful energy I felt could be seen as well. "It's just a trick of the light, I'm sure." I said, noticing his outfit—a pink polo, green and purple plaid shorts. "Hey Jack, it's not really a good idea to dress up in clown before we're ready to put on the nose and really go for it."

He stopped in front of me and inspected himself. "I'm not. These are my everyday clothes."

Is he serious?

"Oh...really?"

"Yeah, really, I've got my 'sewing' stuff in here." He held up the maroon duffel bag. There weren't very many rules in the world of clowning.

Don't hurt yourself, don't hurt others, and don't break anything.

When we were in front of an audience there were only two additional guidelines. The first, was to never touch or mention the nose. The second, to abstain from referencing clowns or clowning. We had been trained to deflect any direct inquiries with code words, and Jack had chosen 'tailors' and 'sewing' as his cover for clowns and clowning. He winked at me as he said it and smiled. I caught a glimpse into his life, saw the Robert Ludlum novels stacked on his nightstand. He was American and, like most of us, had grown up believing in a military system, relishing in the intrigue and subterfuge of international conspiracies. They made such great movies. His clown often played Mission: Impossible or James Bond or some other secret agent.

"So what's the score," he whispered to me.

I sat down on a concrete bench and played along. "Well Jack," I looked both ways, searching for the commandos waiting to infiltrate our organization, "we're going to get up real slowly, then we're going to walk around the back of those bushes there," I gave a slight motion with my head, "no, don't look yet...we're going to get changed, put the noses on and let the clowns out to play. And God help anyone who gets in our way."

He nodded in solemn agreement. "Understood. What's the game-plan?"

"I thought I just laid it out for you?"

"No, you didn't. You just laid out the score. I want to know the game-plan." He moved closer to me and whispered, "what impro?"

"Ah, of course, of course. Thanks for that. I thought we would do Object/Admirer."

His face scrunched. "You think so? I don't really like that one."

"Okay, no worries. How about Expert/Assistant?"

He nodded. "Perfect."

We walked around the bushes and put on our costumes. I rolled up my purple pants, pulled tight my knee-high red and black stripped socks, and slid a pair of rubber galoshes over them so only the tops peaked out. Then, I put on a green surgeon's smock and yellow hard-hat. Jack stripped to his underwear and dressed himself in high-heels, jogging pants that were too small, a red polka-dotted vest, and a magician's hat.

We stood looking at each other, noses dangling ready around our necks. I didn't know what to expect, didn't know what to do next, and this was the part I hated most, just before we began. My ego was flexible. I had trained it through so many flushes, so many unexpected experiences that I was good at letting go, but that didn't stop the fight-or-flight response rise up from my gut. As soon as I put on the nose, my clown would emerge, and there was no telling what would happen. It was an extreme change, and it scared me every time I did it. I guess that's why I did it. I knew that it was true, that some part of it was real because it demanded so much. It was an exercise in faith, to put on the nose and go with the flow, to ignore my own bashful tendencies and preconceived notions.

"Who do you want to be?" I asked.

"Uh....I'll be the assistant," and Jack vanished behind the rubber nose.

"Got it."

I put my nose on, and a shiver moved my body up and down until I was shaking to some silent music in my soul. When it had calmed, we turned, and walked towards the corner. It was a bright Saturday afternoon, and there were plenty of people strolling the streets.

The impro was simple. My clown would be an expert from somewhere, and he was to express his passion, which would remain unknown to everyone, including me and my clown, until something happened, and the passion revealed itself naturally...if it revealed itself at all. As our clowns walked towards the corner, I had many ideas what he could be passionate about, but I tossed them away. They would be no good to him. He had to wait until it presented itself, and trust that it would. That was the line that the clown walked, the present moment. Jack would follow my clown as his adoring assistant. It seemed like nothing, but with that role already created, the clowns had a strong structure upon which to create themselves.

They stood at the mouth of the alley for a moment, just on the edge of their stage. My clown fixed himself with self importance, folded his hands behind his back and clunked out into the open.

As usual, the first response of the people walking by was surprise and shock. It's not everyday that a strangely dressed creature from another world pays a visit, although it was becoming more and more common in that small town. My clown smelled a burst of fear from the couple walking by. He kept

Manifesting the Monkey

his distance and smiled at them, which worked well in dispelling their discomfort. It only took a minute before there was a small group gathered around the clowns. My clown marched the perimeter of the stage, and they all backed away, respecting the invisible border.

The smell of fear thickened around them, and my clown had to suppress the urge to wretch. Fear increased exponentially in crowds.

My clown looked over the audience, further inflated by their perceived adoration.

"Hello, hello!," he bellowed. "Thank you all for coming." My clown closed his eyes in sanctimonious pride.

"We're very glad to see you," Jack's clown assured them. "And you're in for a very special treat." He looked at my clown with shameless admiration. "You're all very lucky to have this honor, to hear the great and wonderful...Doctor...Nasam...Buttermilk...enstein."

The naming of my clown provided a new structure, another piece of the puzzle. Suddenly, he had a name, an identity. His chest puffed.

"You're too kind, too kind...Bob," his name slipped out of the mouth before I could interfere. The crowd chuckled. The pressure in the impromptu stage increased along with our chances of cracking reality.

Doctor Nasam Buttermilkenstein and his assistant, Bob.

The clown, connected to imagination, saw the history as it formed. I leaned over his shoulder and watched Bob and the doctor traveling the world in an old wooden stage coach, helping others, spreading their message, but what was it? That part of the story was still blank, but Doctor B could feel it coming. He could almost touch it, but not yet. It wasn't right. The crack wasn't ready. First the clowns had to trust.

The Doctor's face turned grim and serious. "Bob's right, you know. You are all very lucky to be here. I've spent my life investigating this particular subject. Even at a young age, I had intuitions that something must be done." Doctor B stopped pacing and looked the audience in the eyes, the drama of his driven life seeping out of him.

Bob took over. "Something must be done." He stepped forward, and my clown felt the attention of the audience focus on his assistant. The crowd had doubled. "Something absolutely must be done. I remember when I first heard about it. The good Doctor saved my life. And for that, I am eternally grateful. He's such a good, great man. He's so smart and brave, so strong, and so...handsome." Bob batted his eyes and inched his way closer, until he was shoulder-to-shoulder with Doctor B. And then Bob began to rub his body against the doctor, who froze, his eyes full of embarrassed discomfort. He leaned over to Bob and pretended to whisper. "Now, now, dear assistant. Remember what I told you? We may be in California, but I don't play for that team."

The crowd laughed.

Bob blushed and moved away. The pressure was mounting. The crack was almost ready. My clown could feel it. Memories of childhood had begun to swirl in the minds of the people watching. With nothing to do, something had to happen. A pressure to give up, to break through and push my clown aside welled up in me. I wanted to look everyone in the eye, apologize for my incompetence, and admit that I had no idea what I was doing, that it was all so very stupid.

Instead, I took a deep breath and trusted. I followed the thread, just like Professor Ping-Pong had taught us. "Bob's not the only one, you see. I have spent the last six years traveling the world, telling everyone about this mind-blowing realization." He stopped his pacing and looked at the audience. "You know...saving lives. This is the real deal, a huge key that can unlock the Secrets of the Universe." My clown stretched his arms out wide, stood on his tip-toes and his face stretched out to contain it all. "It's the next step towards the total comprehension of the meaning of life. It's the one thing that can save us all from the horrors of old-age and its continual degradation." The pressure was full, Doctor B and Bob had built it up strong, and they still had no idea what they were talking about, but the crack was ready.

Now or never.

So my clown just started speaking, trusting that something honest, something human would flow out. "I've traveled across three continents to deliver my message."

What message?

"I've spoken with thousands, tens of thousands and passed on this secret."

What secret?

My clown stopped in the center, feeling the pressure, the hopes of the audience that he would succeed.

"I have come...to tell you...about...," the faulty car alarm interrupted my clown. It stopped a moment later. "...about the inherent dangers of neglecting the maintenance of your car." The raucous laughter of the small audience drowned out the thunderclap that accompanied the crack.

I breathed deeply and reveled in that space, feeling the rush of energy from the Otherworld as it passed through me out into the hearts of those watching. I sniffed, but the fear had vanished. It had all been transmuted by their laughter into the sweet fragrance of love.

32

Let go of the past and go for the future.
Go confidently in the direction of your dreams.
Live the life you imagined.
-Henry David Thoreau

Everywhere I went, Cathy was boycotting. She was in the park, meandering among the people, handing them fliers and laughing gently at their disbelief. Most were pleasant and curious, but skeptical. What could a boycott really accomplish? And why would they want to make the effort? People who were honest with themselves saw consumerism's insatiable appetite, the corporate psychosis, its detrimental effect on the planet, and the suffocation of the human spirit. But they didn't see their own participation in it. Not using a dryer or the microwave was manageable, but when Cathy explained to them how the television was the biggest tool of mass mind-control, they lost interest. No one wanted to believe they had been conned.

She was at the farmer's market, wide-eyed and enthusiastic about her project, buying organic vegetables and convincing local farmers of Lecoeur's need to be the first town to boycott, to lead California, and then the nation into a new era. They listened to her with kind eyes and took the bright orange squares of paper she handed them.

"It's the only choice we really have," and she'd wait patiently for the information to sink it. "Sure, we could revolt, but that wouldn't work well or for very long. The government would come in with their tanks and their guns and oppress us. I mean, the government works for the corporations, not for us. How many times have we seen this?" And she would smile at the nods and the 'uh-huhs' as they remembered all the broken promises. "I mean what about the oil. Every president since Carter has insisted that we wean ourselves off of foreign oil, but, really, we've only become more dependent on it." A lot of people could never admit that they agreed with Cathy because, in doing so, they would have to re-evaluate their belief system, and that terrified most.

"It's obvious to hard-working Americans that we have become trapped by giant corporations and their interests." I heard her say one evening in the Irish pub, with an interested crowd around her. "Everyone notices it at some point in their lives, but most have made the hard choice to forget it because there's not much any one person can do. But Martin Luther King, Jr. and Gandhi have taught the world that a peaceful assembly of many has real power." She mindlessly twirled a finger through the party-end of her mullet. "I mean, we're up against a whole system, massive institutions of incredible power and influence, broad-reaching manipulations. Structures that began as our servants, but somewhere in the mists of history, they have become self-aware. They're not going to give up control just because we ask for it. Civilization has turned into a monstrous machine that's gonna plod along, making mountains of money." She took a sip from her pint glass. "Our society is gonna keep going until it kills itself and us along with it. I think it's obvious to most people that corporations, are, generally, psychotic with obsessive one-track minds—money. The Bible doesn't say, 'money is the root of all evil,' it says 'the *love* of money is the root of all evil.' And I think we can say most corporations love money, and they're the ones in control, not you and not me. They're steering the ship. 'For the people, by the people,' has transformed into 'for the Corporations, by the Corporations'."

Someone near the back spoke up. "Not all corporations are bad. I'm the CEO of a small corporation. Are you saying I'm part of the problem?"

Cathy took a moment to organize her thoughts. "Well, Jeremy, I guess that depends on what kind of businessman you are. You moved here about five years ago, and I can honestly say that I've never seen you do anything that would make me think you're part of the problem. No more than I am, or we all are. When I say that corporations are bad, I don't mean all of them. That's why I said 'generally.' There are some corporations that practice business in an ethical manner, and even manage to do good for the community. Does that make sense?"

"Yeah...it does, but I'm not convinced, Cathy. It's easy for you to stand there and say these things, but for me," he looked at the people around him, "for us, it contradicts the life that we've spent our whole lives believing in. And that's not easy."

"I know, I know, that's what makes it so difficult. What I'm saying is contrary to popular belief. And you don't have to believe me, Jeremy. All I ask is that you listen, and you make your own decision, okay? That's all I'm asking of everyone here."

She took another sip of beer. "You know, I said that there are some corporations who do good in the world, but I really think they are the minority, or, at least, the ones who do a whole lot of bad are so influential, so vast as to blot out the effects of those that are conducting business in an ethical manner. And, yeah, I'm talking about polluting the environment as they see fit, getting away with as much as they can instead of finding a healthier way of doing things, but that's not all I'm talking about. Sometimes, it's a lot more subtle, you know, minimizing the masses into increasingly isolated boxes."

She took a deep breath. "It's the way they've snuck into our mind, and convinced us all that we need this shit. They use proven strategies to change the way we think about the world. That's the real problem, that they convince us we need to have a thousand different kinds of toothpaste to choose from or a hundred and one different scents of deodorants. I mean, why do we even need to use deodorants? Oh yeah, I forgot—because the industrialized food we eat is total garbage and makes us smell like shit. It's not natural to use that crap. It's not natural to have teeth that glow in the dark. It's not natural to buy food wrapped in plastic, but some greedy nit-wits have convinced us that it is." It wasn't one particular person Cathy was talking about, but the unidentifiable power that had gotten us all into this mess.

Someone spoke up. "You know what, Cathy, I hear what you're saying, but it sounds like...like bullshit to me."

Cathy stood straighter and smiled, like a cartoon cat about to catch a mouse. "I know, I know, it's the exact opposite of what we're programmed to believe."

"I'm not programmed!" A woman yelled from the back.

"Well, Deborah, I hate to break it to you, but you are. We all are, and that's okay. It's just a natural part of life. Everybody's programmed. It's how the human brain operates, and that's a fact. You can call it 'socialized' if that makes you feel better, but it amounts to the same thing."

"But you said choices are bad. I like having a lot of choices."

"And I like wearing deodorant!" Another woman said.

"Okay, okay. I hear you. I agree that the right amount of options is a healthy thing. It makes us free, but too many and we're liable to fall under the tyranny of choice."

"The tyranny of choice?"

"Yeah, and I'm sure we've all experienced it as well. Can you remember a time when you went to the grocery store or the mega-mall or any shop that has a lot of products? You stand in front of the toothpaste or the deodorants or the toilet-paper or the shaving cream or the tennis shoes or the blue jeans or the picante sauce. And you're overwhelmed. There are so many different kinds that you can't make an informed choice because if it's informed then you've got to examine them all. And we don't have time for that. Can you imagine really investigating the entire range of options for everything you buy? It would take forever. We'd have to outsource it to India." She smiled, and her joke helped ease the tension. "So there you are standing in the aisle, paralyzed." Cathy's face stretched into an exaggerated expression of utter confusion. "Do I take the one with extra-fluoride or extra-whitening power? Cool Mint scent or Jasmine Blossoms or Cinnamon Sticks or Forest Dew or Midnight Ocean or Spring Breeze or Sexy Spice or Manly-Man?" The choices were too much for Cathy, and she pretended to enter a psychotic fit. The crowd laughed.

"And do you know which product wins that little competition in your head? Do you know how you make that final choice, if you don't just choose the one that you always buy?" She paused. "You choose the one that was most successfully advertised to you. So the corporation who has the loudest or the biggest or the most devious message—whatever it takes to make it stick in your brain—will be the one you buy. Because after you give up trying to make a conscious decision, you're just gonna pick one. You'll come up with a good reason why you pick Uncle Earl's baked beans over Aunt Maggie's, but it's not true. Maybe you'll think it's random, but nothing a human being ever does is random. It's all driven by the unconscious mind so we make the choice based on the most effective advertising jingle that's lodged somewhere in the back of our psyches." She paused to let the crowd swallow what she had just said.

"And what gets me the most is that none of it's necessary. Seriously, if we returned to a more natural diet, if we ate healthy, we wouldn't need to wear deodorant or bleach our teeth. Yeah, I am for a little hygienic responsibility, but we wouldn't need most of what's sold to us if we, as a culture, made health a first priority. If you ate a really natural diet for a few months, you wouldn't get all stinky from walking around the block. But the stuff we eat has got chemicals in it, or it's been so processed as to be devoid of any real nutritional value, and we eat way too much meat. A little will go a long ways, but three times a day is...is...obscene. And dairy, no way. How can it be a good idea to drink milk everyday? We're not infants any more. What animal, living in the wild, drinks milk all it's life? There isn't one!"

"Well, that's your problem there, little lady. You're comparing us with animals!" An angry man shouted. "We're not animals, we're God's children, and we can do as we please."

"Sure, Henry, we're God's children, and you can do as you please. I never said that you couldn't. It just may not be a good idea, is all. We can go around doing whatever we want like spoiled children, but all I'm saying is that maybe there's a more mature way. What I'm talking about is taking responsibility for ourselves."

"You're talking hog-wash. I take responsibility. We all do." Henry responded. A few nodding heads murmured their assent.

"Well, Henry, I never wanted to single anyone out, but since you stepped up to the plate." She moved forward and took another deep breath. "I've heard you moan and complain about your bowels, about a constant constipation for years. You bitch about it damn near every day to anyone who'll listen." The crowd laughed. Even in the short time I had been in Lecoeur, Henry had told me a few times of his infrequent visits to the toilet. "But you go on heaping your coffee with sugar and milk, you eat your ice-cream, and your sweets. You go on doing the same things over and over without changing anything. I'm sorry, Henry, but that's not taking responsibility."

Henry, now red-faced and looking as if he'd pop either from embarrassment or anger said, "that ain't got nothing to do with it. I've got a sensitive digestive system is all."

"You don't think what you eat is related to how well your digestive system works?"

Henry didn't react, and Cathy let the question hang in the air. The answer was self-evident.

"I mean is it really so hard to believe that a lot of us drink milk because we've been bombarded by messages from the dairy industry? Milk, it does a body good!" Almost everyone laughed. "But is it true? Does milk do a body good? I don't think the answer is that obvious. I think the information we get about milk doing a body good is biased. But I don't really know."

Manifesting the Monkey

She dropped her voice into a concerned whisper, as Henry and a few others walked away, unable to listen anymore. "I mean, we live in a world that's totally cut off from the cycle of nature." Her audience leaned forward, hooked on the emotion at the heart of her words. "It's not the world I want to live in. I mean, when I was a kid...I never imagined life to be like this. I never wanted to grow up and be a wage-slave or to be tyrannized by choice in the supermarket. I never wanted to be hypnotized into a couch potato or turned into a thoughtless consumer. I mean, when I was a kid, I just wanted to live a good life, to explore the world and its marvels. To be happy, you know, to have fun, to solve the mystery of life. Isn't that what we all wanted?" The heads nodded vigorously, and the 'uh-huhs' were laden with the nostalgia of their own forgotten dreams.

She's right. What child dreams of working forty-hour weeks, making someone else rich, or the commercialization of every conceivable facet of human life? Children dream of bigger things, of a life filled with zest and excitement, not the watered-down version we're convinced is the right way. Even you may remember how you once believed a better world was possible.

"Then we grow up, and we start to learn things about the world, things that shocked us in our youth, things that today are just...normal. We give up those dreams...we say things like, 'well, that's just the way it is. I can't change the world.'" She paused again. "But you know what, we can change the world. And it all starts with everyone of us, every individual standing right here, listening to my words. All you've got to do is ask yourself, 'what can I change,' and you go on asking yourself that question, making little changes. Yeah, at first, it may be hard, but it'll be worth it, and one day, it'll all add up to something real, something we all dreamed about once upon a time."

When Cathy finished her talk, she laughed and went to the bar to order another pint.

Most often, she was on Main Street with her boycott. The dryer, TV, and microwave were soon followed by her hair-dryer, curling iron, waffle-maker, espresso machine, electric pencil sharpener, vacuum cleaner, and other items she deemed no longer necessary. She arrived in the morning, unloaded her stuff out of the van, spent the day boycotting, and then loaded her things up in the evening. I asked her one time why she bothered to move them everyday. Why didn't she just get rid of them and be done with it?

"That's a great question, Ten." Her blue eyes smiled at me. Every time I spoke with Cathy, I had the feeling that I was in the presence of a well-mannered seven-year-old. It wasn't a question of immaturity, but a quality of innocence. She was a glowing soul, and I often wondered how she managed to arrive at the age of fifty-three with such a radiance. "I thought about doing it like that, just letting the stuff sit there on the sidewalk until it was gone, and then I'd be done. But, you know what, I bet the cops would complain. I bet they'd come and find me and give me a ticket or even put me in jail. They already complain about me having my stuff here, but you know what, I'm not doing anything wrong. It's my right to boycott. Freedom of speech and all that. But the real reason, Ten, the real reason that I don't just let this stuff go is precisely that—because I'd be done. And if I'm done, then I can't boycott anymore. And if I don't boycott anymore, who else is gonna carry the torch?" She smiled at me.

I shook my head in awe. "You really are something special, Cathy."

She blushed. "You're such a sweetheart." She pulled me in and gave me one of her well-known bear hugs, then she stepped back and looked at me. "Are you on a special diet? You sure do look younger than the first time I met you."

It became her thing. She lived the boycott with a passion that most people would never feel. They were buried under the things that Cathy was getting rid of. But passion, like fear, was contagious.

Mary was the first person to join her, and it was an obvious choice for a disciple—she was Cathy's best friend. They rode their bikes, drank beer, and played bingo together. Mary was nearly sixty and plump. She brought her small television and set it timidly atop Cathy's, who smiled proudly and put her arm around Mary. "You're free now. We're doing it." She backed up for a high-five and nearly knocked the older woman down. And just like that, it happened. Mary was joined by her grandson, and then, he brought his girlfriend and their two friends. The high school principal caught wind of it and dollied his washer/dryer combo out to the street corner, saying how he always found it rewarding to wash his clothes by hand, even if it was a pain in the ass. He said that, next, he'd probably have to narrow his wardrobe to cut down on the washing, but it wasn't that big of a deal. It would just take a little while to get used to, and then in a couple of weeks, it would be normal for him. The math teacher came with her husband who worked at the dump. The rest of the dump guys soon followed, carting large televisions and a gas-powered weed eater.

I saw her at the post office one morning. "Hey Cathy, I've got this little riddle that I've been asking people."

She rubbed her hands together. "Oh, I love riddles. Let's hear it."

"Alright...how is your heart like a parachute?"

She thought about it for a moment and closed her eyes as she searched for the answer. When she found it, her face brightened into an expression of delight. "It won't work unless it's open!"

I stared at her. I was at ground zero, the focal point of the 100th monkey, and as soon as Cathy answered, the waves of change rippled out from her. "Whoa, did you feel that?" she asked. All I could do was nod. She smiled. "I don't know what that was, but it sure felt good, like suddenly, it just seems obvious that everything is going to be alright, you know?" I nodded again.

Cathy was the 100th monkey, and the activation of human love had happened. I felt it in my own soul as I finally let go of the remaining baggage I lugged around with me. With the snap of some cosmic fingers, I accepted the plausibility, no, the inevitability that the human race would realize their true identity as creatures of love. The background chatter of the post-office employees stopped, and in the silence, I could hear the sound of their hearts creaking open as they remembered their natural state of innocence.

33

Magic is believing in yourself,
if you can do that, you can make anything happen.
-Johann Wolfgang von Goethe

Cathy was the tipping point, and the process of awakening humanity now developed independent of any one person. We had won, and it was only a matter of time for the new paradigm to manifest into the physical. Nothing changed instantly. Remember? That's what I told you in the beginning. It wasn't like what we had seen on TV. There were no explosions, no computer-generated effects. Just the slow certainty of a fertile field. Once Cathy answered the riddle correctly, the healthy seeds of our future were sown in the minds of every human being in our society, and all we had to do was wait patiently for them to bear fruit. That was how it worked with manifesting. It was like we were always looking into the past, at the ideas we believed yesterday which created today. Wherever Cathy went, love sprouted and flourished, hastening the bloom of the new paradigm.

Jason was neutralized. Since I had dropped out of my war, I saw him less and less. When I did, I acknowledged him, sometimes I even waved, but my main focus was on what I wanted. And now that I had found the 100th monkey, all I wanted was to find Aurore and live happily every after.

You always get more of what you focus on.

I walked out of the gate and something in my heart tugged me to the right instead of left towards the center of town and my usual clowning corner. The gentle breeze that accompanied the intuition counseled me, once again, to take an unknown path.

I stopped a few times, turned around, and watched the street behind me. Although mid-autumn, it was a hot day, and the heat rising off the cement gave Lecoeur the shimmering effect of a mirage, as if any life I had there was just another of my dreams. It seemed like I was always waking up, dissolving from one truth to the next, where previous certainties became utterly false. I had the urge to go back, to assure myself that it was real, that I hadn't just fooled myself again, but every time I took the first step back towards the Ping-Pong Club, the wind blew against me until I turned around and continued on the path. For the first two hours, I was an unwilling participant in this game. The Universe wanted me to go somewhere, but I resisted. I still hated being told what to do, no matter who was doing the telling.

Just before the sun set, a sleek black car crested a hill and descended towards me. It caught my attention right away. Off Main Street, especially as far out of town as I was, dusty pick-up trucks and the occasional mini-van comprised all of the local traffic. The car drove by me, and, as usual, I waved, a common gesture in small towns. It made a U-turn and stopped next to me. The passenger window slid down, and a beautiful woman leaned over from the driver's seat. Her hair was long, blond, and dreaded. Feathers and shells dangled from their tips. Her arms were tattooed with birds, lady bugs, plants, and trees. She wore a green velvet vest and a top hat with an entire wing of some poor bird in it.

"Hello," she said in a giggly New Zealand accent. "I'm looking for a trance party, and I'm lost." She fumbled with a crumpled map. "It's supposed to be around here somewhere." She batted her eyes. My body reacted, but I was quick to move the sexual energy up along my spine, not to suppress, but to direct.

"I'm sorry. I'm not from around these parts."

"Oh shit." She gazed out the windshield.

"But I could have a look at that map, maybe I could help."

"Oh would you? That would be lovely. Get in."

I opened the door and entered her air-conditioned world. The electric blue light from the stereo made me feel as if I had been abducted by a very attractive alien. I sniffed and was happy to find the very strong smell of jasmine covering only a dash of fear. She handed me the yellow Post-it with scribbled directions and the deteriorating map. It took me a few minutes to find both our current position and the location of the party.

"There it is," I circled it in pencil, "and here we are, *mas o menos*."

"You found it? You're amazing!" She looked at me, and I felt her casting a spell on me. It wasn't anything malicious, just the normal game of attraction between the sexes.

"It's not that big of a deal."

"You saved me," she said, suggesting that there may be more intimate ways I could save her. "I'm Xena."

"Xena?"

"Yeah," she blushed, "you know, the warrior princess."

"Ahh...okay, of course. My name is Ten."

"Ten? Is that some kind of play on words?"

"It's just an old middle-school nickname that stuck. No big deal." I opened the door, relieved to disembark from the spaceship. "It was nice meeting you. I'm glad that I could help."

"Thanks so much. Hey...do you want to come with me to the party? I mean, I don't really know anyone there. Well, maybe one or two people, but it'd be really nice if you came with me." She smiled, and an old part of me knew what that smile meant.

"Uhh...you know, I'm not really into trance music, and—" the wind gusted against the car, pushing the door closed, "—but you know what, it's always nice to give new things a try, isn't it?"

"Really," she squealed like some adolescent on a sugar high. "That's awesome. I'll drive and you navigate, okay?"

"Alright."

"Perfect." She put the car into gear "So what are you doing here in Cali?" she asked.

"Uh, I'm here learning about communities and..."

"And?"

"And I'm looking for someone." Part of me was reluctant to admit it because it betrayed my trajectory. Most of me was happy to restrain myself from falling back into the seduction game, but the animal part of me wanted nothing more than to romp around, to mate. Of course, I was free to do what I wanted. I mean, Aurore left me. But the wind whispered in my ear, even there in the car, and convinced me to keep it in my pants and find my wife. Isn't that what made me human? The ability to resist the more primitive motivations?

"Oh, I see. A woman?"

"Yeah...a woman...the woman."

"Well, let's just leave it at that for a moment, see where the night takes us, shall we," and she turned up the music before I could answer.

"Take a right here," I shouted when we reached the T-junction. She turned and then swerved erratically.

"Oh my god," she turned the music off. "Do you see it?"

I looked to where she was pointing. A lone coyote sat watching us, its tongue hanging out of its mouth. Our eyes locked, and a chill ran up my spine as I remembered my imprisonment with Dawn.

Is that Maya?

An intelligence looked at me through those animal eyes, and I stared until we disappeared around the next bend.

"Whoa," Xena was nearly out of breath. "That was *amazing*. Did you see it, sitting there watching us? The coyote watching us. Wow, that's a powerful sign."

"How's that?"

"We're on our way to a party, and we've just seen a coyote. It's a message from the gods. Coyote is the symbol of music."

"I thought Coyote was the trickster."

"Well, he's that, too, but we'll just look at the bright side, don't you think?" She let out another squeal and turned up the music before I could answer.

We pulled onto a dirt road and entered the former scout camp. The full moon had risen high, and its silver light illuminated a magical world of bright trees and mysterious lakes. We could see far, and when I looked out over an open field, I saw something running towards us. "What's that?" I asked Xena.

She stopped the car and leaned over me to look out my window, putting her hand on my thigh for support. "Oh. My. God. I don't believe it. It's a fucking coyote." Her voice, although still excited, carried a deeper feeling as well. A quick sniff told me that she was afraid, but playing cool. Something wasn't quite right.

"What does that mean, now that we've seen two coyotes?"

She paused a moment before speaking. "It means we're going to have twice as good of a time." I didn't need my nose to tell me that she was hiding her fear. The thin mask she wore obscured nothing from the observant eye.

We reached the small party just as it was kicking off. The scene was typical of trance parties—neon glow paint, streaming strips of cloth hanging in the trees, and loud monotonous rhythms. Although I wasn't a big fan, I understood the allure of trance music. Its repetitive nature was designed to put the dancer into a trance. Since the beginning of human culture, rhythm and dance had been effective tools to enter the Otherworld.

Xena introduced me to the massive group of friends that she wasn't going to meet there. I knew that she had lied to me and well, I guess that's just how it went with some people. What else could I do about it, but accept? I couldn't force my own quest for integrity on anyone else. I said hello, then kept away from the group. Their fear smell was too strong, and even Xena's stink increased while she was around her friends. I sensed the love-seed growing inside them, but it was still incubating, and there'd be weeks or even months before it bore fruit. They were all fashionably dressed in the style of their group—leather and fur, some of its patchwork worthy of the homeless—looking cool, with that aloof, uncaring expression on their faces, as if nothing could faze them. Each one of the Feather Hats had escaped from the rat-race of modern society and seemed to believe that to the be the end of the journey instead of its beginning. Had they not realized that they had only begun to unravel the mystery? Their clothes, the designer perfumes, and the exotic love affairs were the new coping mechanisms for their fear. They had gone through life, like most, sure that something about our collective reality wasn't right. This certainty had led them to escape from mainstream culture, sure that the problem was FOX news or Republicans, and enter the world of the Feather Hats.

I passed the party on the dance floor, moving my body to the rhythms, slowly entering the Otherworld. After a few minutes, my senses opened past their normal tolerance. I felt the pressure as the energy needed to crack reality built up around me. I had to incorporate the altered vibrations of those around me. Most had taken something to cope with the oblivion of dance, but I stayed sober. My supernatural work assured me that to have real power, I had to abstain from such shortcuts. There were truly powerful substances, like the medicine of the Amazon or of the Mexican desert, but even those must be taken with respect, and always in a context of spiritual evolution.

I felt Xena breeze past me every so often, and she invited me over towards the fire with her group of friends, but I stayed away. Their fashionable comforts stunk of the boogeyman. I kept to my strategy—I noticed him, but stayed on the dance floor, where Jason had no place. The pounding feet broke him to pieces as I stomped my way to the Otherworld. If I was to make use of this spontaneous synchronicity to dance, I would have to stay alone.

Xena wanted to love me. She blushed and batted her eyes. She 'accidentally' bumped into me again and again, kept smiling apologies and invitations. Her attempts became more and more overt, and the resulting tension hastened the crack. She danced close, swaying up against me, nearly triggering my body past a point of no-return, when that part of my mind would click into 'fuck' mode, and everything else would fall by the wayside. But each time I neared this point, a gentle gust of wind blew me back on course, and I re-focused on my goal. I closed my eyes and evoked an image of Aurore, her infectious smile brightening the world. I concentrated on that thick cord connecting us, opened my heart to her, sent the intention on the wind and the music.

When Xena finally got the message, she ignored me. Although there was something I really liked about her, I knew she was wearing a very complicated mask. I wasn't sure what it was, maybe the same as with some of the other stylish nomads—that she had forsaken a real window of knowing for the witchy image she created of herself. Sometimes I was sure that there was something substantial under the layers of leather vests, velvet pullovers, and felt hats, but at other times, I thought she was just another flaky woman, an unwitting succubus waiting to feed.

Left to my own devices, I danced. Slowly then quickly, a thunder resounded and reality cracked. Suddenly, a luminous fissure opened before me. Without deliberation, I danced my way through it. It was the first time that I shifted into the Otherworld while I was awake and sober. It was disorienting, like passing through a thick wall of wet fog. Waking up in a dream was easy. I'd go to bed, notice the ants in my dream, and follow them to the next portal. I'd feel the exponential swirling of the flush as I passed through, and everything would go technicolor. When things returned to normal, I was already in the Otherworld. Dancing my way there was totally different. I had to both concentrate on my goal while not caring if anything happened at all. A detached observer. When I finally stepped through, I had the distinct impression of being in two places at once, as if I had replicated my consciousness. I was still at the party, my body now responding automatically to the trance music, but my spirit flew through the Otherworld. I passed strange beings and beautiful worlds, a galactic convention, never-before-seen colors. I wanted to stop and to explore, to know more about the octopus' garden, but something pulled me onwards. A reality materialized in front of me. I was in a redwood forest, the massive trees twisting towards the full moon. In the clearing ahead, a yellow light shone from the window of a yurt. I heard the comforting laughter of women and moved towards the building. A familiar energy pulled me towards it. I phased through the door, and immediately everyone stopped talking.

"What was that?" A woman with glasses asked.

Her only answer was silence. Seven women looked towards me. I couldn't see them all, but Daisy and her spirally smile tattoo sat at the front of the room, as optimistic as ever.

Can they see me? And why have I come to see Daisy?

"Oh, it was nothing. Probably just that old ghost of ours," an older woman said.

The rest of the group laughed, restoring the cheerful ambiance. I walked further into the room, careful to be as inconspicuous as possible. The older woman glanced in my direction, and I smelt her fear. She didn't see me, but she knew I was there.

I followed my heart to the source of the energy, and a tremendous wave of love almost knocked me out of my trance. Aurore looked up in my direction, and our eyes locked. She smiled, and a small tear spilled down her cheek. My heart pounded waves of raw emotion to her, through that silver rope that I could now see was attached squarely in the middle of her chest. She looked down at it and smiled bigger. My heart thumped nearly as fast as the music back on the dance floor. I took a deep breath.

Always Be Calm.

I had found her. After the initial shock passed, I spent the next half hour watching my beautiful wife work. She looked at me quite often, smiled, and blushed. It was like I had believed. Our wounds had healed, and we could finally be together again.

The women were sitting around a table piled high with massive marijuana buds. They all held scissors and clipped the leaves from the psychedelic flowers. When finished, they placed the manicured bud into their own separate plastic containers that would be weighed at the end of the day and added to their running totals, paid at $200 per pound.

Back on the dance floor, someone bumped into me, and I lost my focus. In a snap, I was sucked back into my body and the crack disappeared.

I moved closer to the fire, looking for answers.

Aurore is close.

Where was she?

There's no way to tell more than we saw. The odds favor Northern California. Much more marijuana is grown in this state than Oregon.

The landscape? Any navigable markers?

Sorry, but no. We can't even say that it's farther north than here. It was colder, but that could be due to elevation as well as latitude.

Shit, what can you tell me?

That's she's alive. And that she loves you. That much was obvious.

She did know that I was there, and her look told me everything I needed to know. That she was alive and well, that she was happy, and, maybe, if I judged the tears appropriately, that she missed me.

Xena joined me by the fire. "Hey, you having fun?"

"Yeah, it's great. Thanks a lot for bringing me here."

"No worries. If it wasn't for you, I wouldn't be here." She glanced at my left hand and took it in hers. "Hand tattoos are a commitment. It's a statement to the world." She pointed to the red and black swirly design on my thumb. "That's a nice one." Then she moved her gaze to my ring finger, and the blue wave tattooed there. "Is that your wedding ring?" I nodded. "That's so sweet." Her eyes went wide for a moment. "Wait a second, I've seen that tattoo before. Her name is Aurore, right?"

The music stopped, and in that interminable pause, the mournful cry of a coyote shattered the silence.

34

Smile at each other,
smile at your wife, smile at your husband, smile at your children,
smile at each other—it doesn't matter who it is—
and that will help you to grow up in greater love for each other.
-Mother Teresa

Xena dropped me at the Ping Pong Club the next morning, just as the sun rose. I waved good-bye, certain we were connected in a way that I didn't understand. To her, it was obvious—we had seen a coyote three times together, and this meant it was one of our animal spirits, that we were both accompanied by and contained an essence of the coyote. In some way, we were Coyote. But for me, it was different. I could never be sure, but I thought the coyote was Maya, that she was still after me, that I wasn't done with Jason Muscoph and his stupid games. I took a deep breath and focused on what I wanted: a healthy reunion with my wife.

Xena had met Aurore where she was working, the place I had seen in the Otherworld. Xena had stayed there for a few days doing energy healing for the owner of the farm, and she assured me that Aurore was happy and making good money, and she would be there for another few days. Every Tuesday evening, the trimmers made the two-hour journey from the farm into the town of Bluing to wash clothes, supply themselves, and take a much needed break from the meticulous work of marijuana manicuring. There was only one laundromat in town, and Xena told me I could find her there, sometime early Tuesday evening. And from what Xena had heard before she left the farm, the work was almost finished, and, then, they would leave to find another job somewhere in Northern California. I had one chance to find Aurore.

I found Professor Ping-Pong bent grooming his plants and talking softly to them.

He smiled big when he saw me. "So, when are you leaving?"

"How did you know?"

He waved his hand at me. "Don't ask silly questions that I can't answer."

It was Saturday. I would leave on Monday morning and arrive at the laundromat sometime early Tuesday.

"You know where she is?"

"Yeah, pretty much. I'll know where she'll be."

He put his hands on my shoulder, like some overweight grandmother, smiling with so much love. "Now you see? That's how things work out, isn't it? Where is she going to be?"

"Bluing."

"Ohhh...she's working up in the hills, huh? Be careful around there. It's not full of old, peaceful hippies like Lecoeur. Just drunk rednecks, and hard-up cops." He looked me hard in the eyes. "I'm serious. Be on your best behavior. Keep a low profile. It's harvest season, and this part of the world is a crazy place."

"I will...no worries."

I walked back to Jackie and Lester's shack. They were covered in mud. "Hey Ten!" Jackie's voice was sweet and twangy as always. Lester grunted his usual hello. They were in the middle of building a cob oven for their home, to protect themselves from the fierce winter in Lecoeur. The oven's mouth would be outside, and the back of the oven would rest inside their home, forming a bench. A small fire would warm the oven, and it would hold the heat for most of the night, keeping the entire shack at a tolerable temperature.

"Can I give you a hand?"

"Absolutely!" Her rush to accept betrayed Jackie's hope that I would offer. The sun would set soon, and it was already growing cold. I spent the next couple of hours mixing cob for them. Two parts dirt, one part water, one part sand, and a handful of chopped straw. It was dirty work, mixing those ingredients into the thick, putty texture that Lester pounded into oval bricks. By the time we were finished, I was dirty and smiling. It had been a long time since I had played in the mud.

I told them my news. Jackie's face exploded in girlish delight. "Oh my God, Ten! That's amazing! You actually saw her? And then this other woman, this Xena, told you where she'd be." I nodded, proud of my achievement of non-doing. "That's a miracle! When do you go?"

"I'll leave on Monday and hitch up there. It's not too far, but I want to make sure that I get there, you know?"

"Absolutely. You don't want to miss this."

"Well, we'll miss you, Ten." Lester said, relaxed and smoking his pipe now that the day was over. "But, you know, a man's got to do what a man's got to do."

"Should we do it, Lester?" Jackie looked at her companion. Lester shrugged. "Well, Ten, we've got a deal for you. If you're interested, of course." Her face slackened into a business expression. "You see that old car we got there?" She pointed to the old '88 Chevy Nova. "Well, we really need to get it out of here. We don't want it anymore. You know, we're going underground, as far away from the system as we can manage. And well...would you like to have it?"

"Seriously?" She nodded. "Does it run?"

"Runs like a champion, Ten. Granted, I haven't started it in a few weeks, but the engine's in top shape. Not a thing wrong with it," Lester said.

"Wow...and you're serious?"

"Yep, you'd really be doing us a favor, you know." Jackie smiled in such a way that I believed her.

I'll be doing them a favor by taking their car?

"I would be honored. I mean, if you're serious, I'd love to have it."

"Christ, boy. How many times do I have to tell you that we're serious before you believe us." Lester demanded.

35

*Twenty years from now you will be more disappointed
by the things you didn't do than by the ones you did do.
So throw off the bowlines, sail away from the safe harbor.
Catch the trade winds in your sails. Explore. Dream. Discover.*
-Mark Twain

This time it had all fallen into place. Everything I needed came to me on its own, more precious gifts from the Universe. I walked to the edge of town, to look at Lecoeur for the last time. Although the small eclectic village had been good to me, I was ready to go, tired of the incessant struggle with the palpable paranoia. Aurore was only a day and a half drive north. If everything continued at its current pace, I would be saying hello to her under the full moon. Our separation had only been a means to an end, a necessary step for us both to develop as individuals before continuing our path together. My heart assured me of it with every breath. I thanked the Divine in all available moments. Although I had caught glimpses of him in dreams and in the shadows of collective reality, I assumed that Jason was dying, that my lack of attention to him, and the slowly increasing effect of the 100th monkey would eventually nullify him. And not by any war I waged, but by the acceptance and integration of fear, and the sprouting buds of love in every person's mind. It was only a matter of time before that image manifested into the external world. Peace would sweep over the world and save us from killing each other. We had just begun the rise into a Golden Age.

Everything changes.

The Great Awakening is upon us...

I took a tour of the town, walked its small streets, said good-bye to the corner where I had clowned and where I had regained my youth, to the people I had affected and who had affected me. Most of the locals knew me. Even in a town as bizarre and as psychedelic as a Lecoeur, everyone took note of a reoccurring clown parading through the streets.

The day was bright, and the light in my heart was glowing and

Manifesting the Monkey   245

growing. A joy threatened to consume me, threatened to burst out of me and onto the world. And it was in this moment of potential that I was truly happy.

I said good-bye, thanked the professor for his kindness, for his education, and most of all for his leading me to my clown. I hugged him, and although he wore the same cool smile as when I first met him, he was sad to see me go. I didn't have much, but I packed it all neatly in the back of the car. My plan was very simple. I was going to drive north to Bluing, then stake out the laundromat and wait for Aurore. And after that, my plan was to stop making plans.

I'm going to trust.

Part of the reason that Aurore had left me, had flown away with that umbrella just over a year ago was because I was stifling. I thought often of the future, planned out all my moves, looked ahead with such a tight laser sight that I killed any seedlings of spontaneity before they flowered. Without that spark of creative chaos, it was impossible to live fully as a human being. I could see myself, could see how I was before, how obsessed I was with fear, how I had poisoned my marriage with that fear. But all that was done—I had saved myself.

I drove out of Lecoeur with the windows down despite the chill in the autumn air. In four days it would be Halloween, my favorite holiday. It reminded me of being a kid, of pretending to be someone else, of taking on a role and believing it true, even if only for a night. My mind wanted to think about what I would do, where I would go, what I would say to Aurore, but I kept bringing myself back to now. Life flourished in the present moment. I was my strongest, and it wasn't only because the fear cannot live in the now.

Each present moment is a doorway to an eternal oasis of love and possibility.

It was just before noon when I saw the hitchhiker. I didn't even think about it. I had gotten so many rides that it was instinctual for me to stop. I knew what it was like to be there on the side of the highway in the middle of nowhere, and I was happy to give back. I stopped, and the man walked quickly to the car. He was wearing a backpack, and before I even saw him, I felt something familiar about him.

"Where ya headed," I asked as he bent over to look at me through the passenger window.

"Anywhere but here." A red baseball hat was pulled down tight around his face and cast it in shadows.

"Well, I'm headed north. I can take you a few hours if you're interested."

"That'd be great." He sat down after he put his small canvas backpack on the floor of the backseat.

I left the shoulder when he slammed the door closed, and I enjoyed that moment of quiet between two strangers, both looking into an unknown reflection. We were careful not to rush the conversation, lest we force it, turn it into something fake that we'd both later resent. I was too occupied with my good feeling to pay much attention to the small quiet voice in the back of my head, heeding me to be careful.

Careful of what?

"My name's Ten," I glanced at him quickly as I navigated a curve and stuck out my hand. He shook it. "Nice to meet you, Ten. My name's Diez."

I laughed.

"What's so funny?" His voice was soft, but strong, like the warning hiss of an asp. It was a voice I had heard before.

"It's not too funny, I guess," the road was windy, and I enjoyed the sinuous drive. "It's just that diez is Spanish for Ten. Kinda a strange, coincidence, don't you think?" I risked a few seconds off the road to glance at him. He turned his head towards me, and I jerked the steering wheel in surprise and shock. I was looking into a mirror, into my own brown eyes. The only difference was that awful scar. The mirror was polished, and finally, I saw clearly.

"Yeah, I guess that is a coincidence." The smile that spread across Jason's face intensified the nip in the air. The growing darkness of a sneaky thunderstorm blotted out the light of my shining sun.

I slammed on the brakes, ready to force him out again, but the 4X4 behind me laid on the horn. In the twists and turns of the magnificent Highway 1, the shoulder had disappeared, and there was no place for me to dispose of my unwanted guest.

"It took me a while to find you, Ten. It took me a long time to get back to you, but you know Mother Culture doesn't give up that easily. She's got one last little surprise for you, and this time you won't get away. I've been trying to catch up with you in the waking world ever since you threw me out in Dinamarca." His laugh heralded the first clap of thunder. "You were good, Mr.

October. A worthy adversary, a fine...hero," he spit the words. "And you did it, you found the 100th monkey and her stupid haircut. She answered your little riddle, and the world is on the brink of a great change." His shrill voice pressed the limits of my eardrums. "Love, love, love. Stupid-fucking-new-age-bullshit! Love will save the world. All you need is love. Fuck that! I'm so sick of it, so godamn sick of it. But I found you, I found you just in time. I won't go down alone. You're coming with me. She'll make sure of that." He smiled, and my stomach turned.

I might be a little late, Aurore.

The silence between us stank of fear, of him. It was too much, and the car swerved as I retched. He just laughed. "Oh, don't worry, you'll get used to it, just like you did before. You'll even forget about it in no time, just like everybody else. Where you're going, there won't be any light to look for, and sooner or later, you'll succumb to your fear. Sooner or later, you'll take me back. I know what you're thinking, that the 100th monkey has been found, that we've passed the tipping point, and you may be right, but before you're saved, I'll watch you suffer. I'll turn you into your most pathetic possibility. Mother Culture is going to throw you down a hole, and it'll take a long time for Cathy and her change to reach you."

"What do you want? Why are you doing this?" I pleaded, glancing at his hideous face and wondered why I didn't see it all along—how I had unleashed my fear onto the world, that it was me I had been fighting against all of this time. It was my own foolishness that had created this story.

"Why are you so intent on doing this to us? Why are you even here? What's the point?"

"Why am I here? Why are you here? Life wants to live, it wants no more reason to exist than just to exist. Why do you expect more from me?" Jason said.

"Because you aren't life. You're contrary to all of life. If it wasn't for you, humans would live in paradise, we'd live in a perfect world, in a utopia."

His smile shook my confidence. I stared at the road ahead, suddenly ambivalent to my predicament. I wouldn't see Aurore tomorrow. Jason Muscoph had manifested himself into physical reality, and I was going to have to do something about that.

"You don't really think that, do you? You don't really think that it's only me that keeps you from living up your potential? What a load of crap!

What scapegoating!"

For a moment, I was almost pulled into his argument. I almost tumbled down, but the clown spoke to me in that quiet voice, and I remembered. I took a deep breath and relaxed, remembering that the boogeyman couldn't hurt me because he was just an illusion I had created when I couldn't understand the world. Even if he was flesh and blood, he couldn't directly hurt me. If I wasn't careful, he could cook up all manner of situations where I would inflict some damage upon myself, but I was awake, present, and safe. I focused on my heart, and let it open. I trusted.

I kept driving, long after I could have let him out, I just sat back and let my heart open more, silently thanking God for this chance to make things right. I heard Antonio's medicine song from the jungle float by on the wind.

My curación *is finally coming to an end.*

I had the choice to be whole, and it was all happening right now. Jason had a plan for me, but, maybe, if I refused to play his game, I could defuse it.

I could tell that he was getting nervous. The smell of fear that wafted in with him got increasingly stronger, and that only made me empathize more with him, love him even more. The calmer I was, the more open my heart, the more afraid the boogeyman became, and the closer I was to being a mature person. I thought of Aurore, and Jason's tendrils probed my heart, looking for weakness, but there was none, not connected to Aurore, not connected to anything. My mirror was polished. I had seen, and I had accepted. I still didn't know what was going to happen anymore than the next guy, but I trusted that whatever came my way was intended to help me

"The earrings? How did you manage to get them into the dream?"

He laughed, and I cringed. "Oh, that was simple. This world isn't as a far away from the dreams as you people would like to believe. The surprising part was how you got it out. That wasn't expected, and that's when I began to worry about you, that perhaps you had more than the others who came up against me. And then, I knew I was really in trouble." Jason's voice was feeble and naked, and my open heart reached out in compassion towards him, but he swatted away my invisible attempts to console him. "I knew that you could win, that you were smart enough to figure this whole thing out when you stopped fighting me. The only people who had done that were soon silenced by assassination or by the perversion of their message. I was always the enemy. It was then, when you embraced me, just like you're trying to do now. That's when I knew it wouldn't be long for me."

He was getting weaker. His voice was quiet, and his skin paled. No matter how much Jason had taken from me, the only way for me, for the world, to be rid of the boogeyman, was to love him. Any oppositional strategy would manifest fear and its offspring in other ways. Although simple in principle, I found my American background very difficult to reconcile with this belief. For my whole life, I had been taught to fight, to argue, to oppose. It was in our films, in our books, and in our politics. We were constantly at war with someone or something—terror, drugs, poverty, illiteracy, pollution. We fought the English, the French, the Indians, ourselves, the Germans, the Germans again, Russia, North Korea, North Vietnam, Iran, Afghanistan, Iraq. There had always been an enemy, and we had always been at war.

In the car, watching my former enemy waver, watching him wither in front of me, it was hard for me to love him. All I wanted was to be free of him, to live my life in varying degrees of bliss.

Don't all humans deserve that? Why is that we must struggle to meet our needs, why is that we have chosen competition rather than cooperation?

No matter what the response, and there were many, they were all laden with one fear or another. I knew that all inequalities were born from that scarred hitchhiker, that we had chosen scarcity because we were afraid of choosing abundance, convinced that, at least some of us weren't worth it. I calmed and centered myself, loving the boogeyman. A well of emotion boiled through me, and tears began to slip down my cheeks.

The next time that I looked at him, Jason was skinny, pale, and coughing. I stopped the car on a nice overlook. The storm had disappeared, leaving the sky clear. We were atop a cliff, and the Pacific spread out before us —blue, sparkling, and refreshing. I acted without thought or malice, but, instead I remembered my days as a Christian and acted with compassion. I helped him out of the car, and we sat down near the edge, watching the undulating canvas spread out before us.

"I'm sorry you have to go," I said.

He laughed, "No you're not."

I shrugged. "Okay, well, maybe I'm not sorry, I really believe that life will be unrecognizable without you. It's just...I'm sorry that it had to come to this."

"It won't work you know? It's too much to ask from people, to love their enemy. It's too much."

I smiled. "But they don't have to, you see? For this to work, the only thing people have to do is believe it's possible, to believe change is possible and to look for it. That will give those of us who want to learn the lessons of love, it will give us enough space to create the transformation for everyone."

He smiled at me, kept smiling and just before he vanished, he winked, and said, "I'll see you soon, October." After he was gone, I could hear him laughing.

I stayed there, entranced by the eternal fluctuation of Pachu Mamma. And then I got into my car and continued, elated and positive. It seemed too easy, but I was finally done with Jason.

The drive was slow and relaxing. I stopped often under the canopy to gaze up at the giant redwood trees that surrounded me, thankful for them, for everything around me. In the silence of the wind, and the swaying of these grandparents, I heard them whispering the wisdom of the ages, offering me everything I needed to live in harmony with myself and the world.

As night fell, I pulled off on a deserted road. I cooked a small meal on my alcohol stove. As I prepared myself for sleep, my heart urged me to move on, to find a safer spot. I looked around, but there was no sign of danger. I was tired, and wanted to get to bed as soon as I could. That way I'd wake up sooner and continue my journey. Tomorrow, I would be with my wife. I squirmed into my sleeping bag, and as I was getting comfortable, I heard a coyote howling. Again, my heart urged me to move on, but I ignored it. When I heard the howl again, much closer this time, I sat up, but the only things I saw were the flashing blue and red lights of the Humboldt Country Sheriff.

Oh shit.

36

*The wise man in the storm prays God
not for safety from danger, but
for deliverance from fear.*
- Ralph Waldo Emerson

As soon as that massive constable asked me to step out of the car, I remembered Jason's bag on the floorboard in the backseat.

"What do we have here?" He asked, as he picked up the small backpack and pulled out the paper half-stuffed into one of the side pockets. It was a page of stamps, at least two hundred of them, each one adorned with the face of a grinning cartoon coyote. When the constable said the word felony, I knew I was in trouble. I sat in the back of his cruiser, watching my few possessions flying through the air and landing somewhere in the darkness as he searched my car for more contraband. After that, everything shifted to the surreal, a vague reality that I floated through with little volition. Just like Jason had said, Mother Culture had caught me. And this time, I wasn't going to get away.

This is a dream, isn't it?

It took an hour for the constable to drive me to the county jail in Eureka. My head was spinning, but I trusted. In this whole adventure, I had learned that a big portion of what happened to me was based on how I perceived it. Yes, going to jail was scary, and yes 'felony' was even scarier, but I trusted that I would get out, and when I did, I'd find Aurore.

It's an endurance race, that's all. We can do it.

I closed my eyes and allowed my roots to extend down into the ground. Even as the car raced along the highway at eighty miles an hour, I could connect to the natural world outside. Pachu Mamma comforted me and assured me that, somehow, everything was going to be alright, that even if I couldn't see it, this was all part of the plan.

When we arrived, I was processed into Humboldt county correctional facility and charged with 'possession of a controlled substance' and 'intent to sell'. In total, Constable Agneau pulled four pages of LSD hits out of the backpack. He was curious to see if the D.A. would charge me with 'intent to overthrow the government' as well. It was something he'd heard about, but never experienced. He seemed like an overgrown kid, hoping to get the All-Star player in a pack of baseball cards, a curious collector, adding drinking stories to his repertoire with which he could impress his dwindling circle of friends. Age and life continued to push him into an ever-narrower slice of society, and deep down, Constable Agneau was ready to crumble, but even on him, I smelled the faint aroma of jasmine. He had been affected by the 100th monkey, and the love was growing in him as well.

At the jail, three more constables rummaged through my possessions. They all laughed when they pulled out the red rubber nose. "What's this?"

A light clicked on in my heart, and I felt the clown moving around down there, pushing to the surface. "That is a key to the survival of the human species," he said in all seriousness. They laughed, but I knew that they were even more afraid. Representatives of the former government did not like the unknown, and that's what I was to them.

"I have seen the world naked, seen her embarrassed and scared, lacking in nothing but love," the clown said. The constables looked at me quietly for a moment, before dismissing the words with a quick judgment. "Too many drugs."

After a few hours of waiting with the other inmates, all of them arrested for alcohol offenses, I was fingerprinted and absorbed into the next level of the system. In the dehumanization process, I undressed in front of an officer who ordered me to turn around, bend over, and grab my ankles so he could see if I had hidden anything up my ass. Then he told me to dress in the same clothes I'm still wearing today, though now, it's by choice. State issued tighty-whities, Fruit of the Loom T-shirt, orange jumpsuit, white socks, and orange slippers. All of them (save the slippers) were changed twice a week for clean ones. I was scared, but somehow protected from it. The clown was lighting all the torches, preparing for that marathon.

Since it was the middle of the night by the time I was processed and fully absorbed, they placed me in a maximum security cell, and in the morning, I would be transferred to my dorm. The heavy metal door closed behind me with a thud that echoed though the caverns of my soul. I was alone in a ten-foot by five-foot room. A bunk bed and a metal toilet claimed most of the space. Thankful to be alone, I lay down on the lower bunk, while the clown waved one of his torches at the shadows that descended upon me. The lights were dim, but the buzz of the fluorescent tube prevented any real sleep. This was only one of the techniques the county jail used to alter my consciousness and program me to be a good inmate. The lights never went out, and the effect on the mind was profound and long-lived.

After the 100th monkey effect reached us in the correctional facility, adjusting the light cycle to something more natural was one of the first things we decided to change.

About an hour into my stay, the door thunked open, and another orange-suited man was escorted into what I had mistaken for my solitary cell. He had straight long black hair and the dark complexion of a Native-American.

"Shit, mother fucka, you don't know who the fuck you messin' with," he shouted as the door slammed shut. "I'm motha fuckin' OG up in this bitch. Cracka ass motha fuckas betta have some motha fuckin' respect. I'm fuckin' Indian, motha fucka. Best be careful 'fore I take yo fuckin' scalp."

I tried to ignore this new addition to my reality, but, given the size of our living arrangements, it was impossible. By the smell of him, he was as scared as I was, despite the act. He paced (only three steps in each direction) with his chest inflated as if he were the toughest man on the block. He continued his rambling rant for another five minutes and then jumped up onto the bunk above me, where he punctuated his unanswered monologue with the longest fart I have ever heard and, then, drifted off to sleep. By the time the smell reached my nose, he was already snoring.

As promised, the next day I was moved to a dorm, and I laughed as I stood waiting in front of my new home. The room number was 555. 5+5+5 = 15. The Devil. The same tarot card that came in Colombia, the one that had taken Aurore away from me and started me on this crazy trip. The Devil had now taken my liberty. The door buzzed open, and I entered the dormitory. I didn't know how long I would be there, but the boogeyman whispered that it would be more than enough to destroy me. I was greeted with the glances of my sixty-three new roommates.

The seed sown by the 100th monkey was there, but buried deeply. Inside, the boogeyman was everywhere, and I had no trouble seeing him. In that place, he had no need to hide. He usually leaned against something, just there in the corner, just there, in case he was needed, his red eyes watching everything. The change sweeping through the world pounded on the walls outside. The Cathy Effect was well underway and gaining momentum. I felt it in my heart as the waves slammed up against our metal cage. Bit by bit, they would chip away at the institutions, at those words frozen into cold, hard steel. But inside, fear feasted upon itself, a ravenous snake pit, a screaming hell. I smelled it. Everywhere. It was harder to keep it at bay as it whispered to me all the time, just there, explaining the world to me. I took a deep breath and focused on the few points of light in the darkening skies surrounding me.

In jail the routine was simple. We woke at 5:30 and had breakfast at six. For every meal (lunch at 11:00, dinner at 4:30), the correctional officer regulated the line by calling out bunk numbers. Two volunteers served us on three-inch-thick brown plastic trays (thick because thin makes a better weapon). Milk was served with every meal, and that wasn't the only quality of jail-life that made me feel like I had returned to an age where I couldn't take care of myself. I guess that's what jail was, that place where people go when they can no longer function according to society's rules, or if they blatantly disagree with those rules. We ate every meal sitting at the same tables, and at every meal people would trade food.

"Bread for desert!"

"Milk for meatloaf!"

"Corn for potatoes!"

After eating, we were quarantined to our bunks for the next forty-five minutes, and the rest of the day was as free as time could be. There were two TVs and most of the inmates were gathered around one or the other. There was chess and checkers, cards and board games. There was Bible Study at 8:30 every evening, and 10:30 was lights out, but the lights never really went out. They were only dimmed to a dull buzz, and the constant interference loosened our selves so that we could be better re-conditioned. During our free moments in jail, myself and my new roommates walked in circles around the room. It was our only form of exercise and a way of passing time. We had plenty of time.

Once or twice, my clown made his way out and cracked reality. Each time it was a necessary recharge for my heart, an act of survival, a gasp for air. The guards' expression suggested I might not let him out too often, but the other inmates laughed, which was a bit surreal—clowning in front of muscle-bound meat-heads with Hitler and swastika tattoos. The guys they made the movies about. Or the Mexicans walking with their *vato* limp. Or the ripped black guys talking about their bitches, bling, and basketball. We were all pretending to be caricatures of our racial stereotypes.

One of my most successful clowning moments was when I reflected the fact that the guards knew most of the inmates outside of jail. They had even gone to high school together. The jocks and the cool kids became criminals. The nerds and the fat kids became guards. That made everyone laugh, even the guards...because it was true.

I focused on the love. I had no other choice. If I looked too long at the boogeyman, it would be only a matter of minutes before he overwhelmed me. So I looked for the light, for the love in the world, and though it was hard to find, it was there. And every time I looked at it, it was brighter. One day, I walked by a TV, and I was surprised to see Cathy. It was the first time, but not the last, that I saw her on the news. Her boycott had gained media attention. It wouldn't be long before her ideas swept across the nation, and the world changed.

Everything changes.

I was in jail for five days before I saw a judge, an old man with white hair and many years since his last free thought. He looked at me and grimaced. "Son, you're charged with 'possession of a controlled substance', 'intent to sell', and 'intent to overthrow the government', which I see is based on the substance, seeing as you had nearly a thousand hits of this...acid." Officer Agneau wasn't in the courtroom, but I hoped he'd get wind of this. I really wanted to make his collection. "That's a mighty big charge, and we don't take lightly to mind-altering drugs around here." The judge continued rambling, lecturing me about the ins and outs of society and how we all had to fit into the right places, how we all had to do our part, focus on our futures and not escape into drugs. It was our duty, he said, to do our part to uphold the values of our country.

I couldn't afford a real lawyer, but the public defender did the best he could. I tried to explain that the bag belonged to a hitchhiker, but that didn't hold much weight in court because they found my fingerprints all over it and everything inside. In the end, I was only charged with 'possession of and intent to sell a controlled substance,' but even that earned me six months in county jail.

After a month, I figured out how to choose whose dreams I entered. It was simple, really. All I had to do was ask the ants, and they led me to where I wanted to go. And, although it was horrible, every night, I went into another inmate's head and helped them see how to fix the fundamental trauma in their lives. It was as much an act of survival as it was of compassion. After all, I had to live with them, and every day, life in jail became a little easier. Their dreams were filled with terrible images and murderous memories. It seemed that all of them had been molded into a criminal by some early emotional wound that they were never able to heal. Either they lacked the internal fortitude or the external support, and then the pressures of life built up until they chose to break the law.

But, of course, before I did all that, I asked the ants to take me to Aurore.

37

We are what we repeatedly do.
Excellence, therefore, is not an act
but a habit.
- Aristotle

It took a while, but the 100th monkey effect made it into prison. It was inevitable. The flowers and fruits of love blossomed. The guards relieved themselves of the inhuman responsibilities their jobs imposed upon them, and the prisoners uprooted the weeds that had turned them into criminals. Literally, in a few hours, everything changed, and we all reclaimed our authentic humanity.

Everything is okay.

The guards put down their weapons, took off their badges, and opened our cages. Strangely enough, we didn't immediately run from our former prison. In fact, we decided to wait until today to leave. We knew that the 100th monkey was still sweeping across the world, and we thought it wise to give the change more time to unfold before we re-entered society.

We caught glimpses of what happened outside our walls on the TV. Cathy's boycott reached the East coast, and some businesses crumbled, but newer, more flexible models sprouted up instantly. They were the first prototypes of a cooperative capitalism. The huge corporations and conglomerates imploded because they could not adapt to the changing paradigm. A CEO threw himself out of the 82nd floor window of his massive glass tower before the 100th monkey reached him. As the world grew ever more beautiful, a part of him could not accept that he was no longer more important than anyone else. He wasn't alone. Some people couldn't cope with the fact that reality changed so thoroughly. Everyone had a choice, and some chose to end their lives rather than change their beliefs about the world. Nobody liked it, but, by then, we all understood that people were free, and if some chose to hurt themselves, it was their divine right and to be respected.

Public transportation and green technologies became the first priorities of both science and society, and not because humans believed that they were in danger of their own filthy ways—we were no longer motivated by the fear of a human-induced environmental cataclysm. We chose to make life more efficient, more natural because we believed it was representative of our integrity, and the 100th monkey united everyone towards that goal. It was unconsciously agreed that doing, being, and creating to the best of our abilities was the new standard. Supermarkets went out of business, but most of the owners and employees learned quickly and changed their tactics. They converted their huge stores into meeting places for consumers and producers of the growing amount of local fresh food.

The TV changed a lot, but we still have it. TV, like money, is neutral. It's how someone uses it that determines its character. TV has transformed from an entertainment device to an educational tool. Now, the news reports only stories about the healthy aspects of life because finally, we all understand that we get more of what we focus on, of what we watch. Yes, of course, in the first month or two, as the armies disarmed themselves, there were many 'terrorist' attacks all over the world, but we followed good advice and turned the other cheek. Our new strategy was to deny them any media exposure. It's not that we wanted to keep the public in the dark about these agents of chaos. Rather, we didn't want to reward those rogue groups with nourishment. There was so much 'terrorist' activity in the early 21st century precisely because we gave them so much sensational coverage. In a sense, the abundance of media attention fed their cause.

I know that the changes haven't reached every place or every heart, that we're all still in the midst of an unconscious, intelligent, self-reorganization of humanity, and that sometimes the road may be bumpy, but we're going to a beautiful place. Today is the day we march forth into a beautiful world.

Today is the day I leave my prison behind. Aurore's outside, waiting for me. It's all been wiped clean.

It's already been happening.

In the beginning, I said I had a gift for you, and if you haven't discovered it in the previous chapters, then I shall offer it to you again:

Reality is a flexible substance molded by your belief. You have the power—the

Manifesting the Monkey   259

divinity—to change anything, everything in your life, and it all starts right now, by making the choice to look for what you want. Once you start looking, you can't help but find it. Belief is the most powerful force in the Universe. Use it wisely, for all of our sakes.

The change has been made. If you haven't noticed that ever-brightening glimmer of love in your life, just be patient, look for it, and, quicker than you may imagine, you'll find it everywhere.

<u>Acknowledgements</u>

*Observations not only disturb what is to be measured,
they produce it.*
-Pascual Jordan

Although it only took me a year and a half to write this book, it's been forming in my head and heart for more than a decade. Thank you very much, dear reader, for taking the time to listen to this story.

The concept of 'Mother Culture' comes from a book called <u>Ishmael</u>, by Daniel Quinn. This was the first book to shift the way I saw reality, and I'm very thankful to the writer for bringing this idea to life and to the special woman who gave it to me on my birthday.

I would like to thank Michael Saxe for his time, patience, and collaboration on this project. He acted as an editor/mirror and helped me sharpen the images and ideas that I wished to communicate. I'm forever grateful for his support.

I would like to thank my mom and dad for this life and all the sacrifices they made while I grew up. I know that we didn't always agree on what was best, but I'm thankful for everything that you both gave and gave up for me.

My brothers James and Timothy. You're both really great people, and I feel blessed to have grown up with you two. We had a lot of fun, and today, as adults, you both inspire me in very different ways. Keep on keeping on!

As a whole, I'd like to recognize the Pumphreys. I feel so lucky to be part of a fun easy-going family. You are so creative, tolerant, and supportive. Thanks for being there for me.

A huge part of this project happened at a little place called Rocky Creek, a veritable wonderland in the Texas hill country. This opportunity was made possible only by the generosity of Paul and Ann. Thank you so much for the use of this place. It was a true godsend, and I look forward to enjoying that space again soon.

To a man named, Pax. Thanks for being my friend, for cultivating your beautiful mind, and for getting me started as a guerrilla ontologist.

And then there was a woman. We met, fell in love, and got married. We decided that we'd determine for ourselves what was best and follow that path, even when it wasn't easy or contrary to conventional wisdom and tradition. There's been some ups and downs, but we laugh together almost every day, and that's sign enough for me that we're doing great. Thank you so much, Hélène, for the support, the inspiration to change, and the love you shower upon me every day.

To: Delfin, Doug, Mr. D., Rod G, Jessica, Marcel, T-Bone, Mike P., Carne, Dylan, Janel, Vanessa, Hugo, Anne, Sara, Markus, Monique, Sai, Sarah, Nancy and Randy Marfin, Pam, Heather, Tommy, Annastasia, Danny Two Times, Justin, Inksia Butterfly, Morris Kaplan, Vivian Gladwell, John Trimble, Professor Ghose, Louise, Laura, Miguel, Lucille, and Jeremy. Thank you for being yourself, for challenging me, for teaching me, for supporting me, for laughing at my jokes, for believing in me when things looked grim, for seeing my potential when I was blinded to it, and for encouraging me along the path of my life.

I may have missed some people and for that I apologize, but thank you for being such a strong influence in my life.

God bless, and may the Force be with you, always!

Please leave some feedback at the homepage:

www.manifestingthemonkey.com

or a review at Amazon!